"After reading Patterson's first novel, 'Sweet Dreams,' I was really looking forward to reading 'Dream On.' This book was amazing. I couldn't put it down. If you're looking for an exciting read, read this book."

—*Paul Carson, Boise, ID*

"I read the first book by Aaron Patterson (Sweet Dreams) and was very anxious for this sequel. I was not disappointed. This book kept me guessing with every page turn. It's very well written and I really enjoyed the technology employed, which makes it just a bit futuristic without being over done. This was a fantastic suspenseful thriller that kept me guessing throughout the entire book. Mr. Patterson has become my favorite fiction writer."

—*Donna H. Boise, ID*

"This is the second book of Aaron's I have read and I have to say he is a very talented writer!!! I read this book in under 12 hrs; it was so good I couldn't put it down. He managed to surprise me with a twist that I did not expect! It is filled with suspense and keeps you guessing throughout. I will be suggesting this book to everyone I know…"

—*Amanda Garner, Oklahoma*

D0249791

Copyright ©2010, 2011 by Aaron Patterson

All rights reserved as permitted under the U.S. Copyright Act of 1976. No part of this publication may be reproduced, distributed, or transmitted in any form or by any means, or stored in a database or retrieval system, without the prior permission of the publisher.

StoneHouse Ink 2011
StoneHouse Ink
Boise, ID 83713
http://www.stonehouseink.net

First eBook Edition: 2011
First Paperback Edition 2011
ISBN 978-0-9826078-6-2 Paperback
The characters and events portrayed in this book are fictitious. Any similarity to a real person, living or dead, is coincidental and not intended by the author.
Airel: a novel/by Aaron Patterson & Chris White
Cover design by © Claudia McKinney – phatpuppyart.com
Model/Jessica Truscott – http://jessicatruscott.weebly.com/
Published in the United States of America
StoneHouse Ink

AIREL

"It takes rare talent for a man to write a novel from a male POV and have it published to great critical and commercial acclaim. But it takes a miracle for that same male, or in this case males, to write a novel from the POV of a teenage girl and have it turn out as incredibly as did the new StoneHouse YA by Aaron Patterson and Chris White, Airel. From the first sentence, I felt compelled to dive into this young woman's story and just as importantly, I felt like I personally knew her, which means I laughed, stressed and cried right along with her. A beautifully written and crafted fiction about teenage innocence, faith, loss and love. A must read for teens and adults alike."

—*Vincent Zandri, International Bestselling Author of The Remains, The Innocent, and Concrete Pearl.*

I am happy to say that this novel is one of my favorites of its kind. I never thought I could read a novel like this and be so swept away! I am always willing to try new books, but I usually steer clear of this kind of novel. Not anymore! Not when I can be so engrossed into the character's story, like I was with the beautiful Airel, that before I know, it's over. I kept turning the pages , wanting to, no-NEEDING, to know what was going to happen next.

—*Molly Edwards, Willow Spring,NC*

SWEET DREAMS

"Sweet Dreams was a book I read in 2 days. I truly enjoyed the read. It kept me wanting to know more. I'm looking forward to Part 2 of the WJA Trilogy!"

—*Sharon Adams, Novi, MI*

"Suspense, thriller with a perfect ending, leaving me wanting more. An on the edge of your seat, all night read. I most certainly will be reading "Dream On."

—*Sheri Wilkinson, Sandwich, IL*

"New authors come and go every day. Very few come on the scene with the ability to weave a tale that will make you sad to reach the end, longing for more. At a time when the world needs a real hero, Patterson delivers big with the WJA's Mark Appleton—an unlikely hero for the 21st century."

—*The Joe Show*

"Aaron Patterson spins a good tale and does it well."

—*W.P.*

"*SWEET DREAMS* is packed with action, suspense, romance, betrayal, death, and mystery."

—*Drew Maples, author of "28 Yards from Safety"*

DREAM ON

"Once again, Aaron Patterson has made a home run! 'Dream On' is a wonderful read from cover to cover! I am now anxiously awaiting his next book "In Your Dreams." I originally purchased his first book by mistake, and was pleasantly surprised at how much I enjoyed it... so now I'm hooked! Aaron has got to start writing faster!!! Although his books are definitely worth the wait! Bet'cha can't read just one! This guy has real talent for writing and keeping the suspense growing... the worst part about the book is the last page... I hated it to stop!"

—*Ruth P. Charlotte, NC*

AIREL

Aaron Patterson
&
Chris White

Also by Aaron Patterson
Sweet Dreams (Book 1)
Dream On (Book 2)
In your Dreams (Book 3)
Airel
Michael (coming soon)
19 (Digital Short)
The Craigslist Killer (Digital Short)
The eBook on eBooks (Digital Short)

LAMENT

Fell from paradise immortal race
Fell from heaven the stars, fell with them grace.
Abandoned love's presence for beauty rare
Beauty buried in waiting there
Fell out from eternity and shackled to time
The festering fouling deception sublime.
With them came each one his own:
Each book of each life, written and shown.
With these they flew, and under sun crashed
Free will's consequence immortality smashed.
Yet ebbed on, slow burning, against extinction survived
Blaze intensified by love
Secret offspring thrived.

PART ONE

THE AWAKENING

CHAPTER I

Boise, Idaho. Present day.

I WOKE WITH THAT horrid feeling in the pit of my stomach — again. I looked at the clock to see that it was time to drag my sorry butt out of bed. School was the last place I wanted to be today, and with the weather starting to get nice again, I dreaded being cooped up in classes all day.

My feet hit the carpet, and I sat on the edge of the bed looking at nothing in particular. My body was refusing to respond, and it wanted nothing to do with this morning business. *Come on Airel, no time to be dragging.* I stood up and looked at myself in the mirror that hung on the wall next to the bathroom door. Its rounded corners and unflinching honesty made me wonder if my idea of who I was and what I looked like actually lined up with the truth.

My dark brown hair had just a touch of curl and fell just below my shoulders in crazy tangles. I had thought a thousand times about coloring it — I know, who doesn't nowadays — but never could bring myself to take that final leap. I was weird about some things, and that was one of them. Not that I was against hair coloring or thought anyone who did it was vain or anything. I just liked to know that it was me all the way down to the core.

Dark circles surrounded my boring brown eyes. I had always wanted blue eyes, but oh well. I rubbed at them as if doing that would help me wake up faster. I smiled at my reflection and looked at how my face seemed to light up, then laughed aloud at how ridiculous I must seem to anyone who might be watching. My imaginary fan club...

Whatever! I have a great smile and if I have to use it to wake myself up, so be it!

"Airel! Are you up? School is in ten minutes and you need to eat something. If you keep skipping breakfast then you... " Her words trailed off in a mom-ish rant on the importance of the first meal of the day.

My mom was just that — a mom. She and Dad had a great relationship, which was rare in the world today, what with divorce and deadbeat dads — and deadbeat moms for that matter — running rampant. I was glad at least I could depend on one thing in my life, or so I hoped.

I yelled back, "I'm not hungry, Mom!" then pulled on my favorite pair of True Religion jeans and a dark blue shirt that I had picked up yesterday at the mall. I ran my hand through my hair, pulled half of it back and clamped it down with a funky clip I bought at a small boutique downtown. I slapped on half of my make-up figuring I could finish with eyeliner and mascara in the parking lot before class.

As I pulled back the sheer curtain, looking past the glass and into the front yard, I was glad to see the sun would be making an appearance... well, for today, anyway. Around here, the weather was about as reliable as the people who reported it. I packed my backpack with the necessary books, make-up and extra clothes, just in case we had a running day in gym. Once a week, we were forced to run, and I ended up sweaty and gross. Ten minutes from the time my feet hit the floor, I was in my trusty Honda and on my way to school... or as I liked to call it... Hell!

I didn't really think it was hell, but it had its hell-like days. I was running a little late, even with my record time getting out of the house, and to top it off, I had a wicked craving for a coconut latte.

I looked at the time and decided to just go ahead and commit to my coffee obsession. After all, it was only high school and I had priorities. I pulled into Moxie Java — I was a diehard fan. The gunko, — yep, gunko is not a 'real' word, but if I say it, then that makes it real in my world — they served at Starbucks would peel the paint off the walls. I liked good coffee — not burnt gunko.

My car squealed to a stop outside the coffee shop, reminding me once again that I needed to have Dad do the brakes. I should have asked him to do it last weekend, but it rained the entire weekend, leaving me stranded at home doing homework. To my dismay, the place was packed. *Looks like 'late' just turned to 'criminally late.'*

I looked behind the bar and saw that Lacey, my latte buddy, was working today. She smiled at me, feigning a panicked look and nodded to the line of sleepy people she was trying to serve. I came here often enough that she knew me and exactly what I'd be wanting. We had a good relationship worked out. She would have my drink ready before I made it through the line to the register, and I always gave her a nice tip for her extra speedy work.

I didn't dare look at the time, but surprisingly, the line seemed to move rather quickly. With latte in hand, I turned, doing the hair flip thing. It was supposed to look like I was a pro at the order-pay-and-I'm-out move, but as I turned to go, someone walked through the door and everything in my world came to a screeching halt.

He was a tall boy — man -- with spiky blond hair. As he walked in, I felt my heart jump. It was like destiny. I felt something begin as he filled the doorway. It was like he and I were made in that moment.

He was so perfect and beautiful. I could feel my face flush and my heart pound within my chest.

He walked past me as if I didn't exist and got in line. All at once, I was moving — or falling — who knows? All I know is that I rammed into some poor old guy and proceeded to dump my precious coconut latte all over his coat. "Oh. I'm so sorry. I, uh…"

The short bent-over man looked up at me with confusion and amusement as I pawed clumsily at his wet coat, looking around for some napkins. I felt my heart race even faster as a hand reached over my shoulder with about ten of them. I turned and followed the hand up the arm, and at the other end of that glorious arm was — him.

I then turned into a puddle of mush; a fumbling idiot. He

smiled, and I felt my face grow hot. "Let me... " he said, as he handed the old man the stack of napkins. I could feel my cheeks flush. I wanted to die. I just stood there like a moron with my mouth hanging open.

The old man took the napkins and cleaned up most of the mess. He insisted that it was no big deal. "Happens to the best of us!" he said. He was so nice, and looking back on the terrible situation, I wonder who ran into whom.

My legs were shaking now, and I was freezing. I looked around, then down at my feet where this ever-so-gorgeous-guy was wiping up the spilled coffee. Then he handed me my empty cup.

"Thank you! I, um..." There they were. My first words to him — oh, wow... what a line of brilliance. What words to utter in this moment. I stood holding my empty cup, and he rose and nodded with a smile. Before I knew it, he was gone. Poof! Whoosh! Just gone. I somehow ended up back in my car and on my way to hell, and yes — today it was just about guaranteed to be hell. *Argh!*

I pulled out my phone and saw that I was not late after all. I was actually two minutes early. How did that happen? Weird. I considered the coffee splatters on my shoes and dismissed the idea that the coffee shop was all some kind of hallucination. I pulled my little Civic into the closest parking space and shook my head. What *was* that? It was like he had this aura or something that reached into my very soul. I didn't believe in love at first sight. Well, not necessarily. But this morning was making me think twice about a few things.

His eyes, so blue, and the way he looked at me! It was as if he knew me or knew what I was thinking — how I was feeling.

I ran my fingers through my hair, interlocked them, and pressed my thumbs into my temples. I didn't get headaches often, but I could feel one coming on.

Two boys that I never talked to... and never would... walked by, staring. *Ugh. Some boys are just born clueless.* I glanced at myself in the rear view mirror one last time, smoothed my hair, and took a moment — since I had one — to finish my eye make-up. *I guess I do feel pretty today. Just clumsy, that's all.*

I headed toward the main building of my school. Lip gloss could be done on the way... if I didn't trip trying to walk and do something else at the same time.

The smell of golden leaves and morning dew filled the air, and I closed my eyes and took in the sweet fragrance as I walked. I loved fall. The colors, the smells, the fresh rain in the morning made me want to break out into song. Lucky for anyone within earshot, I kept my composure. No one wanted to hear my melodious voice. Just the idea of cooler weather made me forget my embarrassing morning. I was glad that I would never see that boy again.

I was not what some might call a beautiful girl, but I could hold my own if the need arose. The invention of make-up was a great thing, and I was an expert in the use of it. My skin was pale. I guess a nice way to say it would be that my complexion was fair. I had a few too many freckles, though, not to mention the fact that I was short. Not like, "Wow, dude! Check out the circus freak!" But I was just short enough that I got teased relentlessly. I felt self-conscious, but would I ever admit to that? "Cheeya!" I said, out loud, and then checked to see if anyone had heard. I would never admit to it. The teasing would only get worse if I did.

My frame was petite, and I had delicate features. On a bad day I would break the hundred-pound mark, so that was at least something. I might not have been the hottest girl in school, but I never had to worry about my weight.

I was a little smarter than I let on. I didn't want to be the smartest kid in school. That was never good. The last thing I needed was to be labeled as a geek, even though I did adore a good book, and I had my quirks. I stood out when I wanted to stand out, but blended in most of the time.

I liked to learn, and I was a good student for the most part. I got A's and every now and then a B. None of my friends were interested in their grades because they were all too interested in their boyfriends or girlfriends and who was doing what with whom, or who broke up with whom... Blah, blah, blah.

The walk from my car to my locker helped to clear my head. The walk and fresh air made me feel better about my day.

I had a few friends that I hung with, but for the most part, I used them like camouflage. I flew under the radar. I mean, I liked my friends, but only one or two of them were real. Everybody knows this except for dumb guys who can't even buy a clue. Sometimes I watched all the popular girls, wondering if they actually had brains or if they just ran on batteries, plugging in at night to recharge their ever-so-perfect personalities. *No bitterness here!*

I made it to class without incident. "Nice shirt." Kim, my best friend and shopping diva, gave me a mock glare and sat down next to me. "So. You see the new guy yet?" She looked around and lowered her voice as if it was a crime to be interested in someone new to our little school.

"Ah… no. And what does it matter? It's not like he's going to talk to us." I rolled my eyes, assuming some super hot guy had just caught her attention, giving her something new to talk about. Kim loved to talk, that much I could count on. I opened up my history book and pretended to read, hoping she would drop the subject, but I knew better.

She was always so energetic. Most people had good days, bad days, and most people's moods could go from hot to cold… but not Kim. She was full speed ahead, no on-off switch. I loved her for it! Besides, she helped to keep me looking on the bright side of life.

"Come on girl, when he sees you, he'll fall madly in love and beg you for your hand in marriage." She giggled and then quieted down as Mr. Brashear started the class. I didn't respond, and Kim didn't seem to notice. She pretended to read her history book and began texting whoever she was always texting.

Kim had friends at other schools, and they literally texted non-stop. I kicked her leg and she grunted, dropping her phone. It clattered on her desk and I smiled. She shot me a death stare and threatened me under her breath.

I zoned out like I did every time the word "history" came up. After all, this class was all about what had already been done before. When it was over, I didn't have any idea what the teacher had said.

But there is one thing I will never forget as long as I live. The person who changed my world forever…

CHAPTER II

"MICHAEL ALEXANDER IS NEW to the area. We, as a class, would like to welcome you to Borah High." Mr. Brashear introduced Michael and showed him to a seat just one over from mine. It was as if the world stopped and everyone in the room froze. I somehow stepped out of time and space. His blond, almost wheat-colored hair spiked up softly, wildly, in the most out-of-control, amazing way. As he moved through the motionless room, I felt his presence.

I was staring, but I was too numb to realize it. As he looked around the room smiling, I felt my heart speed up as his bright blue eyes fell on me. It was him, Mr. Napkins, the same guy I saw at Moxie Java. I was Miss Coffee Spill, but I *so* wanted to be Mrs. Napkins. I turned my head away as I felt the heat rise to the surface of my face like boiling water.

Michael moved with smooth, musical grace. I was gawking at him. I hoped he wouldn't notice my staring. This was so stupid. Why was I acting like this? I wasn't boy crazy. I knew, somewhere inside, it was not just because he was hot. Ridiculously, impossibly hot.

Something else drew me to him. Something that felt — dangerous. It wasn't *'I'm going to be suddenly hit by a bus while crossing the street'* dangerous; it was more like biting down hard on an achy tooth. It was a delicious pain. It was as if the universe was not only calling my number, but that I realized I had been waiting in line all this time, and I was stunned to find the ticket in my hand. I held my breath without realizing it. The feeling was overpowering. *Come on Airel, you don't believe in this sort of thing! Snap out of it — now!*

He looked straight ahead, and I shook my head ungracefully. Just as fast as the room had stopped, it began to speed up and I felt a hand on my shoulder. Kim had a big dumb grin all over her face and her eyes were sparkling. "Wow, girl! You are as red as a lobster!"

"What?" I said. It came out like a raspy, forced whisper, but it was all I could manage. Kim was trying not to break out laughing. I slunk down behind my history book. "Shut up, Kim!" But she just smiled and blinked as if she had no idea what I was talking about.

The next thing I remembered was the class bell ringing. I jumped up and rushed out the back door, desperate for the bathroom. I turned on the cold water and ran my wet hands over my flushed cheeks, trying to cool myself down and shake my groggy mind from this maddening fog.

"Aw, man!" My face looked like I just had my first kiss and then sat under a heat lamp for the fun of it. I didn't hear Kim come in, but I could feel her stare as she stood by the door with her foot jammed at the bottom of the door to prevent anyone from coming in.

"So… you see the new guy?" She was trying to keep from laughing, and her voice squeaked as she hugged herself.

I shook my head and rubbed the back of my neck. "Whatever! I was hot! That classroom… it's always so muggy!" I pulled my hair into a ponytail and splashed more cold water on the back of my neck. I was relieved to see that I was returning to my normal, somewhat pale, complexion.

Kim just grunted and smirked as she looked down at her nails, inspecting them, and looked up at me in little snatches of concern. "Well I think he's ugly. Besides, what kind of a name is Michael Alexander?" she said in a mocking tone. "It's like he has *two* first names." She was pushing it now and her face was calm. Much too calm. She was totally messing with me.

I smiled, and his face filled my mind for a split second. I could feel the heat rising again. I thought of all the dumb 80's song lyrics that my parents continually tortured me with. "Hey! You and I both know he's gorgeous. I don't know what came over me. The room was spinning and I lost track of time. It was weird."

I couldn't make my mind stop. It was racing, replaying every second of our first meeting — the coffee, his hand, his smile. He looked at me, looked me right in the eyes, and I could feel him searching, as if he knew me. My heart fluttered, and I had this insane desire to cry and laugh all at the same time.

Kim made a kissing sound and ran to grab me, but I brushed her off and locked myself in an empty stall. "Love, Airel! You *so* just went all googly-eyed over him."

I felt a pain shoot through my side, then a wave of warmth washed over me and I was instantly depressed. *Hello, rollercoaster! Wow, what's your name? Could it be Michael Alexander? Ugh. Or maybe it's just barf.* "I think I'm going to be sick."

"Loooove sick!" Kim was enjoying my discomfort, but I turned and instantly threw up, barely making it into the toilet. *Oh, dear God. This is fun.* I was totally heaving in the high school bathroom — not the best place to be sick. Kim snapped out of her taunting and rushed in to help me. After all, she was my best friend.

I lost my dinner and yesterday's lunch and started to wonder if maybe I should have had breakfast after all — was that why I was all of a sudden so sick? Skipping breakfast? Kim held my hair and rubbed my back. I didn't know I was crying until I saw a stream of tears escape and fall to the floor. *I'm crying! Why am I crying?*

My stomach felt like a knife was plunged into it, and my whole body convulsed as I stood up on shaking legs. Kim helped me to the nurse's station and I was soon on my way home, but this time in the passenger seat. Trusty Kim was driving my trusty Civic. Good thing Mom was at work and Dad was, too. I hoped I would be feeling better by the time they came home. They had a tendency to go overboard when I got sick. I think it's a parent thing.

Kim was in the kitchen making some chicken noodle soup for me. My arms tingled, and I was cold. I needed to get some sleep. Even though it was the middle of the day, I went up to my room and laid down.

CHAPTER III

I WOKE UP THE next morning with a pounding headache and dried tears on my face. I couldn't remember what had happened the rest of the previous day. I had a vague recollection of Kim putting me to bed and Mom and Dad coming in at some point with that worried look passing between them.

I remembered parts of a nightmare with a black figure, a horrible cloaked presence, walking toward me slowly, trailing black tar like some enormous, evil snail. I had to admit, that scared the crap out of me. Dreams could be weird, that much I knew from experience, but I had never had any that were quite so vivid.

I lay in bed, processing, trying to wriggle out from the remains of yesterday. It had wrapped me up in a cocoon of thoughts and a tangle of blankets. I finally realized that I had swapped ends in the night; my head was at the foot of my bed and my feet were on my pillow. *Whoa, I must have slept rough — rougher than usual, anyway.* After a few minutes, I pulled myself up on my elbows and looked at the clock. Wonder of all wonders, I had time before school. I rolled my eyes and struggled out of bed — backwards — and trudged to the bathroom. *Guess bad dreams have good points to them. At least I have time for a decent start to my day. Maybe today will be better.*

Inevitably, I thought about him. Michael Alexander fluttered into and around my thoughts, and I started to blush. It was really weird, because I could see his face just as clear as if he was standing right in front of me. Normally, I couldn't do that with guys I liked. *Come on Airel. Get a hold of yourself. What a moron!*

I turned on the shower to super hot and waited for it to kick in.

I looked in the mirror and noticed that the dark circles under my eyes were surprisingly faint. Man, I would think after a night like that, I would look like the corpse bride.

I flashed a fake smile into the mirror and that made me smile for real. I didn't really think that I was all that, but I knew I had a few good things going for me. In this case, I was going to use everything I had. *Jeez, Airel, what are you thinking? What, now you're going to ask him out? What if he didn't even really notice you? You're going to look like such an idiot when he turns you down, or worse…*

After a long, hot shower I pulled on my blue jeans and my favorite t-shirt; the one with Bob Marley on it. I pulled my hair back in a ponytail. I always had to do that after a shower, otherwise it would get frizzy and curl like no one's business, turning into a puffball or a fro.

My house was like most houses. There were several bedrooms, a family room and a kitchen. My dad liked to go overkill on everything though, so we had stone arches in between the living room and kitchen and the best, plushest carpet money could buy. Upstairs was my room, my parents' room and two spare rooms: one for guests and one for Kim.

Kim stayed the night at least three times a week. Mom had set up a room just for her, but most of the time she slept in my room. We would end up talking all night about boys, clothes, or whatever we happened to be thinking about at the time. So the spare room collected all her junk and turned out to be more of a storage room than anything else.

I put two strawberry pop tarts in the toaster and noticed that it was raining outside. *Great! One day of sunshine and I was sick all through it.* I made a mental note to grab a light jacket before I left the house. I felt fine today, I noticed. Other than the bad dream, I felt good. I wanted to get out and do something after school, but that wouldn't be happening, not with this weather.

Boise, Idaho was like any other mid-sized town in the west. We thought we were a bigger city, but we still had that small, hometown feel. I liked that we got all four seasons; a good wet spring, a nice summer that would hit the dry hundreds for a few weeks, and a long fall with cool mornings, mild days, and changing leaves on some of the nicer drives, such as Warm Springs or Harrison Boulevard.

The winter wasn't ever unbearable. Snow in town would usually melt after a day or two, but would stick around on Shafer Butte from October to April. Up there, in the foothills, was Bogus Basin, named after an infamous gang of outlaws from the Old West times. Bogus was also the closest ski resort to town, and it got a lot of use from the locals.

I wasn't much of a skier, though talking about it makes a girl look cool in the right crowd. I never really got into it. I liked it warmer, so summer and fall were my favorite times of the year. Stick me out by a pool with a good book and the warm sun rays, and I would be a happy camper.

I loved the energy the town had. Everyone seemed to always be doing something or planning events or trips to somewhere, whether it was out into the woods or off to Seattle or Portland for the weekend. It had this unexplained energy, as if something great was about to happen. Nothing ever did, but it still felt like it was just around the corner. Kim and I would practically live at the river in the summertime, or we'd be up hiking in the foothills.

I ate a pop tart, which tasted good all the way down to my painfully empty stomach, and tried to banish Michael's face from my mind. I had to squash any thought in my head that he would ever even look at me, let alone talk to me.

What would he see in me? I don't really stand out. Then again, why would I want him to notice me? Sure, he's hot, but what else is there to the guy? He probably gets girls falling all over him everywhere he goes. Especially the rechargeable kind, the ones with perky, dumb personalities and nothing to say but nonsense. And guys are so stupid, anyway — always falling for blonde hair and blue eyes and cheerleader uniforms. He's probably just like every other guy — just let it go. Ignore him, girl — he's bad news.

But the more I tried to convince myself about him, to stop thinking of him, the more I couldn't help myself. He was this force that wound its way into my subconscious and lodged there.

What would happen if he did talk to me? Something dangerous?

Hmm, sounds like fun. Aw, who am I kidding.

I grabbed my jacket and started for the door, trying not to wake up Mom. She never slept in and today was her day off, so I knew she would want to. My mom was like most moms. Protective and a bit overbearing, but she meant well. She worked at a flower shop. Not that she had to, but she liked to keep busy.

I was an only child, and since I was in school most of the day, she would climb the walls if she didn't do something, so Dad told her to go find something she would enjoy. She had found a little shop called Just Flowers and started working there years ago. I teased her constantly about being so old-fashioned; such a stereotypical woman, working at a flower shop — but she loved all things plants. If it was nice out she could be found, without exception, in the yard planting, digging, or pulling weeds. We had the nicest yard in the neighborhood.

As for Dad, well, I wasn't sure exactly what he did. And why should it matter? He was a quiet guy and didn't talk about his job much at all. I thought it had something to do with sales, though. He got bonuses sometimes, which we always used to go on family vacations.

Last summer was the best. Dad took us all to Disney World, and I even got to bring Kim along with us. Kim's mom is cool with stuff like that. Her dad left when she was young, so we're like sisters and do everything together.

My dad was long gone for work by the time I was getting ready to leave. He had left the house at an ungodly hour. That was the usual, but he was always home with Mom and me in the evenings. I figured either Mom or Dad must have taken Kim home last night after I had gone to bed. I must have fallen asleep instantly, because I couldn't remember anything. I figured I had caught a bug or something, because I was out for the night.

I walked outside to the curb, where my Civic waited for me in the rain. My stomach felt better now that it had something in it, though I won't go into the nutritional value of a breakfast that can be cooked in a toaster. I was still a little weak from yesterday, and the wet weather made me feel it.

I opened the driver's door to my Honda and sat down. Before I could turn the key, I felt sharp pain running its claws up and down my arms and legs. "OWWW!" I cried out before I could stop myself, but just as fast as the pain had hit me — it was gone.

What's that supposed to be, some kind of growing pain? Am I seriously ill here, or what?

CHAPTER IV

I MADE IT TO school without any more bizarre episodes, but I still wondered why I was getting sick all of a sudden. It was irritating. True to form, the rain was just a light drizzle, and it made the wipers chatter across my windshield, *bdraaaap, flaaaap.* So I walked the dangerous line between embarrassment and annoyance and the need to see where I was going. I was clicking them on and off all the way to school. *Lame...*

I cringed when I pulled into the parking lot. Kim had told me that Michael Alexander drove a sweet, white Chevy truck, and there it sat gleaming, even in the rain. My heart stopped for a split second like everybody's always does when they're in love. Or when they think they are. Or when they are, but aren't ready to be. My stomach did a flip, and I sucked it in and found a parking space. *Isn't that great! Here I am... I haven't even hardly met the guy and I've already had an entire relationship with him in my imagination. Just go in and get this over with. He's just a dumb boy like all the others. Get a grip, Airel!*

I made it to my first class with no sign of the mysterious new boy. I was a little glad about that because I didn't want to face him and risk the chance of a repeat of yesterday's disaster. I felt off my game. My body was fighting this illness — no doubt brought on by my idiotic and uncontrollable feelings — and even the thought of him made me panicky, or worse, made me want to cry.

I knew I would have to see him in the hall. We would probably have more classes together, too. I ran ideas through my mind about how to avoid him. That seemed to work for most of the morning.

Kim found me in the hall on my way to lunch and wanted to know if I was feeling better. "Are you going to live?" She had that familiar smile on her face.

"Yeah, I think I might make it today. You may want to stay away from me, though. I could be contagious." I coughed in my hand and felt my forehead as if I had a fever.

"Ha! Only if you can catch the *love bug*." Kim's eyes sparkled and she had yet another dumb grin on her face.

"Funny. He's way out of my league. Besides, he doesn't even know I exist."

Kim was silent — which should have been my first clue. She was looking past me with a blank stare on her face. Like an idiot, I turned around to see what she was looking at.

There, standing two feet from me, was Michael Alexander. My heart jumped and — I swear — it stopped. Now he was right in front of me, with a slight smile on his face. He had the most gorgeous crystal blue eyes I had ever seen in my life. I didn't know how I kept from fainting.

Kim stepped into the middle of all of us, cutting in between us. Some other jock guy I hadn't noticed was standing next to Michael. "Hi, I'm Kim… you new to town? How do you like it here?" I groaned, hiding my face behind my locker door, secretly peeking out, wondering what I did to deserve this. *Kim and her big fat mouth.*

Michael looked at her, then around her, in my direction, and smiled. "Hey, I'm Michael Alexander." Clearly, he was answering her politely, but not talking to her at all. I looked at him from behind my locker door and flushed.

"Michael…" Kim said, as if pondering his name for the first time. "Good to meet you! This is my friend Airel." She pointed to me and I could see the wicked smirk on her face. I was going to kill her. Murder, kill — and then for sport — unfriend her on Facebook.

"Hi…" I trailed off. Yep. I said, "hi," and probably sounded like I had some disease — which I wasn't ruling out just yet. Nothing cool. Nothing memorable. Just, "hi." I tried to say my name but

Kim had already spilled those beans, and besides, I couldn't for the life of me remember what my name *was*. I flashed back to the coffee shop, blushing even more, which made Kim giggle. From the smirk on his face, I could tell Michael was enjoying my discomfort. *Boys are just evil.*

"You're Airel? I heard you got sick yesterday." The smirk took on just the slightest hint of compassion, which nearly killed me. "You okay today?" Great, he knew I was a sicko… that meant the whole school knew. *Perfect.*

"Yeah, she's doing better today. Her name *is* Airel, and she's glad to meet you." Kim jumped in to save me, which made me even more embarrassed. *Say something. Get that mouth moving and stop gawking at him like he's perfect.*

"Uh…" *Nice start, stupid!* "Yeah, much better. Must have been a… a twenty-four hour… sort of… thing. And yes, I am Airel, like she mentioned — this is Kim." I deflected to her and hoped Michael would just go away and not notice that all the introductions had already been made. No wait — I wanted him to stay.

He had this way about him. Something magnetic; I couldn't place what it was. All I could think about was the way he looked at me. His eyes were like a deep pool of the bluest water I'd ever seen, and there was something in them that moved me deeply, shook me. I liked it as much as I feared it.

"Kim, nice to meet you… again." The smirk once more, directed at me, *God help me.* "I guess I'll see you around, yeah?" He smiled, looked at me, then Kim. He lifted his hand with a half wave, then turned and walked toward the cafeteria. His jock friend followed, and I could hear them laughing. I saw Michael hit the other guy in the arm.

I didn't realize until then that the hallway looked like a scene from a side show. Everyone had stopped to watch this new very gorgeous boy talk to the resident sicko. Then, as he walked away, giggles from the girls filled the stifling air, and a few football players rolled their eyes.

"Hi? Way to go Airel!" Kim was a little beside herself. "Good thing I was here! You might have stood there just gawking at him."

21

Kim shoved her backpack into her locker and stood now, grinning from ear to ear, looking like a stupid cartoon character. *What is it with her lately?* It seemed she was full of dumb looks.

"Whatever, Kim! I wasn't ready for that. Thanks for totally setting me up! You could have warned me!" I stuffed my backpack into my locker and glared at her. Great — now everyone will be talking. This was a bad start to a bad week. All I wanted to do was go home, curl up under the covers, and sleep the rain away.

CHAPTER V

SO I MADE IT to the weekend without embarrassing myself any further, thank God. The school was buzzing about the new guy on set, and it made me — well, I guess I'm not sure what it made me.

I caught myself trying to be jealous, but I wasn't! Then again, I had this thing: if I had a friend, felt like I had a small claim on someone, then they were mine — dibs.

From what I hear, guys have this so-called "code" where they can't date a girl if their buddy dated her. Well, we had our code as girls, too. If you put a claim on a guy, he was yours until you released him. Whether or not he liked you back had nothing to do with it.

I went over to Kim's house pretty early to pick her up. We were both up for a day of retail therapy, and since I had the money, I decided that I needed a new pair of jeans. Okay, maybe "need" was too strong a word, but I wanted to go shopping.

As I drove the Honda into town, Kim chatted up a storm. We were both *so* over all the lame and weird events of the past week and I had to admit that I was looking forward to a day of nothing but girl time.

It was nice out, unlike the day before, and the sun shone in full force. Kim was going on about her latest crush, James Carver. He was the new star quarterback, a transfer from another school, and way out of her league. But who was I to burst her bubble?

I pulled in to the Sunrise Café and parked. I needed breakfast and a cup of coffee with lots of cream. I guess Mom was starting to get to me. The unrelenting rants on breakfast were beginning to sink in. Maybe she was right anyway, and I should take more time in the mornings to eat. Then again, maybe she was just being a mom.

"Did you see him at practice yesterday? Like, he had his shirt off, and man-oh-man was he buff! I wonder if he saw me. I think he was waving at me." Kim smiled and tugged on her purse strap as we went into the little mom-n-pop café.

"Kim, you do realize that he's the quarterback? He's the one that all the cheerleaders and every other bimbo are after. Believe me, you don't want that guy anyway; he has a big enough head as it is." I grabbed a booth and looked at the menu, hoping she would wise up. Knowing her, it was a lost cause.

Kim shut her mouth and stuck out her lower lip. "Thanks for raining on my dreams. You can't help who you fall in love with."

"Come on, Kim. Love? You've talked to the guy like what — once?" I hated to be the voice of reason. I was beginning to think I should take some of my own advice. I tried to stop thinking about *him,* but everything I looked at, every billboard, sign and newspaper, all reminded me of him. It was as if his face or his name was everywhere.

"Look who's talking, miss 'in love with the hottest guy in school!' No — in the entire town!" She had me. *Busted.* I hid a smile behind my menu. Just in time, the waitress came by to get our orders.

"I'll get the Sunrise breakfast and a coffee." There were lots of individual creamers in the little dish on the table, plus Splenda to drown out the bitterness. I'd learned how to make coffee my grandpa's way — he loved cream and sugar. Now I couldn't take it any other way, except I substituted Splenda for sugar.

Kim looked at the choices and decided, but she was still trying to hold on to her pouting lip. It made me laugh. "Give me the French toast with a side of bacon — lots of bacon. And OJ, please." Our skinny waitress hurried away with a smile.

I sat back and looked through the crowd — local farmers and regulars reading the *Thrifty Nickel.* The place had a hometown feel to it, with a huge wagon wheel on the wall, painted saws with mountain scenes on them, and Old West stuff. We were a bit out of place surrounded by farmers and construction workers, but I loved eating at the Sunrise Café. It was nostalgic. I used to pop in for breakfast with my dad back when he had more time off.

I loved my dad, but somehow he and I had grown apart over the years. It might be that I was growing up and that's just what happens, but I missed him and our little dates. I was thinking about the first time I came here with him, when I noticed that Kim was not talking. That was not an everyday occurrence with her.

"What?" I asked a bit defensively. She was looking at me as if I just had a nose job or something.

"Did you change make-up or do something different today?" She was leaning closer, and just like her, had to touch my face. People talk about their bubbles. Kim's bubble was much bigger than mine. Actually, she had no bubble.

I sat back as politely as I could, just out of her reach. "No, just the same old thing I always do. Why, what's wrong?" I pulled my compact out and looked at my reflection to see what all the fuss was about — did I have a zit coming in?

"I don't know… just something looks different. Like, in a good way. You look like you have a smoother complexion. No little blackheads and tiny bumps like normal."

"Oh, well thanks. I didn't know my face was inspected every morning by the zit patrol!" I didn't see anything worth getting all worked up about, but I did look good, considering how I had jumped out of bed and just pulled my hair back in a pony. It was Saturday; I was going shopping with my best friend, and who cared about anything else?

"Hmmmm. Well, maybe it's that new cream I got you. Anyway, you look good. Maybe I'll have to use it some more. We all know I need it!" Kim flipped her reddish hair and it bounced like a shampoo commercial. She was pretty. She had three faint freckles on her right cheek. She hated them. She plastered on the cover-up to hide them, but I thought they were cute.

Our food came. I took a bite of my fave — the wonderful

scrambled eggs. I savored the flavor, when like a freight train, barf-o-matic showed up in full force. *Come on! Not on my weekend... I need a break — please...* My chest felt tight and a wave of nausea flooded over me. I almost lost it right there all over my delicious eggs. I jumped up, knocking over my steaming cup of coffee, and ran to the bathroom. Yet another great start to a perfect day — spilling coffee and puking in the bathroom. *This is starting to get old!*

Seconds behind me, Kim burst into the bathroom and saw me hunched over a grungy toilet, having a close conversation with the porcelain bowl. "Awww! Airel, what's wrong? Girl, you need to see a doctor. This is not normal! I mean, you've got some sort of bug or something."

I heaved one more time, then started to feel like it was going away. I walked to the sink and avoided looking in the mirror. "Whatever it is... it sucks!" I splashed water on my face and washed out my mouth. The water tasted sickening and sweet. *Ugh! Probably better ask Kim if she has any gum...*

"Are you pregnant?"

I looked up in the mirror at my friend, shocked, and shook my head. "Kim! A million *other* girls..." Only Kim would blurt out *that* question, and at a time like this, in a dingy café bathroom after I had just thrown up. "Pregnancy requires sex, which I haven't had. I am not pregnant!" I was wondering, was she just joking around or did she really think I could possibly be pregnant?

"Hey! I had to ask. I mean, hello, it's the most obvious question."

"Yeah, but do you understand what asking the question *means?*"

"Okay, fine. I'm sorry. But you need to go see a doctor. Something is definitely up." Kim fiddled with her hair and looked at me with her big green eyes. She looked really confused and concerned all at the same time.

"I hate doctors." It made my stomach hurt just thinking about going to a doctor. "I'm fine; it's just the flu or something like that." I stood up all the way, testing things. "See? All better. Got any gum?" Kim gave me a stick of some over-marketed tropical-vacation-in-a-wrapper, and I took it, chomping into it savagely. "Let's go. I'm still hungry, and I need to get to the mall quick. I gotta put this bad start to the day behind me." I lifted my hands in the air and spun around like a little girl in a summer dress, as if this would show how good I was supposed to feel.

After one last look at my hair, we left the bathroom and headed back to our booth. I tried not to look at the grizzled old people, other customers, who were regarding us as if we were from Mars. I didn't care at the moment. Besides, they were all scrappy old men anyway. But I did have a feeling, an undeniable sense of being watched. It took over all my senses and I felt the hair on my arms stand up on end. I didn't even know I had any hair on my arms, but it was all excited about something.

Standing in the doorway were two guys. One was James — yeah — *the* James, as in, star quarterback... and walking through the door right behind him was Michael Alexander. It was a slo-mo moment. He was *gorgeous,* and I probably looked like I was about ready to drool, my mouth hanging open.

Kim and I both stopped dead in our tracks. As soon as we did, they both looked at us. Michael looked like a Greek god as he stood tall in the doorway with a light colored t-shirt on that made his shoulders look like they were going to rip the fabric apart.

I looked away quickly, as if I hadn't seen him, and started for our table. My face flushed yet again. Kim, on the other hand, gushed and giggled as only Kim can do. "Hey, I can't believe you guys are here! What are you doing?" She walked toward them invitingly, which was a bad thing. That meant *he* was going to end up at our table, and then...

You can do this... don't be a baby. Act normal for once in your life and talk to him. Don't think about what to say. Just act like you're not a total idiot. Michael had an easy walk as he moved toward our table. He was wearing a faded pair of blue jeans. I can't remember what James was wearing. Who cares?

I sat down, smoothing my hair, regretting that I had not spent more time on it this morning. I was caught with a grab-a-handful-and-be-done-with-it ponytail and there was nothing I could do about it. My hair was probably sticking up everywhere, like I was seriously one of those girls who went out in their pajamas. I cringed inside, hoping he wouldn't get the wrong impression.

"Kim and Airel, right?" Michael's voice was deep and smooth, sending unwanted shivers up my spine. This was just plain stupid, not to mention the way he seemed to not even notice my discomfort. I thought that he was a nice person and that he probably made every girl feel like this. Maybe I was the one with the problem.

Kim was a little breathless. "Yeah, Michael Alexander and James Carver. Who doesn't know your names?" She stood and looked at James as if he was on clearance at Vanity, which was her favorite store at the moment.

James looked at me and smiled but didn't say anything. Michael slid into the booth and looked at Kim, who then joined me and pushed me in toward the window. I guessed they were joining us. Not like I was having a bad day or anything. Then again, seriously, not like I minded. I just wish I would have known. I was glad for that stick of gum, though. I tried not to chomp it.

"Mind if we join you guys?"

Now that you're already seated! I smiled.

"Oh, we'd love for you to join us. We just got our food and… well I'm sure they can get you a menu." Kim couldn't wipe that retarded smile off her face and James looked as uncomfortable as I was.

So now we were sitting. James and I were looking at each other like caged animals. Kim and Michael chatted it up like old grade school friends. My heart was beating faster than I thought possible, and I tried not to think about the guy who sat a few feet from me. I could see his eyes sparkle as he talked. The way he held his glass of water… every movement was flawless, like he was some billionaire's son who spent hours learning how to hold and drink from a glass in the most perfect way. But there was more to him… something fine and sinewy and cat-like. I had to look away and try not to breathe hard. Looking at him was like drinking from some forbidden pool, and I could not get enough, ever.

"So, Airel." *He said my name!* I tried to look as calm as I could, but I responded clumsily. "What are you and Kim up to today?"

He gazed into my eyes, and for a second, I felt like I knew him or that maybe he knew me. It was so weird how he seemed so familiar.

Don't just sit there, answer him! "We're going to the mall, and then we thought we might go see a movie." I was amazed. I talked like a normal girl, no hint of a stutter or of my voice cracking. *Yay.* I even sounded calm and collected. "What about you guys? What brings you to our favorite café?"

"Well, James here offered to show me around. My dad and his dad know each other from high school. I used to play with this guy when we were like four." He smiled at James, who was loosening up, or so it seemed.

"Yeah, we even got my sister to eat mud after we convinced her that it was chocolate!" James smiled and hit the table as he laughed, making the forks and knives clink a little. He was shorter than Michael and had dark wavy hair. He glanced at Kim every now and then to see if she was still staring at him. She was.

Kim was not shy. She was not subtle, sensitive, or secretive. She didn't play games because she wasn't sure of herself — no, she played games on her terms, for fun. She liked James, and she would not hide it, even if she could have. "You should *so* come with us! We could use your opinions as guys. It'll be fun. We'll show you around." Kim's big, fat mouth. I could have killed her. I wasn't just terrified to the bone... I prayed fervently that they would decline her offer. What had happened to girl time? Besides, what guys wanted to hang out with a couple of girls as they went shopping?

Michael smiled and looked at James. I was relieved to see on James' face a hint of the same horror I was feeling. Michael took a sip from his glass and grinned crookedly. I began to melt, but recovered quickly.

"That could be cool. We wouldn't mind, right, James?" He elbowed his friend, the quarterback. "James here isn't much for conversation, and he drives even worse. It would be nice to hang with somebody interesting." James half-smiled and looked over his shoulder for the escape hatch.

I hear ya buddy. I'm looking for it too. I had to interject. "That is," I said a little too eagerly, "unless you already have plans. Ya know, like, I don't know, playing… catch, or… something." I trailed off, *yet again.*

Michael Alexander, brutally handsome, answered my plea with a rejection: "No plans."

"Cool!" said Kim, sealing my fate for the day.

CHAPTER VI

WE PULLED INTO THE mall parking lot, cruising for a parking space. I hated walking half a mile just to get to the doors. Michael and James followed us, and I saw his big white Chevy disappear from my rearview mirror. I figured Michael had just pitched it into the first open spot or even took up like four spaces way out in the middle of nowhere just so his baby wouldn't get dented or whatever. Typical guy.

"I can't believe you just invited them like that. And you think it's funny! Sure, laugh it up," I said through gritted teeth.

"Airel, they are like the hottest guys in school." She busted out the baby talk: "Come on, lighten up!"

I really, truly and honestly wanted to harm her right then and there, but I knew I had to drop it or the teasing would only get worse. She'd start in on how short I was soon enough, so I brought up James. Yeah, that worked well. She began talking without breathing. *James, James, James.*

They had built the Boise Towne Square Mall in stages over the last twenty years, with the last renovation finishing up not too long ago. It had a much cooler entryway – new towers, skylights, and all the old-looking wooden handrails had been replaced by sleek metal and glass. It felt like we finally had a mall I didn't need to be embarrassed by.

By the time we found our space and parked, the guys had walked up to my car. Kim was rattling on and on about James' massively gorgeous arms. Michael opened my door for me, scaring me nearly half to death. The poor guy was just trying to be a gentleman, but

31

here I was, nearly blasting him with the pepper spray keychain my dad had forced me to carry around with me.

Kim was in full-on flirt mode now, talking at — not with — James.

Michael was making me nervous, walking by my side as we headed toward the front entrance. James and Kim lagged behind a few feet. We went to the new Borders bookstore — my favorite place. I loved to sit there by the window, sipping a coconut latte, reading a good book. I preferred a good thriller, and liked to take a weeknight every once in a while just to be by myself.

"So… how long have you lived here?" Michael looked down at me with his big, beautiful eyes. I kept it together and decided that I should make the best of the situation. What choice did I have anyway? Kim had planned out our day now. Michael, clueless to her wily ways, was all agreeable to it.

So I dove in. "I pretty much grew up here. I guess I like it well enough, but I haven't really lived anywhere else." I pulled on a strand of hair as I talked. I was very aware that I was doing it and that I only did it when I was nervous. I hated knowing my own habits while being totally unable to stop them.

"Cool. I moved around a lot. My dad's job takes him all over the country. I hope we stay here for a while." Michael spoke smoothly, and he didn't seem uncomfortable or out of his element at all. The thought of him not living here, possibly moving away, sent a shock through me. *Why should I care? I only just met the guy, and ever since, he has made me sick — literally!* Ah, but he was gorgeous.

"What does your dad do?" I couldn't emotionally afford to get attached to someone who might move in a year. *Who am I kidding? The chances are slim that he would even remotely think about me as anything other than a friend.* He was angelic, and I was — well, average. One thing I knew was that a guy fell in love with what he saw. This guy could have anyone he wanted, plus he was good looking and kind — the whole package. Yet somewhere below the surface was fire. It kind of scared me, but not in a bad way.

"He's a private investigator. He handles high profile cases, so he's out of town a lot. You remember the kidnapping last year? The

Smithson's? They had a six year old daughter who was taken. He found her after the Feds gave up."

"Wow — that must be a cool *and* bad job, all in one. I think I remember that story on the news." I kept making small talk. I found out his mother died of cancer when he was a baby. His dad never remarried, and the two of them were close. He had lived in Oklahoma, California, Texas, New York, Chicago… and that was the short list. So far, he said, Boise was the nicest town he had ever lived in.

"The streets are so clean, and the buildings are all new. When we were in Oklahoma City, it was like a dump. Dirty rivers and everyone honks their horn when they drive. Chicago's all right, but it's dirty too, and then there are all the gangs and crime. You can't drive down some of those streets — it's just not safe. Everything here in the west is much different, much better." His eyes lit up as he talked, looking at me. I thought that he might be good at making friends just because he always had to make them every time they moved. Different schools, towns, and cities, and having to adapt to it, probably made it easy for him to make friends.

We walked around the mall, and I went into American Eagle to look for a new top. I didn't notice that Kim had dragged James into Vanity. I did, however, notice every time Michael said my name. He would hold up a t-shirt and say, "Airel, this would look great with your eyes... Airel, this is way cool... Airel... *Airel.*"

My head was swimming. Every time he said my name, a small shiver ran its way up my spine. Before I knew it, I was smiling, laughing, and for some reason, completely comfortable around him. He had a way of making me feel like I was the only person in the world. We ditched Kim and James. I sent her a text to let her know we were hungry. After an hour and no reply, Michael and I went up to the food court. I had a craving for Panda Express and their Orange Chicken… yum.

Michael didn't care for it, but went to the Great Steak and Potato Company and got a prime rib sandwich. I liked that he didn't just get what I got to be polite or act like we had *so* much in common. I liked Dr. Pepper and he liked orange soda. I *know,* orange? What was he — a kid?

He looked intently at me, very seriously, and said, "Airel, you are the strangest girl I've ever met." I stopped chewing and looked up at him. I hated, seriously *hated* the idea of some boy just staring at me. That kind of thing just creeped me out. But this was not just any boy or any guy. This was Michael Alexander. For some reason, he was looking at me, almost worshipfully — except, since it was him, I didn't mind so much.

Was I about to let him off the hook? Not a chance. "What, did I take too big a bite or something?" He was laughing, which didn't exactly put my wandering mind at ease. "You never saw a girl eat before?" He just sat and laughed, which settled down comfortably into a smile that was just like my favorite book. *He's totally flirting with me.* And I liked it. He was funny and could hold a conversation. Most boys my age were boring and couldn't hold a conversation beyond sports or cars.

When Michael laughed, it was wonderful. It rang out across the food court, striking the heart of every woman and girl within earshot. His strong jaw made him seem so much older, yet still so young. It was an interesting combination. I could feel myself start to giggle, then he looked at me again and I had a revelation. That was it! It was his eyes! In them was his open soul. He did not waver, didn't blink. He just held my gaze and locked me in. I wanted to look away, but I couldn't. His eyes, blue and calm, were like a morning after a terrible storm.

"No, you're not like other girls I've known. I mean, you're sure of yourself, confident… without being a snob. And… I think you have absolutely no idea… how beautiful you are." If anyone else would have said that to me, I would have laughed in his face. It would have been cheesy, dumb, overkill. But when *he* said it, when I saw the look in his eyes—I knew that it wasn't just some dumb line, it was what he believed.

He thought I was beautiful.

CHAPTER VII

OKAY, I WAS IMPRESSED. Or maybe I was weirded out that Michael spent over four hours shopping with me.

Kim and James were off somewhere together. I was sure he was going to kill Michael later for leaving him with her. And if Michael was just putting on a good face to make me think he was having a decent time, he was doing a good job.

I got a text from Kim saying that they were ready to go, and if I was up to it, James wanted to see a movie. Shocker. He was having fun. One thing about Kim, if you were around her long enough, she was like a drug... very addicting. Poor James was getting an overdose, and after today, he would be a hopeless case.

"I think your friend has a thing for James," Michael said under his breath as we walked out of the mall and into the late afternoon sun.

It was shaping up to be a nice day, with a few lumbering, puffy clouds just hanging around like ancient gods.

"You think? She's liked him ever since she first saw him. But she's not a cheerleader and he's the star quarterback. I think if it wasn't for you dragging him along today, he wouldn't have ever looked twice at her. It's funny how things happen." I saw a hint of something in Michael's eyes. Was it anger? No. Frustration?

"He's a good guy. He's not like you would think... not the usual jock." His blue eyes looked down as if he was losing himself in a nearly forgotten memory that was now rising to the surface. "But yeah, Kim is cool. A little gabby." He gave me a playful glance. "But overall — cool."

I laughed and said, "That's why I love her. She's her own person. Not like the lifeless drones dragging their black skinny jeans and chains all over school. Nothing says, 'I'm my own person,' like dressing all alike, thinking just because you're weird you're an individual."

"Whoa, easy!" Michael held up both hands in surrender.

Oops, too deep. I had a bad habit of over-thinking things. My dad said I was an old soul. Judging from experience, it was not exactly a good way to keep a guy. Most guys wanted to think they were the smart one in the relationship. I was never one to hold back just because the underdeveloped guy couldn't hang. I had driven away more than one potential boyfriend that way and I cringed. *Hold the phone. Relationship? So we spend a day with the guy and you're thinking relationship? Stop it Airel. Over-thinking…*

"Sorry, I just get worked up about stuff. I do have my own thoughts and ideas, but in this world, that is kind of a turn-off for most guys."

Michael was silent as I unlocked the car door. He was different in a good way. I mean, a really good way — but nothing seemed to faze or shock him. I bet I could go into talking about the meaning of fear and the hold it has on our society. *Oh yeah, that's totally hot… guys dig that.* I could talk about how the media plays on our fear to keep us in line, and he would respond with the idea that not everyone could be controlled. *Ha, ha. Yeah.* Then, I could maybe throw in how there is still a silent majority that would not hold their peace for much longer. *And then we'd be talkin', baby… about nothing.*

But all of a sudden, he broke the silence, picking up the thread I had clumsily dropped on him. "No, you're right. I call them robots — all trying to be different by being exactly whatever their master made them do. Like a collective consciousness." He smiled and looked into my eyes. In that moment, I totally forgot what we had been talking about. I even forgot where I was. "So what do you want to see?"

"Uh — what?" *Great, I'm stuttering like an idiot.* "Oh. The movie?" *Yeah, duhhh…*

"Yeah, what did you want to see?" He had a small smile on his face as he moved closer to me, into the gap between my open door and the car.

"Hey, Airel!" Kim hollered as she ran toward the car with James in tow. "You aren't going to believe the deal I got. They had a buy one get the second one half off! I mean, I only needed one, but you have to get the second one if it's half price... I mean, come on!" I breathed a deep sigh of relief that she showed up right then. Things were moving pretty quickly.

"So, James, you're still alive." Michael shot a smile toward James, who just nodded. Kim told us all about the deals and the food and everything else that she had seen and experienced. James even seemed to be enjoying himself. He wasn't much of a talker, which was fine with Kim.

"Okay, what are we seeing? Are we in the mood for scary, funny, or a boy movie?" I looked at Kim.

"Boy movie? What's a boy movie?" Michael asked, tossing the keys to his truck to James. Clearly, he intended to ride with me.

"Glad you asked. It's an action shoot-em-up with pointless gore and violence. Guys like it because it makes them feel like the dominant male they all wish they could be." I smiled and looked at him and shoved my hands in my back pockets.

Michael didn't even hesitate. "Or, we could see a girl movie. In case you were wondering, that's a movie with a sappy love story where two people hate each other, fall in love, then one betrays the other — in most cases the guy is the jerk — then they have fifteen minutes of sad time where they reflect on their relationship. Then they get back together in the end. Girls like it because it makes them feel like there's a dream man out there for them, and one day they'll fall in love just to be disappointed to find that, in reality, there is no perfect guy. But who wants to think about that?" Michael smirked with challenging playfulness.

There was a lengthy silence as we all looked at each other.

"Comedy!" James and Kim said in unison.

I laughed, and for the tenth time today, I actually felt good. It was nice to be with friends, old and new.

CHAPTER VIII

WE MADE IT TO the theater before anything disastrous could happen. After I parked, Michael opened my door for me, and on the way to the ticket booth, he grabbed my hand and held it, and would not let go. I was glad, but terrified. On one side of this shiny new coin, he was not shy about his affection for me, and didn't feel like he needed to ask permission for anything. On the other side, *what the heck was he doing holding my hand without asking permission?*

We bought our tickets and went in to the theater, but not before Kim and I had a conference in the bathroom to compare notes. She insisted on digging for all the dirt on me and Michael from the five minute trip over to the theater and dished me all the dirt that I didn't really want to know about her and James.

"Guess what? Guess who his favorite band is? Just guess!" She was giddy. It was cute. They were both crazy about the exact same music. We walked out holding hands and giggling. Luckily, that discouraged any more handholding by Michael as we found our seats. But, of course, I let him sit next to me. I couldn't be rude. Besides, I wanted to sit by him.

Darkness filled the movie theater as the previews started rolling. It was girl, girl, boy, boy — Kim on my left, Michael on my right, and James next to Michael. Kim didn't seem to mind, or maybe she just didn't care. Michael was making jokes about the different movies that were coming out and leaned over, whispering in my ear, "Do you want anything? Popcorn or a drink?"

Just the sound of his voice in my ear made the hair on my arms stand up again. Not to mention the goose bumps. "Sure. Diet Pepsi and popcorn. Thanks, Michael."

"No problem." He slipped out and James followed.

"They went for a junk food run," I whispered to Kim

"Good, I'm starved." Then she changed gears again, almost giving me whiplash. "So, I see you and Michael are getting friendly…" She had a glint of sarcasm in her voice.

"He's nice, but he's a little out of my league, if you know what I mean." I didn't dare even think about anything more with Michael other than friendship… even with the handholding. It could have been a fluke. *Or maybe I'm being neurotic.*

If there's one thing I'd learned about guys, it was that they can hurt. I was going to be as cautious as possible about all of this. Michael was friendly with everyone, anyway, and I had no reason to believe he was seriously considering me as one of his many, many options.

"Come on, he likes you. Anyone can see that. Don't worry about anything, just leave it to me." I gave her that *don't even think about it* look and hit her in the arm. "Ow, so mean!"

"Ha! You deserved it. Now don't try anything or I'll tell James you're a stalker."

"So? I am." Kim laughed, adjusting her purse. She flipped out her phone and left a movie theater check-in on Facebook, moving quickly on to Twitter. I guess a girl's got to stay in touch with her peeps, but Kim was a little overboard. I was on Facebook too, but that was only because Kim had set it up for me. If I didn't get on it often enough, she would hack in and post stuff on my behalf — just another reason why I could never lose her.

Michael came back up the stairs and slid in next to me. He handed me a large soda and smiled. "Big enough for ya?"

"Yeah, ya think? Holy BUCKET." I giggled like an idiot and turned my face away. *What was this guy doing to me?* "Where's James?"

"He had to go to the bathroom. He should be back soon. Unless he's running scared from… ahem…" He pointed with his thumb over to Kim who was busy checking her reflection on her phone.

"Ha, she would find him," I whispered in his ear. I could smell his shampoo and feel the warmth of his skin next to mine. His arm brushed mine, and I almost embarrassed myself by screaming. It probably would have come out really weak, given the heart palpitations I was having to deal with.

James came back a few minutes later and took a handful of popcorn. *Sheesh, help yourself, pal.* The movie started, and I scrunched down in my seat, wondering what I was doing. *Was I a glutton for pain? Did I just like to have my heart broken?* Just the thought of…

My thoughts were instantly cut off by something I had never felt before. It was like a splitting headache in the back of my skull. Everything went fuzzy. I closed my eyes and tried to focus, and for the second time today, I felt like throwing up. This time it was not as strong, though. I controlled my lunch, breathed in deeply three times, then opened my eyes.

The people in front of us, all the way down to the front row, were all a blur — all but two, who sat in the second row. It was a tall man with short blond hair and a shorter man with a ball cap on. They were talking, and from where I was sitting, I could tell they were not happy.

The tall, blond man leaned over and whispered something to the ball cap man and he stiffened. I had a bad feeling that something was going to happen, but I wasn't sure. *What are they talking about?*

Then, I saw it. The glint of a blade, catching the light from the movie screen, appeared from the blond man's coat. I saw his arm wrap around the ball cap man's shoulder, reaching around to cover his mouth.

I tried to yell, but nothing came out. I just opened and closed my mouth like a fish. There was no way this was real. Everyone else seemed not to notice the two men, but I could *feel* what happened.

The tall man jerked his arm, making the ball cap man's body twitch crookedly. A second time, he thrust the knife in, and after a few more seconds, the ball cap man went limp in his seat. I was speechless. I had just witnessed a cold-blooded murder. I couldn't breathe, let alone talk. It looked like the ball cap man was napping in the darkness. There was no way anyone would see he was dead until the end of the movie.

Now, just as if I had shouted at him, the tall man with the knife turned and looked dead at me. His piercing dark eyes shot a hole right through me. I jerked my gaze away and tried to act like I was lost in the movie. He stared at me and refused to let me out of his sight. I managed to grunt something like, "I have to go to the restroom." I stood and slipped by Michael and James.

I hiked down the stairs and past the killer's row, and I could feel him watching me hatefully. He sat still as I passed. I didn't look his way. I could feel his gaze follow me as I turned to go out into the lobby. I was scared and in a panic, not sure what to do. My mind felt like sludge and would not work like I needed it to.

I hit the lobby quickly and ran full blast to the bathroom where I promptly threw up in the sink. I looked into the mirror. My reflection was the image of a stranger — I wondered at all of this for a split second. Questions came tumbling in, all jumbled up and twisted together with answers that didn't fit. I fumbled with my phone and dialed 911. *Come on, pick up!*

"Nine-one-one, what's your emergency?"

I was just about to answer when I heard the door open. I turned and rushed to an empty stall. I shut the door as quietly as I could and crouched down on top of the toilet. I quickly turned off my phone, but it played that irritating jingle that's always way too loud, giving me away. There was silence for what felt like eternity. Then, I heard heavy footfalls. Someone was walking slowly through the room... toward me.

Like a crazy person, he was whistling some random tune, very low, like a whisper. At first, it was unintelligible, total nonsense. But then, he came even closer to the stall where I hid, and as he did, I swear I could recognize the tune. It was beyond me to put a name to it, but it filled me with horror.

I shivered as he came closer, the footfalls like heavy machinery, dropping like lead weights on the tile floor. I saw under the door the shine of a pair of men's dress shoes.

Oh God, oh God...! Don't let him find me... I was crouched like a jungle cat on the toilet, and if I could have pinned my ears back, I would have.

I could see him hunch down on the balls of his feet, his coat touching the floor around him like a tent. He started looking under the stall doors, crouching lower. His hand dropped down and a bloody eight-inch long knife was in his hand. I just about screamed, but I clamped my hand down over my mouth, only allowing a frightened gasp to escape.

I watched him through the crack of the door, his body tensed like a vicious predator. He sniffed at the air. Then, his hands slowly came down and rested on the floor, balled up on his knuckles with silky elegance. It was more frightening than the anger and violence I was expecting. He seemed to be completely calm and collected.

Down he sank, and as he did, he slid his feet back away from his hands. Lower and lower to the floor, as if doing a push-up, he descended, the knife in the hand nearest to me.

I could not bear it, but I knew I would see his face... it was inevitable. I dreaded the seconds as they ticked along with me riding inside them, but I also dreaded those that were coming for me.

Then it happened. His face appeared in the small space under the door. He was looking directly at me. I could not bear his gaze. My body twitched, and I turned away and trembled in panic.

Then, just as fast as he came in, he was gone.

I started to sob and shake uncontrollably. I stopped myself when I heard the door open again. "Airel, you in here?"

Kim! "Oh God, *Kim!*" I burst from the stall crying. As she stood there stunned, I clung to her.

"Whoa, hold on, girl — what's going on? Are you okay?" Kim held me up as I cried. "Airel, it's okay. I'm here. Everything's gonna be alright."

I was sobbing and shaking uncontrollably. The total panic of what had happened was made complete by the sound of screaming people in the lobby outside.

CHAPTER IX

1250 B.C. Arabia

A TALL, COLD MARBLE god stood in the snow-driven wind, wrapped in fur and leather. He did not shiver or move as he gazed out from the precipice of a stone cliff that dropped dizzyingly below him. The frozen landscape moaned in protest as the wind pushed stiff tree branches and pulled on strands of long, dead grass. It was as if he was not present in that moment — or perhaps he was dead on his feet — frozen in the standing position, only a statue; a carving of someone once strong and brave.

He inhaled the icy air and let out a cloud of vapor that was quickly carried away. His eyes were dark and sparkling under his thick eyebrows. His face was pale, smooth, almost white. Even in the frigid morning light, he seemed to be quite comfortable.

A feather of smoke hurried from the top of the small hut behind him. Across the wooded hills, through the trees, a thousand more huts sent up their own smudges of smoke, signifying that life was still smoldering in the little village. Even with the long winter only halfway gone, the people took heart in the simple fact that they were not alone in the dead world. They would not suffer through it in miserable solitude. The human heart could endure much in the company of others who shared the same plight.

The powerful man cocked his head when he heard a woman's pathetic cry escape from the hut behind him. He turned, walking toward the rough door, his easy strides giving him an air of self-assurance. He ducked inside and lashed the door shut with a leather strap.

The one-room hut was drafty, even with the door shut. Cold air pushed its way through cracks into the room. A makeshift bed sat in the corner, and a fire crackled in the center of the room where it jumped and leaped, fighting to displace the cold with its warmth.

An uncommonly beautiful woman lay in the bed, in labor with child. She was covered with a blanket made of skins. Her face was twisted in pain, but even in her anguish, she was stunning. The fire filled the room with an orange light that danced off the walls.

The man pushed the hood from his head and leaned down, placing a gentle kiss on the beautiful woman's cheek. His wife forced a smile, then arched her back and bit her lower lip as another contraction wracked her body. The contractions were getting stronger and closer together. The baby would soon arrive. All the pain of labor would be forgotten, if only for a little while.

Taking a black pot from the fire, he placed it next to where she lay and let his coat fall to the floor. He wore rough hand-stitched leather pants with a white woven shirt that tied at the chest. His skin was hard and stony.

Even in the dim light, faintly visible markings could be seen on his forearms and on the side of his neck, winding their way in and out of his skin. They appeared to be tattoos, but were more like a birthmark. They appeared in the firelight and disappeared with the shadows.

The man took a cool piece of cloth, placed it on his wife's forehead and smiled with concern hidden behind dark eyes.

He hummed a soft melody and worked with skilled hands, tearing strips of warm cloth with which to wrap the baby when she came. She... he had a feeling the baby would be a girl. Something deep inside told him that she would be special, too. He longed for a daughter, longed for the child to be a girl. His wife cried out again and looked directly into his eyes. He knew: it was time.

Pulling the blankets back, he waited as she pushed with a shattering scream. The wind answered her with a burst, shaking the room. She was in her second day of labor, and the effort and strain on her body was beginning to show as her strength faded. He wondered how much longer she could endure, but he said nothing, praying for it to finally end for her sake.

She hunched, pushing so hard that she could not breathe for a moment. Then... cries... sweet, soft cries. The baby's voice filled the small hut as mother and father looked into each other's eyes, smiling. The baby looked impossibly small in his huge arms. He gently wrapped her in warm cloths, giving her to his exhausted wife.

It *was* a girl! She was beautiful, with her mother's dark wispy hair and the same dark eyes as her father. She ate for the very first time, then the little family gathered together under the warm blankets by the fire to sleep, glowing with the spark and joy of new life.

For that one night in their little world, everything was perfect.

CHAPTER X

HE STOOD OUT AGAINST the morning sunrise. The tears that fell from his eyes took hold of the sunlight and sparkled like crystal. Looking down at the bundle in his arms, he pulled the smooth woolskin blanket back and looked into his daughter's eyes. She was perfect. Her skin reminded him of his beloved bride. It was smooth and olive-colored. His grief came in a fresh and powerful wave again. Now she had her place amongst the stars.

He knew that even in his own village, he was an outsider. He still remembered how his kind used to be part of a civilization, a culture, a society. But they had been required to disperse, separate and scatter — because of the Brotherhood.

They harbored the deepest hatred for anyone or anything different from them. They would hunt down and destroy anyone who resisted them. Everything about him and his kind was always exactly opposite to the Brotherhood.

The man had a name, but none could pronounce it in human tongue. The people of his village knew him simply as Kreios.

The cold wind was whipping but dead, along with his wife. He felt all of it was forced on him with equally outrageous swiftness by the cruelest winter he could remember. He wished only to honor her, not to compare such empty things to one so full of life, warmth and beauty.

He dug a shallow grave in the rock-hard, frozen earth under the very oak tree where they had proclaimed their love for one another only five years earlier. He could still feel her heart in his memory, fluttering with anticipation. He had gotten down on his knees, poured out his soul, and vowed to love only her forever and into eternity.

Now he poured out his soul once again, drowning it in her grave — and he felt the unjust spitefulness of a life lived in subjection to reality. He placed her cold body into the colder ground. Now, the snow made everything look clean and fresh, providing a bitter irony in contrast to what would be the last thing he would do for her.

The baby cried and wriggled in his arms. Kreios turned and went back inside his mud hut and shut the cold out with a *thud*. He wrapped his daughter tighter in the warm skins, put her in his own bed and lay down with her. When she fell asleep, he rose again, restless. She would need milk soon. He knew where he had to go to get it. Two days walk from his small village was a town called Gratzipt. His brother lived there with his wife, and she was with child. She would have the precious mother's milk his daughter would need.

Crouching down, poking at the fire in the center of the small hut, he tried to think. No matter how he looked at it, he would have to take her there. Milk was the only life source for a newborn child — nothing else would do. But there was not one mother in this village who would give suck to his little girl. Not in the winter and not for someone like Kreios. This village had written him off years ago. They were scared of him and his odd skin color, his strange ways. Even under the scorching summer sun, his skin always kept its pale tone; never burning or darkening. Local myths cast him as a wizard or worse.

Brother will take me in or I shall die myself. I will not let my sweet girl starve to death. With the sure and steady hands of a warrior, he pulled on his thick heavy coat. He gathered all the scraps of dried meat, putting them, along with his few worldly possessions, in a leather pack. He took a sling and placed the baby into it, then hung it around his neck, carefully tucking her close to his chest under his heavy coat.

He tightened the thick leather belt around his waist, in preparation for his journey, and walked out the door into the crisp winter air. The howling wind had subsided now, and he reflected on the change now undeniable in his life and that of his little girl, and felt an overriding peace — if even for a moment. *It is you and me now.*

He thought about the long walk that lay ahead and the chance that the Brotherhood might be watching the roads. She had no chance of making it for two days. She needed to eat within the next few hours. He knew she would be dead by the time he reached his brother's village if he delayed any longer.

It will draw out the Brotherhood and would violate the pact. "I must," he said simply, into the thinning winds. In this statement, the future, with all its potential for good or evil, seemed to be encapsulated.

Kreios shook his head heavily and padded silently through the snow toward the road with the village to his back. In about one hundred paces he would be in the woods, under cover. *They will know — they have eyes everywhere.* He did not bother to argue with himself further. There was no use fighting nature. For his beautiful child, he would risk his life, as well as that of his brother, if that was what was required.

Kreios reached the edge of the wood. The forest had been named for the small and remote village it hemmed in, the place he had called home for ten years now: The Whispering Wood. The Storytellers had said that God would whisper truth to travelers there if they had a pure heart. But no one had ever claimed to hear the voice of this God. In this world, no one had a pure heart.

Looking around him, Kreios turned from the crude dirt road and trudged off into deeper snow, through the dormant undergrowth, into the forest. He could feel his baby girl breathing softly as she slept next to his skin. He knew she would be warm. The cold would not reach her there.

DO NOT DO IT! His inner voice screamed at him, warning him not to provoke the Brotherhood.

He stepped into a small clearing. Kreios shut his eyes, calmed his nerves, and forced himself to be at peace. He listened carefully and looked around once more for any watchers, scanning the bleakness of the wood for a lone traveler, perhaps a merchant caravan traveling on the road far behind. After a moment, he satisfied himself and was certain that he was alone.

He looked down at his hands. They began to radiate; an internal glow cast itself against the bright snow behind. Turning his eyes upward, he bent into a crouch.

Kreios shot straight up into the sky and turned west, speeding as fast as a shooting star. All around his body, the air waves formed the appearance of wings. Light trailed him as he shot across the sky.

CHAPTER XI

THE WIND WAS BITTER cold. It sliced, knife-like, at the thick coat that covered the baby girl Kreios was holding tight to his chest. He touched down, soundless, in a heavily wooded forest. He was just outside of Gratzipt, his brother's village.

Stealing a glance at his daughter, he couldn't help but smile and breathe her scent in deeply. He was relieved, and his heart calmed some when he saw that she was sleeping soundly.

It had felt so good to get back into the air! Flying was like a drug – with every draw, the feeling grew stronger and more intense. With each flight, he could feel his need and hunger for the experience grow, and unlike any drug, it filled him with power.

He could feel a thousand chilling stares arrayed around him like weapons. His flight to Gratzipt was like a torch in the night to the Brotherhood, and he knew that he would be followed. *What choice have I been given? Am I to watch my daughter perish? Am I to bury her in the cold ground as well?* He did not know how they knew when his kind took flight. He did not know what mystic connection his kind had with the Brotherhood, but it was deep and unbreakable. He could feel blackness coming for him.

The Brotherhood had one goal — the destruction of the Sons of God.

Kreios remembered having lived in peace, walking the streets, dodging happy children's games, listening to the sounds of their laughter. It had been safe. He and others like him were able to live unhindered, free. It had been so long ago... the memory was a vapor in his imagination. He sighed heavily.

He walked through the trees with smooth steps. His eyes closed partially as he looked around using his senses, aware of every creature that moved about the forest, every breeze. His ears heard the icy, subtle movements of the air and the muffled hard-packed crunch that his moccasins made in the snow as he walked.

Quaking aspens and ancient redwoods loomed above him as he came to the natural boundary of the woods. Beyond, the sky opened up into a long valley. In the summer, it would have been filled with lush grasses, teeming with life. But winter held it firm within its clutches and nothing stirred; it was deadly quiet.

He scanned the small village of Gratzipt. It was not much different than his own. Quaint mud huts with thatched roofs dotted the valley randomly. Smoke rose from every one of them; the only hint of life or movement. At the center of the village, there was a much larger structure with a spire piercing the sky. It was the temple.

The temple, the marketplace square, and some other town buildings were built from hewn trees that were stripped, cut to length, and shaped. They fit perfectly together. This construction method had been proven in the most adverse conditions. The town would come together whenever it was time to erect a new building, laboring together. The small huts that surrounded these meticulous buildings were far less glamorous.

Kreios was a family-oriented man, and to him, that was all that mattered. His brothers and sisters, grandparents, uncles and aunts had settled in places far from here. He never saw any of them, though, because the danger was too great. That was the difficult part.

He made his way out from the forest to the main road that ran through the center of the village. Stones had been spread on it by the villagers to keep mud to a minimum in the rainy season. Since it was so cold, not many townsfolk wandered outside. The few that were outside cast glances at him and hurried on through the cold, looking away. This answered his unasked question: no one here was willing to help a stranger.

"We are almost there, baby," Kreios whispered. "You will love your uncle. He is not as strong and handsome as I am, but he is a good man." Straight ahead, the temple spire rose into the sky. It had large wooden doors set with heavy bronze handles that put a strange face on it. Glass windows were built into the walls, which were a radical innovation to the humans at that time.

The people of Gratzipt had discovered a large deposit of iron in one of the valley walls some distance from their village. Lightning strikes were a regular occurrence in that spot during summer storms, and with that regularity, they tested all kinds of materials against it. Soon after, they discovered what the intense heat did to sand, and they began heating it in their brick ovens to make glass without the aid or limitations of lightning, shaping it at will. Glassmaking became a viable trade, and Gratzipt became the merchant hub for the various products that could be made from it.

Kreios knew his brother had been involved in the discovery of this process. He was the chief glassmaker artisan in the village. Kreios, in his own turn, was the master of wisdom in his village. The people would come to him in much the same way the people from the old tales had come to Solomon. Because of his enormous past, he, like his brother, knew things no human could know. They had to be very careful as to how much of their gifts they would reveal. If the people saw too much, they would become frightened. Soon after, rumors of witches or seers always spread like wildfire.

The baby wriggled against his body and cooed, cutting him right to his heart. He loved her more than he could have imagined possible. She was only a few days old, but the love he already felt for her seemed to be as old as the earth. He hurried his steps. She needed to eat, and soon.

Kreios saw the medium-sized hut to the east of the temple and walked directly to the door. Before he could knock, it opened and a dark-haired man with the same features as Kreios stood in the doorway. There was a smile on his face and a hint of concern in his eyes.

"Welcome, my brother, and come inside. I have been waiting for you."

CHAPTER XII

ZEDKIEL SMILED AND EMBRACED Kreios. It had been ages since they had allowed themselves to see each other. The bond they shared ran deep. Kreios stepped inside, closed the door behind him, and looked around.

"I am sorry, my brother, for putting you in danger like this."

"Do not worry Kreios, we are family. If that means we fight, then we are prepared to do that."

"You are a good brother, Zedkiel. I only hope we never have to face the Brotherhood. You have built a fine village, and I can sense that you love it here." Zedkiel nodded and pulled the hide away to reveal the baby girl's sweet face. She was awake, and looked up at her uncle smiling.

"She is lovely! Looks like her mother, thank God." Kreios laughed a deep throaty laugh and allowed his brother to hold her. Zedkiel looked down at the newborn girl and kissed her on the forehead. Without a word, he turned and gave her to his wife.

"Maria is due by the next new moon. We will care for your daughter as if she is our own. You have blessed us with a gift, Kreios." He embraced his brother again and they sat down by the fire that blazed in the center of the room.

Kreios knew that family was the most important thing in the world to all of them. Just the fact that they had offspring to carry on their bloodline was a miracle. Zedkiel and Maria had tried for years to have children. After many painful losses, it looked like they, too, would finally be blessed with a child.

The fire crackled as Zedkiel tossed another log in, making sparks jump up and pop in the air. It was a cold day; the wind starting to beat against the small village as Kreios talked to his brother, telling him everything that had happened to him in the last few years.

Kreios shed his long winter garments, and both men sat on hand-crafted wooden chairs.

"I am trying to be strong, but the pain of losing…" Kreios looked down into the fire. He had a long scar that ran down his right arm and a jagged tattoo-like marking across his left bicep that looked like eagle feathers. His powerful arms and upper body moved, and in the firelight, his skin appeared translucent.

"I am sorry Kreios. I know how much you loved her." Zedkiel had the same light skin tone, but he was not as big as Kreios. His hair was long and dark, pulled back and tied with a leather thong. His massive legs were pure muscle, hardened from many years of labor.

"I remember the first time I saw her." Kreios smiled and looked away, calling up the memory. "She was so beautiful, and filled with joy and so much fire. I know that leaving heaven was wrong, but for her… she was worthy of the consequence I continue to pay."

Zedkiel nodded. "I have been by your side for a long time. I too have no regret…"

Kreios sighed and poked the fire. He watched the flames as they licked up the wood hungrily. "What are we to do about the Brotherhood?"

"We must face them, destroy them." Zedkiel spat in the dirt. "We cannot hide forever. I felt you coming here. I understand why you had to hurry, brother. I felt both of you as you took to the air, but I fear what I might feel next." One of Zedkiel's lingering gifts that he retained after the fall was the ability to sense imminent danger.

Kreios could hear him thinking about the Brotherhood, and he considered their options. He shook his head, knowing that what he had done, in taking to the sky, had been like the sounding of the Battle Trump from the top of the highest mountain. It had been nearly a call to war, his desperate attempt to save the life of his little girl. Certainly, it may have voided the agreement, the pact, but only time would tell.

"We cannot face them and win. They sap our power the nearer we get to them. The only way is to fight them one at a time. Pick them apart, alone and unaware. With speed. We must be even more merciless than they."

Kreios remembered his dearly purchased training involving the Brotherhood in close combat. He had learned that if they were within close range, his power and strength would fade quickly and they could kill him. The Brotherhood always fought in pairs; a demon and a man. If divided, they could be killed, but together it was much more challenging.

Kreios was pure-blood angel and could heal from almost any wound, but the Brotherhood could prevent this process when they were near. The strategy Kreios had finally settled upon was to fight them in small groups, try to kill the demons, the monsters, fast — the men afterward. Then he would hide until he had enough time to heal.

"We must fight smarter, Zedkiel. Ensnare them, separate them from their partners. And we must put to use what is in our hands now." Kreios stood, picking up an object as he did so. It shimmered like water as it caught the light. He held out the invisible weapon and ran his finger down the broad side of its length.

Zedkiel stood and whispered, "Where did you get that?" His eyes were large and round as he realized what he was looking at.

"I recovered it a year ago. It is my sword from the days of old. I tracked the wretch who took it from me and killed him with it." The Sword was sheathed and concealed. The scabbard reflected its surroundings, rendering the Sword mostly invisible.

Kreios took hold of the grip of the Sword and slowly pulled it from its sheath. The room filled with light as he held it up. Zedkiel shielded his eyes as the Sword shone with the brilliance of the sun. Kreios touched the blade and said in a hushed voice, "The Sword of Light. Never again will I let you stray from my side." He turned to his brother, "With this, we will wage war and restore hope to our people once again." His eyes were burning with pure fire.

CHAPTER XIII

Boise, Idaho. Present day.

I WAS LITERALLY IN shock when the police showed up. The ball cap man's body was discovered by an unfortunate boy who was looking around for the source of the smell — the tangy, rusty smell of blood and urine — during the movie. He had been craning his neck, trying to see if he could catch the eyes of anyone else who might have smelled it too. A daylight scene on the screen provided the sudden illumination he had needed.

The situation got worse from there and the police were called, the movie stopped, the lights turned on, and everyone came pouring out of there as if the place were on fire.

Michael found me in the lobby, gave me a reassuring hug, and asked if I was okay. "What happened? Did you see anything?" He asked as if he was excited, hoping I did see something so he could hear all the gory details.

I blurted out, "I saw the whole thing! Didn't you guys see it? He did it right in front of everyone."

I pressed my fingers into my temples, as if by doing so the images of the event would flee like frightened children. It didn't help. All it did was bring up the image of a bloody knife and the sound of footsteps on the tile floor. I could picture it in my mind, the way the knife just hung there in his hand as if he would drop it any second, so careless and casual.

The police locked down the theater and interviewed everyone, including some people who had been watching other movies.

Maybe someone had seen the killer in the ticket line, or in the bathroom in between movies. James and Kim stood around with us as the place gradually cleared out. The police had interviewed everyone they could. Even though they had locked down the building in an attempt to trap the killer, I knew he was long gone.

They interviewed me too. I told them everything that had happened, even the part where he followed me into the bathroom. I wanted to cry but couldn't. It was like the world was running on its time and I was lost in my own slow and haunting version.

"You are one lucky girl!" The officer in charge said. He had a heavy brow with deep set dark eyes. He flipped his notebook shut, mumbling something to another cop, bigger than him, as they both moved away, talking. *Lucky?* I thought how unlucky I was to have seen the murder, but then again, I was alive. And that was something.

The officer with the heavy brow turned back to us and said, "We need you to come on down to the station to meet with a sketch artist. You can... "

"I'll take her." Michael broke in. I didn't interject. I thought it was a good idea, me not driving.

"Miss, Miss!" The other officer broke in, a fat man with a balding head. "You'll be riding with us. We still don't know where the suspect is and Detective Lopez would feel more comfortable if you were under our protection." I nodded to him.

I started to hand off my car keys to Kim. Michael snatched the keys from her hand. "We'll follow you and wait 'til you're done."

"You don't have to come. I'll be fine."

Kim rolled her eyes and said, "We're coming!"

I called my parents and dropped the bomb. Boy, that was fun. My mom was freaking out, in tears, and I could tell that Dad was ready to kill someone. I reassured them as best I could and told them not to worry. I would be home in a few hours.

My dad insisted on meeting me at the police station. To confess the truth, that made me feel a lot better. "Dad, it's fine. I'm okay. Besides, I'm the only one who saw him, so I kinda have to go down and talk to them."

I hoped I wouldn't just burst into a big fat blubbering mess in front of everyone. It just felt so good to hear his voice. There was strength in it, and that's just what I needed.

"I'll see you there," he said flatly. He hung up and I breathed in a sigh of relief.

The overweight officer made small talk as he drove and talked on his radio every now and then. I could picture him with a big cup of coffee in one hand and a donut in the other... the stereotypical cop. His fatness didn't really fit the lean and mean look of his Dodge Charger. I thought about how sometimes these things just don't make much sense, how life just throws us all kinds of curve balls, and how nothing is actually what it appears to be most of the time. Overweight, balding cop, sexy new car. It was just weird, the real world. *Where do I fit into this mess?*

The police station was a small brick building with a single glass door leading to an over-crowded entryway. The woman at the front desk was middle-aged and had nice hair. A little too red, really, and it was up in a messy bun, topped off with two number 2 pencils sticking out of it, making an X.

"Just this way, Miss." I followed Officer Jim — baldy told me I could call him Jim — back to a cramped office, which looked depressing. There was one window that looked out onto the street. A single metal desk and a chair were all that was in the room.

Michael and the rest of the gang had come in the front door and were ushered to a waiting room. On the south wall stood a rack with magazines. There was a soda machine next to a row of uncomfortable looking chairs.

A few minutes later, the cop from the theater with the heavy brow and dark eyes entered and introduced himself. "I'm Detective Lopez. Looks like you got gypped!" He slammed a thin file down on the desk. "You went for comedy but got horror instead." He slapped his thigh and smiled broadly at me.

Wow, dude. Pretty lame joke. He had a comforting way about him, though. He told me he was just trying to lighten the mood. His smile was reassuring, a lot like Dad's, and I could see in his dark brown eyes that he really cared. Either that, or he was just really good at his job.

He had another chair brought in and I went over everything that had happened, step by step. What I saw, what I heard, everything. My heart sped up when I told him about that horrific scene in the bathroom. The only thing I held back was how the murderer had looked at me. That was too weird, even for me.

The artist came in. She was a shy small woman with thin black hair.

"Now," Detective Lopez continued, "I know it was dark, but what can you tell us about him? Was he tall, short, fat, thin, scars, weird looks? Anything you think of will help."

"He was tall with blond hair…" As I gave the description, the artist began her work. After getting the basic shape of his face, she began to sketch the killer's eyes. Looking at them on paper, they still cut right through me. *What if he tried to find me?*

She continued her work, filling in the details, making corrections, adding features, thickening the nose, thinning the eyebrows, squaring the chin. When she finished, I was amazed. The sketch looked just like the man I had seen in the theater.

"That's him!" I felt sick to my stomach.

After Detective Lopez and the sketch artist left, my dad came in. I held on to him and would not let go. I needed someone stronger than me. He told me that Mom was home making dinner, busying herself to keep from worrying. "I'm fine Dad, really!" I lied.

"You sure? Kim filled me in. I'm so glad you're safe." His eyes said what he could not: *"You could have been killed!"* He had a scared look on his face, and I hugged him again.

"Well… I'm safe now. No need to worry." I knew that was weak, but I couldn't think of anything else to say. My brain was moving like sludge, and yet I felt like I was still thinking clearly. I looked over my dad's shoulder and saw Michael. He was standing a few feet behind and I caught him staring at me. I blushed and he turned away. I wondered what he was thinking.

Did he really like me or was I just seeing things again? How could he really like me when I was just… me? Then again, he had totally held my hand just a few hours earlier as we had been walking toward what was a defining moment in my life. *Maybe 'defining moment' is not a good way to put it.* Anyway, it was all shaping up to be too much to handle for one day.

"Well, I'm just glad you're okay."

"Thanks, Daddy."

How could I explain the things in my life that I had chosen to keep private? Not just to Dad, but to anyone at all? The most perfect boy I had ever met was digging on me like I was chocolate cookies or something. How crazy was that? And I was getting sick at random times for no good reason.

Now, as my dad curled his strong arm around my shoulder, taking me toward the car, all I could think about was how I was glad he had paid for my kickboxing lessons. At least I had some kind of self-defense training.

As we walked out, I remembered Kim saying something about taking the guys back to their truck and that she would bring my car over later. I knew there was no way she was staying at her house tonight, not with her Airel having gone through hell today. We had a lot to talk about.

CHAPTER XIV

MONDAY. IT WAS NEVER a good word. The day that came along with it looked to be living up to its name. I looked at the clock. Two a.m.... great. I was lying in bed with my eyes open, unable to fall asleep. The cool night air drifted in through the crack I had left in the window and made me shiver. I pulled the covers tighter around my neck.

Kim was in the guest bedroom, passed out. We had made up for lost time after all that movie theater craziness, watching nothing but girl movies all weekend and eating pizza and popcorn like — well, like a couple of football players, I guess. Maybe the only difference was the tissues, the tears, and the lack of a blue dart contest. Guys are seriously gross.

All of these thoughts came to rest on Michael Alexander, inevitably. I had to face facts. I was pretty tangled up around the idea of him being in my life. And the romance — or the — well, I couldn't say love yet, but whatever it was, it was putting down roots in my heart. I didn't feel there was anything I could do about it, even if I wanted to. I was so anxious to find out what was going to happen between us that I was actively trying to shut up whatever alarm bells I heard in my head. Michael was perfect. For me, I mean.

I don't know if there's the *one* out there for me. I always thought that idea was pretty corny anyway. So many of my friends were so hung up on their idea of the *one guy*, that they were seriously having some issues with reality, just waiting to be found by destiny or whatever. I always thought that was pretty weak. I felt like I was

67

meant for more than that — like I was made to *be* more. I can't explain it, I just knew it. I didn't have any idea what part Michael might play in it, but I couldn't help being drawn back to him in my heart and in my thoughts all the time.

I could hear Kim snoring in the next room. I had to laugh at her. I was giving her a hard time for crying at one of those girl movies yesterday, and she chased me into the bathroom with a bowl of popcorn. It was then that I had noticed my skin. I was really starting to grow up into a woman... somebody lovely. It was amazing, really. I didn't know if this was how it was supposed to go, but I was really digging the results. My skin was clearing up and causing me to do a double-take on myself in the mirror. It couldn't be real.

None of it could be real. I mean, it almost made me angry, thinking about it. I couldn't get the events of the weekend out of my mind. It was like a bad movie that I couldn't help replaying over and over, no matter how much I hated it. I guess it was just another turn on the rollercoaster of my life for the past week or so. It was starting to get really crazy, and if it kept up, I didn't know what I might do.

He looked right at me. Talking to myself at two in the morning wasn't helping things. The thought of that tall killer was creeping me out the more I thought about it. He had looked so composed, so massive, so calm. I shuddered. Then the thought of one person taking another person's life had me thinking that I had to do something. *What are you going to do, go all 'Detective Airel' and hunt the killer down?* I didn't know what to do. I knew I should let the police do their job, but something deep inside of me wanted to get involved.

The moon was full and made long scary shadows on the walls. There was a big oak tree right outside my window, and in the moonlight, the shadows looked alive. I normally loved the moonlight. There was something soothing about it. Tonight, though, it wasn't a good moon. It was somehow dark and had its own agenda.

I rolled over and closed my eyes. I needed sleep. I had school in the morning, and if I was up all night, I would be a zombie. I turned over onto my stomach and thought about math. Nothing like math to put you to sleep. *Boring, blah, blah, boring, nonsense, boring. I'm tired. I—Am—Tired.*

Crap. Tossing the covers off, I slipped into a warm pair of slippers, stole down the hall, and tiptoed downstairs to the kitchen. It was almost as bright as day, the moonlight splashing off the tile floor through the window.

I opened the fridge and took out the milk carton, pouring myself a little mug and nuking it for 30 seconds. Mom used to make me warm milk like that when I couldn't sleep as a kid. I sipped it slowly, trying to relax.

My pink pajama bottoms and brown t-shirt weren't super warm. I shivered a little bit. The night air was cool... on the border of being cold. I hoped it might get me in the mood for sleep once I crawled back into my nice warm bed.

I was restless, though. I found myself wandering around the living room, looking out the front windows at the lawn. I took my little mug of milk and stepped to the front door, being careful to turn the deadbolt slowly so I didn't wake anyone else up. I slipped out onto the front porch, closed the door, and looked out over the neighborhood.

It was so very quiet. Some sprinklers a few doors down hissed and popped up unexpectedly and I hugged myself, chilled by the night air. I finished my milk and left the mug on the porch rail. My thoughts turned back to my upcoming math test, and I remembered that I left my backpack in the car. I walked down to it at the curb and tried the door.

Locked.

Great. Now math and homework all seemed like too much work. I just needed to breathe, to calm myself. But walking around alone at night was like being in one of those stupid hacker movies. Some dumb blonde running around as a killer slowly stalked her. Not exactly real life.

The neighborhood was quiet, and most of the houses had their lights off, but I could see everything with the moon looking over my shoulder. My slippers made a smacking sound with each step, and I thought of each house, how they had someone inside them sleeping. It made me feel alone, but I didn't mind. I kind of liked that feeling sometimes. It was a little exciting, even, like I was cheating, being up and awake for a part of the night that most people slept right through.

I stopped.

Something crashed in the alley in between the two houses to my right. I looked over into the dark alley and saw a glowing pair of eyes. My heart was pounding a mile a minute. I looked into the bright yellow eyes, a million thoughts running through my head, and the hair on the back of my neck stood up on end. A dark brown cat ran from the shadows and took off down the sidewalk. *Stupid cat!* It was weird. I had crouched down into my defensive stance. *Kickboxing's really starting to pay off, Dad. No worries!*

I was scared, and the more I tried to fight it, the worse it was. I tried to calm down but couldn't. Just like trying to sleep. Here I was taking a walk because math couldn't make me sleep. *What next?* Now everything in the dark was scary and a hidden killer lurked behind every trash can on the street.

I started back to the house as my heart beat harder and harder. *Don't run! That will make it worse.* I took off running anyway. I was now completely terrified. I clamped my mouth shut, trying not to scream, when I saw a lone figure standing in front of my mailbox.

I stopped instantly and looked with wide eyes at the man who stood between me and the safety of my home. He had short, blond hair and stood well over six feet tall with a muscular build. He was wearing a black leather jacket and blue jeans. My heart was in my ears. All I could think about was getting out of there. I turned the other way and ran, going past my next door neighbor's house, stumbling over their sidewalk on the way. I ducked into their side yard and ran for the back.

Now I was petrified.

It was the same man from the theater. I was sure of it. *How did he find me? What did he want from me?* I thought I knew the answer to that, but couldn't bring myself to say it or even think it. I scrambled over my neighbor's fence and ran across their backyard, circling around toward my house again. I stopped at the gate and quietly unlatched it. I could see part of my front yard through the crack. I had to get back inside my house where it was safe, but it wouldn't be safe if the killer knew I was there.

I had to get closer if I was going to be able to see anything. My house had the perfect shrub to hide behind. I got down low and crept out the gate along the side of my house, hugging it closely and squeezing behind a large evergreen shrub. I parted the branches to look out. I was safe enough as long as he didn't see me. *Airel, you are being reckless and putting your life in danger. What are you doing?* I peered out and looked around.

He was gone.

The mailbox sat with the door open and the flag up, but no one was around. I looked up the street and back down again. I couldn't see the killer anywhere. Was he hiding, just waiting for me to show myself? Then, a horrible thought struck me. *He might be in the house.*

I waited a few minutes and finally decided to risk it and make a dash for the front door. It was only a few feet from where I was hiding, and even if he was waiting, I could probably out-run him.

Taking a deep breath, I jumped up, ran to the front door, and burst inside, slamming the door. I couldn't believe I didn't wake anyone up with that racket. I looked around the kitchen and living room as I stood with my back against the front door, gasping, trying to catch my breath.

Everything was quiet. I sank to the floor and put my face in my hands. I wanted to cry, but I was too mad to let it escape. *Who did this guy think he was? Coming to my house and scaring me to death.*

So much for going back to sleep. Then, I heard the sound of footsteps on the porch. I scrambled to the island in the kitchen and ducked behind it. My heart beat in my ears, and after a breathless minute, I peered up and saw the shadow of a man looking in the window.

I gasped and clamped my hand over my mouth. He didn't see me and turned and walked away. I stood up and watched him walk down the sidewalk and disappear around the corner. The mailbox door stood open.

CHAPTER XV

THE NOTE WAS WRITTEN in the most elegant cursive I'd ever seen, yet it chilled me to the bone.

I know what you are!

I stared down at it. I sat down heavily on a bar stool. What did it mean? I know *what* you are. Shouldn't it say *who* you are —? The killer was leaving me notes and following me to my house, and I was fully creeped out.

What could I do, though? What would I do?

I decided, for the moment, that I was overwhelmed enough to go back to bed. I was suddenly very tired. I trudged upstairs and plopped down onto my soft bed, pulling the covers up to my chin. As my body began to calm down and the bed began to warm up, I relaxed. I began to drift off to sleep, even as my mind raced with how to handle my bigger-than-life problems.

I didn't know who to talk to — the police? My dad? My mom? *What should I tell them?* Exactly how much could I reveal, even to my closest friends and family, without sounding totally insane, even to them? Could I tell the detectives about my stalker, the murderer? I mean, should I?

What about this note, though, and what if they wanted to use it as evidence — what did that mean for me? And how, exactly, could I break any of this to my dad? He would totally flip out and run out to stock up on ammunition or something. That's all I needed, for Dad to answer the door with a shotgun all the time.

And what could I tell Mom — that I'm like, barfing all over the place, unexpectedly?

My mind was finally starting to shut down, but not because I was ready for sleep. It was probably because I was in over my head and I knew it. My life had officially become berserk.

As far as I knew, the rest of the night was uneventful. I slept through the night and even had a nice dream about Michael Alexander. Nothing too weird, just about our afternoon at the mall and how he looked at me. He could look at me one minute like I was a science project and the next, I was beautiful. Did he like me, truly? Or was I some sort of sick dare that he had with his guy friends? "See if you can get that girl to like you," or, "I dare you to get her to go to prom with you." So juvenile.

A few short hours later, I got out of bed. Rubbing the sleep from my eyes, I looked in the mirror to see if my skin had gone back to normal. *Nope.* Not that I was disappointed. I was beginning to like my new, airbrushed look. If this kept up, I could be on the cover of *People* or something. Hopefully it wouldn't be the *National Enquirer.* I guess I didn't need to put on make-up today. I ran my hands through my wet hair after a shower, pulled it up, and twisted it into a messy bun. I found a #2 pencil, stuck it through the center of the bun, and smiled. Why not? City worker *chic.* Sweet.

Kim sauntered into the room and looked like she was the one who was up being harassed all night by a killer. Her red hair was off in crazy-land and the bags under her eyes had their own zip code. "Morning, hot stuff!" I said as she waved me off.

"Shut up! I need coffee and a bagel — in that order." She dragged herself into the bathroom and turned on the hot water. I looked at the clock.

"If you want coffee, you'd better hurry." We had less than a half hour to get to school. We had a hard-nosed teacher in our first class together, and cracking down hard on tardiness was a part of his motivational technique.

On the way to school, I couldn't help but tune out some of Kim's chatter. It was like I was a magnet, and the fridge I was drawn to was all this crap that was happening to me. My thoughts were so crazy that they seemed like they didn't even belong to me half the time.

Thank God for history class. Come on, like I cared what Chinese dynasty was what, or when they built the Great Wall. But this time I wasn't thinking about how my jeans fit, or how Marcie should really not be wearing a 6, or if I would get asked to prom by Michael — and if he did ask me, why was I so scared of the question?

No, I was stuck with the face of a murderer looking up at me from a dark movie theater, the footsteps sounding on a hard tile floor, the echo that made him far scarier. I could have very well lost my life.

Or maybe I was just over-thinking again. It was almost painful to be this confused. Kim would have laughed and joked about that nonstop, if she would have heard me say it.

I looked for Michael, but he was not in school that day, as far as I could tell. I wondered if he was sick — maybe he got what I had, or what I was getting over — or if something worse had happened to him. *Airel. You're acting like a lovesick head case. Then again, maybe that's exactly what's happening here.*

After school, I went right home. Dad's orders. He had made it perfectly clear what he expected from me, until this killer was caught and locked up. No negotiation. Not that I was any good at it anyway.

The sky had a large gray and black cloud hanging over part of my fair city, like a schoolyard bully waiting for the nerd to come around the corner so he could blow off a little steam. It smelled like rain, and I didn't care. Rain, snow — who cares.

I was stuck at home until my own personal cloud passed over and my parents decided it was safe for dear little Airel to go out and play again. I was about to pull into my neighborhood when I felt that all-too-familiar feeling rise up in my chest. *Not again!*

I pushed on the brakes just in time to throw my door open and lean out to lose my school lunch. Weird, it didn't look much different than when it was served to me a few hours earlier. *That's what a buck-fifty buys ya — it looks like barf.*

And with that, my mind was made up. Time to call the doctor. Doctor Gee had been my doctor since forever. He had white-blond hair and the brightest blue eyes I'd ever seen. I flipped open my phone and called his office. I hoped I could get in. It wasn't flu season yet, so I didn't think it would be a problem.

"Doctor Gee's office," the chipper secretary said.

"Yeah, hi. This is Airel —"

"Airel, oh, how nice to hear from you!" She cut me off. I knew it was Mrs. Birch, a sweet woman who had been with the office for longer than I had been alive. "Are you feeling alright? Oh, that's silly of me. You must not be or else you wouldn't be calling."

"I've been pretty sick... " I croaked, "and I was wondering if I could get in to see the doc." I tried to sound happier than I was feeling, not that it mattered. She didn't care if I muttered and complained about how I was feeling.

"You know, we just had a no-show. If you like, he can see you right away. Can you be here in ten minutes?"

I was only five minutes away, so I told her I would be there. I managed to hold in the next round of queasy feelings on the way over, and as soon as I pulled into the parking lot, I started to feel much better. Murphy's Law, I guess. You feel sick until you get to the doctor's office. Then, miracle of miracles, you're healed.

Mrs. Birch's mess of silvering hair was all 1982, and her glasses were tethered with a thin gold chain draped around her neck. She smiled and looked up at me as I came in.

"Oh, sweetie, come on back. He's waiting for you. My, my! How you have changed... so beautiful!"

I blushed and turned my face away. "Thank you, but it's just me... the same Airel as always." She squeezed my shoulder and showed me into a small room with a table and a counter. In the corner, next to the sink, there was a jar of tongue depressors.

"He'll be just one minute." She smiled and closed the door, leaving me alone. I felt just a little scared, even though I was in my family doctor's office. I went to the table and sat down, making the paper on the table crackle. My feet hung over the side, and I felt like a little kid again. I sure hoped he could find out what was wrong with me. I didn't know how much more of this weird sickness I could take.

CHAPTER XVI

"SO, AIREL, I'VE BEEN told that you're feeling a little under the weather." Dr. Gee smiled with his bright white teeth all showing, which made him look like he should be on the set of a soap opera rather than in front of me in a dress shirt and a tie.

"You could say that! I think I might be dying." I smiled back and faked a cough just to try to make myself feel better than I really was. Not that I was feeling like death at the moment, on the contrary, I was feeling great. That was what made it all so much worse. It was like never having a chance meeting with a cute boy when you were ready to. No, girls like me only ever met cute boys over breakfast, without make-up, wearing sweats and a t-shirt, and with our hair totally beyond help. Nothing ever worked out the way it was supposed to.

"Well, tell me what's going on — don't butter it up for me. And tell me what you think it *might* be as well." He looked at me with his blue eyes, and I felt like I was looking straight into a cold sky in the dead of winter. I think I even shivered a little.

Dr. Gee listened to my breathing through his stethoscope and looked into my ears as I began to explain the past few weeks in as much detail as I could, without explaining what each chunk of barf looked like.

"And no — I know what you're thinking — it's not possible."

He nodded and grinned with just the left half of his face. "No boyfriend?"

"No. Besides, I'm partial to waiting until marriage, if you know what I mean. I've got the ring and everything." I held up my left hand and flashed him my ring finger, which had a thin gold band on it. "My dad gave it to me when I was thirteen." I was a little embarrassed to be talking about this with my doctor, but he got the hint after I looked at the floor, leaving my sentence unfinished.

"That's great." Dr. Gee sat back on a little round chair on wheels. The silence was more than uncomfortable as he slid back a foot or so with his arms folded across his chest.

"So what do you think about my little problem? Am I going to die?" I laughed a little, but deep down inside, I was thinking I might do just that... either from this mysterious illness or by the hand of some psycho killer. Is this what people meant when they talked about being lovesick, or what?

"I don't think you're going to die, Airel, but I'm not sure what it might be, and I would like to run a few tests, if you don't mind. I think it might be viral, and I would like to rule out some things before we dig any deeper." He saw the look on my face, pushed forward in his chair, and leaned forward to touch my arm. His orange tie hung down like a breezeless flag. "Don't worry, you'll be fine. I just want to be sure. I don't want to overlook anything, okay?"

I nodded and sighed with relief.

"Now. I'm going to have Sue take some blood, and I would like a urine sample, as well. If you get sick again, I want you to call me right away, then come in. I would like to run a test when you're feeling your worst, okay?" He pulled out his card and scrawled his cell number on the back, handing it to me with a serious look on his face. "I mean it. You call me as soon as you feel anything."

"I will, I promise. I don't think I want to live with the ability to vomit without any warning. It doesn't really fit into my social agenda, doc." I winked at him, which for me, was uncharacteristic, and it made me blush. *Man, I hate when I embarrass myself like this.*

Dr. Gee laughed aloud and stood up, making him seem like a giant. He left the room, and once again, I was alone in the chilly office listening to the only sound in the room... the crackling paper under my legs. I was not looking forward to having my blood drawn.

My mind wandered and came to rest on vampires, of all

things. I remembered a book I read about someone who was bit and changed into a vampire — it made him sick, but he got better afterward. *If you could call it that.* Anyway, no one had bitten me — except for the *love bug,* as Kim would say. I didn't know of any vampires at my school, anyway; they weren't even real to begin with.

I put my hand to my cheek, felt its uncharacteristically smooth, soft surface, and closed my eyes. "Changed... " I muttered in a whisper. I hadn't had a zit in like forever. Which, contrary to everything holy, actually gave me cause for concern. *I should have paid more attention in science.* "Chaaaange, Meta-MORRR-phosis," I said to myself, in my TV announcer voice, which made me laugh. But... my skin was smoother, and all but a few of my freckles were disappearing. *No, it can't be. There's no such thing! Humans don't undergo metamorphosis.* It was probably just hormones making me insane. It's all a part of growing up.

Sometimes life is just sucky and unexplainable. I finally had the perfect skin I'd always wanted, but along with that came the spontaneous barfing... a package deal. *Or does all of this mean something worse?* Was I going to grow fangs and start craving blood?

As I was thinking that, the hair on the back of my neck stood up on end, and I nearly followed suit. I could feel a presence in the room with me, as if something invisible had just allowed me to take notice of it and didn't care how I felt about it, one way or another. Whatever it was, it wasn't evil. I knew that much, because I wasn't scared of it. In fact, it seemed like it was good all the way through to the core, filled with brilliant white light. It was just startling because I couldn't see it. Whatever it was, I had a feeling it was here to stay.

It spoke to me, not in a real voice or audible words, or even as my conscience, but a third voice beyond my own being. It laughed a faint little giggle and shook its head like a parent who had just heard me say something incredibly naive about silly old legends.

It stretched like a cat, settled down and fell asleep. I had to laugh out loud about it. I had a new friend, and I was not entirely sure if I wanted one or not. I had a feeling I didn't have a choice about it. Great. More drama. Just what I needed.

CHAPTER XVII

MY SIMPLE LIFE OF school and the occasional pizza and movie night had been turned on its head. I not only had a genuine stalker, who seemed to like killing people and mocking me with cryptic notes, but I also had a weird disease that crept up at the most unexpected times. As for everything else, well, yikes. What was I supposed to think? I was probably certifiable now. Schizophrenic.

I had a strong feeling that Dr. Gee wouldn't find anything, no matter how many tests he ran. The new little voice in my head told me that it was all nothing. I had a feeling that all of this was simply pointing back to what was going on with my skin and those occasional intense growing pains. Now, as I looked in the mirror on a normal Tuesday morning, there was something more. It had been a week and still no change, 'til last night.

I had been startled awake at three in the morning by the most hellacious nightmare I can ever remember having. I had a headache to end all headaches, and my hair was dripping wet, tangled on my face as if I had just come up for air in the river. I couldn't, for the life of me, remember what the nightmare was about, and I was glad about that. I summoned the courage to get up and turn on the light in my bedroom, which instantly seemed to dispel most of my fear.

I felt really gross. Maybe my dream was about pre-season practice with the football team. Now that *would* be a nightmare. I shuffled to the bathroom to clean up, cool down, and try to pull myself together. I changed into my back-up pajamas: my favorite blue sweats and an old long sleeved t-shirt. They were so comfortable — but so ugly — that I didn't dare wear them unless I had no other choice.

I felt better after that, but still had a raging headache and no idea why. Grabbing a couple of Advil from the medicine cabinet, I filled the glass by the sink with water. I tossed back the tablets and took a long drink of cool water, then carried the glass into my bedroom.

When I sat down on the bed, with my feet dangling off the floor, the glass suddenly shattered in my hand. I gasped as shards dug into my hand, and I dropped what was left of the glass. I was in total shock. It hit the carpet with a thump, and I bit my lip to keep from screaming out in pain.

Blood ran freely from two different cuts on my palm. From the looks of them, they were deep. I started to get woozy but forced myself to keep it together. *Don't pass out Airel. You've got to stop the bleeding.* In that moment, I wished I had woken my mom up. I jumped up, dodging the glass on the floor, ran to the bathroom holding my bleeding left hand, and got to the sink just in time to catch the first drips. *Mom would have a cow, maybe a calf, too!*

I turned on the cold water. It stung, and I winced in pain as it flushed out the wound. Blood pooled in the sink. There were two large, deep gashes in my hand; I feared I would need stitches. I pulled the largest pieces out with my fingers. There were a few that I just couldn't get, and though I was brave, I wasn't that brave.

I found some bandages and gauze strips under the sink, wound them around my throbbing hand, and made a bandage that looked like something out of one of Dad's war movies. Not the best, but at three in the morning, I wasn't about to wake my parents — at least, not now that I had everything under control. I guess I just needed a stiff upper lip and time to heal.

I made sure the bathroom didn't look like I had just killed someone and went back to bed. I still don't know how I fell asleep with the rhythmic throbbing in my poor hand, or the thoughts running through my mind of what I was going to tell my parents when they saw my enormous gauze mitten. And what would I tell Kim — Miss Talks-a-lot?

Stuck in the back of my mind was my new friend, whispering *Why did the glass break?* It was a good question. It wasn't one of those thin cheapie glasses. It was heavy, thick. I could have tossed it across the living room and it wouldn't have broken. It would have left a dent in the wall. So that's how I spent my night: horror show, sweat shower, headache, my own real-life episode of CSI, and back to bed.

In the morning, I stood in front of the mirror in the first rays of sunshine, more beautiful than I dared to be, especially after a night like that, hearing those words in my head: *Why did the glass break?*

I unwound the tape and bandages, wanting to assess the damage before showing Mom my handiwork. That's when I knew there was going to be big trouble. There was more to my little mysteries than vomit and perfect skin, anyway. I stared at my hand. *Impossible!* Then, I stared at it in the mirror, thinking that in there maybe things would look normal. *I'm going crazy and that's that!* My hand was not cut, bleeding, bruised or even starting to heal.

It was completely healed.

The alternative version of reality was that I was never cut, the glass never broke, and it was all just a bad dream. But there were bloody bandages and fragments of broken glass in the trash can that sat next to my dresser. I turned my hand palm up to inspect it again. Nothing. It was fine. But there was something gritty and shiny on my palm. After a closer look, I realized that somehow, my body had rejected the tiniest shards of glass that had been embedded in it... the ones that I could not get out the night before.

I reached down and pulled the bandages out of the trash can. They, too, had little shards of glass. I looked again at my palm and realized that there weren't even scars. I looked up into the mirror again, looking myself in the eyes, blinking as if meeting myself for the very first time.

Then, I did something I still don't believe I had the guts to try. I reached back into the trash can, took a knife-like chunk of the remains of the glass, and held it up in front of my face. There, between the mirror and me, was a moment like ripples in a pond.

The girl in the mirror looked defiant and brave all at once. The real girl, if I could call myself that, felt scared but impulsive. The shard of glass looked wicked, dangerous. Now, I felt it down to my very bones; I knew what it felt like to be completely crazy.

I laid my hand palm up on the top of my dresser. I grabbed an old t-shirt from the drawer and bit down hard on it. I raised my right hand and stabbed the glass knife into my left. I screamed through the t-shirt with clenched teeth. If Mom heard, she would probably just think I stubbed my toe or just remembered some unfinished homework.

Blood. Both hands were now badly cut. My right palm was sliced to ribbons where I had grasped the weapon, and my left was absolutely pierced. The glass was stuck through it into the top of my dresser like a dagger.

I pulled, and with some effort, dislodged the glass shard from the dresser top, dropping it back into the trash can. It chimed abruptly as it hit the other pieces of glass. I looked down at my hands with a look of horror on my face. *What have I done?*

CHAPTER XVIII

1250 B.C. Arabia

KREIOS SLEPT BY THE warm fire that had died down to coals, casting an amber glow on the hard-packed walls. Just before he had fallen asleep, he let his mind come to rest on part of his talk with Zedkiel.

His brother had mentioned a large city, two weeks' journey to the west, where they were building structures out of stone and granite. He remembered living in a city much like the one his brother described, but a long time ago. That was another time, another life; but he allowed his mind to dwell in those memories as he drifted off to sleep.

It was now very late. Nothing moved.

A dark shadow crossed the room without a sound. Kreios awoke, becoming alert without opening his eyes. He had been trained for combat, and his sleeping habits had not changed much over the years. He slept soundly, yet very lightly. The slightest sound that was out of place was enough to wake him fully, and he had disciplined himself to awaken without changing his breathing pattern in the slightest.

He waited, unmoving. Now, he could hear something moving around inside the hut. The heat from the sword that lay under his arm confirmed the danger he felt.

Cracking his right eye open, he looked around the room. On the other side of the fire pit stood a figure cloaked in darkness, a long haggard robe draped down, dragging on the floor. Kreios' hand rested near the grip of his sword and he moved his fingers slowly, wrapping them around it and enclosing it like a band of iron. Every muscle in his body tensed. *You will only have one chance. Make this count.*

In a blur of speed, and in one motion, Kreios jumped to his feet and unsheathed the Sword of Light. The hulking dark visitor screeched in pain but did not shrink back as blazing light filled the room. Kreios could feel the demon drawing on his life force. But an unexpected sensation interrupted all of this. With sword in hand, Kreios could now feel it resisting the demonic draw. It was restoring him, renewing him, and he regained what had been stolen as energy returned, flowing up his arm, into his chest. He betrayed himself with a faint smile flashing across his face.

From the corner of his eye, Kreios saw another filthy black figure stepping from the next room. He decided to begin the fight by ending it. Quickly, he swung the Sword and split the midsection of the closest enemy, spilling his bowels onto the ground.

Before it could roar with indignant pain, he had begun fluidly moving the Sword back into the attack, arcing low, barely touching the dirt floor, and coming back around to shoulder height. He was poised and did not hesitate. With a backhand swing, he took off its head and watched as its jagged sword clacked to the ground, its body crumpled in a bloody heap.

Kreios immediately felt a surge of power returning to him, and his birthmark glowed up his arm as if on fire. *Now for another.*

He turned toward the second intruder, closing with it quickly. As Kreios drew back to strike, the beast savagely plunged a crooked black dagger into him. Kreios felt searing pain as the blade penetrated his chest. His thoughts turned toward his precious daughter in the next room. As he fell to his knees, stunned, he prayed desperately for her safety.

No words passed between the two enemies as they stared at each other. Kreios still held the Sword in the vise of his grip as it flamed brightly, the white light revealing the hideousness of his enemy. It was disgusting, pathetic. A dirty, waxy hood concealed its face, revealing only the glow of eyes within that were fueled by the fires of Hell itself. Leaving the dagger jutting from Kreios' chest, the demon raised its wickedly curved black sword high overhead, savoring the coming strike at the heart of his foe.

Its stinking, festering body tensed in preparation for the final blow. Abruptly, however, the thing retched; black liquid gurgled up from its throat, and its sword fell, clanging to the floor. Its mouth hung open wide, and in the light of the Sword, Kreios could see the sharpness of steel sticking through the beast from the back of its head, protruding from its gaping mouth.

Zedkiel!

Kreios pulled the beast's dagger free of his own chest and turned it homeward, burying the smoking tip within the sickening folds of the robe of the demon. He rose up, ignoring the pain shooting through his ribcage, and swung the Sword violently across its neck, severing the head. The demon fell to the dirt floor, dead. Tacky blood spilled from its body. Zedkiel put his foot on the head and pulled his sword free, standing over the lifeless form with contempt.

"Are you wounded?" Zedkiel looked at Kreios and leaned down to examine his injury.

"He missed my lung. I can already feel it healing. I will be whole by sunrise." Kreios grimaced. "Thank you." He struggled to remain standing. He placed a hand on his brother's shoulder, leaning on him for support.

Kreios wiped the blood off the Sword, sheathed it, and slung the scabbard over his shoulder, keeping the sword tight and snug to his body.

Zedkiel placed more wood on the fire, which began to roar lustily. Then, he cut up the bodies into pieces so he could burn them. As Kreios helped his brother with this grisly task, he could not help but feel like something was amiss. He could not place the feeling, but something was not right.

Kreios walked out the front door and looked up at the clear night sky. The air had a bitter quality. The sulfuric smell of the fuel now burning on the fire did not help matters. He listened for the sound of horses. Maybe he would be able to discern, by straining his ears, the approach of the Brotherhood coming to finish the job.

The village still slept and did not know what had just transpired. It was better that way.

"I believe they only sent two of them. It would have been an easy kill if it was not for the Sword you carry." Zedkiel stood in the doorway and searched the sky with his deep dark eyes. The night was still and calm, completely clear. The stars illuminated the valley in resplendence, and it reminded him of another age.

Kreios did not like knowing that he had brought the demons there. His problems were not his brother's. In his haste to save his daughter, Kreios had put the whole family at risk. "I fear you will have to move away from Gratzipt. They know you are here now. They will send more." Kreios knew his brother would refuse, but he was compelled to speak the truth, no matter what his brother might say.

"I cannot remove us from this life. We cannot rebuild again. Maria could not endure it, especially now. The child is nearly here, and we have a good life in our little village." He paused, and the moment was heavy. "No. We will wait and set snares to protect ourselves. With you here, with the Sword, our strategy can be adjusted. We do not need to run."

Kreios said nothing. He was sure that his brother would see how the decision to stay would rain down hellfire upon all the innocent villagers, punishing them for daring to live next to angels who provoked battles with the Brotherhood.

He turned, walking back into the house. Kreios knew his brother would not listen to wisdom just now, so he decided to drop the subject. He wanted to be sure his baby girl was still snuggled in safety.

Kreios found Maria sprawled crookedly in the corner on his brother's bed. "Zedkiel!" He called to his brother as he ran to Maria. Zedkiel came quickly and they sat her up, cautiously. She began to sob, moaning with her head in her hands. Kreios jerked his head to where his baby girl was sleeping. He rushed over and pulled the skins back.

She was gone.

Maria sobbed and looked up at him with grief in her eyes. "They took her, there were four of them! Two went after you and the other two left with the child. They would have killed me as well, but ran with the baby when they heard you." She had red puffy eyes, and her face was wet with tears. Kreios wanted to scream. He filled with rage as a knot bound up in the pit of his stomach.

"I tried to scream when they took her, but they struck me and everything became dark. I thought I was dead! Oh, Kreios, I am so sorry!" Kreios went to her and embraced her. He was glad that his brother's wife was alive. She would bring Zedkiel a child soon, and it was by the grace of God that the Brotherhood had not killed her.

Kreios stood, malice flashing in his eyes. "I must go. They want me. They will not harm her as long as I am alive!" It was a pleading prayer. Kreios hoped it was true, but deep down, he suspected he would never see his daughter again.

Kreios took a sling and filled it with some barley cakes and then quickly grabbed a skin for water. He waved off his brother's attempt to go with him. "You need to be here to protect Maria. They will come back for her... and you." Zedkiel wandered about with a lost look on his face; the inner turmoil he felt was obvious. He pulled Maria close and watched as Kreios prepared to leave.

Kreios donned his coat and tied his belt tight. If it was battle they wanted, it was battle they would taste.

He stepped out and looked up at the star-filled sky. With an agile movement, he sprung up, shooting into the night sky, leaving a small light trail behind.

CHAPTER XIX

THE AIR HAD A cool bite to it as Kreios flew through the sky. He knew that the Brotherhood had taken his daughter, and he was having a hard time controlling his anger. His thoughts were racing with recklessly crafted scenarios in which he was slicing the enemy to bits and pieces. He was shouting at them on the battlefield, running toward them, praying for more demon flesh to cleave, and when he had exhausted these fantasies, his mind turned toward what he would do to the Seer when they met.

His body was shaking with rage, and his eyes burned with righteous hatred for the cowardly, sneaking, filthy beasts that had taken his daughter. He had every right. He would send every last one of them to Hell personally.

After having lost his wife, he was broken and desperate. Now that he had lost his daughter, and he wasn't sure if she was dead or alive, he felt the eyes of the heavens upon him and his quest for justice. Now vengeance would belong to Kreios, and he would deliver it without mercy.

Kreios breathed heavily. Tears streamed down his face, but he wiped them with the back of his hand. There would be a time to mourn, but this was not it; he needed to be strong for his daughter.

He descended into the trees and alighted softly, deep in the dark woods, near the main road from Gratzipt. He could smell horse manure. The demon horde would be on horses, moving fast through the forest to make as much time as they could. He moved toward the road quickly.

At its edge, he stopped. He could now smell dust in the air, along with the scent of the horses and the unmistakable choking signature of decay. They had passed by this spot not long ago.

Softly, he retreated to the cover of the woods and climbed a tall tree. He had ascended to its uppermost reaches within seconds. He observed the terrain for miles around, looking for any trace of his prey. He could sense that they were near but now he could hear the clatter of hooves on the road, toward the setting moon. He knew which way to go now.

Kreios wanted to go in with sword drawn and slice them to pieces, but he feared what would become of his sweet baby girl. He pulled his hood low on his head and silently dropped to the ground in the dark shadows of the forest. With deceptive speed, he began to close in on the enemy, running in complete silence along the roadside, dodging brambles and leaping over fallen trees.

He could feel his strength start to fade, felt them feeding off him with every step he took. He had to move fast and with a sure hand if he was to see his little girl reach her first birthday.

Up ahead, at a wide spot in the road, there stood two horses, black as night. Sweat was pouring from them, and Kreios could tell they had been ridden hard. He could hear the murmuring of a stream nearby as he stopped to take cover and observe them. The riders were taking a drink from the stream that flowed through the center of the clearing. *These two must be the rear guard of the army.* The rest would have gone on ahead and probably had his daughter.

Kreios took a moment to listen to the sounds of the woods. An owl called out. The little creek steamed as it flowed over rocks and under old logs, and the smell of snow and deep forest decay filled his nostrils. Every sound in nature, including some that were not of the world, flooded his senses. He could hear the sound of their blackened hearts beating, the lapping of their lips as they drank like dogs.

There was a small adjoining meadow by the wide spot in the road, filled with dead, moistened stalks of tall grass left over from the heat of the summer. Kreios slipped into the field and moved forward like a panther stalking its prey.

He could hear a baby's cry close by, muffled. He saw a jiggling movement in one of the saddle bags. One of the horses moved in reaction to it, which brought the cry to his ears again, this time more insistent. It made his heart soar to the heavens. *She is alive! And not with the horde, but here, with these two.* He had to act with haste. His presence would very soon be felt by them as they fed more and more on his energy.

The stench was nearly overpowering already. Beast-like creatures, they smelled of fire, sulfur and smoke. But it went further than that. The smell of decay and rotten flesh, the parasitic smell of an ugly life form feeding on another, growing like a fungus, was ever present. If Kreios had not been exposed to it many times before, it might have overpowered him.

He knew that one of them was human and one was not. He could smell the one that was of the original clan. These were bigger, had sharp shoulders and long arms that almost touched the ground.

Kreios was nearly upon them when the bigger one, the beast, stiffened and sniffed the air. Kreios silently drew the Sword of Light, knowing full well he had to kill the demon first, then the man, if the wretch could be called by such a name. The demon turned as he pulled his long black sword from his side, breaking the silence with a screeching, scraping sound.

A blinding light flashed out like a shot and the Sword cleared the air. It filled Kreios with a burst of power, and with every bit of it, he swung high and down, slicing the demon's head in half. He jerked the broad side of the Sword in a snapping motion and the head of the creature fell to the earth in two pieces. Kreios was expecting it to be more difficult. The man, standing before him in awe, must have thought the same thing.

Kreios was not in the mood to be taking any chances, however. He lifted his Sword high again, pointed toward the earth, and plunged it downward powerfully into the beast's heart. Thick, black blood gushed from its neck and up into the air as Kreios pulled his weapon from the twitching body.

He turned to the man and held out his glowing sword. The demon's carcass fell beside them with a dead thud, but the eyes of the man and the angel were locked upon one another.

The man was tall, with thick arms and broad shoulders. His long black hair streamed down from his head, crowning him in greasy filth. His sword was drawn, and he held it like a man who knew how to wield it.

Kreios stalled, waiting for his power to return, by asking the man a question. "Before I kill you, tell me why you took my daughter. What is she to you?"

The man looked at him, then up to the sky. He shifted his weight as if bargaining with a merchant, then spoke with a hideous voice. "We knew you would come for that, pawn. We do not want it — we want you." He spat on the ground as if completely bored by the situation. "You puppet. You fool for a lost cause! You think you know. You know not. The power now ranged against you and your blood-mates is more than you could imagine. We wanted to draw you to the canyon just beyond the forest edge," he motioned over his shoulder to the west, "then capture you alive and deliver you to the Seer." The man flexed his shoulders and planted his feet.

Kreios looked to the west and cocked his head. "Why tell me now? You know I am going to kill you."

"Our numbers over that ridge are many. If we, the rear guard, do not ride into camp tonight, *they* will come for you. We know where you and your brother are hiding. We will kill the entire village for sport." His smile turned more wicked and filled with evil delight as his eyebrows arched. "We will stop at nothing." Then a sneer escaped the man's lips and his face contorted as he bared his teeth at Kreios.

"I have nothing you or your kind could want. Leave now, and I will let you live to tell your Seer to forget this foolish mission." Kreios saw instantly that his offer would not be taken. This man was determined to die.

"We want you — and we will take you — for reasons that I will not reveal to you. It is what the Seer has ordered, and we will deliver no matter the cost." The man rolled forward onto the balls of his feet, ready to strike. His eyes flashed with hatred as his grip tightened on his sword, which was still pointed at Kreios.

"You would dare kill me when you are ordered to bring me

alive to your Seer?"

"He can revive you as long as you have your head intact. *He* can bring you back. *I* will kill you, bring your body to him and regain my place as captain of a hundred. Please do not tempt me."

"As you wish." Kreios sheathed his sword and stepped back toward the horses, in between the attacker and his baby girl. Kreios had caught the man's mention of having been demoted from the rank of centurion. He was amused that the man thought he could stand in battle against one of the Sons of God without his demon to give him strength.

The man started forward, turning his sword across his body. With two steps, he was upon Kreios faster than he had thought possible for a human. The man's sword slashed across and sliced deep into Kreios' chest. The man stopped and looked at him in shock when he didn't respond to the wound.

Kreios grabbed his coat where the sword had cut through and tore it from his body. His pure white skin had a faint glow to it and a bright red slash bled from where the man had cut him.

The human stared at Kreios' perfect skin. He took a step back as the wound healed right before his eyes. Kreios smiled and thought about how he was not even cold as he stood bare-chested in the freezing wind. He only wore human clothes to better blend in with them. A naked man with pure white skin would not go unnoticed very easily.

Kreios looked over to the wriggling saddlebags and his anger rose, boiling over. This human had dared to steal her away from him. In a flash of speed, he grasped the muscular man by the hair and flung him into the sky, sending him high above the treetops. Jumping after him, he met the man in the air, burying a shattering fist deep into his abdomen.

The man tried to grapple with him as they began to fall back to the ground, but his will had left him, having been replaced by terror. Kreios was hurtling downward, the man in his iron grip, with all the speed he could muster, like a bolt of lightning. The ground thundered as they made impact, sending grass and chunks of hard, frozen dirt into the air.

Amid the crater, Kreios stood up. He dusted himself off, wiping blood and rubble from his chest and arms. The man was dead. Every bone in his body had been shattered from the impact. Blood began to pool where he lay.

Kreios found his torn coat, and taking the baby in his arms, he wrapped her tightly in it. Like a shooting star, Kreios sped through the night sky. The dark firmament held many shooting stars, but on this night, it played host for an ominous observer. The hollow, glistening eyes of the Seer looked on as Kreios raced across the sky.

It was time.

CHAPTER XX

KREIOS TOUCHED DOWN IN the woods just outside Gratzipt. The smoke from the huts hung low to the ground like a blanket. Kreios ran the rest of the way into town and down the main road to the humble house where his brother had hid his little family. It was just before dawn, the moon long ago set. A crackle of firelight on the eastern horizon prophesied the coming day. Not one townsman had awakened from his deep sleep, though death and evil surrounded them.

Zedkiel opened the door. Hugging his daughter, Kreios said, "She is safe, but we cannot stay any longer."

Zedkiel waved him in. "We have packed and are ready to leave. We must go now if we are to survive the day." He had a large makeshift pack filled with the essentials on the ground next to the door. Blankets, dried barley bread, a knife, wood and bone utensils, and a few things for cooking. They did not need much food, only enough to keep Maria nourished. The rest they could hunt and cook over an open fire.

"They are camped a few miles from the gorge with an army. The Seer is with them… they are planning something," Kreios said. He stuffed a bundle of rope and more dried food in his pack as he spoke. "I killed two of them. The Sword has restored me faster than I have ever experienced. I actually healed from a mortal wound right in front of the man. Something is happening — and I must confess that I do not know what it is."

"You have your daughter, and that is all that matters. I must take Maria away and keep her safe. I fear I will not be able to accompany you on your journey. But we will keep your baby safe." Zedkiel called Maria from the other room and gave her a kiss on the lips. It was tender, speaking much more than words could say.

Kreios was glad Zedkiel had changed his mind about staying. He thought Zedkiel must have decided that, with the horde so close, it was not worth the risk. Zedkiel knew that Kreios would go after the horde and find out what was going on. It was the only way.

Kreios looked down at the soft eyes of his sweet baby girl and bathed his heart in her smile. She had her mother's complexion and soul, he could feel it. *They want me?* He could not believe it. He knew they had really wanted her, but he could not guess for what purpose — especially since they had let her slip from their grasp so easily. He looked at his brother, and they shared a moment of mutual yearning and pain.

Kreios broke the silence. "We will go to the mountains of Ke'elei. In it, there is a city where we can all be safe. They dare not go to it. It is one of the last places where our kind are free. I will show you the way brother, but after that, I must track the Seer. It is time we are rid of him and his witchcraft."

"I have heard of this place. I did not believe it was real. I believed that they had scattered us, all of us. I thought that the last of our villages had been either buried or taken to the sky for eternity." Zedkiel was lost for a moment in thought and reflection, during which, his shining face dimmed and his eyes cooled, losing their passion.

"…But you and I both know that there is no going back. We are outcast, cursed." He lowered his head and a tear ran down his cheek as he remembered the home from which he had been in long, painful exile. It had been a very long time, but the remembrance of the smell of perfect air, a sunless sky that never gave way to darkness, filled him with hope.

Kreios thought about it too, remembering when he had walked into the Sea of Crystal and let the cool white water flow between his toes. He remembered the beginning times, after they had been banished and El had turned his back on them. He had every right, but it still cut him deeply into his very soul. "Remember, even though we are outcasts, without a country or a place to lay our heads, we still feel and receive blessing from El. That love is like flowing water breaking hard rock. We cannot begin to hide from it... or Him."

Zedkiel nodded. He stood up straight and embraced his very pregnant Maria, whose smile was radiant, like the first spring dawn after a very hard winter. They looked at each other knowingly and packed anything else they might need before setting out.

Kreios led them around back to the ramshackle stable, where three white stallions stood, ready to ride. "They are the most potent line ever bred. This is the tenth generation." Zedkiel grinned with pride as he helped Maria into her saddle, then he sprung up onto his own mount. The stallions were massive, standing well over twenty hands tall, and would be looked upon with terror on the field of battle. From this breed would spring the mighty Percheron of France — horses bred for war, for strength, for power.

Kreios was given the largest. He ran his hand over its muzzle and neck, whispering into its ear. The horse grunted as if understanding, even as if in agreement.

Soon, they were on the road, riding out of town. Zedkiel looked back at the home they had built. His heart sank. He could tell it was not going to be an easy ride. Kreios had told him that it would take three days and nights to reach their destination. They could not take to the sky, so that the secret of the mountain city could be kept. It was not worth any amount of risk. Besides, Kreios had an idea of how to throw the Brotherhood off the trail.

"I will go with you as far as the head of the Two Rivers. Then, I will take to the air in a new direction and try to find an old friend. He might be able to help us." Kreios smiled slightly at the corner of his mouth, pulling his baby girl close in the sling next to his chest.

Gathering clouds filled the sky to the north. They were dark and thick with snow and frigid air. He knew that Maria could not make it far on horseback. The pass was very difficult terrain to ride, even for an experienced horseman. Kreios would need to find his old friend. The tables would turn. *This is a matter of life and death now, Yamanu. I pray you can live up to your name.*

CHAPTER XXI

THEY HAD REACHED THE headwaters of the Two Rivers, and Kreios felt a pang of regret. He did not like parting ways with his brother and daughter so soon. He knew, though, if he did not find Yamanu, they would never be able to make it to the safety of the City at Ke'elei. He had to do the one thing he did not want to do — leave his daughter yet again — but he had no other choice.

He sent his beloved brother a message in his thoughts, and it was returned with a blessing as well as a warning: *"Be careful, brother! Remember, you are only one, but they are many."*

The cool night sky flickered with stars beyond number, peering down into his soul as he walked in peace through darkened woods. Kreios had left his mighty horse with his brother. He would need to travel light for now. He decided to wait an hour before calling the enemy's vision to himself, making the path clear for his family.

His old friend was called Yamanu. He was a Shadower. In another age, it was a very useful talent for combating seers, medicine men and wizards. He could draw a shade over himself, or even a group, into which the enemy was not able to see.

Kreios grew up with Yamanu and could remember when they had learned to fly back home, where the streets were gold. *Life under the sun provides such bitterness, and very little sweet.*

Every member of the Arch race could fly, or at least were supposed to. Yamanu had not taken to it as well as the other boys. One day, he and Kreios stole to the entrance of the white tower, where only the warriors were permitted. Kreios had been twelve, Yamanu ten. The doors stood as tall as five men and were over

101

an arm's length thick, with iron bands running throughout like spider legs, holding them together. They heaved the doors open and walked into the darkness, closing them behind them with great effort. Shafts of light illuminated the circling stairway through windows as it led upward, beyond them.

None had ever ascended to the top of the white tower just to jump off and learn to fly. It was a lookout post for the army; the warriors. Without a doubt, Kreios and Yamanu were engaging in flight practice far before the Old Masters would have permitted. But Kreios had the heart of a king and nerves of steel. He was not content with the safer jump-off points where everyone else learned. At the tower's top, he felt as if he could regain the heavens long lost to his fathers.

"Come with me, Yam, if you want to see things for what they really are! You will not be disappointed." Kreios had run two steps at a time, with Yamanu close behind him. Kreios was not afraid of death. It was a foreigner to them in that age. The only ones who knew of death were characters in old tales. They had grown up hearing stories of the old battle-scarred Ones, their fathers from very long ago, who fought in the Original War.

Kreios didn't even bother waiting for a response from his friend, for Yamanu was a quiet sort. He raced up the stairway, up and up, through the sunbeams, with the innocence of a little child.

The tower pierced the sky. Even clouds were sometimes dashed against its white stone walls and cleaved in two. It was a beacon, a great statement of daring, just to stand upon its battlements, amongst the peaks of the mountains God had crowned with such glory. The tower had been cut from a single piece of pure marble countless years ago, and felt cool to the touch.

Yamanu came to a screeching halt when they reached the top and burst into the light of the unbroken sky. Since it was his first time at the top, he had not yet seen the expansive view, the breathtaking drop below them. Gusts of wind such as they had never felt, wild and unpredictable, greeted them as the white gold in the light kissed their faces.

They were standing on the roof of the tower, and all that

surrounded them was a short wall, perhaps waist high, with one opening. A platform jutted out into thin air there, both warning and daring them to come closer. The tower was a perfectly circular spire. All that intruded upon the symmetry at the top was the rectangle cut into the floor that admitted the stairway, which, as was agreed upon between them, was a one-way ticket: the only way down from the top was to fly.

"It is very far to the bottom." Kreios stated with excitement. They were both breathing hard. "The wind current up here will keep us aloft for a little while," he said, poking Yamanu in the ribs, "even if you do not know how to fly."

Yamanu looked over the edge and took a step back as a spasm of fear ran its icy fingers up and down his spine. "Are you sure this is safe?" he asked, but knew the answer. He did not relish the idea of testing the stories he had heard about their immortality. The idea of experimenting, to see just how far they could take that truth, scared him.

"My friend, you and I are as safe as a babe in his mother's arms!" Kreios grinned at him from ear to ear. "The worst that can happen to us is a bruised ego. And trust me, friend, I will not allow you to forget it if you fail to catch *these* wind currents."

He slapped Yamanu on the back, powerfully, and looked over the edge with a smile. Kreios gazed with appreciation at the pure carved marble, veins of black twisting through creamy white, like the vessels in his own body, and he could imagine that the entire structure surged with power.

He walked forward to the opening in the wall in front of him. As soon as he went out past it, the unpredictable gusts turned suddenly violent. A weak boy would have been tossed in one fatal instant. But Kreios was not weak. He took another deliberate step toward the end of the platform, stopping two steps from the end. He looked over his shoulder at Yamanu, who had been putting on a brave face. But Kreios was intrepid, and his expression had become mischievous and daring. He looked forward, ran the last two steps, and jumped with his arms out like a bird.

CHAPTER XXII

Boise, Idaho. Present day.

BLOOD POOLED ONTO THE wood of my dresser. I managed to stay on my feet, looking at my hand and hoping that I wasn't crazy. I prayed that I wouldn't have to get Mom up and ask her to rush me to the emergency room for... *for stabbing myself!*

But, if I *was* crazy, and oh how I wanted to be — the wound would heal. I didn't know how or when. This complicated things. No matter what, either I was a psycho who heard voices and stabbed herself, or I was a freak of nature who, admittedly, could be a cover girl. *When I'm not spontaneously barfing.*

Now I would not only have the difficult and thrilling job of making it through high school and the whole teenager thing — but I had to figure out *what* I was, as well. No matter what happened after this, I knew there would be consequences.

It was surreal. I stood there and watched my gaping wounds as they dripped. Gross. But it was like watching the invisible hands of an expert surgeon reorganize the twisted remains of my tendons, arteries, and whatever else was in there. It itched like nothing I had ever felt, as if my hand would tear itself apart. Everything was placed back in order, fused together, and my skin covered it all without a trace... well, except for all the blood.

All I could think about was the chorus to this song I had heard once. All it said was "stupid girl" over and over.

I shook my head, wiped the blood from my hands in awe, and cleaned up my dresser with a ratty old shirt that I had been meaning to throw out anyway. Then I took everything out back and dumped it all into our big outside trash can. I went back up to my bedroom and grabbed a frilly looking doily my mom had made and used it to cover up the gash on my dresser.

I kept looking at my hand. I touched the place where just moments ago a bloody gash had been. It didn't even hurt, and there was no trace of a cut anywhere in sight. Maybe most people would be happy with that news, but it terrified me. I didn't remember being bit by any radioactive spiders lately, or even hit over the head by a meteorite out in a corn field.

Okay, so I heal quick... I mean really quick. It didn't seem to keep me from getting sick, though. *Maybe I have a tumor in my brain or something.* I'd read about that sort of thing happening. People got weird gifts like being able to read people's minds or something, and it turned out they had a baseball sized tumor in their brain. A month later they were dead.

I remembered the note the killer left in my mailbox that said, "I know what you are!" Not *who* you are but *what*. As if I was some sort of thing or animal.

The cut itched so badly when it was closing together that I had struggled to keep from ripping open a new wound just to get it to stop. What in the world — or beyond this world — was going on? Somehow, death seemed better than this. Not that I couldn't find use for a... a gift, talent, or whatever this was. But what would happen when people found out? I'd be on Oprah in no time. Everyone would be looking to interview me and dissect my brain on national television. A freak. No, thank you.

I know *what* you are!

Maybe someone else already knew. Maybe someone else did this to me. Maybe when I was an infant, they injected me with some sort of drug; some secret government project trying to create super-humans. *Seriously, Airel?* I felt a shiver run up and down my spine, and I got that same feeling I had at the doctor's office. It was as if I had this thing, this other voice, that wanted to help me or watch me.

I listened as I stopped to look in the mirror. All was quiet, and in the back of my mind, I heard the sound of someone sighing, as if it was impatient and wanted me to figure things out a little faster.

I felt as if I stood on the edge of something big. "Look, if you've got something to say, say it!" I said into the mirror. I was on the edge of something, all right. I wanted to scream and kick my legs and throw a tantrum, but what good would that do? I was still alone.

I recalled having read *Frankenstein* last year for English Lit. That's exactly how I felt just then. A freak, totally alone. Still, I couldn't shake the feeling, deep down where it counted, that I was not alone at all.

I looked at the clock. Six a.m. The sun was going to be up soon, bringing on the morning. I groaned at the thought of it. Sometimes my moods were just not in sync with the sunny weather. I prayed for rain.

I was not very excited to go to school in this state. My world was completely upside down. Outside of faking a cold, I had to go. I thought about this, but decided not to. Mom usually didn't buy it, anyway. Besides, it would give me more time to think this mess through without Mom checking my temperature every five minutes. Maybe I could even get Kim's advice.

School didn't require a large part of my brain anyway. Seriously. If you learned to nod and grunt in the right places, you could skate by without breaking a sweat. The rest could be found on Google.

I turned on the shower, cranked it to scalding, then opened my closet to decide what to wear this fine screwed up morning. I picked out a blue button-up top and then got in the shower. It felt so good that I almost felt normal again. I decided to scrap the button-up top and wear my hot pink tank top with a white lace-lined shirt under it. Pink was my "feeling good" color, and if I put it together with my worn-out jeans, I was unstoppable.

The morning proved to be better than I thought it would be, with large cartoonish clouds filling the sky like daisies and the sun blazing through them. I made it out of the house just in time to retrieve my coconut latte on the way, this time without incident. I had half an hour until the school parking lot would start to fill up, and I emptied my mind of all thoughts about my weird life.

I didn't want to think... just feel... *Feel.* The word rolled through my mind like a summer thunderstorm. *Feel...*

I heard the flutter of wings in the back of my mind.

Opening my eyes, I saw Michael Alexander pulling in next to my Honda. My heart jumped into my throat, but I downed the last of my coffee anyway.

Michael slammed the door to his truck, leaned down, looked through the passenger window and waved at me. I smiled as he opened the door. "Hi, what brings you here so early?" I even sounded like a normal person, unlike how I felt inside — wind, waves and butterflies.

Michael's eyes lit up and he shot me *that* smile. "I just had a feeling you would be here before everyone else. And here you are."

My heart did flip-flops in my chest as Michael slid into the passenger seat. I could smell his shampoo. There was also the faint odor of bacon and eggs lingering on his breath. Coming from literally *any* other person, I would have thought it was nasty, but on him it was magical.

I looked at him without looking at him, and he smiled and stared at me. It was as if he didn't mind me knowing that he was interested in me, or maybe I was imagining it and he was just being a nice guy. I was running out of excuses.

"So, you hear anything from the police about that murder?" Michael asked. I was a bit shocked that I had forgotten all about it, but maybe it wasn't so surprising with everything else that was going on.

"Uh, no. I think they're still looking for the guy. Kinda weird being there in the theater when it happened."

"Yeah. Not every day you get to be in the middle of real live action like that." Michael sounded excited, as if he enjoyed the experience. Then again, he had not been hiding in a bathroom stall about to be attacked and cut to pieces by a psycho killer. "It was just like in the movies! All the police cars and everyone screaming and running all around..."

"You sound like you enjoyed it. Personally, I could have been killed. And then what? Would you have been all excited that you knew the girl who was murdered?" I was getting mad at his happy-go-lucky attitude and the lack of fear he seemed to have.

"No, no, I'm not happy! I uh — come on, Airel — it's just that it was crazy, ya know... and you're alive. Besides, it wasn't just a random murder. They even said that the victim was a serial killer." Michael's eyes lit up like blue embers.

"What? Where did you hear that?"

"What do you mean, 'where did I hear that?' It's been all over the news. They've identified the body as some child killer from Vegas. He killed like ten kids and even made it onto the top ten Most Wanted list. I guess they're hunting their own kind now. Killer killing killer." Michael shook his head in amazement and said, "Anyway, where have you been? The whole school is talking about it. You're like the local celebrity... the girl who got away."

"Great. So much for flying under the radar," I muttered under my breath. I didn't want to be famous for anything. I just wanted to get through high school and maybe go to college. I got lost in my own thoughts for a second when I looked past Michael to his truck. I noticed movement. James was sitting in Michael's truck drinking a Red Bull and staring out the window as if lost in a deep dark dream. I was so confused that I didn't say anything for a minute.

Michael followed my gaze and laughed. "Oh, James needed a ride this morning, so I picked him up. He didn't want to be the third wheel, so he stayed in the truck."

"Wow. I didn't see him, so it kind of freaked me out. You two are becoming fast friends, I see. Gonna go out for football?" I didn't know what to think, but the James thing made something in the back of my mind twitch. I wondered what it was. Maybe it was just my conscience being over-sensitive, or maybe a sixth sense, like in the theater.

"Well..." he laughed. "James is a cool guy. He's going to talk to the coach for me, since the season has already started. I'm not that into it, but it could be fun." Michael ran a hand through his perfect hair and turned to look at me. I turned away, not knowing what to do, or even what might happen. His eyes were so crystal clear, as if he could read my every thought.

I could imagine Michael playing football. He had the body for it. I glanced at him, deciding that yes, he was... of sturdy stock... *and I sound like my grandma now.* He was a beautiful man, and with this thought, I realized that I *did* think of him as a man, not just a boy.

He was powerful. He had eyes that could look right into my soul, but under it all, there was something dark. I've heard of those underground rivers that go for miles. The water down there must be cold, black. That's the feeling I got, but it was fleeting, hard to put my finger on. He was dangerous. That was it. Maybe that was why, in that moment, I knew I was falling for him.

Michael felt my gaze and met it without a smile. All of a sudden, my little car started to feel hot inside and I wanted to roll down my window. There wasn't even a hint of humor in his face, which was not the way he looked most of the time. He always had a joke or a funny comment to make everyone laugh, but as he looked deep into my eyes, I saw something that made me gasp. It was a deep and clinging desire. It scared me more than I could have imagined. *So... this is what it's like.*

I felt as if I was an ocean — unpredictable, wild, stormy — and I could feel, intensely, that his single wish in life was to be given the privilege of drowning in all that I was. But it was more than simple desire. No, I could tell. He loved me. In it was something more powerful than all the stars crashing to earth.

I tried to look away but couldn't. He held me captive, and I could not — knew I would never — resist. Just as fast as it had emerged, the burst of passion in his eyes passed, sinking under lapping waves of self-defense. A smile pulled at the corner of his mouth, and the mask — the one we all wear — was back in place.

"I wanted to ask you something." Michael grinned and looked down at his hands, abruptly shy. "I was wondering if you would like to go to dinner with me sometime. You know, not anything fancy. Just hang out, get to know each other. I think you are... well, you're very interesting."

I couldn't help but smile. He was asking me out and he was shy. Or playing shy, whichever, I didn't care. I was the last person he should be shy around.

But I caught myself saying these words: "I would love to." My heart pounded, and my entire body buzzed with excitement. It occurred to me that I just might throw up all over this amazing guy sitting in my car.

"Great, great..." he said, smiled awkwardly, opened the car door, and was gone. He and James headed into the school.

I looked around, sank back into my seat, and fought back a tear. I was *that* girl. The one everyone wished they could be. I didn't know why, and I was afraid to ask, but I couldn't help it. I balled up my fist, curled my arm, and gloated, "Yes!"

CHAPTER XXIII

1250 B.C. Arabia

KREIOS FLEW HIGH IN the evening sky, just under the low-hanging clouds that were forming on the western mountains; a fortress of jagged black rock peaks.

He did not have time to stop until he found the Shadower. Pulling his shoulders back, he poured all of his energy into the increase of speed, breaking the sound barrier and leaving a powerful sonic boom in his wake.

Kreios touched down with a crack of static electricity on the doorstep of his old friend Yamanu, who sat on the front porch of his shack. He was in a wooden rocking chair smoking a pipe, and probably, Kreios thought, dreaming of the old days in another world. Kreios walked up the three creaky steps, took a seat next to his friend, and sat down without a word.

Kreios took out his own pipe, filled it, and it lit without the assistance of fire. He drew on it slowly, allowing time to savor the sweet, relaxing smoke. It tasted like serenity. It was wholly unlike anything mankind had ever known. He let the smoke roll out of his mouth like a waterfall and curl up on his chest, drifting slowly down, draping him in a cloak. He leaned back to gaze at the stars with his old friend.

Yamanu did not look his age. He had a full white beard and a bald head that shone in the moonlight. He was lean, just as he was as a kid, and a dark aura hovered around him; a shadow. "I have been waiting for this day," he said, breaking the silence. Both of them still looked ahead at the stars, not at one another. "You come with haste." Then, Yamanu turned to regard his old friend and said, "I know why." He took a long drag from his pipe and looked back up to the heavens, regarding the stars.

"Do you, indeed?" Kreios looked at him. "My daughter is in great danger, old friend, and we must take her to the mountains of Ke'elei."

Yamanu turned, looking with wonder at Kreios. "The City of Refuge." He sighed. "This is more than I had imagined." He paused again and looked at the ground. The smoke was pooling at their feet, fusing itself to the shadow that clung to him always, in symbiosis. "Tell me, is it true that your wife is dead?"

Kreios had to take a moment. His hands were trembling as he nodded, "It is true."

Yamanu reached a hand to Kreios' shoulder, touching him affectionately. The tears around his eyes mingled with a furrowed brow. "I am sorry, my old friend. She was a pure heart." There was only a moment more of silence and consideration until a fire was lit within the eyes of the Shadower and his decision was made.

Yamanu stood. "We must go." He descended the rickety steps and began walking briskly in a little circular track that signified nervous energy. "I can feel your urgency," he said; then paused, looking to the west. "With that westerly wind, I fear the Seer is closer than you might have guessed."

Kreios stood and came close. Yamanu moved behind him with agility and spoke in a whisper, "I will fight with you to the death, my friend." Then he added playfully, "I will also beat you into the sky!" Yamanu was a rocket, gone in an instant, leaving Kreios looking up at his light trail with a smile. Kreios bent his legs, launched, and shed a sonic boom almost instantaneously.

It was the beginning of the end, they both felt that. Even as the world slept, unaware of the existence of the monsters and incredible beings living amongst them, Kreios knew that what was destined to happen would change everything.

CHAPTER XXIV

Boise, Idaho. Present day.

KIM AND I SAT in the third row of the bleachers under the mild late-September sun. The football team was running drills for an upcoming game. Borah liked to win more than anything else.

Coach Dennis was a machine. If he had his way, the football team would practice all year long. Football was his life. He was short and pretty fit for an old dude. The man had arms the size of most men's legs... gross.

He stood with his feet spread apart like he was going to swing a sword or something. Every once in a while he blew a whistle, commanding the attention of everyone on the field, as well as a few in the stands. He barked out a few orders and the guys began running wind sprints.

I watched the bigger ones lag behind the other guys, like James and Michael, who seemed born for it. I wondered, as they killed themselves for their conditioning, why guys pushed themselves so hard for a *game*. It was just a stupid ball. They fought and clawed their way up and down the field over it, thinking they looked impressive, then what?

I had to admit I didn't get it, but it was kind of fun to watch, all the same. I tuned Kim out — she was talking my ear off — and watched Michael run the field back and forth, up and down, in perfect rhythm to some hidden clock that he alone could feel. He moved like a cat, light on his feet; and quick — much quicker than the rest of the team.

"Did I tell you that James asked me out the other day? We're going to see a movie. Oh, no wait... maybe that's not such a good idea." She looked at me as if I was made of glass. "Well, he said he had the perfect place in mind for dinner. I hope it's that new Brazilian place. I hear that you need a reservation just to get in. Gosh, he's so strong! Just look at him run!" She gave a lovesick sigh, and I gave her a sisterly look that said, 'If you keep this up, I'm gonna barf on your shoes.' *Who knows? Maybe I will.*

Michael glanced up at me as he ran by, flashing me a little smile that gave me shivers. I was not entirely sure I should even be allowing this kind of thing. How is it possible to know someone for such a short time and feel like this? If Dad, or even Mom, knew how I felt... wow. Danger. I looked at Kim. I guess I had to take the plunge.

"I have news of my own, but you have to promise not to make a big deal out of it... I mean it." I knew that it was like asking an addict to quit cold turkey, but I had to try.

"Michael asked you out, didn't he?" Kim had a look of glee stamped on her face, and the look on mine must have been confirmation. "I knew it! He asked you out! Yesss!" She made the same gesture I had made in the car, like she had just scored a touchdown. "I was hoping he would, and he is sooo hot! Oh my gosh!" Then she looked alarmed. "You said yes, didn't you? You had better have said yes, or I'll kill you."

Death by Kim. Chalk up another murderous stalker. How many does that make now? I nodded and shook my head in defeat, grinning helplessly. "Kim, it's not like I could have said no..."

"Oh, Airel! I'm so excited! You and Michael, and me and James, we can go on, like, double dates! And hang out and talk about stuff! Oh my gosh! We should go shopping and get a new outfit for our first official dates of the school year!"

Seriously, I don't know what I did to deserve this. My best friend was going to drive me insane with the shopping and the — and the — my mouth went dry and my lips felt like they were thick, swollen shut from lack of water. I sat straight up, my back stiff, and all the tiny hairs on my neck and arms sounded the alarm.

Across the field on the visiting team's bleachers sat a blond haired man with black sunglasses hiding his evil eyes.

Kim felt me tense up and stopped talking. "Uh oh. Do you need a barf bag?" Then she followed my gaze across the green grass to the man in the far bleachers. "Who is that?" Kim asked in a whisper. She pushed her sunglasses down to the tip of her nose and peered out.

I tried to respond, but I couldn't because my mouth was so dry. A wave of raw heart-stopping fear rushed over my body. Kim was ditzy, but not dumb. She touched my arm, leaned over close to me, and whispered in my ear — so softly, I almost missed it, "It's him!"

It was him. He was right there. He was watching me; watching with careful consideration and... something else. He knew. He knew that something was wrong with me. He wanted to see what it was. Or, maybe... he wanted to see what I would do. Maybe he wanted to scare me into silence.

If he wanted to scare me, it was working. I was so scared that my hands were shaking. I felt weak. *Oh, neat. Here's something new and impossible. I totally need more of that.* I saw it happening. It wasn't slow-mo, not like a movie at all. This was real. The seat of the bleacher below came at my face shockingly fast, and I knew this was going to hurt later.

CHAPTER XXV

I OPENED MY EYES to see a black sky. The sun above was enclosed in a womb of smoke and smog. I saw jagged rocks the color of coal sticking up from the ground below at sickening angles.

I was in what looked like a huge bird cage, except this one was square and made of rough iron bars with a plank floor. I could see that I was high above the ground in a tall and ancient tree.

I looked out over the vast valley beyond the black rocks. Row upon row of mountain ranges were stacked against each other, rising and falling. The distance beyond me seemed to be impassable, even if I could get out of this cage. It was another world. It was so dark and so dead that nothing grew or lived. This ground was cursed – even the sun wore a cloak.

I thought I was dreaming, but the bump on my head proved to me that I was somehow… not. I did, indeed, pass out and eat the bleachers. I didn't know quite how to explain it to myself. Wherever I was though, it was not beautiful. The air had a chill as a slight breeze made its way through the iron bars, making me shiver. There was no way in or out, as far as I could see.

I stood, and I felt my little cage sway back and forth, bobbing up and down as I shifted my weight. I froze. I was hanging. I peered out through the bars to see that my cage was wedged between a couple of branches, balanced on them. Maybe if I got too jumpy it would topple over, causing me to plummet to my death.

I wondered then, if I died in this dream or in this world, would I be dead in the real world? Maybe I was in a hospital right now, with a nasty cut on my head, and the doctors were trying to revive me from a coma.

I made my way slowly to the center. The whole thing groaned with each step. Long, fat floor boards spanned from one end of the room to the other. I counted twelve across. Each one was held in place with rusty nails.

Not wanting to fall to my death in some crazy dream world, only to find out that was where I would spend eternity, I stopped and looked around for something — anything I might have missed that could help.

I figured if there was one rule for this situation, it was simply this: do whatever needed to be done. I really didn't know what to do, though. Nothing came to mind other than one stupid, harebrained thought. *Maybe death is the way out... in a dream...*

I heard pages turning and that strange, seemingly friendly voice in the back of my brain whispering to me. Now I could pick it out from my other more normal thoughts. In other words, I could tell when something wasn't Airel. It was like this tiny yet powerful voice that I couldn't push to the background. I had to listen.

"Be careful, Airel, things are not what they seem."

I ran toward the bars of my cage and slammed my shoulder into it, grunting as I did. It hurt. My little cage rocked, groaning in protest, and I felt my world turning horribly. I could feel the rhythm of the swinging I had created and decided to exploit it. I pushed hard, throwing my weight into the wall. The cage leaned crazily on its side, and I looked straight down to the sharp daggers of rock below. I felt a lurch and heard the snap of dead branches as the huge old tree gave up its grip.

I was falling.

The cage tumbled, turning over and over, and flashes of black shards reached up for me from below. It was all happening too fast. I screamed, hoping but dreading that someone would hear me crying out for help. Deep down, I knew there was no one who *could* help me.

The ancient tree had to be over two hundred feet tall; it took an eternity to hit the ground. The explosion of wood was deafening at impact, and the clang of iron against stone ran right over my ears, drowning me out as I screamed.

Then there was pain. This couldn't be a dream. The impact hurt badly, and to my surprise, I was injured. I supposed that was a good thing because, if nothing else, it meant I was alive. I lifted my head, which was pounding like a church bell on Sunday, and surveyed the destruction.

The bird cage had left wooden shrapnel in a radius around me. Some of the bars lay at my feet, twisted and bent.

I checked myself for damage and found that I did have a problem. My left arm was broken, hanging, and ripped almost completely off at the elbow. Blood squirted out with each heartbeat, and I could see the bone sticking out like a tooth. Blood ran down my arm and dripped off my dead fingers.

I was going to bleed to death.

The panic I thought would come never did, though the pain was so sharp and overpowering, I could feel myself going into shock. This was it. I was dying, and in a matter of minutes, I would be dead in this godforsaken place. I would die alone and confused, not knowing how or why I was here, or where here even was.

Then, I felt something cast a thin shadow over me. A thick wave of nausea washed through my stomach. I was sitting in the pile of debris I had made, holding my wrecked arm in place with my good one, my back turned to whatever was standing behind me.

I could smell the stench of rotten flesh and mold. It was so strong I could taste it in my mouth, making me want to spit it out. It was vile.

The sound of clicking and gurgling sent shivers down my spine. I didn't want to look. But I had to know. Something within me was demanding that I turn to face whatever was there. I turned. What I saw made me wish for death.

The *thing* had a long black cloak with a massive hood pulled low. All that could be seen in the darkness were two dark red glowing eyes. Something wet and slimy dripped from the lip of the hood and made a puddle at its feet. I was frozen in fear, staring at it, unable to look away.

It reached up slowly with white and withered hands and pulled the hood back to reveal a dark mass of nothingness; an empty void where the face should be. It managed a grotesque smile in spite of this, staring down at my arm, drooling clotted slime all over the front of its robe, leaving a long stinking stain.

I felt something move by my leg and jumped with fright. I wrenched my gaze away from the figure before me to find my fingers brushing against my leg. My arm was whole again. The blood had dried, and I let go of my arm, stretching it out to test it. It was good as new, as if it had never been broken, gushing blood, or hanging by a thread of flesh. I flexed and wiggled my fingers. There was no shooting pain; not so much as a scar was left where the bloody mess had been.

The thing screeched like a dying owl and splattered me with brown snot and slime. I recoiled and crouched down, ready for the attack. It came right at me, and I reached out to resist the monster. But as soon as I did, a bolt of lightning exploded between us, throwing me backward. I landed some distance from the screeching thing. I saw it coming toward me with unreal speed and a huge black rock in its withered white hands. It raised the rock overhead, meaning to crush me. I rolled, but not fast enough. The rock caught me on the side of my head, crushing the right side of my face.

I saw bright white light, and the strange world vanished painfully.

CHAPTER XXVI

1250 B.C. Arabia

KREIOS AND YAMANU WERE fast. Not long after they set off from Yamanu's shack, they made their rendezvous with Zedkiel, Maria, and Kreios' precious baby girl, before sunrise. They were encamped among giant ferns in a thickly wooded forest, the sound of the river not too far distant. They were half a day's journey from where Kreios had left them.

Maria must not have been able to go any farther. He hoped they were in time to save the baby that grew in her belly.

Kreios felt a tightening in his gut every time he heard water moving. His kind could survive great wounds, but drowning was a great danger. He had never been close, avoiding it at all costs.

Zedkiel stood when his brother arrived, glancing at his wife with a worried look. "She is losing strength. I believe she needs sleep and a good bed in which to rest for the remainder of her time." In answer to an inquisitive glance from Kreios, he added, "We did not have any trouble along the way, but something tells me if we do not hurry, the trouble will come."

Kreios looked toward the small tent his brother had pitched, listening for his baby. She was lodged in Maria's arms, fast asleep, her content and beautiful face radiant. He then turned back to conference with the warriors now assembled. "You remember Yamanu. He will help us to Ke'elei and then we will find out what this Seer wants with me. We will go at first light, after she has had a full night's rest."

As he spoke, Kreios was searching the woods around them. His senses filtered through the noises and movements, picking out anything unnatural or out of place.

Zedkiel took Yamanu by the hand. "Thank you for coming. We would be lost without you."

Yamanu smiled in the darkness, causing all his teeth to gleam in the moonlight. "I am at your service, friend. I only hope we can make it to safety without our enemy seeing through my shadow."

The camp did not have a fire that night. Kreios left the group to stand watch in the boughs of a tall tree. He did not trust his senses completely; he needed every advantage. The Seer, the powerful leader of the Brotherhood, might be able to track them in spite of every precaution they took.

Kreios let his mind drift back to his childhood once again; to times when war, violence and death had not yet been fully tested. After he and Yamanu had learned to fly, they could not get enough of it. They took to the skies whenever they had the chance. Yamanu was slower but could keep up as long as Kreios gave him a chance. Kreios grunted, amused, as he thought how he had even let him win a few of their many races just to keep him interested.

But when he was alone, Kreios would go to the tower and launch himself straight up as fast as he could, until he reached the outer edge, where the clouds stopped, the sky becoming black. He would turn then, to look below him at the majesty of his home.

In a flash of speed, he would throw himself, rocketing downward toward the ground; pushing himself faster and faster. The first time he made a sonic boom, he thought he would die. After all, it hurt so much. The flesh of his face and arms, he reminisced, felt like they would rip from his frame.

A subtle and irregular sound brought Kreios back to reality; alert, with all of his senses standing at attention, ready for whatever was waiting. He closed his eyes in the darkness and listened.

The river in the distance swirled over rocks, under the remaining ice. But back behind him, he heard something so faint that it could have been nothing at all.

Breathing.

It sounded soft but ragged, coming in short intervals. The sound of crickets and night owls masked it for the most part, but there it was, just behind all the other sounds. This breathing was not coming from a man — or even a beast — of this world.

Kreios knew what it was. He froze in place, a cold stone statue of a god in a tree. He allowed it to hide there, behind him. Both supernaturals were waiting for an exact moment.

Kreios shut down the sounds of the wood, the animal life all around him, and listened... in, out... in, out... then nothing. The foul beast knew Kreios was aware of its presence and shriveled, flying off to make its report to its master.

It was time to go. They had been discovered. The faster they found refuge in the City, the better.

Kreios was on the ground, sprinting silently. He shook Zedkiel awake and said, "We must go — now!"

CHAPTER XXVII

Boise, Idaho. Present day.

I WAS ALIVE. NOT in a world of black mountains or shrieking monsters. Nope. I was on my back on soft, green grass with the whole football team looking at me as if I had three eyes. My head throbbed. I reached up to touch the bump that was forming on my forehead. *That's probably nice and ugly.*

"Are you okay, Airel? Can you see how many fingers I'm holding up?" Coach Dennis looked down at me with a concerned scowl on his face. I could tell that he wanted to yell at me; command me not to pass out again because it interfered with his practice, and football was serious business.

"I'm fine!" I shouted at him because I was scared out of my wits and more embarrassed than I could ever remember. "… Just slipped… hit my head," I lied, looking for emotional cover. "I wasn't paying attention and..." Kim shot a look my way, but miracle of miracles — she kept her mouth shut. I glanced over my shoulder and saw that the blond man was gone. I guess I wasn't surprised. I wondered if he was just a figment of my imagination, but then, Kim had seen him too.

"I'll have one of the boys walk you to the nurse's station to get looked at," said the coach, snapping his fingers at his minions. "Never mess with a head injury."

Michael piped up, "I'll take her, Coach." He was already at my side, lifting me into his arms like a helpless victim before I could reject this huge escalation of embarrassment.

My mouth was not responding to my frantic attempts to say something. Kim had a stupid grin on her face that suggested I had fallen on purpose, just so I could get carted off in Michael's arms. *Yeah Kim, it's a total conspiracy — I'm not actually your friend, either.*

Coach barked one last order at Michael. "Fine. Come right back, though! We have two more drills to run, and you need to run them." Michael nodded, and I could smell the sweat from his skin. I didn't mind it. It smelled kind of good, anyway, and I couldn't help but get carried away with the fact that my dream guy — heck, any girl's dream guy — was not only paying attention to me, not only close to me, not only holding me... but he wasn't afraid to sweat on me, either.

Michael whispered just low enough for me to hear. "You should be more careful. Next time you might break your neck." He had a smirk on his face.

I tried to sound mad, but it came off as weak instead. "I'm fine." I thought I sounded a little like Lady MacBeth, protesting too much. "You don't have to carry me. I can walk just fine on my own."

"Sure you can, but it's more fun to carry you." I nearly fainted, feeling his strong arms enfolding me. In spite of everything that had happened these past few days, all the chaos and weirdness, I felt secure in his arms. I could have died happy and did not want him to let me go, ever. "We wouldn't want you to slip and fall again. That could be embarrassing."

Oh, noooo. We wouldn't want me to be embarrassed.

He smiled at me. I was in heaven. All was gone, forgotten, forgiven. *I just really love the whole entire world right now...* I wrapped my arms around his neck, to *help* him. If I was a daring girl, I would have rested my head on his chest, but that wasn't going to happen. *At least not right now.* "Yeah, like this isn't embarrassing, you holding me like this and... and..."

"And what?" He laughed.

"Never mind. Just walk, mister, and try not to drop me if you can manage it." Kim ran ahead of us, catching up from flirting with James, and opened the door to the nurse's station. She smiled at me as we passed, rolling her eyes obnoxiously.

Michael set me down on my feet, and for a moment, he was Superman and I was Lois Lane, and we had just had our moonlight flight. I wanted to pull him closer to me, but I didn't dare. I decided to sit down, just to be safe. He sat right next to me. *Thank you, God!*

Michael looked at me with concern, staring into my eyes. Our faces were only a few inches away and I could feel his breath. He smelled like PowerAde and laundry soap — and sweat. His eyes held me in a magical lock that I couldn't break as they searched for something. But I couldn't tell what he was trying to find.

"Thank you," I said in a soft whisper. It was like a kiss. I was all too aware of how I must have looked, with a big goofy-looking face and a big fat lump on my forehead. I felt flushed and turned away, breaking the spell. He stood up and said, "'Kay, then," waved his perfect hand at me, and left. I didn't know what to think.

Kim plopped down with a sigh in the chair he had only seconds ago occupied. I was a little jolted by that sacrilege. "Fell," her voice was sugary sweet and her eyelashes fluttered. "What a load of crap! You passed out because you were scared to death." She was pointing and poking at me.

"Dude, ow! Chill!" I grabbed her pointy finger angrily and shoved it back at her. I was a little offended at how my fantasy world had been so suddenly and rudely broken. She, of all people, my best friend, ought to have known that I needed time to come down from that high. *Dang it!*

My life was a struggle again and things were impossible, unexplained, and dangerous. And then, front and center in my memory was the face of a cold-blooded murderer. It all came pouring back in on top of me.

The killer had found me at home, left a calling card, and now he had been watching me at school, for who knows how long. I felt like my back was either up against a wall, or like the wall had jumped onto my back and I could not get it off.

"Airel." Kim sounded like she knew what I was thinking, and I realized I was holding my head in my hands. "He's stalking you. We should go to the police. I mean, like, now. This is getting a little out of control, don't you think?"

"We can't, Kim. I don't have a good reason. I mean, he knows something about me and…" I caught myself and clamped my lips shut before I could say any more. What was I supposed to say? That I heal and have some kind of power? That he might be the only person who knows what's going on with me? That I needed to let him find me? Or that I needed to find him so I could get some answers?

"You're not making any sense, Airel! This is not a game. You could get killed! Is that what you want?"

I looked away. It occurred to me that the killer might be some other kind of villain that I had not yet considered. I let my imagination go for a sec. I wondered: what if I was some kind of freak science experiment gone wrong? God only knew what kind of research some of these big pharma companies were doing, and who knew what kind of things the CIA might be up to. I felt crazy, but what if this dude was sent to bring me in? What if he was my handler, my boss? Crazier things have happened. I looked back at my best friend.

"Kim?"

"Uh, yeah, crazy girl?"

"Never mind." I couldn't begin to explain, and I dismissed her with a wave of my hand. She reacted by recoiling from me, mouth open in disbelief, as it dawned on her that I was totally shutting her out.

The school nurse walked in just in time. The last thing I wanted to do was inform my best friend that I couldn't tell her what was going on. But I guess I just did that, only without words. I didn't want to hurt her, but I decided right there to figure out what was happening to me on my own. Even if it meant putting myself in danger, I didn't want to drag anyone else into it — especially Kim.

Kim stood up and stormed out in a huff. *Oh boy. That will take some time to fix.*

As I followed the nurse into the exam room, my heart was flipping around inside me, doing cartwheels. I had just trampled all over my best friend. But necessity, or survival, focused my entire mind. If I could only figure out how to go about figuring this riddle out. *Airel, you really are nuts.*

I felt like I was trapped inside a game I didn't want to play.

CHAPTER XXVIII

THE DREAM OF THE cage — now that I was alone — mocked me and haunted my every waking moment. I could feel the dust fill my nostrils with the stench of the demon as it hovered just inside the back of my mind. My world wasn't very exciting on most days, but now it seemed that every turn I made brought me into a situation that might kill me; or maybe something worse. Much worse.

I sat on the exam table, wondering what it all meant. It was fitting, being on yet another exam table. Perhaps I was sicker than I knew. I felt really bad about Kim. She was a good friend, and I was being unfair. But I wanted to keep her at a safe distance from this — from me — for a while.

Then — and this is where it gets crazy again — there was the voice in the back of my head, sometimes accompanied by the fluttering of a bird's wings, or the sound of pages turning in a book. *She*, I called her. Like an extension of myself. No. Kind of like Mom, I guess, but not. Whenever I heard *She* speak, I felt like I was hearing wisdom. I knew that I was changing. *She* had told me as much, and I accepted that somehow. *She* knew and reassured me.

I felt bad for keeping Kim in the dark, but seriously, what the heck was I supposed to tell her? And where in the world would I start? I knew that no matter what, she was my best friend, but I hesitated.

Michael. I could tell him, couldn't I? Not that I had any logical or sane reason to trust him, other than the fact that I was beginning to fall for him. That wasn't it, though. There was something in the way he looked at me that made me feel like I could tell him anything without reservation.

Miss Parks, a youngish woman, flashed a bright light into one eye and then the other. The light brought me out of my daydreaming. I liked to dream, but lately, I seemed to have lost control of my thoughts.

"You look fine," she said. "Nothing more than a bump on the head as far as I can tell. Are you feeling better? Do you have a headache?"

I didn't have a headache or even feel bad. A terrible thought came to me. *What if the nasty throbbing welt on my forehead healed and disappeared right in front of Miss Parks?* I figured it would be smart to fake a headache, because most people in my situation would have a whopper. I winced and put my fingers to my temples.

"Yep. My head feels like it's stuck under a school bus. Do you have anything for that?" *Hey, Miss Parks, don't worry about it. It'll heal here in the next few seconds… just watch.* Yeah, that would go over like a turd in a punch bowl.

Miss Parks smiled a weak smile, pursing her lips compassionately. "I'll get you some Tylenol. That should help." She hurried into the other room.

I stood up and walked toward the door so when she got back, I could get out of there as fast as possible.

Miss Parks came back into the room, handed me a little packet of Tylenol, and put her hand on my shoulder. "Take two now and two more in a few hours if you still have a headache. And try not to faint the next time you see a bunch of boys in football uniforms." She giggled at herself and I faked a light laugh.

"Thanks for the Tylenol," I said and turned toward the door.

I opened the door. First, I saw green and gold, then a football jersey, then Michael. He must have hurried back from practice after it ended. I grinned compulsively at him like an idiot, and then tried to wipe it from my face, hiding behind my hand. But that only made it worse.

He looked incredible. I tried to tear my eyes away from his, but did a double take. Something in his eyes refused to release me. It was shock, amazement — then fear.

CHAPTER XXIX

1250 B.C. Arabia

A TENT STOOD IN the darkness, ringed by hundreds of other tents at a distance that suggested supreme command, fear of authority, or both. Choking smoke filled the beaver skin tent as the Seer looked deep within his pulsing bloodstone.

The blazing light was otherworldly. Even though it was sucking the life from him, he could not pull away. He desired and lusted for the glow of amber light so much that it filled his obsessive dreams every night; whispering to him things he never before imagined. A faint glow escaped from the seams in the tent. The light dimmed, flared up, then faded back to a fragment of its former self.

The camp numbered a thousand men and a thousand demons. They were weak when the men, the hosts in the parasitic relationship, were separated, and the demons were manifest in their true forms.

Demons, agents of the kingdom of Hell, sought a lodging in the minds of the men and fed on their life force parasitically. Men followed the Seer blindly, obsessed with every filthy lust to which they could give themselves, or to which the demons could tether them. To the men, the demons were men too — they just possessed higher — kingly — authority. This was rarely questioned. They had been blinded and cursed by the power exchange — power they thought they received from the demonic relationship, but which, in fact, they gave and re-gave time and again to the agents of Hell that fed off it. This deception was an addiction both parties found irresistible.

And their foolish hearts were darkened, blinding them from the truth...

The army was trained and seasoned by war. They were fiercely loyal, so long as plunder was available in plenty, but they also feared the Seer. Remarkable was the fear that the bloodstone he carried around his neck garnered. The light that ominously bloomed from his tent at night unnerved them. For this reason, not one tent stood anywhere near a stone's throw of the Seer.

"Yessssssss... yes, show me what you will have me do... sssssspeak." The Seer groaned, his body writhing shamefully. His face washed out in the ruby red light, his eyes empty sockets filled with blood, glowing with consuming heat. He looked featureless in the glow as the demon light took his human features and replaced them with something entirely different. The figure that stared into the pulsing pendant was ancient; repulsive, suggesting *real* evil – something that went far beyond description. The Seer was careless of the sucking leeching properties of the bloodstone. He was addicted to it, bound to it, dependent upon it; even as it rotted him from his core.

His hollow sockets blazed their way into the world that lived within the walls of the small thing. His lips parted, showing rotten jagged teeth. Inside the bloodstone, the red cleared just enough to allow him to see in. A man — no: the angel Kreios stood in a wooded place listening and watching.

"Argh!" The Seer spit and cursed at the sight of his arch enemy.

In answer to his question, pure red hatred split the bloodstone open in a tight beam that spread wide, covering the Seer in a bath of evil. The old man writhed, rocking back on his heels and toppling over, sprawling on the dirt floor. Dust clung to his filth.

Arms curling into cadaverous claws, the Seer opened his mouth to scream out in pain, but nothing came forth. The bloodstone became hot and burned his hand, melting the skin, filling up his mind with a vision of the future; breaking his will even further. His body nearly snapped as his back arched and he thrashed against it, fought it, spewing and retching — but to no effect.

A silken voice then spoke to him in a lost tongue. He could

not have dared to try to speak it, but here in the wretched dirt, he could at least comprehend it. *"Listen to me, Seer. You will never be what you are supposed to be if you "fight" like this. I am here to bring you life… a life of which you have never dreamed. You do not have much time. The immortal Kreios draws near to the City of Refuge. You must seize the child before they reach the walls… or shall I have no use for you anymore?"*

The Seer lunged upward from the ground as the red fire from the stone blanketed his body. He hovered wildly and upright, eyes wide and knowing. Clutching the stone, he whined like a whipped dog as spittle drenched his cracked and bleeding lips. The bloodstone went dark, abandoned him. He was thrown violently to the ground.

Crumpled on the floor like so much waste, the Seer groaned, coming back to himself. He shook his head and got to his feet. He looked at the now cold pendant with dim recognition, as if he was not able to recall something very important. He replaced it around his neck and tucked it under his robe. Hanging over his mind like a ready avalanche was the certainty of the next step the army was to take. He flattered himself that he was a partner with his master. But that was why he was Seer — he was so simply persuaded of his own importance. He did not dare to dream that he was completely replaceable.

He needed air. He pulled back his hood, revealing the face of a young man with smooth black hair and unblemished pale skin.

Wickedness housed in a single grin crossed his face. His black eyes simmered in a stew of hatred. He brooded over what he would do to Kreios. The smile pulled taut. He contested with voices in his mind about what would be done with the girl, and as he did, hellish light flashed in his expression. So much enjoyment awaited him. He would try to savor it this time… and Kreios could watch.

CHAPTER XXX

THE THREE ANGELS SILENTLY but speedily packed their small camp, burying the fire and anything else that might leave a trail. Kreios knew they had been spotted, but he didn't want to throw any bones to the dogs. Since they had a Shadower with them, he knew that the Brotherhood could only track them by following their physical trail — if they left one.

Kreios glanced at Maria, then Zedkiel. Maria was obviously exhausted at this point, but travel was a necessary evil. No amount of rest would rejuvenate her until she delivered the baby. She needed skilled help for the remainder of her pregnancy or she could die along with her baby.

Zedkiel had made a decision. "No need to worry about hiding the camp. We must take to the sky and hope that Yamanu can hide us from the surveillance of the Seer." He shoved the last of the deer jerky into his pack, tied the drawstring, and slung it over his shoulder. His face was drawn tight with worry, but when Kreios smiled, he loosened up; bringing back the sparkle in his eyes.

Yamanu cut in. "Do not be troubled, my old friends. I am as strong as I ever have been, and with the presence of the Sword of Light, I am even more powerful. The enemy hordes will have been wandering in the woods for days by the time they realize we are gone." He snapped his fingers and dark dust floated in the air, shedding foggy blackness. Whenever he moved, it fell off his body to the ground.

Kreios was itching to go. "The time for talking has now passed us by. We must move. I can feel the army over the nearest rise to the west, and they are moving fast. It will be impossible to fight them in the air while also keeping my daughter and Maria safe. It will leave us outnumbered, with too much distraction from the fight." Kreios was a practical mind, but now he seemed like he had no sense of humor at all. The message was received. This was not a game.

Zedkiel took Maria in his arms and Kreios hugged his baby girl tight to him. He could smell her skin. It was intoxicating. She smelled like sweet lavender with a hint of something that Kreios could not determine — it was not like anything he had ever smelled. But it was the most wonderful scent in the world.

Kreios sent the horses away with a glance and placed his daughter carefully in her little sling. The magnificent war horses hid themselves deep in the wood, far from where any man would tread.

The angels rose from the ground in battle formation: Kreios on point, Zedkiel at his right hand and Yamanu on his left, already difficult to see. The air was cool under the brightness of a full moon. A touch of spring could already be felt, a prophecy of hope to them.

Kreios looked to the west. The unholy flicker of war torches greeted his gaze. Black and gray mist hovered around the airborne cluster of angels like fingers of dark smoke, masking them in shadow. They quickly faded into the night sky.

Turning north and soaring like eagles on desert updrafts, the travelers coasted gracefully toward a City to which they had never been. They hoped and prayed it did exist. But something they all felt was that it might not be easy to find.

The sword grew warm against Kreios' back as if it knew the way home and would lead them. He breathed in a sigh of relief mixed with hesitation. The sword had a definite connection to his daughter — he could feel that very clearly, though he was not sure why. It was difficult to see and perceive the truth after so recently losing the only woman he would ever love; and so bitterly, so unexpectedly.

He wondered, almost aloud, what this connection was and

what role the Seer might play as well. These questions, and more, bothered him as they soared northward. He would not rest until he was sure that they were safe; in the safest place on earth.

CHAPTER XXXI

Boise, Idaho. Present day.

WHEN THE DOOR OPENED and I saw Michael Alexander stand up stiffly, I stood paralyzed, hoping with everything in me, that what I feared was not happening, that this was all just a bad dream. He was staring at me with an unsettling mixture of awe and disbelief.

"Your head... the..." His voice was soft, questioning and scared. "It's gone, I mean it just disappeared!" He reached out, muttering something incoherent, trying to touch my forehead. But I ducked and took a step backward. He lowered his eyebrows and folded his arms across his chest.

"Airel—"

My mind refused to function. Despite the fact that I needed it more than ever at this very moment, it hid like a stupid kid on his first day of school, refusing to come out from under the bed. Should I pretend that I didn't know what was happening? Play innocent? Or should I fess up to the only person I was comfortable fessing up to about this subject? *Why can't I let myself bring Kim in on all this? But with him...* I looked at the gorgeous guy standing before me. Maybe I knew deep down that he would understand it... or me. If that was possible. There was no getting around it, though — I was a turncoat. A backstabbing fiend, for sure, because I was totally trashing the feelings of my best friend for... some dude...

I reached a trembling hand to my forehead and touched

the place where, seconds ago, a large goose egg throbbed. It was smooth, cool to the touch. Healed.

I stood there with my best impression of a confused, blank look on my face. I looked up at Michael, who was standing so close to me now that I could smell his skin.

"I, uh…" The brilliant words that flowed from my lips in that moment would have made the great poets of the world stop, slack-jawed, and gaze at me in wonder and amazement at the brilliance of my answer. Michael had a tentative hand on my forehead and touched ever so gently the spot where my fatty welt used to be.

"Does it hurt?"

"No…" I responded, leaving all kinds of loose ends. What blanks would he fill in?

"Weird, it's gone. Like it was never there. You sure that doesn't hurt?" He pressed harder to test out his theory.

I pulled away, breaking free, and scowled at him. "Well… what? So it's gone. Maybe it wasn't as bad as I thought it was. Maybe I didn't hit it that hard anyway." Pretty weak, lame, and worst of all, chock full of *maybe*. It sounded like a lie to my own ears, and from the grimace on Michael's face, I knew that he didn't believe a word of it either.

"Come on, Airel, what's going on? You know more than you're letting on, and now you're lying to me." He sounded angry and a little hurt, as well. I sighed loudly and pulled on a few strands of my hair, then shoved my left hand in my back pocket.

I decided right then that I was going to tell Michael everything and hold nothing back.

I could not stop thinking about him and was afraid that if I didn't let him in on everything, I would lose him. Lovers don't have secrets — right? And that's what we were becoming, quickly. How could I keep secrets from him?

I didn't want to lose something with him that, at this point, hadn't even happened yet. I didn't want to risk the destruction of something that felt so fragile in my heart, especially by keeping such an important part of myself from him. *He might even be able to help me.* I knew I was reaching for reasons to keep him close.

I sighed, surrendering. "Michael… I'll tell you on our date." *Hook, line and sinker.* "I just need some time to think things over." I nearly begged him with my tone of voice. "Please don't be mad! And don't worry, I'm fine. I *promise* I will tell you whatever you want to know. Just not now."

Uh oh. I had promised. And when I promise things, planets start to pop out of their orbits. It's serious business. That's what this was now, things were getting… complicated.

He looked at me with a calculating gaze. Then, as if weighing his options, nodded with a small smile. "Okay." He took my hands in his and enfolded them. "But you promise to tell me everything?"

"I promise."

CHAPTER XXXII

Eagle, Idaho. Present day.

THE PICTURE ABOVE THE bed was large. It was an original painting; the master who had produced it unknown. On the canvas, simply depicted, was a drawn sword. It stood against a black background, alive, shining and luminescent, even as a representation in oils. It was the Sword of Light. It hung above the massive bed in a stone alcove in an ornate bedroom of immense size; the architecture ancient, stately.

A killer lay sweating under the painting, spittle dripping, tears flowing from twitching eyes. The mattress, as well as the thick blanket that covered him, was damp with the manifestation of his toil. The room was well above ninety degrees, but he still shivered. His hair plastered itself wet against his scalp. He was more than simply sick.

The things he saw within his bedroom made him consider death as an exit strategy for peace. But he wondered if what was swimming in space above his bed would follow him when he left this world.

There were three lizard-like demons flying about the room. The two smaller ones were bird-like, over ten feet long at full length. The third was twice that in size, with huge, sharp spines rising from its back. One of its wings was torn, and around its neck pulsed the red glow of molten stone. The character of this pendant was decidedly unholy. Upon the face of the creature, if such a thing can have such a name, was the embodiment of hatred, the essence of malice, the expression of self-prostitution to vengeance, at any cost.

The demon stood, legs spread on the bed, straddling the man, who was curled into the fetal position. It wielded a long, curved dagger, which it moved slowly downward; calculatingly, obsessively, until the tip touched the killer's chest.

With greater force but no greater speed, the tip of the dagger pierced the blanket, the shirt, the skin, the ribs, and blood began to boil outward from the wound, against the dagger, accompanied by spitting smoke as two realms came into collision. The wings were vibrating with hideous pleasure.

The killer struggled, trying to escape, but unable. He turned his face toward his enemy, with bulging eyes. The big demon was fixed with burning, red eyes as a hunter fixes on his prey. It was an apparition of black smoke mixed with tar, dripping as if wet.

Sickly green smoke came in bursts from the snout of the thing. It crouched, hovering just inches from the face of the tortured killer. The pulsing red stone dangled and came to rest upon his chest. The dripping maw housed hundreds of sharp teeth, discolored by putrid breath and coated in filth. Two horns sprouted from the top of its skull and enshrouded its face protectively. A long thin tongue slithered out and caressed the face of the killer.

The killer flinched and whimpered something unintelligible. The demon smiled above him and laid back its ears, ripping a scream through the air and the killer's very soul.

Tengu seized the killer's shoulders and its claws dug in. The glowing eyes of the demon flared brighter, singing eternal death. The killer cried out for mercy. Tengu shoved a closed fist into his chest and slithered into the killer's body as if it were a pool of water, not a body of flesh. The sharp tail disappeared with a snap and a twist.

Bolting upright in his bed, soaked, a killer opened his own eyes, gasping for breath as if surfacing in the sea. He was drenched in sweat, his heart pounding like a hammer, his right hand curled as if grasping a weapon. Heavy in his mind, glowering and cloudy, he beheld a rotting, staring hooded face — one of the very few things that could cause him real terror — but he would not speak name or title tonight. *It has to be tonight or never — there is no more time.*

PART TWO

THE DISCOVERING

CHAPTER I

1250 B.C. The City of Ke'elei

KREIOS KNEW FIRSTHAND WHO it was that had His large, powerful, hand under the universe. It is — was — will be — God; the Most High. Kreios had looked into His eyes and saw the flame of fire that burned there. He felt the Presence, and in those eyes, he saw more than he could ever say in one lifetime — even a lifetime as long as his would be.

Kreios feared God in a way that gave bedrock meaning to the word. The All-Powerful Knowing Master that ruled and reigned could, in an instant, know every choice that would be made in a single life. Even the earth knew Who had spun it into existence. Kreios knew Him as El, or the power of El. The saying was true that El was *all in all.*

Kreios' thinking was best done in the air, where the cool scent of the earth filled his nostrils and mind. He could think clear thoughts in the blank canvas above, where the land below rippled in undulations and trees seemed to grow from nothing, in an order known only to El.

He was glad that Maria, wife to his beloved brother, was safe — and his daughter as well, in the hidden city at Ke'elei — most simply called, "The City." No more was ever needed. It was the most beautiful place on earth. A long valley of tall, green grass led up to it in a lush carpet, shouting out with the truest color he had seen since he left home.

They had been in The City for two days now, and Kreios took

his morning flight over the vast valley that lay nestled between snow-capped peaks, rising sharply like teeth toward the sky. On the north end was a sheer cliff of rusty red that stood in stark contrast to the calm green valley. It reminded Kreios of what he had seen in parts of the world where deserts gripped the earth and the sun was king.

He turned and surveyed The City from the sky. He was just a speck against the light blue, and as he looked down, he admired the thick fortress walls that ran along the boundary edge of the great City. They were laid with white stones, each one as big as a village house, five or six stones high, arcing smoothly in a line. The City was hemmed in to the north by the cliff, to the south by the wall, and to east and west by the mountains.

Horses and chariots would race side by side on the top of the wall at the year-end festival. Great oaks and elms tangled with the deepness of an unknown forest at its base, and giant ancient redwoods towered in front, hiding The City from the view of anyone in the valley below. The City fathers had planned well for its defense, making it impenetrable to any known assault.

Behind the walls, The City spread like a delicate flower over the fertile soil of the valley and up the side of the mountain, sometimes cutting directly into the stone face. These stone houses led to tunnels and paths that wound deep into the heart of the mountain, making use of the protection that only a natural granite fortress could afford.

The City was surrounded by a courtyard of grass with a stone pillar at its center. The pillar was crowned with a bright flame that burned by night, providing light and warmth and consuming no fuel. It was evidence of the Presence, that it was not forgotten, that it was prized. The fire flared up each night, appearing at dusk and illuminating the entire City, snuffing itself out at dawn's first light. Outside The City's walls, no light was visible, keeping safe the secret of the City of Ke'elei.

"It is El," Kreios thought. "He wills it — and so it is."

The rest of the buildings in The City were constructed with the same materials as had been used to build the wall and to form the mountains. Glass, and another gifts from the angels — mirrors — reflected the mountain around The City as well as the sky above, making it nearly invisible.

Kreios liked how clean the streets were, and he loved the sound of the young children who ran there, filling The City with laughter. It took him back to another age, when creation was, as yet, still filled with innocence. These young would be trained as warriors; every family member was to be trained in the art of war.

Kreios descended, landing by the stone pillar at The City's center. The grass under his feet moved, as if it was aware of and had reverence for the Sword he carried. He would attend a gathering with the elders to learn what counsel they had in regard to the ever-approaching battle with the Seer and his horde.

Today, though, he would take another long rest and enjoy the beautiful, warm weather and hold his darling baby girl. He would kiss her and give her one extra for her mother.

CHAPTER II

Boise, Idaho. Present day.

LIFE WAS GETTING MORE complicated with each passing day. I was getting more beautiful by the second, which was amazing, but also was a problem. Plus, I had promised to reveal to the most amazing boy, whom I hardly knew, that I could heal supernaturally. The problem with making promises is that they have to be kept — or broken.

Michael was there in the back of my mind. I was annoyed that I could not distract him from the fact that he had seen my welt disappear right in front of his eyes.

Kim was chomping at the bit to call the police. I wondered if she was on my side, or if she just thought it would be cool to be involved in a police investigation. It made me seriously want to pull my hair out. Either way, it was more than I wanted to deal with, for sure. I had to rein her in before I lost my chance to get some answers.

I wished Michael would let me ease up on my promise, but I doubted he would. One way or another, I was going to have to tell him or show him. As crazy as it sounds, I thought showing him might be easier, because otherwise it was like telling some impossible story that nobody would believe.

After an awkward phone conversation and an apology, I had somehow talked Kim into ditching the double-date idea. I promised her that later we could share all the juicy details between us. I convinced her it would be more fun that way. In the end, it was enough to convince her, and I was relieved that I would be alone with Michael so I could fully explain to him what was going on — if only I knew, myself. All of this was extremely frustrating. How was I going to explain this craziness to the guy I was falling for?

It was date night. Cue the ominous music. It's a good thing my mom was busy fussing and hovering over me, because my emotions were getting pulled in so many different directions. How could I dread, so completely, the one thing I had been wanting with all my heart for so long? It was just crazy. Mom was there, though, to run a brush through my hair and help me decide on the right shoes — but we both knew it wasn't about any of that. When you need your mom, you just need your mom.

My hair looked like spun silk, but darker, and kind of metallic looking. When I touched it, I gasped. It was so soft, but so strong that when I pulled a strand from the brush and tried to break it, I couldn't. With each stroke, it got smoother and smoother. Maybe I was going to die — but at least I would die looking good.

It was just after six, and Mom and I shared a glance between us. I pulled on a cute little dress that I had picked up at Forever 21. Kim had insisted that I buy it, and I had to admit that it did look great. It was a light springy material, sky blue, with silver lines falling down the right side and curling up the hip into a flower with silver petals. The thread was so beautiful and delicate that I was almost afraid to touch it. It was a sleeveless v-cut with the delicate hem at my knees. It was so flattering that I blushed at my own reflection in the long mirror on the back of my bedroom door.

Mom helped me complete the look with strappy black high heels. I pulled my hair back with a barrette and let half of it fall over my shoulders. I was amazed. *No more flat iron for this chick.* I chose the same shade of eye shadow as my dress and some clear lip gloss. I felt amazing. Was this how it was supposed to feel?

Mom excused herself from my room. She said she had to get dinner ready downstairs, but as she left, she was dabbing at her eyes, and I think maybe she was just as emotional about date night as I was.

As she blew me a kiss and closed my door, Kim called, my phone bouncing on the dresser. I answered it, sure that she could hear me smile. "Yes, my dear Kim. I take it you're still trying to decide what to wear?" I could imagine her standing in front of her bedroom mirror with a frustrated look on her face; the two dresses in question hanging next to each other like a line-up at the city jail.

"Yes! The red one... is it too fancy? Maybe we won't be going to a very fancy place. The black one is hot, though... but I'm so pale! I should have gone tanning last week. Argh, Airel, what am I going to do?"

"The black one's better. You know how red and your hair mix. I don't know why you even bought that one." Kim had seen the red one — and when I say red, I mean in-your-face bright red — and had to have it. Her red-orange hair made her look like a cooked lobster if she ever wore anything red.

"You think? The black is so...well, so cliché. You know, every girl has a little black dress. But on a first date?"

"Kim, since when do you care about what anyone else thinks? Go black and don't look back. I gotta go. I'll call later tonight, maybe in the morning if we stay out late." I didn't want her texting every five minutes for an update.

"Okay, I'll wear the black one. Oh, I can't wait!" She giggled. "Call me!" I hung up and tossed the phone into a tiny clutch I was going to cart around with me, more to complete the look than anything else.

I heard Michael's truck pull up out front and I moved to the window to look out. I wanted to run down and open the door for him to block his path to my dad, but Dad had already told me to stay in my room until he had a chance to meet "the guy." "The guy." He was more than "the guy," of course, but dads will be dads.

I heard the doorbell and a dry voice downstairs. I paced the room and double-checked my make-up and hair. Spinning around, I smiled at the way my dress looked. *Not bad, girl! Not bad.*

"Airel, you ready?" Dad yelled up the stairs and I nearly jumped out of my skin. I grabbed my purse and bolted, glancing one last time in the mirror. I took the stairs far too quickly for the blasted heels I was wearing.

Michael stood at the foot of the stairs in a pink Oxford shirt and jeans that were faded in just the right spots. He looked like a model for GQ.

His jaw dropped, and my dad blushed for me as I came to a stop one step from the bottom. I did a little curtsey and smiled. I looked Michael up and down in a critical manner as if to judge what he was wearing. "Hm. Pink, eh?"

"It's off-red." His smile intoxicated me. His light blond hair looked almost white and stood up all over in soft spikes that I wanted to touch. He smiled, holding out his hand.

I took it. "You're trying to score points here." He smelled *so* good. No cologne-bomb here — just something naturally irresistible. He looked at me with the biggest smile on his face, as if he wanted to say something but was unable to find the words.

Dad broke the spell. "Now, you two be good. Have her home by midnight. If you need anything, call, and if you're gonna be late, call. Have fun and remember what I said, Michael."

I looked sideways at Michael, then at my dad. He smiled and shook Dad's hand. "Yes, sir. We'll be good and she'll be safe — you can count on that, sir." Mom stood there, Dad holding her, and her eyes were misty.

Well, how wonderful. The guy could be a gentleman. I couldn't resist him, and what's more, couldn't think of a single reason why I ever should. I suppressed a laugh. I kissed my dad on the cheek and gave my mom a little hug. "Love you guys. We'll be fine. Don't stay up waiting for us. Get some sleep, okay?" I knew they would wait up anyway because parents are like that. They were like a masterpiece portrait as they stood there watching me walk away. It was striking and so sweet, and thoughts of my own romantic future stirred my imagination.

I waved over my shoulder as Michael opened the front door for me. The evening air was warm and sweet, filled with pumpkin spice and golden leaves. I breathed in deeply and Michael took my arm, leading me down the front steps.

"So, he gave you the I-will-have-my-revenge talk, huh? You

were all, 'sir,' and, 'yes sir!' Did he show you the 12-gauge, too?"

Michael lifted the latch on the passenger side of his big Chevy truck and helped me in. "Oh, yeah. He even told me that he has a 'special understanding' with Coach." He smiled, indicating that he was probably joking. "He and I had a man-to-man, nothing big. Nothing you'd understand. Besides, I've got you now... " He looked at me in the oddest way just then, but it was brief, and before I knew it, he had moved on. And you look more beautiful than anything or anyone I have ever seen."

I blushed and looked away, but he reached up and gently turned my face toward his. All I could think of was that my parents were probably watching, and it was all I could do to keep from dying over it. "I mean it! Stunning, hot, Audrey Hepburn, however you want to describe it. You are the most beautiful woman I have ever seen."

Audrey Hepburn?! I was going to die a happy girl. I had spent many an hour with Kim watching her in *Roman Holiday* and *Sabrina,* fantasizing about being the chauffeur's daughter or the princess. I had memorized those movies, awestruck at how Audrey carried herself and how beautiful she was. If only we could live our lives in black and white. It was poetic, in a way. But for him to compare me to Audrey, favorably, out of nowhere — it just sent me right over the moon.

I could tell that he was dead serious about it. He looked like he was about to cry. The moment shocked me to the core. As long as I live, I will never forget that look on his face.

Michael stood staring into me, drinking me in. I imagined that if I had never said anything, he would have stood there all night looking at me in a way that's only allowed in fairytales. This had to be a dream. Michael was not just handsome, he was kind. He had a way of making me feel like the only girl in the world, and he was here, looking at me like this. I felt his hand as it held mine, and his pulse as his heart beat in harmony with mine. It was as if we were made for each other.

"Well then, mister. Are we going or not?" Michael grinned and shut the door reluctantly, and as he walked to the other side, I had about two seconds to compose myself.

He was winning my heart, and no matter how I tried, I couldn't help myself. He was so wonderful. I was afraid that something terrible was going to happen to mess it all up.

CHAPTER III

THE CHEESECAKE FACTORY WAS one of my favorite places to eat. It stood connected to the side of Boise Towne Square Mall and was right next to Borders Books and Music — my fave. I found myself in Borders every chance I got.

I always had to buy a book, even if I wasn't done with the one I was currently reading. I loved to read. I felt like the turn of each page echoed inside the world between the book's covers — and each book had its own rules. There, within the mystique of that connection, was something special, and it was addictive.

Michael found us a parking spot, actually four of them, about fifty miles from the doors. I will never understand how guys are about their machines. One minute they're burning rubber and playing in the mud, and the next they're crying because some heartless soccer mom dinged their door. And they think *we* have issues. So he was going to make me walk fifty miles for dinner. I really didn't mind too much. It meant I got to hold his hand that much longer.

That's exactly what we did — we held hands from the passenger door of his truck to the front door of the restaurant. I felt the deliciousness of his warm-almost-hot skin and fluttered inside. His fingers gently gripped my own, making me feel like glass. I liked it. I felt that there was no safer place for me to be, especially in that moment.

"How'd you know I like the Cheesecake Factory?" I wondered if Kim had ratted on me. It was no fun if he didn't have to at least try.

"I have my ways! I figured that we could go hang out at Borders afterward if you want." Oh yeah, Kim was the big fat rat.

Michael followed me inside. As he did, his hand brushed the small of my back, sending a shiver up my spine. *Come on, get hold of yourself. He's just a guy!* The shiver ran its course, ending up somewhere in the back of my head, where that new flutter was. *She* loomed in the back of my mind, watching the whole thing with silent curiosity. I had a feeling that *She* disapproved somehow. Inside the Cheesecake Factory were enormous domed ceilings with paintings of angels on them held up by huge columns. Colored glass and plastered walls accented the interior, giving it a decently convincing European feel. It may not have been real, but I didn't care tonight — I liked everything about the ambience.

"Table for two?" The hostess smiled at us, showing us to a booth near the back. The place was packed. How Michael got a table with all the people waiting in the lobby was beyond me. I didn't ask, though. I felt like a princess and *my* prince had connections.

We sat down. I left my menu where it was. I always got the Orange Chicken, at least the three or so times I had been there before. I loved it, so why change now?

"You already know what you're getting?" Michael asked as he looked at the menu.

"Yup. Orange Chicken's my favorite, and I just can't ever seem to get past it." I smiled and avoided his eyes, knowing I might blush. "I've heard that everything here is good, though."

He studied the menu, his eyebrows lowered in thought, and I took the chance to look again at his face. He had such a smooth complexion, not a single blemish in sight. My dad used to talk about "gunslinger's eyes," the kind of eyes you'd expect to find glinting at you from underneath a black Stetson, along with a single-action .45 revolver. Dad was a bit of a gun nut and some of that rubbed off on me, but I thought about the eyes. That was the important part. As I looked at those eyes, I knew: they *were* gunslinger's eyes.

"I think I'll get the steak. It sounds good, and I'm hungry. I need more protein anyway. All that running for football gives me a killer appetite." He leaned his forearms, which were impressive, on the table and looked at me. There was a question sparkling in his cold blue eyes. I knew what he wanted to know.

"Later," I said. "I promise, but not here. I have to show you… not tell you." He gave me a doubtful look. Then he sat back and folded his arms across his chest.

"Okay, but I'm holding you to it. You look good. I mean, your forehead looks perfect. I mean, it looks fine. No welt, not even a bruise or anything." In spite of his awkwardness, he was cute. He leaned forward again and I felt my skin heat up.

"Stop staring at me like that. I'm not some experiment. I'm a human being with feelings." It came out of me a little too forcefully and I wondered where this sudden aggression came from. After all, this was Michael Alexander I was talking to here.

Wings fluttered and *She* calmed me down, but I still gave him "the look." It was what my dad said I needed to work on, that ultra serious "I-ain't-takin'-none-o'-this" look. Dad had told me that I needed practice before it would strike fear in the heart of a man. I secretly hoped it wasn't *too* effective.

"I'm sorry, I didn't mean to stare at you." He sighed. "I just can't help it when you're around me. Here. How about we try this," and he closed his eyes, looking down. When he opened them, he looked directly at me, and now, instead of the gunslinger, there was something that made me want to give myself to him, forever. Deeper still, savage wonder was there, as if he saw something to be feared when he looked at me.

My eyes must have widened. "Okay, stop, just — if you don't stop it I'm going to cry." I was so getting in over my head. "You can only use that on special occasions." My heart was racing, and I was starting to feel like I needed some fresh air.

"But isn't this a special occasion?" He looked at me with calm curiosity.

"Well, yeah. Yes, it is. I mean, it's our first date, and I have to say, so far you're picking up some points: perfect restaurant, and you look good." I raised my glass of ice water to him, and like a perfect gentleman, he clinked his against it.

"Thanks, Airel. I try. There oughta be a law against how you look, though, really. You might cause an accident just by walking down the sidewalk." I laughed and blushed. At the same time, he thundered with a deep low laugh that was absolutely wonderful.

I was trying to savor everything. This, I thought, was a moment that I would be able to look back on and remember, maybe even tell stories about. Not that I was making long range plans or anything, but a girl can dream. Even if it's a little wild. But even though I was literally having the time of my life, something was nagging at me, pulling me from — or in — a direction that was uncomfortable. My stomach was a little unsettled, which worried me, but it went beyond that. Something wasn't right. I didn't know what it was, or even if I was sure about it, but I wasn't about to let it ruin my evening.

CHAPTER IV

A SLEEK BLACK GMC Yukon sat under a scrubby pine tree in the mall parking lot. The man inside liked everything to be just-so. With blackout tint on the windows, oversized rims, and forgettable license plates, the SUV looked like something someone in the Mob would drive.

The back seats had been removed. Installed in their place were two reclining bucket seats made of hard plastic and equipped with locking five-point harnesses. There were straps on the armrests and footrests. It was like a paddy wagon designed for the criminally insane. The extra dark tinting and sound-proofing ensured that even if the victim screamed after the doors were shut, not a sound would penetrate to the outside.

The man at the wheel took a drag from a hand-rolled cigarette. His window was cracked, and a thin curl of smoke made its way out into the goldening sunlight, then fell downward onto the lines of the pavement. He looked up and down the parking lot with sharp eyes hidden behind dark sunglasses.

He took another drag and thought about what he was going to do, what he had to do, and wondered if the boy was going to be any trouble. He didn't want to take him, but it seemed he must. It would slow things considerably. He figured the lad would put up a fight, but he had no fear of being overpowered. He wanted the girl, and if that meant taking her beau as well, so be it. But the boy had a part to play in this — truth be told — and he was curious to see how it would end.

He studied the smoke from his cigarette, watching it wind

around his hand. He really enjoyed smoking. He couldn't understand why so many people these days were scared of their own shadows. It was too bad, he decided, and flicked the cigarette out onto the pavement.

He ran a hand through his hair. It had to be now. After all, he wasn't the only one pursuing the girl, and he had done so much to get to this point by himself. Nowadays, they called it "situational ethics," but in days gone by, it was understood that killing a man wasn't always a sin. He checked the revolver on the seat beside him. It had two rounds — at this he smiled, because it was poetic. Symmetrical. Two would be enough. If it wasn't, he didn't deserve her.

CHAPTER V

I SAT BACK IN my chair and watched Michael eat the last of his steak, studying his face. I hoped he would understand whatever was going on with me, with my sudden sickness and freakish healing ability. They were the only words I could think of — ability, power. I tried not to think about it too much, because it was making me insane. I just wanted some answers, and for some reason, out of all the people I knew, he was the one I trusted the most.

Maybe it was just that I *wanted* to trust him with it. I laughed out loud, thinking how absurd the word "absurd" sounded in my head. He looked at me quizzically. "Something funny?"

"Oh no," I laughed. "I was just thinking. Sometimes my thoughts are just funny to me." I twisted a strand of my hair and he watched my fingers as if it was the most interesting thing he had ever seen.

"You are just gorgeous." He smiled with the corner of his mouth and I couldn't help but laugh.

"Shut up, Romeo." I kicked him lightly under the table and then looked around, signaling my desire to get going. I wanted to sit here forever, but the time did not allow us to dillydally around. If we wanted to do anything more than eat, we had to get moving or my dad would have the police out after us.

He flagged the waitress and she told us that she'd bring the check. Michael looked at me. "Do you like surprises? I have one in mind, but you'll have to be open to the extraordinary and the extreme." Michael pushed his plate toward the center of the table.

"I'm all about the extreme — where were you wanting to go,

Borders?" I thought he was going to spit his water all over me; I made him laugh so unexpectedly. "Anyway, you want extreme? Just look at these babies." I flexed my arm for him, tapping my bicep like a weight room thug, making a grimace. If there's anything I could do, it was sell the joke in a way that *always* got a laugh.

"Du-hude! Nice guns, Airel." He was still slightly wheezing with laughter. "I guess you know how to handle yourself."

"You have no idea." He really didn't. He just sat and smiled at me. "Well, Michael?" His name was delicious on my lips. "How about that surprise?" He slid some cash in with the check and took one last swig of water. I stood up, and he took my arm as our waitress thanked us. We left the restaurant like a fairy tale pair, *nothing but blue skies from now on.* I hummed a tune from another old favorite of mine, *White Christmas.* I loved those old movies.

The sky was now dark, but the air was warm and hinted of sage and juniper. Floating from all the surrounding restaurants was the scent of garlic and butter.

"It wouldn't be a surprise if I told you." He grinned and leaned over and whispered in my ear. "I think you are going to love it, though." His breath in my ear gave me goose bumps.

I was hyper-aware of Michael's arm on mine. I was in heaven being next to him. I just wanted to stay like this forever. He towered over me, and next to him, I felt safe and small, too, but not in a bad way. It was the kind of protection that allowed me to be free, to be whoever I really was. The *real* Airel.

The parking lot was full now. Cars had been parked all the way out, nearly to where Michael had obsessively taken up four spaces with his truck, near the end of the row. As we walked toward it, I heard the fluttering of wings in the back of my mind. *She* moved. Something about it made me stop. It was different this time — a warning. Something wasn't right, and my mind instantly raced back to earlier in the evening when I had felt only a fraction of alarm compared to now.

"You okay?"

"Yeah, I just have a weird feeling, like we're being watched or something."

He looked around. "I wouldn't doubt it. You look amazing. Anyone within a mile of that dress would definitely be watching." He smiled, and I smiled weakly back, but still something inside made me uneasy. Was there a chink in the armor of my hero? *No, that's not it.* His compliment was cliché, but he meant it, and what's more, I wanted it, so it was okay.

I looked up and down the parking lot and noticed that no one was in our row. People milled about, going into the mall, coming out with their shopping, but our row was like a no-fly zone or something — devoid of any life at all.

I kept looking around as we began walking again. A creeping fear moved from my heels to my back and over my head like a hood. As I began to wear it, everything in me wanted to bolt like a deer in the woods.

Then I heard *She* say something I will never forget, *"Do not be afraid."* I was scared, frightened, concerned. But not nearly enough. It's almost as if I heard destiny calling, giving everything a kind of symmetry.

The next thing I remember, Michael fell like a corpse, hitting the pavement so hard I heard his head crack against the hard blacktop. As I turned toward him, I saw a man standing next to a black Yukon with a gun in his hand, aimed at me.

I could not see his face in the dark. A light pop sound came from his gun, and I felt a sharp pain in my neck. I reached for it and felt a tiny dart sticking out of my neck. I yanked it free, and crazy with rage, I rushed him.

He met me, expertly, as I passed between the Yukon and the blue truck next to it. He had me by the shoulders and twisted me around as if I was a rag doll, easily getting me into a headlock. My purse and cell phone went flying, and the sound of it hitting the pavement stuck in my memory.

I began to realize that I was acting rather foolishly, charging a man with a gun. He was obviously not worried about being seen, and not worried about 98 pounds of me, kickboxing lessons and all, taking him down.

His arm was like iron around my neck. I took hold of it and

dead-weighted, throwing him off balance for a split second. I pulled his arm forward as hard as I could. I didn't think it would work, but shockingly, he flew over my shoulder and slammed into the blue truck, upside-down, with a dull crumpling sound.

I stood there like an idiot. He was instantly on his feet and back at me. He charged me, shoving me against the Yukon with so much force that it knocked the wind out of me. He spun me, getting behind me again, and took me down, his knee in my back and his arm around my neck. The noose was tightening, my windpipe was cut off, and blood rushed to my head. He had me in the very sleeper hold that my dad had tried to teach me a few years back. If done correctly, I would be unconscious in less than four seconds.

CHAPTER VI

I KNOW WHAT YOU are. The words reverberated through unconscious randomness inside of me. I had heard stories of comatose people having dreams, sometimes hearing what their loved ones were saying, but being unable to respond. That, to me, was hell, assuredly: to be trapped and screaming, "Hey! I'm alive, don't give up on me!"

"I know what you are," came the words again, voiced vaguely, the tone probably resembling my dad, but mixed with every memory I ever had, and somehow, not Dad at all. Was someone speaking them? And if so, who?

There was a fight, a gun. But those things were wrapped in cotton, insulated against the touch of my awareness, and shifty. Every time I tried to come to rest on something concrete, it would vanish in smoke. Everything I had known to be real was a distant abstract world, and I was not a part of it anymore. I feared at any moment I would wake up, caged again in the dark, in a broken world, kept by my demonic jailor — and that was a nightmare I did not want to be having, not again. Certainly not for real.

My dreams turned hazy and soft. Michael was sitting in his truck and I was sliding close to him, looking out over the city lights from Table Rock, high up in the foothills, where other young lovers were parked in darkened cars. We sat in silence because there was nothing to say. The city lights twinkled below, becoming his beautiful blue eyes into which I poured myself like water. If perfection could be defined, this was it.

"I KNOW WHAT YOU ARE, AIREL."

I gasped in shock. I was instantly aware of cold metal straps around my wrists. The voice boomed off the empty canyon walls of my mind one last time, dissipating into nothingness. I realized that my eyes were open, trying to focus, to register what they beheld.

I knew that the metal straps were real; I felt them against the skin of my wrists, cold and harsh. I was seated in a reclined position, strapped down to a hard chair, and when I tried to move my feet, I realized they were bound.

I started to panic; I was defenseless. My eyes were swimming and reaching for the wall. I wanted desperately to know where I was, but knew I would regret knowing.

Inches from my face, I felt something warm, something that tasted sweet. I turned toward it, begging my eyes to focus. Slowly, taking shape in front of me in the dark, were the important details. A car. I was inside a car. I could see the shape of the open door to my right and the yellow light of a streetlamp filtering in. I heard breathing to my left and knew it was Michael. It just sounded like him, like the way he spoke, the tone of his voice.

My eyes went wide, filled with the horror of blankness, and grasped for sight desperately. I knew I was in the black Yukon, strapped to some chair for crazies that kept them from hurting themselves. That left one possibility. The man with the gun was standing over me, probably gloating over his fresh catch. But that wasn't even half of it.

My eyes began to focus on two dark orbs set into the shape of a face. They were almost black, the surrounding skin fair, pale, stony. Crowning his head, I saw blond hair and heard him whisper to me, "I know what you are, Airel." I gasped, deeply and jaggedly, like my first time through a haunted house when I was 8 — completely terrified.

The killer. The theater. The stalker. The note in the mailbox. My weird dreams. I struggled frantically against the restraints, my breath ragged, throat dry, pulling myself away from him as much as I could, completely crazed.

"If you keep quiet, I will not gag you. It's your decision." His voice was firm and could have commanded tens of thousands. Impossibly, it calmed me, if only a little bit. "If you insist on defying me, I will gag you as well as drug you. Do you understand?" In his voice, was thick and pliable kindness that did not make any sense to me.

My response to his commanding voice surprised me. "I'll be quiet, but if you touch me I *will* kill you — do you understand that?" I couldn't believe my own words as they came from my lips. He didn't look shocked or even amused at my threat. In fact, he looked like he believed me, even though it was preposterous.

"Trust me." He said it simply, and within his words was the implicit understanding that he was as good as his word. Even more than that, I understood that he thought he had a reason for doing what he was doing and that he really *did* believe I would try to kill him.

He turned and closed the door with a final thump. He climbed into the driver's seat and started the engine, which was unbelievably quiet.

I looked at the blacked-out windows, seeing only my reflection. I turned to look out the front window, but the killer pressed a switch and a partition slid upward, separating us from him. I was surrounded with darkness and the soft sounds Michael made as he dreamed. I suppose it was then that I resigned myself to the obvious: I had to go along for the ride. The safety I felt before vanished like a vapor in a high wind. I wondered why I had awakened so fast when Michael was obviously out cold. I must have pulled the dart out pretty quickly.

We drove for a long time, a few hours, which gave me plenty of time to worry about my parents, my best friend Kim, my life, my dreams, prom, homecoming, my trusty little Civic, the paper that was due next week. Most of it was becoming completely worthless except my family and Kim. I alternated between tears of desperation and unbridled anger, as my host, my stalker, drove tirelessly on.

I could feel the road winding, rising and falling, and I figured we were north of town in the mountains. Eventually, I could tell that we turned onto a dirt road. After a brief section of very bumpy terrain and steep inclines, we came to a stop. The Yukon still felt like it was moving and my head was swimming. The silence was deafening.

I had tried a few times to wriggle free but found that it was pointless. He was a professional, judging by everything I had seen so far. I figured, even if I were able to free myself, it was pointless to make a break for it. What would I do, fight off a professional hitman, carry Michael on my back, and go — where? Up a creek? *That's about the size of it.*

The driver's side door opened — Michael's side. There, bathed in moonlight, the killer looked at me, expressionless. He began to free Michael from the restraints, checking his pulse. "He'll be fine. Just a headache in the morning, that's all."

I was taken aback by his gentleness. Why would he care if the two people he had kidnapped had a headache in the morning? Was this guy nuts? Was he just one of those creeps that thought he loved his victims, a tear running down his face as he killed them?

He slung Michael over his shoulder as if he weighed no more than a sack of feathers, and turned and walked away. He was gone for quite a while. I took the time to look through the open door, out into thick woods.

Trees and ferns filled the landscape in shades of moonlit gray, the chilly mountain air refreshing and reviving me. I allowed myself to relax, taking it all in, trying not to think of werewolves or anything else otherworldly. I tried not to be anxious about the open door, and the fact that I was defenselessly strapped to a chair. I tried not to think about what predators might be stalking the deep woods after midnight, and how I might smell to them.

Without warning, my door opened. I jumped in my restraints, jerking ungracefully. The blond man, unknown to me, but awkwardly familiar because of all the times I had seen him, unhooked my restraints. I was free and looked at him dumbly. He backed away, allowing me to climb down out of the SUV by myself.

He looked at me with curiosity and turned, expecting me to

follow him. I did, not because I wanted to, but because as I looked around, I saw that there was nowhere to run. No lights from nearby cabins or anything else to offer a glimmer of hope, so I followed my captor.

We came to a space in the forest. Not really a clearing, just a small space in the undergrowth, barely noticeable, carpeted in pine needles. In the center of it, as if discarded by some inconsiderate squatter, lay a wooden door with an old brass knob. It was decidedly out of place, but it blended into the forest floor, rotting, the paint peeling. Ahead of me, my captor stopped by the door, turned to face me and squatted down, his hand resting on the doorknob.

With a light *snick,* the doorknob released from the catch and opened upward on silent hinges, standing wide open. Below, as if leading down into a storm cellar, were stone steps lit from within. I could not see the end. Lit by this shaft of light, the forest around us appeared surreal, with ghastly exaggerations of color and shadow.

He moved aside, gesturing for me to go first. I *knew* that I was going to die down there. There was no debate about it in my mind, and *She* was remarkably silent, seeming to have abandoned me. The man with black eyes and blond hair was going to kill me down there. My body would never be found.

CHAPTER VII

I DESCENDED THE STEPS carefully, leading the killer on. *What is this place, somebody's grave?* I thought sometimes that he had left me, he was so quiet. Even the sound of my footsteps made at least a small noise, but his didn't seem to make any.

The light ahead swelled and brightened as we neared it. I saw that it was an honest to God torch, flame and all. It was hung in a bracket in the wall by a doorway, and was covered with an intricate web of engravings, twisting up the handle. I paused at the door and looked back at him. He didn't offer me any clues as to what I should do.

I felt the need to reach out and open the door. I didn't seem to have much choice anyway — cold-blooded killer behind me, strange door before me. *I guess I'll be taking the door.*

It hit me that I didn't feel afraid in that moment. I can't explain it, but he didn't scare me as much as he probably should have. It was as if he liked me, but in a weird-uncle sort of way. The door swung in smoothly, and beyond… it was not what I expected to see. All I could think about was Michael; where was he? Was he hurt?

"Where is Michael?" My voice sounded much louder than I intended.

"Safe."

"Where is he?" I said even more forcefully.

He did not respond, but moved forward into a large circular room with smooth gleaming stone floors. It was much larger than a football field. And, far from looking like some subterranean lair, it was clean and airy. I couldn't tell how the space was lit, but I could tell it wasn't the same kind of light you'd get from electric bulbs. The ceiling was domed, supported by a few well-placed columns of marble. It was like the state capitol or something.

I guess he's not going to tell me anything.

At one end was a wall of windows standing well over thirty feet tall, through which shone the ethereal moon. The windows were framed by spidery thin metal and strange-looking glass, reminding me of a massive old church. I don't think there was a straight line in any of it — it was all curves and complex symmetry.

The killer followed me in as I stared in shock. I turned to look back up the dark tunnel. *How in the world does this place even exist?*

I almost wanted to thank him and hand him my coat as if I was a guest. But he had hurt Michael, he had snatched both of us and brought us here against our will, and the thought of my parents looking for me, by now having the police involved, made my blood boil. I wanted to smack him right across the face and rattle his black eyes right out of his skull. "Do you know what they will do to you when they catch you? I will testify against you. I'll even make up lies if it will put you away for the rest of your life." But as my words echoed back to me, I could feel my own desperation and how pathetic it was. I was at his mercy. I could tell that *She* was not one hundred percent on my side, either.

He smiled with his eyes at my tirade, hiding the slightest grin on his face. "I hate to sound arrogant or vain, but I will never be caught — it is not possible." With a gentle turn of finality, he ambled over to the wall of windows, his hands behind his back, stopping there to gaze through them. I followed him meekly, lost and exasperated.

I gasped when I saw what he was looking at. Though we were underground, we were looking out at a view that could only be seen from a mountaintop. Below, basking in cool moonlight, was a valley of trees crowding around a huge meadow. A stream babbled through it, winding its way to the other end. There, a mountain range scratched its way to the heavens, protecting the hidden valley.

I could imagine wildflowers filling the valley in summer, but fall in the mountains was like winter in the valley. I doubted there could be flowers there — but then again — those things I had been taking for granted were turning out to be unreliable.

To my left, I heard the roar of water. Most of the windows on that side, I noticed, were obscured by mist from a cascading waterfall that must have found its source farther up, above us. It reminded me of our family trip to Multnomah one summer; the long hike to the top, the dizzying view from where the stream bed released its charge into the atmosphere. I wondered how I would remember this particular wrinkle if this was really a dream.

The killer said, "I selected this site to build my house many years ago. I thought living under a waterfall would be beautiful." He looked like he was taking a nostalgic turn.

"Sometimes in the mornings I sit here, watch the sunrise come over the mountains… and as it hits the water, it makes millions of rainbows all across this room." He looked at me. I felt unexpectedly bold and wanted to ask his name for some reason, but I didn't. Like a father beholding his beloved daughter, he said, "I want you to know: in time, you'll thank me for doing this."

He paused, and I could feel my anger begin to boil as he continued, "I don't expect you to understand now, but one day you will love me as much as I love you."

My jaw was scraping the floor. "Are you — *freaking* — kidding me?!" I couldn't believe what he had just said. He was crazy. "You are a *sick* man." I started to back away from him and the windows. I turned my back to him, hoping to provoke him. I wished he would just get it over with, whatever he had planned. I'd rather be dead than waste any more of my life in his presence. The way he looked at me made my skin crawl.

Noiselessly, he strode by me at a brisk pace, leading me out of the ballroom. I followed, because what else could I do? I was starting to become aware of my exhaustion — it had been a long night — and what else was there? Would I curl up on the cold stone floor like a dog? That wasn't an option.

I figured I'd take my chances with whatever creepy "hospitality" he had to offer me. If there's one thing I had theorized about people, it's that they used each other, whether they meant to or not. Whatever his use for me, I made a guess that I could barter his interest for something a little more practical — like somewhere to lie down and die, for instance. At least for the night.

I looked around for any sign of Michael. I worried that my captor might have been lying about not harming him.

We passed through a set of massive double doors that led through a large kitchen. There were no appliances; nothing modern. There was a huge wood-fired brick oven in one corner, and massive wooden tables for workspace that were crowded with huge earthenware bowls, full of fresh produce of every kind.

Ornate cabinets lined the stone walls. Some of the cabinets stood like furniture, and I imagined that they were stuffed to the gills with all kinds of things I had never seen. *I'm betting that there ain't a bag o' chips to be found in this place.* No fridge or microwave that I could see, either. *I'm so screwed.*

I took mental notes of the layout of the place so that when I tried my escape, I could remember which way to go. We passed through the kitchen, down a wide hallway, and up a flight of thickly carpeted stairs. He stopped at a pretty, standard-looking door. The difference was this one was secured with a thick steel bolt mounted to the outside with a latch the size of my fist.

"This is your room," he said.

"My cell, you mean."

He ignored me. "Michael is in that room, next door. I warn you, there is no possibility of escape. Any attempt will result in punishment. Do you understand?"

"Yes," I said in a flat tone, ripping an imaginary hole through him with my eyes. I was so furious my hands were trembling. I clenched my fists open and shut to try to control it. I wanted to see Michael, to hold him and to make sure he was okay. Why was this man doing this to us?

He slid the bolt and flipped the latch open. The door opened with a slight nudge and I walked in. Before I could turn to face him, the door shut with a solid boom, with an aftershock of the metallic sound of the latch being driven home. All was quiet. I had been planning on giving him the lecture of his life. I guess that didn't work out.

All at once, the whole night overwhelmed me. I ran to the king-sized bed, fell face down, and cried. I wept so hard that my body ached. I was just trying to crawl through to the bottom of it, heaving in spasms of wretchedness until I was completely dry. My head felt bloated and achy.

I was a captive. I kept going over in my head all the possible meanings of the word, taking it in, trying to deal. When my outburst of emotion was all over, I felt as if I had just run twenty miles. No sound came from the hall or the room where he had said Michael was. I wondered if he was really there, or if he was lying and Michael was somewhere else — or were the rooms soundproof? *So many questions. And so few answers.*

My heart ached and bled for the comfort of my friends and family; especially my mom and dad.

There was a glass of water on the nightstand. I took a long drink to quench my thirst. It had been a long night and between fighting, crying and everything else, I was parched.

She whispered something, but I couldn't make it out. My vision clouded and the room began to spin. Oh, no. He drugged me; how could I have been so stupid? I fought the feeling, but in the end, the drug was stronger than my resolve.

I dreamed.

This time, I was in the beautiful valley I had seen through the windows by the waterfall. I ran in the meadow of summertime wildflowers laughing like a little girl. The beautifully scented mountain air swept through me. The fragrance of honeysuckle was overwhelming. All of it — the meadow, the rushing waterfall behind me, the bluest skies I had ever seen — made me want to dance with joy. I twirled in a sun dress, ribbons in my hair, feeling as if my daddy was nearby admiring me.

But Daddy wasn't there. It was someone else — my mysterious stalker was watching me. His eyes were different, ice blue this time. Deep within, I saw a spark of light. It told me that he knew who I was, and what I was becoming.

I heard pages turning again; like a book was being leafed through, fanned out. *She* stirred and sat up in the back of my mind as if *She* knew this man. I didn't run, but looked at him as he walked toward me through the wildflowers. It was as if they sensed his coming, and parted to let him pass without crushing them. I stood on tiptoes to try to measure up and meet his gaze.

She said, *"Do not be afraid. He will not hurt you. He has something you need. Look for it, and when the time is right, you will know."*

"Who are you, and what do you want?"

She answered, *"I am a friend."*

The killer moved like a predator, scanning subtly, aware of the wind. He stopped and stood a few feet from me and held out his hand. I took it. He led me to the edge of the clearing, where I looked up at the waterfall that hid part of his house underneath its beautiful cascading mantle.

"High up on the side of the cliff you will see it — if you look closely." He pointed toward the top, where the water began its fall over the edge, over a thousand feet up. I scanned the rocks and ferns that clung to the side, but didn't see anything.

I was about to give up when I saw a large nest made of twigs and branches, built in a very thin tree. He smiled when he saw that I did indeed see what he wanted me to see. "Now watch."

I rubbed my eyes and took another look. This time, I saw a skinny baby bald eagle scramble up the side and sit perched on the edge looking out at the valley — perhaps at us. He fluffed his baby feathers and opened up his new wings, testing them. This little bird was making me nervous. I hoped he wouldn't fall over the edge — it was a long way to the bottom. I was sure from the way he moved that he had not yet learned to fly.

The mother eagle swooped by the nest in a tuck and clipped the baby in the back, pushing him over the side. My hand flew to my mouth as I watched the baby eagle tumble in the air, flapping wildly, trying to recover, and not making much progress. "Oh, no..."

Then, just as he was about to hit the rocks, his wings finally got some traction. They bent and filled with air, lifting the young bird.

He fluttered and flapped to a landing a few feet from the sharp rocks that would have crushed him. He threw back his head and let out a tiny warrior's squawk, and then another.

I let my hand fall from my mouth, looking up at my captor. He still had my little hand in his. He smiled and said, "This is why you are here…" It shook me awake, his voice seeming to echo in my room. *My cell?* It was morning and the room was filled with rainbows, dancing across my bed like butterflies, as the light filtered in through the waterfall.

CHAPTER VIII

1250 B.C. City of Ke'elei

GATHERED NEAR AN ANCIENT oak tree, dappled by the sunlight that filtered through it, the circle of elders, wise men, and Sons of El were gathered on a mountaintop high above Ke'elei. The court in which they were seated was encircled by perfect Corinthian stone columns of pure white; the massive old oak at the north side, the beginning and end of the circle. A fine latticework of shimmering silver thread screened the open spaces between the columns, casting wild shadowed reflections on the cobblestone floor.

At the east side of the circle, Kreios was seated in one of the high-backed gopher wood chairs drawn up in a half circle. On the west side were twelve thrones of white marble making up the other half of the circle.

Zedkiel was seated at Kreios' right, Yamanu at his left. His brother and friend were adorned in their best garments, as was custom in this council. Kreios was wearing the same cloak he had worn on his wedding day, and it was bitter sweetness that rode on his shoulders.

His beloved wife had crafted it for him of white elk skins throughout their long courtship, lasting through two harvests. His thick belt was studded with rubies that stood out against the white color of his robe like blood in snow. His long hair was pulled back with a leather thong, and the Sword of Light was strapped to his side in its sheath.

The elders, one taken from every tribe, were twelve in all; immortals representing every race of humanity. Kreios looked from one face to another, studying their eyes, reading into most of their thoughts. He was happy to see that most of them were on his side, wanting to fight, to put an end to the Seer and his horde.

The old man in the middle of the twelve wore his beard long and white, but his face was young. He stood, draped in a golden cape lined with badger fur that touched the ground. His breastplate gleamed of onyx, set with diamonds.

"I am called Anael. I am the Watcher over this land as well as the land that overlooks the Forked Sea. This council will come to order in the matter of the reentry of the Sword of Light, and the matter of the Seer and his followers. We, the council, will hear you well."

Kreios acknowledged him and stood. Anael took his seat, and all eyes were on the barely visible Sword in its sheath; its presence exuding great power.

Kreios' hand moved to the grips of his sword as he strode forward to the center of the circle. When he reached the center of the council he stopped, his eyes locked with those of Anael. The sound of metal against metal rang out.

As the Sword cleared the scabbard, the heavens came loose with the ringing. The skies thundered, the artillery of the Kingdom of God sounding off at once. The Sword was lifted up, its blade held high. It crackled, and a barrage of blinding white light burst from the tip in a bolt of lightning.

Then he spoke. "I, Kreios, Son of El, the keeper of the Sword of Light, give praise to God Most High, who is seated now and forever on the Throne of Grace…" He knelt down. "…and Grace has allowed that I could recover from the Seer what was stolen. Father! Raise up your voice to the storm! We approach boldly to ask what You would have us do…"

Murmurs of praise to El ran through the encircled leaders, like water over stones.

"Praise be to El; praise be to God Most High…" Prayers and awe came from the elders. Anael stood now, his white beard waving in the breeze like a banner. Kreios stood under the blazing Sword as if hanging by it. Anael stood tall and began to weep from the corners of his eyes.

The council remained in this posture for some time, awaiting the Word amongst them. Heads were bowed, Kreios stood at center, and Anael stood at the head of the elders.

The Sword became quiet again and cool to the touch. Kreios looked above him to the Sword, to blue sky beyond. The canopy of the mighty oak that covered the gathering place of the council had been partially consumed in a perfect circle.

He brought the Sword down to his side, looking at it with the familiar respect of a seasoned warrior. It still glowed mildly as he guided it back into its sheath, sliding down to the hilt.

"It is time for the Seer to be numbered with the dead. He must perish. If we fail in this, we will be destroyed along with our children and wives. The time to act is now!" Kreios stood, a statue of stone, staring into the faces of the elders. They whispered to one another. He knew he could not do without their endorsement if he were to gain the support of the other warriors.

He closed his eyes, still standing at center in the court, and ran to the place in his mind where he kept things that — if he were wise — he would never reveal.

In his mind's eye, he could see a long valley much like the one below them, where the city of Ke'elei stood. He went deeper into the void and found what he was looking for. He could not tell what it was — only that somehow he needed it. He understood that it would help to convince the elders they could defeat the Brotherhood.

There was a door standing before him as if floating, without hinge or handle. It was of solid wood, and it bore no marks of having been crafted with tools. It looked to Kreios like it had been simply *grown*. It had suffered many scars and scratches in its dark surface, as if someone or something had tried to open it, but could not.

He felt the Sword of Light respond to the door, but he could not tell what it would mean. Deep in his mind, Kreios took hold of the Sword, unsheathing it swiftly. The door flew open at the very same instant. Kreios was pulled powerfully toward the black opening, but he planted his feet and stood his ground. The scent of moist earth filled his senses, but it smelled of something else that he could not place. Iron? Wood? He gave up on knowing — all he was certain of was that he must not go through the door. Not just yet.

From out of the blackness came fingers of red and blue light, separately wooing him, and wreathing him; pulling him toward the black hole of the opening with insistence.

"Return!" he commanded. The Sword of Light returned to the scabbard and the door slammed in his face, knocking him onto his back. Simultaneously, he returned to awareness in the court, in the presence of the elders, the sound of silence soaking him. The birthmarks, like tattoos, that ran and twisted up his forearm all the way to his neck, now burned hot. The elders stared in blank amazement.

Kreios hid his shaking hands as he moved back to his seat. He did not know if the door he had seen could help them, or if it would end up killing them all. These questions were quickly submitted to the facts. The Brotherhood was relentlessly pursuing him and his daughter. The only way to save her was to stand and fight.

CHAPTER IX

Boise, Idaho. Present day.

THE RAIN DRIZZLED FROM the heavens in a light mist, landing on a black BMW 7, making little droplets on the windshield. There was a different kind of individual inside. His arm hairs stood up on end as he watched a house across and down the street a little way.

His mind flipped over and over about what he was going to do to the girl, if she turned out to be who he thought she was. *Kill her now before it's too late!* "Try to control yourself. We don't even know if it's her."

It was just past midnight, and the street had settled down. He ducked down as the high beams of a Ford Explorer filled his car, then drove on past and turned into a driveway, slinking into an opening garage door.

He thought back to a few nights ago, when he saw her, so close and vulnerable in the moonlight as she ran like a spooked rabbit. He wanted to drag her kicking and screaming back to his deep, dark hiding place; the cage, his toy. He would let the caged beast out to play. "You want to come out to play? I know you do."

Patience. There is no need to hurry, we can enjoy it soon enough. He couldn't wait to feel the thrill of the kill again. He shivered as he gripped the steering wheel. His hands turned white with desire, and he started hacking deep within his lungs. He spit out thick black snot and wiped his mouth on his coat sleeve. He cursed under his breath, washing it all back down with cold coffee.

His chest heaved and bulged as if something inside wanted to get out and the only way out was through his sternum. He clutched at his ribs, groaning, and then his skin began to crawl. He ripped his shirt open, watching the spectacle, disconnectedly wondering if he would die this time.

Around his neck was a steel chain. Suspended from the chain was a black stone that glowed blood red. It pulsed darkly with the killer's heartbeat, speaking to him. The evil that flowed through the killer's veins surged and pulsed with a low hum that no man could hear.

He had a splitting headache and dug his fingers into his skull, hoping the pain would stop. He tipped a bottle of Advil up like a drink and poured some into his mouth. Chewing them up and consumed them, waiting greedily for the calm that would come, if only for a little while. He closed his eyes and felt them burn in their sockets.

The next thing he knew, he woke with the sunrise beginning to warm the black leather of the interior. He hoped he had not been discovered while passed out. The headache had been replaced with a cool dizziness that wafted over him in waves. He pulsed with that rhythm, feeling like he was underwater, moving like an anemone.

Two police cars were now parked in front of the girl's house. His body filled with alarm and dread, but not because of the presence of the authorities. There was a more potent authority he feared. A word now formed in the air before him, draped with cobweb and corrosion, and he read it aloud: *FAILURE*. He repeated it in several languages, even some he did not know. He felt sickened far beyond what he had become accustomed to. He knew there had been a change in the game. He didn't know what, but it was not advantageous to him. Then he reverted to pathetic curses.

His thoughts tortured him with images from long-ago battles that he himself had never fought, of bloody kills he had never administered. He clutched his skull and pressed his fingers into his temples in an attempt to stop the gruesome images from filling his mind.

He could see the girl, her dark brown hair and stupid smile.

Oh, how he hated her. Especially now that she was so obviously in love — he could feel it and it nauseated him.

He remembered he had a job, but he had not been in to work for over a week now. He even had a family, but at the moment couldn't remember who they were. He laughed in spite of himself and damned all of it, all of them, to Hell. He didn't even remember his own name, until he wracked his brain over all the "S" names he could drum up: "Sam, Steve, Saul, Stan... Stan, that's it! Stan's the man..."

Stan nodded and touched the red stone, marveling at how much power he could feel coming through its cold sides. He returned his attention to the house, where the two squad cars were now joined by a news van with Channel 12 printed on the side in big block letters.

He had a feeling that some ill had befallen his prey. Maybe she was dead. Perhaps her blond stalker friend had done the job for him, saving him a lot of dirty work. But he resented someone working his job.

The demon in the back of his mind told him otherwise, and he watched from the comfort of his BMW as a new wave of hate filled his veins. He wanted to kill Airel, wanted to take hold of her neck and choke the life out of her and feel the crunch of her bones breaking under his hand.

Smiling with bright white teeth, he gripped the steering wheel harder. Happiness filled him and bubbled over with the thought of finding her and the blond man from the theater. He would kill them both.

CHAPTER X

1250 B.C. The City of Ke'elei

"WHAT I ASK FOR is this: the Army of Ke'elei. Assist me in eradicating the Seer's horde from the face of the earth. If we do not attack, they will find this city and all will be lost. Word of it will spread like a plague throughout the land. We must act quickly to destroy before we are destroyed." Kreios looked at the frowning faces and continued.

"They are less than a day's flight away. If we move with haste, we can attack them before the next sunset. I believe El has placed the key to victory within our hand already. With the aid of the Shadowers, we can attack them from the air without their foreknowledge." Kreios felt the tide begin to turn as he spoke. He wondered what it was that had begun to turn his peers so quickly — unless he was, in fact, deceived somehow, he wasn't quite sure. His face radiated with the power the Sword had already demonstrated. He was not sure exactly what propelled him forward, and to what end, but he felt he could almost defeat the horde by himself. It was as if he was becoming one with the Sword, and the Sword one with him.

Anael shook his head, and his white beard wagged with disapproval. "If we give you the Army, the city will be defenseless. What will happen if they send a second wave to take the city as you are gone? I cannot allow our women and children to be sacrificed in order for you to embark on a battle that may leave you all dead."

Kreios tried to keep his voice even, but it shook slightly in spite of his effort. "I believe that the Sword of Light will protect us from the drain of power in battle —"

"— You believe, but have no proof. What happens if the battle lasts for days? What if, over time, you lose all of your power? The Shadowers will not be able to protect you as you return to the city and lead the entire horde to our gates. Then, not only will you and the entire army be weak and dying, but also the city will stand at the mouth of its own grave."

Kreios could feel his temper rise, but resisted. "Understand, they will be at our gates on the morrow no matter what we choose to do today. I do not know how, but the Seer is able to see past our defenses. How he does it is not the point. The enemy would not expect us to leave a fortified city in favor of open battle in the wilderness. If we attack swiftly, he will not see it coming." Kreios stopped, looking at Anael, gauging his reactions. He was stone-faced still.

Kreios slumped his shoulders slightly in acknowledgement. "We have to try. I can leave half the Army here to defend the city in case we fail, but we must try! Our lives are all at stake!"

Anael muttered, conferring with the other elders in a hushed tone, occasionally stealing a glance toward Kreios and the Sword that hung at his side.

Kreios had no evidence that his plan was sound. He simply knew what was true and what was not. He knew he would protect his daughter at any cost. If that meant meeting the Seer in battle on his own, he would do it.

"We will have to hold further council over this matter," Anael stated matter-of-factly. "It is a difficult thing to judge. The Sword is back in our hands now, and I have a hard time risking that it be taken away again."

Kreios flinched in fury. "Why is a sword forged, O Great Anael? Why are shields made? For what purpose does a man bend a bow and craft arrows? Why does he train his hands to battle? Is it to hide these things in obscurity when they are most needed? Would you in fact have us run from the risk of battle when the possibility of victory is at hand? If we would but reach out to grasp it! I lost the Sword once. Once! That will not happen again, Anael. I am the keeper of the Sword and the rightful use of it is mine alone. If I must, I will fight the horde single-handedly. But you would open up the gates of the City of Refuge for the enemy to trample our very graves and defile them, to keep safe that which is not even your responsibility. Do you stand with me, or no?"

Anael smirked and turned aside dismissively in his seat. "Kreios, you speak as a fool. You are indeed the keeper, but the Sword belongs to us all. Even you must see that. If you lose it or are killed, we will be lost and our city will have no chance of defense. The enemy army will be here, as you say, in a day or two. Why attack them when we can prepare our own city and hold it when they come? After all, what is the purpose of the City's great walls?"

"You are blinded by your own fear!" Kreios despised the weak of heart. "If we fight them away from the City, we have a chance of keeping it secret. If they find it — where do you propose to rebuild? We will then be locked in perpetual war. Do you not remember why we live in hiding? Our last refuge will be under attack until everything about it has been snuffed into legend — including any of us unfortunate enough to be caught here."

Kreios saw that this got through.

Anael looked at each member of the council with growing concern. Some, he could see, were swayed, and he felt his grip on them slipping. He spoke, finality dripping from his voice. "We will prepare the City for war. I will give you a third of the army and enough Shadowers to hide you and your men. If you fail — we will defend the City with the rest of the army, and pray for El's mercy." He stood, declaring the council was done discussing this matter. Everyone stood and bowed. The council left the circle without a word.

Kreios stood, not as stunned as he probably should have been. *He's given us just enough to ensure our failure.* He watched as the council departed.

The old oak, a hole torn in its canopy, symbolized the emptiness Kreios now felt. It fluttered majestically, moving regally with the breeze.

Zedkiel and Yamanu approached Kreios. Yamanu clapped him

on the shoulder, grinning broadly. "When do we start?"

Zedkiel and Kreios were gazing thoughtfully at the hole in the tree's branches overhead. "A third is not enough," said Zedkiel, "but it is better than the three of us against the horde." He was trying to be cheery.

Yamanu scoffed jokingly at them. "You two look like you're on your way to eternal death. Do you not remember who you are?" His voice bubbled with joy. "Do I need to remind you? You are the Sons of God…"

Kreios and Zedkiel looked at him, and smiles began to break over their dark countenances.

"I will gather the best of my kind," Yamanu said with a dark look on his face. "The old bat has much to fear. A third, two thirds — it matters not. Numbers are like gold to El. What we need will be provided for us."

Kreios smiled at them both and said, "Muster the warriors. We depart soon. It is time now to teach this Seer to see fear in spirit and in truth."

CHAPTER XI

Somewhere in the mountains of Idaho. Present day.

I WAS RUNNING. THE faster I ran, the worse my fear became. The thing that pursued me grunted and howled with rage as it chased after me. I dared not look back, concentrating on digging into the rough terrain with my feet. I felt each power pulse of my cadence as I sprinted, tucked my head, and felt the resistance of muscle on bone.

I exploded into a clearing and a huge tree cast a demented shadow in front of it as if leading the way. I was running through the clearing toward a forest of impossible black trees with dark purple leaves.

I screamed as a clawed hand gripped my shoulder from behind, and I put on an extra burst of speed, tearing loose. A slice of my flesh was taken from me as hot pain ran into my shoulder. The evil-looking forest loomed two hundred feet ahead, possibly within my reach. I felt I would be safe there from whatever was determined to get me.

"Airel… Airel…" The voice was guttural and sweet at the same time, taking on the characteristics of the beast as well as my own conscience. The dark woods parted in a curtain and I dove through. I landed on hard shale and skidded to a stop, opening up new wounds in my back. I clambered to my feet.

I turned and saw the hooded beast as he lurched to a stop at the edge of the forest. He howled, then I heard my name again. "Airel… wake up…"

The beast was hunched over, wolf-like, but standing on two legs instead of four; massive clawed hands, covered with fur, hung at his sides like broken branches. He paced back and forth outside the boundary of the forest, and his robe fluttered like feathers as it clung to his thin frame. He croaked my name and my face burned with heat.

"Airel!"

My eyes shot open. Michael was sitting over me with his hand on my forehead. He had a look of concern on his beautiful face, and somehow he looked as if he had aged overnight. I tried to speak, but my body was wracked with pain and my throat was so dry all I could get out was a grunt.

"Calm down, you're going to be okay. Here, drink this." Michael handed me a glass of water, and I took it with greed. It burned as it went down, but I drank all of it. I knew it might be drugged again, but I was so thirsty that I didn't care.

Michael leaned over and kissed my wet forehead. He smiled at me, but it was weak, and I noticed a tremor in his hand.

"What are you doing here?" I managed, but it sent a fresh wave of nausea through me.

Michael shushed me and said, "You're still here with the crazy man. He let me see you after you fainted. You have been in and out of consciousness for eight days now. He has been trying to heal you with some weird chanting and some other stuff I've never seen before. I've been trying to feed you, in between your nightmares and screaming fits. You really scared me, Airel. I thought you were gonna die." At this, his voice caught, and he held back tears, looking away.

"What are you talking about? What are you doing in here? Where am I?"

"Airel, what do you mean?" Michael was visibly upset.

That's it. I knew I was going crazy now. I seriously had no idea which way was up, what was real, what was safe and what was dangerous anymore. "I was so worried, Michael, I thought you were gone, dead. I don't know. I'm so confused."

Michael was silent, then, "Airel…" And I shuddered. I was

drenched; I felt disgusting. *Eight days?! What in the world is going on here!* I felt insane.

"I'm sorry, Airel, I didn't know it would be like this."

"What is going on, Michael? I think I was drugged." I noticed that I was no longer dressed in my fancy blue dress. I wondered how that had happened. It creeped me out beyond words. I was wearing pajamas, and they were stuck to me as if I had been wearing them for a week. *Gross.*

Michael tucked a loose strand of hair behind my ear and took my hand. "Don't you remember? We were taken, and... I..." He looked down as if he had done something he was ashamed of.

I scanned the room and some things started to come back to me. I remembered having been locked away in this, my "high tower." I remembered rainbows dancing on the bed in the new dawn of some lost day I could not recall as of yet. Like a badly cut movie, random scenes started to come back to me.

I remembered calling out for Michael, banging on the door to my room, which, I remembered, had a really nice bathroom with a huge claw-foot tub. I had been the one who had changed my clothes. *Weird.* I rubbed my temples. *What else?* I tried to conjure the past. I felt fury—*why?*

I was angry. I was angry because I feared the captor had murdered Michael. I saw myself pacing in an angry stew in front of my locked door, and I knew why. I was furious at having been locked up like an animal, no matter how nice the accommodations — and I was worried sick that something horrific had happened to Michael.

The scene shifted, and I was flooded with the realization that I was madly in love with him, that I knew it, that I had reconciled my heart to that reality. That explained what happened next in my spastic movie reel vision. I delivered a crushing roundhouse blow to the door of my cell and it exploded off the jamb into a million splinters. *I had been Bruce Lee, for crying out loud... Bruce Lee on gamma rays, or whatever.*

The movie reel continued. I was running through the obliterated doorway and down the hall. Rooms appeared, covered in years of dust, furniture draped with sheets. Other rooms were clean. Then, there was Michael's room — I knew it to be his room, but when I opened the door, which was unlocked, it was empty, and I feared the worst — that he was dead. I saw myself running down hallways trying to find him, down a flight of stairs, and being arrested by the appearance of the blond killer, the master of the house. He had appeared out of nowhere. I was struck at his beauty for the smallest of moments.

Then the movie reel took a really bad turn. There was vomit everywhere. It was mine. I saw myself as I retched time after time, right onto my captor's fancy carpets, losing whatever I had in my stomach from the Cheesecake Factory with surreal violence. Fast forward, and I was dry heaving as the killer picked me up and carried me to my room.

I looked at Michael in confusion. I smelled bile. *Oh. That might explain the dreams.*

Michael lowered his head, his blond hair matted and sticking to his face from sleepless nights. His shoulders began to shake as he turned to go. I had somehow hurt him. *It must be hard for him, too…*

"Michael, I'm sick or something. Eight days?" I pulled him close and hugged him. He was warm, and at once, I was aware of how I must look and smell.

I tried to pull away, but Michael held me firmly. He was… crying. His back was tight, and I could hear his muffled sobs. "Michael, what's wrong?"

"I…Uh." He pulled back but wouldn't look at me. "I'm sorry, Airel." Turning, he rushed out of the room.

"Michael!"

CHAPTER XII

I WAS CONFUSED AND hurt. Not for myself, but for
Michael. He was in pain and something was on his mind, but I
didn't know what to do. Should I leave him be, give him space?
Relationships were hard. Most of the time I didn't even know what
I wanted, let alone what Michael did. I decided to let him be and
clean up. I was covered with eight days of sweat, and I could feel
my clothes sticking to my body.

Bathing can be glorious. I hosed off in a scalding shower
while filling the tub, then climbed in for a good soak. There were
candles and matches, which I used, as well as several clay pots of
very yummy smelling botanicals. I was guessing that everything in
the bathroom, as well as everything in the bedroom, had not been
touched by any kind of manufacturing process at all. There were
no electronics of any kind that I could remember either, come to
think of it. Not even a clock. Well, not an electronic one anyway.

Everything was rough, but well-made. The tile, the fixtures —
all of it bore the stamp of authenticity in a way that no house in
town could touch. Even the water felt different. Maybe he had
built a massive boiler somewhere in the house that heated the water
to be used for bathing. Or maybe it was coming from a natural hot
spring. Whatever it was, it wasn't running out any time soon, for
which I was grateful. I was starting to feel like myself again.

When I thought about the hallway, my mind flashed back to
my parents, my friends, my whole life as I had known it. I sat
there in the tub for a pretty long time, just crying. It had been at
least eight days — that's what Michael had said — and my parents

probably thought I was dead.

Oh, God! I couldn't imagine how they must feel by now. But I had to resolve myself to the fact that, as of right now, there was absolutely nothing I could do about getting back home. I might be able to set a few things in motion...

I had to get my mind back out of desperation mode. I looked at the candles that illuminated the enormous bathroom, watching them burn. Blackness rested against the outside of the lead glass windows, beyond which was at least a thousand foot drop to the valley floor — I had peeked out earlier. *Hmm.*

I didn't know how, but literally every piece of clothing I owned somehow showed up here, in the closet in my room. Cell. *Wait, is the door still busted off the hinges?* If the door was gone, I was basically free. I dragged myself from the tub and back into the shower, resolving to check on that. First, I wanted — needed — to be squeaky clean.

When I was done and dressed, I took a passing glance at the door that led to the hallway. It was as if I had never kicked it down. I shook my head, trying to hold onto my version of reality. It didn't matter that it was, like, version 6.2.7 by now. It just had to make sense to me.

I went back into the bathroom and peered into the mirror. Gorgeous, of course. Superhumanly gorgeous. Michael would die. So to speak. I ran a brush through my hair expecting it to frizz into a fro, but amazingly, it looked like I had just stepped off a cover shoot for a magazine again, only better. I looked into the mirror, leaning into it to get a closer look. "Aaaaaaaaand... no makeup necessary." *Bonus.*

This was weird, I was not used to being — looking — like this. I knew it was a gift and I decided to enjoy it, because if I *did* have a baseball size tumor in my head, I was dead anyway.

My thoughts turned to Michael. He seemed to be under some sort of pressure. Was he just worried about me? I didn't want to push him to talk to me, but at the same time, I wanted to know what was going on in his head. I missed him.

After a few minutes sitting on the foot of the bed, I opened my eyes. I remembered, more than anything, two words: "I'm sorry." They came to me in a version of Michael's voice; it was recognizable but strange. I knew that he had sat at my bedside for the span of eight days muttering those two words. *Now why would he do that?*

I decided I needed to break with all of this. I was clean, beautiful, and ready to take on the world. "Never mind that it's two a.m." I rolled my eyes. It was time to create something new to look back on at a later date. I walked to the door that led to the hallway, expecting to find it locked, especially since it was dark outside. I was trying to imagine kicking it down again. *How had 98 pounds of me done that, exactly?* I stood in front of it and extended my index finger to it. I placed it on the door and pushed. It swung free, yawning open on the hallway, which seemed to be dark and quiet.

Why do I sense a trap? I went back to the nightstand and grabbed a fresh candle, lighting it. I looked up and down the hall, finding no creeps milling around in the shadows. I took the plunge, walking out in my bare feet so as not to make unnecessary noise.

There were doorways to my left and to my right, and I remembered my last trip down this particular hall. I had been a rabid wolverine looking for someone to kill. They say Hell hath no fury like a woman scorned, and I believed them. I passed on by the room adjacent to my own, which I was pretty sure belonged to Michael. I wanted to go in, to talk to him, but I pushed the thought away.

I came to the staircase and descended it to the main level. It was a grand house, really, like an ancient monument that just kept going and going and going. I found that the house was situated with its front toward the mountain and its rear to the cliff face where the waterfall cascaded. It all looked stately and majestic, except it was underground, which was still weird to me.

I found the kitchen next to the ballroom, separated by three massive stone arches over two feet thick. I went in, needing food; I was all of a sudden hungry. I grabbed a handful of bright red grapes from a clay bowl, popping one of them in my mouth. I stopped and looked down at them, marveling at their taste. *Best grape I've ever had?* I threw another one in my mouth and coolness satiated my jagged throat. I groaned aloud with delight and began to devour them.

Brick and granite ran throughout the kitchen, and the dark wood cabinets were carved with intricate feathers around their tops. A carving of an eagle was centered on each door.

A formal dining room was through the next set of arches, with a glass and silver chandelier hanging from a forty-foot ceiling. The room had to be seventy feet square, with an enormous dark granite table in the center that could seat over a hundred guests.

Okay, so this dude is excessive. I still don't like it. But the grapes were good. So I ate them. I finished the last one and wandered back through the kitchen and across the ballroom. On the other side was a study, if you could call it that, with leather couches encircling a stone fireplace that was forty feet tall, with a mantle that held a few books at about head height. A hearty fire was leaping in the grate, lighting the space happily.

Bookshelves were stuffed handsomely full on every wall. I couldn't resist scanning the spines for titles, seeing some I recognized, and a lot I didn't. Some looked so old I was afraid to touch them. I felt as if I had spent too much time already, so I left that room and moved on.

I found myself standing at the head of another long hallway, this one aglow with wall-mounted torches and curving to the right so that I could not see the end.

I stopped and listened to see if I could hear anything, but all I heard was the faint popping and crackling of torches. Like on the second floor, there were doors on each side of the hall about every twenty feet. I opened a few and found that these rooms were clean and used, or at least ready for use.

I couldn't help wondering if my kidnapper had many guests. Was he a partier or something? *Yeah. This place is party central.* Did he have people over to dance the night away in the great ballroom? *What was he doing, flying them in?* Somehow I didn't think so, but it was strange that he had all this space for a single man. I guessed wealth just made people eccentric. *Which is polite for really weird.*

Toward the end of the hall, I found another staircase leading down. Unlike everywhere else, it was pitch black. An earthy smell wafted up in a draft of cold air. I wondered if it might lead to the outside, and if so, whether or not it would end under the waterfall. I didn't want to find out. My nerves were shot. Besides, in front of me was quite the curiosity. It was a massive double door, filling my end of the hall like a sleeping dragon.

I didn't notice how large the corridor was until I stood in the shadow of these gigantic doors. They were made from huge slabs of wood, carved and inlaid with copper and gold, forming an image of an angel fighting a beast with two heads. It was stunning. The sword in the angel's hand looked like there was light bursting from it, and each ray was accented with silver and glass. At the top, the two doors arched toward each other and met in the middle. Big black pulls stood like hands at about shoulder height for me.

I stood in awe, unable to move as I studied the engraving. It was indeed very beautiful, but it was unnerving at the same time. I wondered who had done the work, but had no illusion as to whom this room belonged.

The killer. He had no name to me. I figured he fancied himself a scholar of history or something. Maybe he brainwashed himself into thinking he was doing the world a favor by taking girls and doing God knows what to them. I had a feeling in the back of my mind that my conscience, and maybe even *She*, did not approve of what I was about to do.

I turned the large handle, pausing to gather my nerves, then pushed. The door was so heavy that for a brief moment, I was afraid I wouldn't be able to open it. At last it swung in, silent on its hinges. The room was dark. But as the door opened, my diminishing candle, aided by the torches in the corridor, threw an orange light into the room. My shadow fell long and fuzzy across thick carpet.

Straight ahead in the darkness was a canopy bed, very ornate. It stood on a raised platform against the wall. I crept in and closed the door gently behind so I wouldn't announce my presence, if I hadn't already done so.

I held my candle aside and down, waiting until my eyes

adjusted a little. I kept my back to the wall. This room was round too, and opposite me were large windows much like the ones in the ballroom, showering the floor with starlight. I sneaked boldly to the bedside. Nothing stirred in it as far as I could tell.

I came to the windows of tall etched glass and observed a setting moon, blood-orange, against the snow of a distant mountain range. There was a trailhead at the edge of the porch outside the windows. It seemed to lead toward the base of those mountains. There was a shed or shack, partially on stilts, that clung to the mountainside. Below it was a square patch that looked like one of those places where gymnasts do their floor routines for the Olympics, but it was washed-out brown and stuck out over the drop as if it were floating.

I forced myself to look away. Though life was getting difficult to assess — *which is an understatement* — I still wanted to be cautious. If it turned out that being savagely murdered in the dream meant certain death in the real world, I had to keep my guard up. It didn't matter if I sometimes couldn't tell what was a dream and what was the real. I was so overwhelmed with my life that it was getting difficult to stay tough.

I took a brief survey of the rest of the room. I found a bathroom, a tub that was more pool than tub, and some odds and ends that I couldn't really place.

I watched the bed curtains to see if I was safe to explore further. I heard respirations barely louder than a whisper.

I moved to the closet, which was like a private Wal-Mart. It was filled with every kind of clothing imaginable, in every style. 80's MC Hammer pants, old suits like the mobsters used to wear, and even robes, all of them appearing to suffer from the occasional actual use. It blew me away. It looked like a costume wardrobe from a movie studio. Of course, there wasn't a stitch out of place; everything was orderly. I think I would have felt more comfortable if there was one thing normal in the place. Like shoes kicked in the corner or even dirty undies in a pile of old t-shirts or something.

I was creeped out, and I'm not sure if it was the thought of killer underwear or not. But I felt the irresistible yanking need to turn around, as if he was standing right there. I grimaced, dreading what was coming — not sure if I was going to die of embarrassment or a knife wound — and raised my hands in surrender, turning slowly around. I almost said, "Okay. You caught me," but I didn't, because as soon as I had turned and opened my eyes again, there was no one there. *Just another unexplainable item to add to the list.*

I was not deterred from my nosiness and continued on, creeping through my captor's private life. I chalked it up to the fact that I figured he owed me at least a little information — and if he wasn't going to volunteer any, I would find some, so help me, and he would be at the mercy of my interpretation of it. *So there.*

It was a bummer that all I found after that was a bare concrete room, it was about the size of a restaurant refrigerator. Killers need storage space too. But that was probably the weirdest part of another weird night strung on the necklace of my existence. Palatial house, in which everything is obscenely overstuffed — then a tiny bunker of a room that's just… empty. I was seriously wondering how many of these kinds of things were going to continue to happen to me.

I wasn't leading a life, I decided. My life was leading me. Where, I did not know, and was almost afraid to ask. But whenever I asked the heavens for explanation, they were silent. *Typical.*

I yawned and decided I was getting sleepy and needed to make my exit sooner rather than later. I retraced my trail to my room, being extremely careful not to leave any crumbs. I fell into the soft bed, and this time I didn't dream of anything. No monsters, no running. Just blank sweet sleep. Was that good or bad?

CHAPTER XIII

1250 B.C. The City of Ke'elei

"THEY NEVER INTENDED TO give even one man," Kreios said aloud, primarily to himself, but in the presence of his brother and friend. Yamanu sat smoking his pipe as if readying himself for a very long sleep, and Zedkiel was pacing by the fire. They had all three returned to the inn where they had found lodgings at the great City of Refuge.

"You read their thoughts?" Yamanu asked, a tone of surprise in his voice. "A bit risky, if you open your mind up to read, you are vulnerable as well."

"Yes, I know. But I am not afraid of the likes of the council; they have grown weak. I am sick of the lies. They had no intention of giving us even one man." Kreios paced the room.

He was not going to let the Seer or the council control him. He knew that the Seer wanted him and his baby girl for some dark purpose beyond his imagination, and the only way to be rid of the Seer and the threat against his daughter was to kill him. Cut the head off the snake, and the rest of the body will die.

Yamanu sat back in a long low chair, feet up, jovially puffing on his pipe. He looked up at the two brothers as if they were two figures in a play discussing nothing more important than whether one lump or two was proper. "I am ready to fight, ladies, but I will require a dinner of lamb and greens with bread smothered in butter, if it please you."

Kreios let out a pinched laugh and swept Yamanu's upraised

feet off the table. "Nothing gets to you, Yamanu, does it?" Yamanu shrugged and looked innocently at him.

Kreios's smile faded slowly as the jest died away under the gravity of their situation. His eyes turned to Zedkiel. "I think you should stay here with Maria. She needs you to help her with the childbirth, and I will feel better if you are here to protect what is left of my family."

Zedkiel protested lightly as a matter of course. "I will pray for you my brother. Every moment."

Kreios did not answer him.

Yamanu regained his reclined posture, regarding the brothers.

"They will stay here, instead of taking a chance to surprise the Seer and wipe the horde from the face of the earth. 'Fortify and defend,' they say, but in the end, the war will be long and hard. Every day that goes by, the horde will grow stronger, and we will grow weaker — they simply need to be led to the foot of the walls and besiege us with their *encampment!* Not even having to raise a sword! It is madness. Why would they risk so much in refusing to risk so little?"

Yamanu took the pipe from his lips, standing at last. "Kreios, we do not have the time to uncover this mystery. We should ready ourselves; grasp what is already in our hands." He poured out the bowl of his pipe into the fire, where it sparked and sizzled. "If you don't mind, I require a good night's sleep and a hot meal. After that, friend Kreios, you and I will go to see how many demons we can kill."

Kreios managed a weak smile, nodding. "We go at sunrise. We will eat and sleep — then we will hunt."

CHAPTER XIV

Somewhere in the mountains of Idaho. Present day.

COOL MORNINGS IN THE mountains, with rain on some nights, made the earth smell so good that it invaded the mind. I sat up and drank it in, feeling better than I ever had up to this point. For the first time in a long time, I felt like I had a good night's sleep.

I took stock of my situation: I knew Michael was alive and well. He was off his game, but at least he was breathing. My host was disturbingly generous and wealthy. Either that, or he was working for someone who owned an entire country.

I let my feet fall to the floor and shuffled into the bathroom. I wasn't going to think about my parents and how they were doing. *Let's at least wake up and clear the cobwebs before we burst into tears.*

A pink sticky note looked at me from the mirror. The handwriting had to be Michael's. I imagined the killer's hand would be cursive. I pulled it free and read what it said.

Went for a walk. Don't worry about me — I was assured I was being watched, so I won't go far. See you at breakfast — 8 a.m. sharp!
– Michael Alexander

I looked outside, down the lush green valley, but did not see Michael. The enormous grandfather clock against the wall was reading… *little hand on the seven, big hand on the nine…* quarter 'til. I was experiencing culture shock, full on. Literally nothing digital in the entire place, unless it was numbers themselves. "Man!" What could I say? I decided to get ready and head downstairs.

I found a hair band, pulled half my hair back, and tied it tight. Smoothing out the rest with my hand, I looked in the mirror. On second thought, I pulled the band out of my hair and let it run wild, hiding part of my face, providing cover. I decided that was better, and pulled on a black shirt and my favorite jeans, trying hard not to think of how they had appeared here *in the middle of freaking Narnia*.

I opened the door and stared straight into the dark eyes of my captor, which prompted a sharp gasp and a long, "Shhhhhhhhh —" aborting the rest of the curse.

He smiled, his lips drawn thin. "Morning," he said. "I hope you're feeling well."

I recovered quickly, rebuilding the wall by reattaching the mask to my frightened face, glaring at him. "Well, actually, I'm feeling pretty good. Better than I have been, since you asked." He turned to walk and I followed. "But I think I may need a doctor to find out what's wrong with me. I started getting sick a month or so ago." I didn't know why I told him, but somehow I felt I must.

"You'll be fine. You need a good breakfast, and there is much to talk about. It will become clear in time — and try not to think of me as your captor or kidnapper," he looked at me. "I only did what I had to do."

He stopped short when he saw the look on my face. I had no interest in being his friend or buddy, if that was what he was looking for. I remembered something from a movie, where victims actually started to like their captors, building a sick version of a relationship — I was not afraid of that happening to me.

"I don't want to be your friend. I don't want to know you, and the first chance I can find to escape, I will. I'm trying to make the best of all this, but don't pretend anything's normal." I didn't care if he had tried to nurse me back to health or any of it. He was a murderer and a kidnapper. And that was just the stuff I knew about him.

His eyes grew hard. "Have it your way. But know this: you cross me or try to escape, I will kill you. Do not mistake my generosity for weakness."

He ground his teeth, turned, and walked away. I followed him, wondering if I had made my situation better or worse. We descended the stairs together, and for the briefest of moments, I imagined what it might be like to descend the same magnificent stairs in an impossible five thousand dollar princess gown on the arm of my Michael. Instead, I was walking at a distance from my kidnapper that more than suggested repellence.

He wore jeans and a tight black t-shirt with a white intertwined ivy design laced from the hip to the shoulder. It was an interesting shirt; I couldn't quite place where he might have gotten it. He moved smoothly for his size; he looked like he was a panther. Maybe it was the black shirt. Nothing about him was wasted. Not even his words. He seemed to think long and hard before he spoke in order to avoid saying something he might later regret.

He led me to the far side of the ballroom and through a set of heavy glass doors. I saw a round table and three chairs under a white umbrella in the morning sun, looking like a slice of Paris. The porch was a hundred feet long at least, and surrounded with bushes and plants of all kinds. I saw Michael standing by the edge of the porch and my heart skipped a beat.

I ran past the killer and threw my arms around Michael's big shoulders, hugging him tight. "Michael," I said breathlessly. "I'm so glad to see you!" I pulled back, looked at him, and hugged him again. I had to hold back a tear. I hadn't had time to realize how much I had grown to care for him, but suddenly it was *realized*. I didn't want to let him go.

"Airel, I was so worried about you. How are you feeling?" He seemed better and back to his normal confident self.

"Great! I'm fine, all better." I *was* fine, better than fine. I was alive, I felt great, and I had Michael next to me. How could I *not* be fine, even in the black-eyed face of my captor?

Michael held my hands and looked at me with his deep blue eyes. These were the eyes that could look into my very soul, and I gladly allowed it. "Are you sure, though? I mean, are you still sick?"

"I'm better; I think it was all the stress and maybe something I ate or drank." I gave our captor a glare and said it just loud enough for him to hear.

Michael smiled and nodded. "Good. You had me worried there... I don't know what —"

The killer cleared his throat and sat down. The chair scraped on the cobblestone as he pulled it closer to the table, and I got a strong sense that it was intentional. "There will be time to ask and answer all of your questions. All the time in the world. Let us eat." He had a calm look on his face as if this was all quite routine for him.

Michael shot me a look and pulled out a chair for me. I could only guess at the meaning of his expression. He slid his chair closer to mine so that we sat opposite from our mysterious captor, the table serving as a buffer. He glanced at us without any concern, even seeming amused by it.

There were three white china plates on the table. Each was piled with fluffy scrambled eggs, bacon grilled to a perfect crisp, country sausage, and crusty cracked wheat toast with plenty of soft butter. Baskets of fruit and muffins stood in the center of the table.

I could see cherries, mango, oranges, papaya, peaches, grapes on the vine (the kind I had discovered the previous night), and fresh pineapple. Glasses of freshly squeezed orange juice were in front of each plate, droplets of condensation forming deliciously on all of them. I took the cold glass in my hand and sipped it. It was amazing.

Michael started on his eggs hungrily, and so did I. The killer took a small bite out of his toast as he studied us. Then, just as abruptly as a punch in the stomach, he introduced himself. "My name is Kale. My last name is of no importance. I thought you ought to know."

I stopped in mid-bite and put the fork down, staring. "I bet you could tell me my name," I baited him in vain. I waited, too, in vain, but I had to surrender. "It's Airel." Michael mechanically introduced himself out of obligation. It was really awkward.

"I need to tell you something so that we do not have another night like the one that put you in convalescence for a week." He was looking directly at me. Then his gaze shifted to Michael, and he continued.

"You cannot escape, so don't try. If you do try, I will lock you away like a dog. If you stay on the property, you will be free within its boundaries." He took a sip from his glass of orange juice, then sighed. He acted as if he was being forced to do this. I wondered if he was like an employee for someone, a hit man for some multinational power broker.

I could not help but wonder how in the world I had ended up there. Kim would have said, "I told you so," and reminded me that we should have gone to the cops. I was shocked at myself as I wondered if I was inside the machinery of one of those human trafficking organizations I had been hearing about.

I was so mad; I couldn't believe we were all sitting at a table eating as if we were all old friends. But I couldn't bring myself to hate Kale or even retain my anger. He acted natural and sure of himself, which disarmed me. He didn't even seem to consider the fact that he would end up in prison for a very long time if he was caught kidnapping minors.

"I have eyes and ears everywhere. I'll know of any plans you make before you have a chance to execute them. I do not want to hold you in a cage like animals. I would rather you were free." He paused, indicating that he was switching gears. "You are to attend to your schooling so as not to fall behind in your studies." Michael groaned, and I sighed aloud.

"This makes no sense," I said. "You kidnap us, and then you act like we're here on a field trip? Now — why did you take us, and what do you want?"

"You will obey or suffer the consequences," he said calmly. The calmness chilled me deeply, and I backed off, feeling with certainty that I was in over my head.

"Easy now, she didn't mean anything by it," Michael was trying to keep the peace. "She just wanted to know what you want — money?" Kale looked at him with what can only be described as hatred. I don't think Michael noticed it; he just kept on talking in even tones. "My dad doesn't have much. I don't think hers does either." Michael tensed, opening and closing his fists as if he was about to strike. This was like cats and dogs, seriously, and I almost felt like I needed to jump up and get in between them.

Kale deflected him. "I do not need money. As you can see, I have money to spare. What I want," he turned to me, "only Airel can give."

CHAPTER XV

Boise, Idaho. Present day.

STAN WAS CHEERFULLY IGNORANT, standing over the demobilized police officer, engaged in what was, for him, a shiny new hobby: abduction and torture. He held the badge up to the light that came from a single bulb in the tiny one car garage.

"Lopez," he read out. The instability in the housing market had done at least one thing for opportunists, and that was that there were plenty of empty foreclosed homes all over the valley.

Stan fancied himself a man of deliberate action. He had considered the empty house for a week before deciding it would work well for his purposes tonight. Officer Lopez was bound with his own handcuffs; his torso and ankles duct-taped to a metal folding chair. Blood seeped from his broken nose onto his white uniform shirt, soaking in, making a beautiful inkblot image.

Stan thought it looked like a bat; maybe a dragon. This image filled him with a sense of power and fear; a buzz to which he had become addicted.

"Lopez, I am in need of information, and I must warn you: if you lie, I will not have any use for you." Stan chuckled and wiped tar-colored spittle from his mouth with the back of his hand. "I will ask once. Only once." He opened a small folding knife with a serrated inward curving blade, bent down on one knee and pulled off one of Lopez's shoes. The officer tried to protest, fighting the restraints, but the rag stuffed in his mouth made it impossible to discern his words.

Stan took hold of his shoeless foot and held it tight. "Now now, Lopez; are we not both professionals? Do you not trust me?" He mocked him. "This is for your own good, I promise you that — for you need to see and understand the seriousness of your situation, and I need to make it known to you, clearly, that I mean what I say."

Stan removed the sock from the officer's foot. In a sawing motion that took several attempts to cut through the ligaments, he removed the little toe from the detective's foot. Lopez wailed and thrashed, but the gag held in place, his body bound.

Stan stood up and looked around the empty garage as if realizing, for the first time, where he was. He fished in the pockets of his suit coat, which he had been wearing for a week now, and produced a cigar lighter. Smirking, he lit the torch-like device and held the flame to the freshly inflicted wound. It sizzled, the smell of burning flesh infiltrated the garage, the detective squealed in pain, and Stan engorged himself on all of it, inhaling deeply.

"There, now. We can be friends again," he chuckled. "At least now I know that when I ask my question, you may prove yourself to be of some use to me." The bloodstone swung freely from his neck, pulsing and humming, hovering slightly with each pulse. Stan was super-aware of its presence. All he wanted to do was caress it with lust and desire, but he controlled himself for now.

"I know who you are, Lopez. I know that you are the lead detective in the investigation into the disappearance of an insignificant girl named Airel... the girl who witnessed that murder..." He waved his hand dismissively. "I want to know who took her and whether or not she was alone. If you refuse to answer me, I will dispose of you — and your pretty wife, of course... and I will find someone who wants to live." Stan looked at him with reddening eyes.

Time seemed so thin to Stan — he was looking straight at something only he could see, and for a time, he was not himself. His own reality tended to come and go nowadays; it was something he had come to accept since the bloodstone had come into his life. Stan looked straight ahead at nothing.

He ran his hand through his hair and glanced down at the cop. Stan's eyes glowed red, and his face became radiant. In fact, his body was tenanted by the parasitical presence that made him what he was for now — the Seer. His eyes took on an intense Satanic red glow, and his face became disturbingly beautiful.

He spoke. "Menial fool. I will remove your gag and wait for your answer. If you scream, you will die." He yanked the rag from the detective's mouth and stood before him, his palms facing upward. The pendant rose and hovered in the hollow of his hands. Fear stole into the cracks of the officer's mind and began to break it apart, piece by piece.

CHAPTER XVI

Somewhere in the mountains of Idaho. Present day.

"I NEED YOU TO try something for me." Kale lowered his voice, and as I placed the last bite of scrambled eggs in my mouth, I noticed that he had brought a book with him. It looked like it had a thousand pages, and it was leather-bound. The edges of the pages had once been gilded, but after time and use, the gold had all but rubbed off.

"Tell me what this is and where to turn." He pointed to the black bound book, sat back in his chair, and folded his arms across his chest.

"I don't understand — what is that and where to turn? That makes no sense." Kale the killer was losing his marbles. I remembered my grandmother's old family Bible, and this book looked a lot like it. This one, though, looked ancient.

"What is this book?" he demanded in a harsh tone. Michael stiffened.

I wanted to shout back at him for making me play this stupid game. All this 'you shall know in time' crap was getting on my nerves. "It's a Bible," I sighed, surrendering to the ridiculous. I ducked my chin and hid behind my hair, thanking God I had had the foresight to leave it down today.

In a softer voice, he said, "Good. Now where do I turn? Don't think about it; just tell me right off the top of your head." I could see Michael was feeling the awkwardness as much as I. I put my hand on his arm. He looked at me and managed a weak smile.

"What are you doing, playing Bible roulette?"

"Now. Do it now!" Kale commanded.

After I got over my initial shock, I sputtered out, "Fine. Six one — Genesis six, verse one."

Kale's face was illuminated with satisfaction. "I was just thinking that. Very good." He even smiled. He opened the Bible, placing it in front of me, and pointed to the passage. He cleared his throat, closed his eyes, and spoke.

"And it came to pass, when men began to multiply on the face of the earth, and daughters were born unto them, that the sons of God saw the daughters of men, that they were fair; and they took them wives of all which they chose. There were giants in the earth in those days; and also after that, when the sons of God came into the daughters of men, and they bore children to them, the same became mighty men which were of old, men of renown."

The way he spoke the text of the old Bible made me think he loved each word. I saw how gently he touched the pages, how sacred the act of closing the cover together was for him. He set the Bible down on the table and stared at me.

He seemed irritated with me, and I guessed what he might be thinking. I shook my head, "So what? You read some random passage that means what?" I still didn't like it. He sighed softly, but I could tell I was missing something important, that he was exercising self-control. My hand was still on Michael's arm, and I was very aware of it. My heart was pounding; just the feel of his skin touching mine in that simple gesture made me warm all over, and I realized that most of me just wanted to go off somewhere with him so that we could be alone.

Kale's voice, velvety, shook me from my reverie. "This story is the only one like it in the entire Bible. It talks about how the angels of God forsook their place in heaven when they saw the beauty of Eve's daughters. They fell in love. They left paradise to marry and create new lives among mortal man — the sons of Adam. These angels intermarried with the race of men, and their wives produced children. These children were different; immortal. As far as you would consider them, they had what might be called…

superhuman powers."

Overloaded with new information, the tumblers in the locks in my mind all fell into place and sprung open instantly. I struggled to hold on, and the only thing that held me was fear. Inwardly, I had already admitted to myself that I had been convinced, that I was in the midst of a genuine epiphany, but the cost of outward admission to that fact was too great to bear, so I kept it hidden.

Then an even stranger thing happened: Kale chuckled. It was as if he had read my thoughts, as all this had flooded in upon me, and thought it was amusing. All I could do was sit there and worry about drooling out of my open mouth.

Now that Kale had my attention, he drove it home. "The half-angel children would grow up normal. Their super powers were never triggered unless they came into contact with what we call the Brotherhood. Don't worry; we will get into that some other time. The point is, if these hybrid children never got awakened, they would simply live normal lives, growing old and dying just like a normal man or woman. The verses you picked out for me tell about their origin. I hope you see what I'm driving at — or do I have to spell it out for you?"

My hands were cold. The pit of my stomach clenched tightly, feeling slightly like hunger pangs. My mind replayed for me the night I had cut myself, how I had healed without even a scar to show for it. I thought about the way my skin had become so milky, smoothed out, pure. I thought about my hair; how it was so perfect, so strong — that was decidedly not normal, not — *human.* And now, as if to complete the internal mutiny against my average teenage life, I heard fluttering. Pages of a book. Wings. *She,* in the back of my mind, stood up.

Everything I had ever known, wanted, dreamed, desired, and planned in my entire life was now almost visibly crumbling before me, and I could not stop it. I was furious.

Kale sat silently, allowing me to ponder the information further. Even Michael seemed to be too shocked to say anything. I figured he was putting it all together as well; he had seen enough to make him wonder what was wrong with me. But I couldn't know what he was really thinking.

Like a shout in the darkness, I heard my name. "Airel." It was Kale. The killer. The stalker. The kidnapper. "Airel, listen to me. I am not your enemy. I am your friend."

CHAPTER XVII

FIRST LOVE. FIRST KISS. First night spent away from home. These are the things that leave their mark on everyone. These were true enough for me, but there was also the time I almost drowned, the first time I rode a horse, and now there was the day I sat in front of my kidnapper and realized that everything in my once-happy life was all just an illusion. *Congrats, girl, you're a half-breed, the love-child of angelic aliens and ancient hut-dwellers. Oh, really? Wow, sweet...*

I didn't remember standing up, or even the long walk down twisting stone steps. All I could feel was the long wet grass on my bare feet as I walked through the meadow.

I felt like I was in a fog, that what I had thought was real turned out to be just a curtain. Now, the curtain had lifted, and what was lying in wait behind jumped out and ravaged my mind. *I can't really believe this lunatic murderer and kidnapper, can I?* I had no way of knowing if what he had told me was true. *But, wait...* I shivered. His last words echoed through my brain, threateningly. I was beginning to understand the meaning of risk — because I was starting to doubt everything I thought I knew.

The end of our conversation played in the large space of my freshly expanded mind:

"How did you know that the story I wanted to read to you was in Genesis chapter six?" he had said.

I had stared at him in utter amazement. "It was a lucky guess," I had said flatly.

"Was it?" He had raised one eyebrow, a small smile lifting the right side of his mouth. "I was thinking of the book and chapter in my mind. You read my thoughts, Airel. I suspected you might have that gift, among others..."

"Who are you?" I had nearly shouted it at him, and would have if my voice had not been on the verge of cracking. It's funny, but I didn't let him answer me — or if he had, I didn't remember what it was. I had stormed off the porch, letting my feet carry me where they would.

I ended up sitting in the wet grass in the meadow, glances of which I had stolen so often from my room. I was a candle burnt from both ends, completely spent. My eyes filled with tears as I felt the dark woods surrounding. *Super-human?* I was just an average girl. But the things I wanted the most were out of reach, permanently, and they were foolish, too.

I became overwhelmed with one thought, and words fail to describe it even near to what I felt, because it soaked into the marrow of my bones in that moment. What I felt, stronger than anything I had ever felt, what faded literally every other concern into the background, including my family, my future, and Michael, was that I had woken up today to find that I was... a super-human... *thing...* but all I felt was *frail.* My mind was firmly trapped in the difference between the two.

Shoulders shaking, and shivering with chills, I sobbed and cried for what seemed like an hour. I didn't care what Michael or that horrible man thought. What did it matter anyway? What did I have to look forward to? Days, months, years, decades, centuries, lifetimes of loneliness — if what he had implied about immortality was true — and knowing that I was not only different, but also different in a way no one would ever understand.

Feeling like, at seventeen years of age, I had cried enough tears for many lifetimes already, the ripples in the little pond of my life began to subside. I felt as if a weight had been lifted from my shoulders, which I needed desperately.

I looked up at the huge house that was embedded in the mountainside. It was so beautiful. I could see the tall windows that looked out over the lush green valley, and the patio where Kale and

Michael still sat. I was glad they let me be alone; it would have been embarrassing to have cried like that in front of Michael.

But I wasn't alone. *She* was there with me, and for once, I felt her almost tangibly. I was glad that *She* seemed to show up when I most needed her. *She* helped me think of something I never would have come to on my own: *"You cannot change this. You are who you are. Live. Live, Airel."*

She was right, of course. I couldn't change who I was or *what* I was, as my stalker had informed me an eternity ago. I was here for a reason. Maybe Kale knew, or he could help me discover it. As I steeled myself to it, it began to occur to me that there had been times before when my answers had proved to be inadequate. I decided that I had more to lose in sticking it out by myself than I stood to gain by asking for help. It was time to find out why I was here, and I needed to cast aside everything that made me comfortable.

I returned, ascending the winding gray stone steps, and rejoined them on the fringes of the patio space, awkward and self-conscious. I hid a little behind my hair, sticking my hands in my back pockets, and managed a weak apology. My chair was overturned, just as I had thought, but Kale stood as I approached and righted it, holding it out for me in a gesture of peace-making. I got the very strong sense that Kale was like a gift from God. It may have seemed like a radical change in my thinking. It was.

I sat down. Still, I had an axe to grind with Kale, especially if he was *indeed* friend and not foe. I decided to cut right to it: "My parents —"

"— Are fine," he finished for me.

I wanted to believe him, but I desired proof. I was thrown. All I could manage was, "But —" I didn't like how these negotiations were going. It was worse than asking my dad for the car keys on a Friday night.

"Airel, you need to learn how to trust me, and how to be patient as you wait for the answers you seek."

"But what does that have to do with my concern for my parents, for my life?"

He was briefly taken aback, I could tell, but he dodged the question a little. "You may not be ready to see the answers yet. And what good would it do you to see anything that you cannot understand?" His eyes spoke volumes of kindness and empathy.

I gave up. It was obvious that Kale wasn't going to tell me anything but what he wanted to tell me, and there was no amount of bargaining that would change that. Which is not to say that I couldn't try. "Okay, whatever. Just why am I here, then?"

He appeared appreciative that I had changed my tack. "Airel, you are here to begin your training."

"Training. Like," I couldn't help giggling a little bit, "superhero training?"

"If you don't learn control, you'll be a danger to everyone around you, including yourself." He had a hint of a smile on his pale face. I turned to look at Michael, still, in spite of myself, feeling like I needed to be pinched.

Michael leaned into me. "We should stick together. I think whatever he knows, we need to know. This is uncharted territory, if you know what I mean." Michael took my hand in his. I could feel his pulse, and I couldn't help but grin. His heart was beating just as fast as mine was.

I turned back to Kale. "Alright. What do we do first?"

"'We?' 'We' won't be doing anything. Understand, children, Airel needs to be here — as for you, Michael, you're here for other reasons altogether."

I was seriously chafed now. "'Children?' How dare you?" I mounted my high horse and looked condescendingly at him from it. "Don't ever call me a child again!" I was so angry at him that I could barely formulate the thoughts in my head, which, I was aware, he would probably be probing.

He sighed in response. "Airel, your training is to be solo. Michael cannot undergo any of it. Most of it, he will not even be allowed to watch. You must learn these things in the quiet of solitude; you must become accustomed to your instruction one-on-one." He stood and walked to a small, rough table that I had not noticed before, standing by the windows. On it were several books, one of which was the Bible we had been using earlier, and all of which were very old. "Your first course of study will be history."

He selected one of the books. It was an imposing looking volume, and me being somewhat of a book junky, although not a history fan, I almost salivated looking at its hide-bound cover. He walked it back to the table, and as he did, my mind flooded with what can only be described as destiny. There is no other way to express it.

"Your history, Airel." His voice was filled with pleasure and pain, and as he said the words, he looked at me the way my dad did sometimes, right before he would tell me that he loved me. He placed the book on the table before me.

I looked at it, and I have to admit, even before I ever touched it, the moment felt heavy. I reached out my right hand to the book, to open its ancient cover. As my hand neared it, it began to feel magnetic to me, as if I could not draw back even if my life depended on it. The tip of my finger rested at last on its front cover, releasing a torrent of sound in my head, a shout of triumph: KREIOS.

CHAPTER XVIII

1250 B.C. The City of Ke'elei

COLD SEEPED INTO THE room where Kreios lay awake, fidgeting. Sleep eluded his grasp tonight, and he resolved himself to that particular fate as he lay staring at the sky, watching the North Star's constancy. He did not like the situation. He was wrestling with whether or not the council was willing to lie to him — or, at any rate, to obscure their motives. It scared him. He wondered, though he attempted to reject the thought from his mind, if there was a secret alliance with the Seer. It was unthinkable. It nagged at him, and he fidgeted again as he wrestled with it in his mind.

"You sleep less than I do; I did not think that was possible." Yamanu struck a flint and piece of stubble on the stone wall, lighting his pipe in one fluid motion. He drew in and let out a puff of smoke. "Your thoughts betray your heart. If you die, how is that going to help your daughter — are you better off dead?" Yamanu pulled his cloak tighter to his neck and looked out past Kreios at the moon.

Kreios kept his gaze on the steady North Star, unmoving in the heavens, and the stars reflected in his eyes like infinitesimal diamonds in a sea of black. "She is all I have. Victory will be victory. Even if small victory is as small as my daughter and I flee with her into hiding. And never return." He looked at Yamanu. "We have a specific purpose, and we must use what tools we were given to accomplish what lies before us."

"Brother," Yamanu said, his eyes beginning to glisten, "we shall

231

be victorious if El wills it. I cannot see any other reason for our circumstances having been drawn up so tightly as they are in this moment. "The council does not see it, or insists on being blind, but I feel very strongly about the purpose of these heavy times. For what other reason would El allow us to be so threatened? Our last remaining option is to stand firm and wage war. It is for such a time as this that we have been born, bred, raised up, brought through many trials, and tasted both the triumph of the conqueror as well as the havoc of failure. The sinews of war are clustered in our hands — we need but to pull on the proper cord at the right time. For *such* a time as this! "We have not yet begun to pour out the cup of wrath that has been stored up for the Seer and his ilk. Father has a plan, my friend… and I believe He is revealing it to us even now."

Kreios cracked a smile in holy submission to El, looking at Yamanu. "You have the faith of a child, my friend. I will take heart, and I beg your forgiveness for my doubt. It is both gift and curse to be such a practical thinker."

Yamanu waved his pipe, moving the headwaters of the trail of heavy smoke that had been pooling at the hem of his robe. His laugh was pure, musical. "Friend, behold: the sun begins to rise. Let us also rise to the purpose of this day and be off. No use letting the Seer's horde have another peaceful day."

Kreios stood up, stretched, popped his back, and let out a grunt. He was getting old.

He found his daughter sleeping soundly in his brother's room and went to her, nuzzling her skin. Memories of his beloved wife flooded over him as he held his daughter close, cradling her up to his face, hearing her breathing in soft snores. She stretched and yawned luxuriantly, her body showing the rustling of her thoughts, and he wondered with loving eyes what she could be dreaming.

He suffered himself to weep silently as he held her, wondering, but not quite asking, why the bonds of the family had had to be so violently shattered; why such a simple thing as his love for his daughter — and the memory of his beloved — would set into motion such a wicked menagerie of events. It felt as if creation might tumble in upon both of them at any moment. This moment, he decided, he made himself believe that he knew, was holy; he, warrior and husband and father, standing with his daughter in perfect embrace. He savored all of it, breathing in her fragrance deeply, remembering. He could not complain to God for his lot in life.

Kissing her softly, he whispered blessings in her ear and laid her down on her bed. She raised a tiny hand, yawned again, and cooed before slipping back into a deep sleep. He left the room quietly so as not to awaken Maria. Zedkiel was waiting for him outside on the balcony that overlooked the beautiful city.

"I will do my part, brother; do not worry your thoughts. She will be safe no matter what. I swear it by the life of the blood that courses through me." They grasped arms, Zedkiel's long hair wafting in wispy strands in the light morning breeze.

"I know," was the simple response. Kreios was not able to say much more.

Zedkiel nodded and said in a hushed tone, "She will have the child tonight! I can feel it in my bones."

Kreios smiled at his brother. "I am glad for you, brother. All will be well, and in the morning, you will be a father." The thought of Zedkiel holding his new baby in his arms brought on a pain so deep that he wondered if he might be jealous of his brother.

Kreios turned from him, gathering up his pack and his Sword. He held the sheath and listened to the voice that seemed to hang in the air, in his spirit. He could feel his daughter through it, and somehow he knew that she would be safe. He grasped the Sword and unsheathed it, running his hand along the flat of the blade, and pulled back in surprise. The blade was warm to the touch.

He closed his eyes, thinking back, going deep into the folds of his mind, remembering the door once again. He wondered how he had missed it for so many years. The door had not been there in the past, but now there was nothing he could do to make it go away. Its presence filled him with elation and fear, because he felt that whatever stood beyond that door was not good. He knew, furthermore, that he was going to have to pass through it. The thought made him want to run far and fast.

❧

Yamanu stood by watching his friend, smoking his pipe. He could see deep lines chiseling themselves into the surface of Kreios' face, and it worried him. This upcoming task *was* suicidal. The only thing keeping Kreios from knowing his thoughts was his ability to shadow them. Yet he would fight, and fight to the death with every fiber of his body and soul. If he were to die, so be it; and if by some miracle they lived…" All glory be to El, and to El alone," he said.

Kreios nodded, sheathing the Sword and strapping it on. Pulling on his cloak, he tied his pack to his belt and lifted the hood over his white blond hair.

The air felt alive. Kreios walked to the open window and jumped out without a moment's hesitation. A crack of sound followed his arc through the clear blue sky as he broke the sound barrier. Yamanu shook his head and muttered under his breath. He shoved his pipe in his pack and jumped from the window. "Show-off."

CHAPTER XIX

Somewhere in the mountains of Idaho. Present day.

I WALKED ON A thin path that ambled its way through massive green trees in full leaf that towered over me. I felt small and so confused, realizing that one of the things about Kale that didn't compute, among the millions of others, was that, if I remembered right, he had kidnapped Michael and me on an autumn evening in late September.

Why then is it summertime in the mountains? I almost said aloud. It was backwards, just like my brain. But like just about everything in my life, I simply had to let go. I decided that I might very well be completely out of my mind — but I also decided that, all things considered, I may as well enjoy it.

Kale had given me that old book, told me to read it. He said it was history, part of my school work, I guess. I held the book under my arm as I walked. I could feel it there, as if it was alive and our movements through the wood were mutual and agreed upon at every step. Green fern fiddleheads peppered the shady areas, and some strange plants with red-tipped leaves grew on either side of the path. Michael and Kale had stayed behind — they had 'things to discuss,' and I wanted to be alone with my own thoughts anyway.

How did we get here? At one point, an eternity ago, we had been kidnapped by a killer. Now, I had let myself slide into the kind of thinking that allowed me to consider the idea that a murderer was to be trusted. He had physically taken us; kidnapped us from the mall parking lot. It sometimes made my head swim in chaos — but

I felt the Book under my arm would provide the anchor I needed in the midst of my stormy existence. I couldn't name the assurance I had, but it was there nevertheless.

A large boulder blocked the little trail, but I climbed over it without thinking. It was as if I was in a dream world. All the woodland sounds seemed closer and clearer than usual. None of this was lost on me, either. I was aware of my awareness; it was like the Book — or maybe just whatever it had awakened in me — was stimulating a dormant seed that God Himself had planted within me.

If I was really descended from a race of immortal angelic beings, it only made sense that that seed came from somewhere farther up my family tree, waiting for the right moment to spring forth. I brushed aside everything I couldn't understand, which was plenty, and just felt the sun beaming down on me through the canopy of the trees.

I saw a patch of sunshine off the path, up on a little knoll. I turned toward it and began to climb. It was a small, natural clearing of wildflowers and meadow grass, centered on an ancient redwood that littered it with broken limbs and discarded needles from years prior. It was so undisturbed and natural that it was irresistible, and I sat down on a clump of soft green grass near the tree to read.

I put the book on my lap and opened the front cover. There, on the flyleaf, were the softly glistening letters of the name of Kreios, fading as if they were not sure if they wanted to be there or disappear completely.

I turned the page, but it was completely blank. I turned to the next, and the next, until I was flipping through the book, beginning to feel either dumb or hopeless. The voice came to me so loudly that I almost jumped up: *"Stop."* Again, I heard it: *"Stop."* This time the voice was softer. I knew who had said it. *She* was becoming so familiar that it was getting difficult to tell the difference between her voice and my own.

I took a few deep breaths, calming myself, and tried to respond as best I could. "Okay. Just what am I supposed to do with an empty book?" I cracked it open again, this time to the middle, and looked up at the huge tree standing guard over me.

"Close your eyes and search with your heart." I shut my eyes, trying to clear everything out. I opened them after a while and looked at the textured, creamy white page. Still nothing. I persisted, though, and began to see that there *was* something there. I couldn't distinguish it, but it was there, hidden with great care.

I touched the page. My hands trembled. In the sunlight, if I held a single page open, I could see the imperfections in it. To me, imperfections went beyond character or charm. Imperfections were what made something *real*. I felt almost as if I had died and gone to heaven. *Perhaps I have.*

Letters seemed to grow from my touch on the page. Like the flyleaf, they appeared and disappeared as if underwater, or as if they were being viewed through a cloud. As they became more recognizable, though, I could see plainly that they were not English. *Of course not!* It made perfect sense, but it frustrated me.

Though you see through a glass darkly...

I closed my eyes again and focused on the positives. I thought of the day I had first seen Michael Alexander; how gorgeous he was, how he said my name, how we had so much in common with each other, how he seemed to accept me for who I was. The real question was, though, precisely who had I been? And much more importantly, who was I now? I well enough knew what Kale had told me... and I was sitting in an impossible place reading an impossible book with impossible figures on the page that probably spoke about impossible things... which were impossible for me to read.

I opened my eyes to find that I had been crying, and that a single tear had dropped onto the page, soaking in instantly with a rainbow of color. I was so worried that I had somehow destroyed an irreplaceable book that I couldn't see straight — but I realized that I was able to understand the text on the page now. It was a smooth script, a beautiful hand, and the ink was so dark and crisp that I thought I might be sucked into the world within the words. The world I had known seemed so thin. Now, as I read, I was sure that it *was* somehow. Thin — and unreal.

1250 B.C. New moon full and low.

The battle ahead weighs upon my mind as a heavy stone. Part of me desires nothing more than to flee, taking Eriel as far away from the Seer as possible. But another part of me desires nothing more than to remove the Seer's head from his body and place it on a pike on the highest hill for all to see. How is it possible for evil to so completely fill up such an empty vessel? There seems to be no end to this madness. I must take my stand against him, though I remain uneasy. I trust El; but it is difficult to do so. Though the Sword of Light has returned to me, I find no rest for my tortured soul.
Kreios

It was a journal. Kreios. I had heard that name when I had touched the Book the first time, too, as if the Book spoke for itself as to who owned it. I had been given the secret history of his life. I flipped through the pages, astounded at the span of time his life encompassed. The beginning date was 2700 B.C., and the last entry was 788 B.C. *That's an interesting wrinkle — how could someone who had lived before Christ know precisely how many years before Christ he had lived?*

I skimmed through more pages and found that they had all been written in the same fluid, beautiful hand. It had to have been written by one person. *There's no way one man could live that long...*

But He wasn't a man. He was one of the angels, or descended from them; I wasn't sure which. That's what Kale had called them: Sons of God. I wondered if they lived forever. Maybe they could be killed. This book did end; perhaps it meant that Kreios had met his end. From the looks of the final entry, it didn't look good for Kreios.

I turned back to the beginning, deciding to read the whole story in order. I learned the whole story of Kreios. I read the account of his time in heaven before The Fall, his love for a woman whom he would never name... and other things as well. The pain I felt for him as he wrote about his beloved, as I read his Book, produced in me tears of my own. I inevitably compared his love for her with my own love for Michael, and I marveled at the pain his love for her endured. I took it as a warning that there would be pain of my own that I would have to bear, as well.

PART THREE

THE BOOK

CHAPTER I

Boise, Idaho. Present day.

THE FEELING OF POWER in its purest form was enough to compel a man to break free of every law of decency and run through the streets naked and screaming. Stan knew that he did not *have* to kill the detective — but oh, how much fun it was to shoot the pig in the head.

Detective Lopez had taken too long. Much too long. There was a schedule to keep, people to see and all that. Lopez did give Stan what he had wanted, though — which made killing him in spite of it feel so much more satisfying. Innocence had so many uses, and quite contrary to what decent people thought. "Stan is very creative," he said.

Stan let his memory flood his mind. The nice thing about memories was the ability to relive a great moment. The moment he shot Lopez was one that he liked. How could something so wrong feel so right?

CHAPTER II

Somewhere in the mountains of Idaho. Present day.

I DREAMT OF THE Book, felt its presence in the room like a living thing. I could swear it called to me in the night the way my mother would, sweetly.

I opened my eyes to see the sun high in the sky, the curtains pulled back, and a warm yellow sunbeam filtering across my bed. I yawned, reaching up with my arms over the forest of soft pillows. I felt my back pop and a rush of wonderfulness flow through me like the unkinking of a garden hose.

"Good morning, sleepyhead." Michael's voice made me start. He grinned and chuckled low.

"Michael, you scared me! What are you doing?" I pulled the covers up to my neck, though I was fully clothed in my pajamas.

"Relax, I'm just here to wake you. I couldn't let you sleep any longer. It's noon already, and the date I have planned for us is slowly slipping away." I smiled and let the covers fall away. I struggled out of their grasp, my feet finding the floor. I discreetly checked my breath and ran a hand through my tangled hair. I was promptly self-conscious. We were dangerously mixing bed head, dragon breath, and Michael Alexander. He was standing only a few feet away, offering a date and looking great on top of it.

"You kinda caught me at a bad time, mister." I could feel my face heat up and my palms begin to sweat.

"Aw, you look beautiful. But anyway, I'll just wait down in the kitchen. That way you can make your stunning entrance. I made you breakfast — well, lunch." He had worked his way to the door as he spoke, but he turned, smiled, and left.

I shook my head at him, smiling. As soon as the door closed, I leapt from the bedside to the bathroom. I got ready just as quickly as I could, dressing in jeans and a pink hoody. I stepped into my sneakers and ran down the stairs feeling better than I could have imagined. One look in the mirror had told me I was beautiful; once again, no make-up required. I shook my head and let my hair sort itself out.

Michael was standing with his back to me at one of the counters, downing a large glass of orange juice. I stopped and looked at him, feeling my heart rise and thump in my chest just at the sight of him. I snuck in and grabbed a stool, sitting on it.

"So, what's the special?" He jumped at the sound of my voice. "Gotcha back," I said. He smiled.

"You look amazing, Airel." When he turned toward me, a large bowl of exotic fruits came into view behind him. He had arranged everything in the shape of a heart.

I clicked my tongue and said, "Awww!" It was such a nice gesture; and it had probably taken some time to do.

"There's fresh bread, too," he said, turning to the brick oven. He brought out a couple of gorgeous looking rounds of sourdough, and abruptly, my stomach turned.

Oh, no. I didn't want to get sick again. Why was this happening? It was like a second puberty — no matter how you sliced that idea, it's bad. I spoke, to try to distract myself. "You make your own bread, too?" I was genuinely impressed.

"Sure, why not?" He looked at me quizzically, cocking his head. "You okay? You look weird."

"Oh, really?"

"Well! Not weird. I mean, you look great. But you look like you just smelled something gross…"

My mind fluttered, going into emergency procedures. Michael's eyebrows lowered, making me wonder what he was thinking. "I'm fine, just hungry. It all looks so good."

I guess I should have seen it coming. For the first time — well, the first time consciously — I heard something: It was Michael's voice, but distant, as if it was coming from a thousand miles away. *"I can't go on like this; I have to tell her."* It was Michael, but not his spoken voice. I was hearing his thoughts. I was reading his mind; I remembered what Kale had told me about the 'gift.' It was a small voice in the fog, but it was *all* Michael's.

"Well, good, 'cause there's plenty to eat here." He seemed to lose some of his trademark spark. I hadn't *really* noticed it until it had gone, but it had always seemed to be toward the back of his eyes, illuminating his gaze. I wondered what he was holding back from me, and what it meant.

"What's wrong?" I asked.

"Nothing." He moved the bowl of fruit over to where I was sitting, serving me. "Just thinking of how crazy all this is. We're in this beautiful house with everything we could want: food, clothes, great trails to hike. No TV or games, but I really haven't missed 'em all that much."

I smiled; he was so cute. He was the one person I could never fear, or even see myself becoming fearful around, like some guys I knew. Deep down, I think a lot of girls have this underlying fear of a man they know could kill them, crush them with sheer strength or will. He was so strong, built like a rock. But I knew he could never use his strength to hurt me, no matter what. His strength made me feel — safe.

We sat and ate breakfast for quite a while, enjoying the luxury of one another's company. I realized that we hadn't really had much time to ourselves, for all that had happened. And if we had an easy time before the kidnapping finding common ground, our present situation was like double-sided tape between us.

We spent the day doing ultimately forgettable things, just enjoying each other's company. My grandparents would say we were strolling, because life was slower then, more easily enjoyable, probably. *Yeah, and there was horse poop in the streets, too.* I guessed every age had its gilded edge. But it didn't matter. I was finally, *finally,* getting to indulge myself in what I wanted the very most: Michael Alexander. And it was glorious.

The air was cool, with a hint of rain. The trees and the undergrowth seemed to open to it, as if enjoined to the sense that something was coming. The woods came alive with anticipation of the life-giving rain, and we stood silently in the midst of it, looking up from russet-colored earth through giant redwood boughs that reached to the darkening sky.

Michael looked great in his worn-out blue jeans and dark blue windbreaker. We had both found hiking boots in our rooms. They were new and lightweight. I guessed Kale had gifted us with such niceties. I winced at the thought of him. I wondered if that assessment was unfair now. I knew I needed to ask him about it and find out what was really going on. Why *had* he killed the man in the movie theater? Was that guy a 'bad guy?' He had to be; I couldn't see Kale murdering someone in cold blood.

"So. We need to talk," Michael said unexpectedly. We were moving along a well-worn path guarded by green shrubs and ferns that brushed our legs as we walked by.

"Yeah, I guess we should try to work out some nagging questions about this whole mess. What do you know so far about why we're here?" I wondered if he believed Kale's claim that I was a descendant of the Sons of God, a half-angel of sorts.

"Well…" He *shooshed* in a heavy sigh as he began, "I think I'm here by accident. He's interested in you, and I just happened to get in the way." His face clouded over.

"Yeah, but somehow I think Kale wouldn't mess up like that. He doesn't seem to do anything on impulse. I mean, just look at how he lives. Everything is just-so." I jumped up on a log that had fallen across the path and Michael vaulted over it without even thinking.

"Well, it doesn't matter why I'm here. He wants you, to train you… to do what? Develop your 'powers,' or the powers he believes you may have."

"Michael…" I wondered if he remembered my head injury, and if he was still fighting the reality of what was going on. "I do have some abilities that I cannot explain. You remember when I fainted at football practice?" He nodded as we kept walking. "Well, it healed. I heal very fast. I've tried it out a few times, and it's true. I'm also strong enough to kick down the heavy door to my room… but that one I'm still trying to figure out." I left out the mind-reading bit. No use freaking him out.

"So he's telling you that you're part angel and part human? That's kinda… unbelievable, really."

"Yeah, I know." I felt like I had to say that just so he wouldn't feel awkward. But I believed it readily enough for me.

"You know, it feels like we're in a movie or something. I just wonder when we're going to wake up. Maybe when we do, we'll find ourselves back in the mall parking lot, where we started. On our first date." He looked at me.

He was *so* romantic. I could die. The memories came back, honestly warm and fuzzy. "I know, it's weird, huh. But for what it's worth, I believe Kale. I don't know why — but I do." Up until this point, I did not know what I really thought of our kidnapper. I didn't like the *situation*. But I knew I could trust him. He seemed to have this code of honor, one he would never cross. They say that chivalry is dead — but what if that age was still clinging to someone who had actually lived through it? How would they go about their days, I wondered. There was something about Kale that was different in that respect.

"I think I trust him," I said, trying to close the deal. "He seems to know something that we don't." I paused for a minute, thinking. "Ya know, it's like he kidnapped me on purpose. Maybe to protect me from something?"

"Yeah, that's true enough, I guess. From what, though? 'The Brotherhood?' I doubt *they* still exist, though they might have a long time ago." Michael was playing with a long blade of grass and the tip bounced in his hand like a bobber on a lake. It was hypnotic.

"Well, it's possible. Who knows?" I said. "All I know is that I need him for now — I have too many questions about these so-called abilities, and he seems to have all the right answers." I looked at Michael. "So far."

He seemed to resist what I was saying.

"Look, I just want to be careful. I need to figure out what I can do, if anything, to get control of my abilities before I hurt someone I care about."

"It's not that." He looked genuinely disturbed and worried. "Airel, you know that even though we don't know each other that well, I still feel you're..." He hesitated, his gorgeous blue eyes hiding behind a momentary shadow. He took my hand in his and looked at it. He was *so* warm. The touch of his skin made me feel a shock in my arm running straight for my heart. He looked into my eyes.

"Airel, I want you to know I'm falling in love with you. And it's not a crush — we all know what that is. But this..." He put a hand to his heart and closed his eyes, taking a moment.

I cannot express in words how I felt, the way all of me was bound up right inside that moment.

"... This is the real thing. This kind of thing is like winning the lottery. You can go a lifetime without ever finding anything real. I love you, Airel, and all I need from you is to know that one simple thing."

My heart hurt as it swelled with emotion. I took his face in my hands and made him look at me. This time, his eyes were clear and brilliant. "Michael, I love you more than life itself. No matter what happens to me, or... or how I change... I always will."

I could almost feel his soft lips about to gently brush my own, in the prelude to a kiss — but I wouldn't, I couldn't. The anticipation of it was killing me. But I knew if I kissed him it was all over. I would be positively head-over-heels and I needed to hold back a small part of my heart until I figured all this out. And I may have been only seventeen, but I knew well enough that the first kiss with that special someone always started a fire that couldn't be put out.

Michael pulled me closer, enveloping me with his strong arms. I laid my head on his chest in surrender. That's where I belonged, where I wanted to be. If I could have stopped time, I would have frozen it right then.

As Michael held me, I could feel his heart beating against my cheek. I searched the spaces in my mind and tried to read his thoughts again, but all I heard was crying. Was he crying? I pulled away and looked up at his face. It was dripping with pain and sadness. There, in the deep pools of his eyes, was a force that I didn't understand.

Something was tearing him apart from the inside out. No tears were in his eyes, but I could hear it in his head. I could picture a little boy crying in a dusty corner. I wrapped my arms around his neck and pulled myself closer to him.

"It'll be okay, Michael. I will *always* love you. Everything's going to work itself out, you'll see." I buried myself in his scent. It was him, Michael, *my* Michael. I could feel that little part of my heart I was trying to hold back slipping. Michael, with all his charm and mystery, was the only man I wanted to be with.

We sat like that for quite a while, the storm gathering closer to us. When the wind began to whip and gust, we both realized we were cold and under-dressed for the weather. We felt a little too far from the house and broke apart, standing. My feet had fallen asleep. I put my hands in my back pockets and stepped back from him a little. He seemed like, whatever he had been dealing with, he was mostly over it now.

He looked at me mischievously and smiled, putting his arm around me. "So. Can I see one of these *super powers?*" His eyes sparkled and a small grin spread across his face.

"Boys!" I laughed, rolling my eyes. "You're all the same." I walked in a circle, looking on the ground for something sharp. "Okay, the one I know the best involves healing. It hurts — but it's really cool." I found a jagged-looking branch on the ground and began to try to dislodge it from its entanglements.

Michael stood up with a look of concern on his face. "Are you sure?"

"Yeah, it'll be fine. Watch." I finally broke off a chunk and examined it. "Yep, that'll do." It looked like a giant shark's tooth. I held it in my right hand and lifted it high over my head. Before I could change my mind or hesitate, and in the midst of Michael's protests, I stabbed it down into my other hand as hard as I could.

"Airel! Are you okay?"

I growled in pain. I held my hand up, the chunk of branch buried and standing up in my palm. I wanted to do that little hopping dance that people do when they stub their toe or whatever. But I kept my courage by looking in Michael's eyes. I could feel my hand begin to itch. I yanked the thing out of my palm and tossed it away. I held my bloody hand out to him, and we watched as the blood flowed, carrying little bits of dirt and bark and splinters with it.

The itch was more powerful than I remembered; I wanted to tear my own hand off in order to make it stop. Tiny fingers of flesh reached out and grasped one another like old friends. A patch was made, then the skin closed over. What blood was left, I wiped on a nearby fern. Michael stared at me with his mouth hanging open.

"I am *so* showing that to all my friends," he said with a look of utter amazement on his face.

"I don't think so, mister. I'm not a party trick."

"Duh, I was kidding. But you've gotta admit it: that's the coolest thing ever!" His eyes sparkled as he looked at me with what I reckoned as new-found respect.

"Yeah, *cool*. But it's also a *secret*. No spreading it around that your girlfriend can heal herself. All I need is a bunch of hormone-happy boys running around sticking me with knives and sticks just to see what will happen."

He laughed in a manly way, making me giggle. "I won't tell a soul." He flashed me puppy dog eyes. "Scout's honor!" He gave me the two fingered salute, making me laugh even more.

CHAPTER III

1250 B.C. Arabia

KREIOS AND YAMANU PULLED up in midair, hovering high above the tree line. They conversed in thought.

"There, west of the lake, in the trees." Kreios pointed to a thick stand of trees on the western edge of a long lake. It produced a tributary that wound down and around in the wide valley, finding its terminus in the sea, which was within sight at this altitude. Yellow flames of light danced within the darkness of the forest, and the sound of undisciplined voices could be heard bouncing across the still water.

"How many?" Yamanu pulled his hood up over his head and tied the leather thong under his chin.

"Eight hundred, maybe a thousand. More would have come if they knew about Ke'elei. I am surprised the Seer allowed them to have campfires… he has grown arrogant and foolish in his old age." Kreios touched the Sword hilt and felt better at once.

Yamanu grunted audibly. *"Maybe. Or, he knows something we do not. Caution and a solid plan will go a long way toward keeping us alive long enough to see beautiful Eriel grow up and marry."* His thoughts made colors of blue and red in Kreios' mind. He did not know the meanings of every color, but he knew that it was never good if black or dark purple surrounded a particular thought.

"Find their weakness and exploit it." Kreios donned his hood.

"Yes."

"We may need some fog…" They cinched down their gear,

double-checking that they would be silent, and turned toward the north side of the lake, downwind, to prepare their infiltration of the enemy camp.

They landed in knee-high grass, silently, the enemy camp within sight. Kreios pulled a short dagger from its sheath, touching the grips of the Sword for comfort. *"We must move with speed. The longer we are in their midst, the weaker we will become. I will signal when I feel my strength failing —"*

Yamanu nodded, unsheathing a dagger of similar size and shape.

There are moments to which men and angels have been brought throughout their destinies that have shaped the paths they have walked forever afterward. Some have been ready for it when it came to call. Some have not, and possibility shifted irrevocably from that point forward. Kreios knew El to be jealously intrepid in His pursuit of the created, however. He would roadblock, shunt, redirect, nudge, push, pull, convince, debate, and tirelessly chase down His children within the circle of the destiny He had created for them until they grasped it.

Kreios knew that he could not ultimately miss his destiny — in a sense — but he knew that it was still possible to fail tonight. He determined, therefore, to rise to the occasion with his very life forfeit, if need be.

Kreios felt Yamanu turn to a deeper place that he could not access; the color of his thoughts turned bright white. The ground slowly began to cover with thick fog, which spread from them outward and rose like the dead in the coming resurrection.

Kreios was ready to deal in real justice now — and as the fog rose around them, enfolding them in concealment, he filled up his Sword with retribution, the wages of sin, the reward of judgment reserved for those wicked enough to ask for fairness.

Kreios opened his eyes and beheld his hand. It was almost transparent, and the dagger in his hand could not be seen. His friends had always told him that he had no imagination. The sight of his own flesh disappearing right before his eyes, however, made him break into a fresh smile.

Yamanu opened his eyes, too, looking at Kreios with a hearty invisible smile. *"You must keep careful track of me. I will let you know if you are in danger of straying too far from my side and losing cover."* He paused, then said aloud, "Not bad for an old man, eh?" He chuckled, slapping Kreios on the shoulder.

"Careful I don't kill you, boy."

"You'd have to see me first, little girl."

Kreios almost laughed out loud. Yamanu turned aside in his mind, Kreios opened up to him, and then they could see one another in the fog through their thoughts. It was an odd sensation to see with the mind and not with the eyes; it reminded Kreios of true faith. *"The evidence of things not seen..."*

They moved through the fog into the dark wood, alert, the fog penetrating before them and trailing after them in the wind.

CHAPTER IV

Somewhere in the mountains of Idaho. Present day.

I DREAMT THE STORY of Kreios, the fight for his daughter Eriel, and the memory of his amazing love. I took great pleasure in fitting the pieces of the puzzle together. He was someone who had loved without fear of death. He was all-or-nothing. A little like me, really, which I liked — though I feared death like nothing else. *In that sense I'm still normal.*

I read the entire book in two days. I loved to read stories that I could relate to. I could relate to the story of an angel — epic battles, soaring sonic booms, deep and meaningful friendships. I guess it's true that the best stories are somehow universally true. I felt like I knew Kreios, that somehow I was linked to him in ways I could only dream and think of with the aid of *She.*

Michael didn't read the book for a couple reasons. One, because Kale insisted that it was for me and me alone, and two, because when Michael opened it, all he saw were blank pages. No amount of focusing or magical wishing could bring the smooth script into focus for him. I, however, grew to love that handwriting and could recite every line. I cherished each letter as if written *to* me.

Kale left me alone as I studied my 'history.' I spent most of my time by a tree, seated on the clump of green grass under its branches. I felt each day that passed drew me farther out away from the only home I had ever known.

I missed my home fiercely. Thinking of Mom and Dad made my heart sick. I wished I could at least call them to let them know

I was okay, though that probably wouldn't help once they started asking me questions. Even so, I was growing apart from that home and into a kind of new life. Could a person forget so soon?

Here, in the heart of the woods, I began to like the quiet. It was the not-so-busy life; like how Jane Austen's characters would just walk and talk their lives away.

I had to admit, the difference between those stories and my own was that I was terribly alone. Though I had no homework, no chores, and no responsibilities, I ached for all of it because it was at least familiar to me. The hardest part was the inescapable feeling that things would only get harder. It was as if I had walked into a dream, and here everything was all about me. Lots of girls, and probably some guys, fantasize about that kind of thing, I bet. Now that it had happened to me, I realized the foolishness of such a thing, and how bad selfishness can truly be.

Michael had left me alone as well, and I had thanked him for it. I had told him, "I know I've been kinda out of it lately; sorry. I should get myself sorted out in a day or two, though." He had smiled and hugged me, acting impressively mature, which had melted me to goo inside all over again. I felt so safe in his arms. I didn't know what it was about this guy, but he was everything I wanted out of life. If I could just have him, honestly, nothing else mattered. It was all so crazy anyway that I was tempted to just throw it all away and start over. It might be easier.

"Take all the time you need, Airel," he had said to me. "We just gotta play along here. I think, over time, he'll get tired of us and let us go." His statement had caught me off guard. He hadn't believed any of it; he thought Kale was crazy, that this had been just some psychopathic game, and that in the end, the cops would show up to spring us.

I returned to myself, wondering if that wasn't what I had thought, too. Or was that what I was supposed to think? I didn't know anymore. The stories in the Book were so real. They were too impossible to have been made up. I knew in my heart that Kreios was a real person. I could sense that his life was as real as mine somehow.

I wasn't having bad dreams, but I wasn't sleeping well. I guess I didn't need it, because I wasn't tired. It was as if knowing the story gave me an energy boost. I used the nights to think and to walk all through the great house. I spent some nights in the huge study with all the books, reading by the light of the fireplace that never, not once, went out.

The house really was very beautiful. I explored every room but one. I couldn't get into it because it was locked — even though I could have broken the door down, I guess. I didn't do that. It would have been wrong. I imagined a great library of old books, or a hidden staircase leading to underground caves that held something unknown. It haunted me, and I thought about it often.

As I fell into bed that night, I relived the adventures of Kreios and his beloved daughter Eriel. She seemed to have been so kind and beautiful. I wished I could know her, and in some weird way, I felt like I did. I was falling deep into a dream when a firm hand shook me awake.

I bolted upright to find Kale standing over me. He wore a white robe, and he appeared monkish in a 21st Century sort of way. "Airel, come with me."

My heart pounded in my chest from the shock. It was like I was ready to defend myself from an unexpected intruder at my bedside. Even though I secretly was beginning to like him, I still tried to fight against it with all of my will. "To where? Don't you knock?" I looked out the windows and said something rude about how it was still in the middle of the night. I was angry, too, for even considering trusting him.

Kale looked slightly dejected, but he left the room. "Be sure to dress in something that doesn't inhibit your movements." He left no doubt in his mannerisms about the expectation that I follow him immediately. I grumbled darkly as I dressed in a gray track suit and tennies. My hair was a mess, but I didn't care — I just pulled it up in a pony. Men — they were all the same — so demanding, and no time for anything remotely sensitive. Well, except Michael, of course.

I left my room and closed the door behind me. Kale was waiting for me in the hallway. He led me out of the house to the shack I had seen on my first solo journey through the house. There, outside the building, just as I had seen it before, was the large floating area where my imaginary gymnasts did their floor routines. My hands buzzed with the excitement of discovery.

The shack stood in the corner of the area, lit from the inside. Kale ascended a stair made of wood and opened the door. I followed him inside. The shack, shed, dojo, or whatever, was constructed of wood and stone. The floor was covered thickly with a huge rough rug. It seemed impossibly large inside, seemed not to fit the dimensions of the shell that hemmed the space in which I now stood. Huge wood beams anchored the roof overhead, and a rustic chandelier, already lit, hung from the middle beam, lending a warm glow to the room.

A perfect square; I could tell in looking around that it was indeed a dojo of sorts. No matter what, it was a place designed for sparring. Against the far wall stood a rack with swords, staves and other weapons I'd never seen before. Kale walked to the middle of the floor and stood in a dark red circle. Farther out from that circle was a faded blue ring, then another red one, and so on about every five feet, I guessed.

"The rings are the first stage of your training and schooling. I will train you in hand-to-hand combat and teach you to use your abilities. You will be able to control them at will soon." He stood with his feet slightly apart, his hands in front of him at chest height in a kind of salute, grasping a long pointy stick.

I was beyond flabbergasted. I responded coolly, cocking my head to one side as if appraising his sanity. "So, it's hand-to-hand combat, then." I inhaled, still trying to take it all in. "Did you not get the memo? I'm seventeen —" Before I could do anything else, he had stepped to one side, drawn back a spear, and hurled it at me with blinding speed. The end of it plunged into the shallow of my gut, shredding me right through, the leading edge exiting through the small of my back. The pain was so sharp that it was indescribable. I began to black out, and I fell to my knees.

Kale was upon me in a flash, standing before me like a warrior thirsting for the kill. I could feel him panting heavily. He grasped the weapon firmly and yanked it straight out from my body, my blood flowing.

He brought the heel of the pike down with a shattering crack on the floor, the weapon standing vertically, a spray of blood showering me as it vibrated powerfully from the violence of his grip. He reared his head back as he towered over me, as I collapsed sideways, and released a blood curdling shout that seized me, head to toe, with icy fear. My head bounced off the matting of the floor and the room started to spin as my eyes involuntarily squeezed shut in pain.

I saw blue, pink and white stars floating across my vision, then an unbearable tingling itch grabbed at my gut in tiny fingers of intense pain. It itched so badly that I seriously considered death as a viable choice for a few seconds. I lifted my shirt, cautiously, in horror, and watched in awe as the huge gash closed up and smoothed over as if it had never been there. The itching subsided gradually, but my track jacket was hopelessly shredded and bloody. I looked up at Kale, quite beside myself with shock and rage.

He smiled down at me and laughed.

CHAPTER V

KALE'S GRINNING FACE LOOKED stupid to me; I was beyond irritated. He held out his hand to me. I looked at his fingers as if they were attached to the hand of Satan. "Nice. Attention getter. Okay then, what's for breakfast?" I finally took his hand, deciding to 'just roll with it,' as Kim would say. I cooed, an aftershock of my injury wracking my body one last time as I regained my feet.

Kale cracked a joke: "You shouldn't train on an empty stomach."

"Hilarious." I placed my hands on my knees and breathed hard. "That's why I'm asking about breakfast — mine's killing me."

I stood there like an outfielder for a while, just taking everything in. I guess you always want what you can't have — now that it seemed impossible for me to die, I felt trapped in my own life. More so than usual.

He must have heard some of my doubtful thoughts. "In time you will have your answers. For now, you must just accept things as they are."

There was real, honest compassion in his voice. It was refreshing, I decided.

"You have been given a gift — will you accept it?" He still held out his hand, though I was standing already.

Kale standing before me like that triggered something in me. I knew it, too. Something had let go way up at the top of some gigantic mountain of me, and an avalanche was going to come down and change everything. My eyes filled with tears. "Do I have a choice?" Destiny was coming for me again, I could feel it.

The moment was beginning to crash in upon me, and I had been stripped of my defenses against it.

"You always have a choice." His words sounded like the Voice of God — very still, very quiet, and purely true. I broke. I heard the sweetest music. I took his hand and collapsed into his enormous chest, heaving in big wet sobs. I felt like heaven, creation, God Himself, were all part of a conspiracy designed to bring me always and forever back to the point where the tiny capsule of all that I was resided on the tip of a pin.

Kale simply held me like a child and let me cry. I didn't know how long it was. And I'm not sure what, exactly, happened. Lots of times I just cried because I had to, to let off the pressure that accumulated inside me, to say with tears what words couldn't describe. Whatever happened in that moment of time, changed everything.

I pushed Kale away and dried my swollen eyes with the sleeve of my track jacket, now mangled and bloody. I took it off, deciding I could manage with just my t-shirt, but that, too, was impossibly destroyed. It made my mind tangle in knots.

"Fine, then. What do we do now? Cut me some more to see how much I can take?" I wiped at my eyes and sucked in a sob.

Kale's voice was gentle. "We need to find out what you're able to do and how much control you have over your abilities. When I say that you have a choice... you do realize that you have the choice to do good with what God has given you, or evil. Which do you choose?"

It was surreal. I felt like I was on a game show. I felt like I was back at the kitchen table arguing with my parents about the SAT and what college I would go to, what major I would declare. I felt like asking Kale how I should possibly know. The truth was, though, that the answer was quite obvious.

But wrapped up inside his question to me was another one, directed right back at him: How can a murderer ask someone to choose between good and evil without being crazy himself? I wanted to ask it — and I unwittingly did, forgetting that he could read my thoughts. *Crud.* I found myself wishing desperately for some privacy.

"Good," he said, willing to gloss over all my mental baggage for now. "The first thing we will work on is hand-to-hand combat." He turned and walked over to one of the racks that held staff upon staff like pool cues, and I followed, shaking my head, trying to clear it. He continued, "You are stronger than you think, but only when you're filled with raw emotion. You will be able to feel it coursing through your veins." He handed me a staff.

Oh, what the heck. Maybe I could use a little workout action to help me think clearly. I took the staff in my hand, feeling a little like Moses at the Red Sea. *What next?*

"Love. Anger. Fear. Whatever the emotion, it must be strong." His voice commanded attention.

I nodded, though I didn't understand what he was talking about. I figured I would learn as I went, me being a hands-on type when it came to kickboxing and such. I turned the wooden staff over in my hand, running my fingertips along the smooth surface. It was dark, very hard, and was wrapped around the middle with a leather grip.

Kale held up his own staff now, made of silvery metal with the same leather grip in the center. "I want you to break that staff over my head." Kale looked at me with eyes that seemed to be lighter than they had been a few seconds ago.

"What?" I looked at my staff, then at him.

"You heard me, hit me. It must be hard enough that you shatter that staff — and I must warn you—that is gopher wood. A rod of that is very hard, almost impossible to break. So you must focus on your anger right now, and try to channel it into your actions."

Well then, no problem.

"Here's a little something to help you out," he said, and whacked me in the shin with his metal staff.

"Ow!" My left shin stung, and I instinctually snapped into kickboxing mode. Kale was not smiling this time, and I knew if I didn't at least defend myself he would punish me further. *Whatever, old dude.* It helped me to 'channel the anger,' anyway.

I moved as swiftly as I thought possible, swinging my staff

overhead and bringing it thunderously down. It collided with his staff with a clang, and the vibration hurt badly. "Ow!" I said again.

He made ready again, elegantly. "That's all?"

"Hmm," I scoffed, and tried again, this time faster, stronger, quicker. I pivoted on my left heel and brought the staff across his midsection with all the force I could muster. I was going to put everything into it, even if I fell afterward.

His staff was everywhere at once. He blocked the blow almost casually, and his unexpected movements caused me to lose my balance. I went down to the floor, landing on my knuckles, my staff skittering off and rolling. Pain shot up my hands. I turned over onto my back, winded.

"Again! Break the staff over my head!"

A warm feeling began to spread through my body as I interpreted his words. I was never super-athletic, but from lying flat on my back, I jumped to my feet in a single movement, grabbing my staff again along the way. I twirled it once over my head like a baton and jumped, swinging the staff in an arc at the top of his head.

He raised his bright silver staff to deflect the blow. He laughed. It's like all he saw was some kid who had just learned to ride a bike without training wheels. I, however, was screaming like a crazy woman. The impact of the two competing weapons cracked like lightning, and just as I had imagined in my mind, the staff shattered into splinters.

I landed on my feet, bending my knees to absorb the shock. I uncoiled to my full height, Kale now off to one side and behind me at the end of our maneuver. I turned toward him, absolutely filled with rage like never before, a little out of control.

I tore the silver staff from his hand and racked him in the back of the legs with it. He went down like a bag of rocks as I reset and brought the metal staff up over my head. Right before I stabbed the end of it down through his face, he rolled out of the way. It impacted the floor, tearing through the matting and wood, digging into the earth below, so deep that the leather grip was only half visible.

My breathing was rapid and my heart pumped furiously. I

felt cold steel against my neck and froze. Kale grabbed my wrist and wrenched it into my shoulder blades. The tip of a knife rested threateningly just under my chin.

"You let your anger control your power one more time and I will show you the meaning of pain." He flicked his wrist, slicing the underside of my chin, which hurt. But it healed quickly. That itching thing was going to take some time to get used to.

I walked over to one of the walls and sat with my back resting against it to catch my breath. I studied Kale from across the room as he wiped the blood from his knife and put it away. The silver staff stuck out of the floor like a gigantic needle. As I calmed, I wondered how I could be so strong. Here it was, right in front of my eyes. Evidence, facts, truth.

The room was littered with wood splinters. It was hard not to feel discarded, in a way. I had sat in class wondering if I was abnormal or normal — whatever that was — so many times. I wondered if I would ever be accepted as is, or if I needed to change part of me. Maybe I was doomed to be on the outside looking in. *Try to fit in now.* Now I would be the kid who had been kidnapped, at least. Or the girl who had super powers. "So bizarre." I wondered if I was concerned about the right things — and I even wondered if that thought belonged to me in the first place.

Kale grunted approvingly at me and picked up another wooden staff from the rack. "Now do it with love."

Love? "What does that even mean?" I was trying not to feel awkward. "How do I do that?"

"Feel that heat, the same as when you were angry — but feel the way love can overpower your emotions and use *that* to break the staff. But this time, break it over your knee." Kale managed a sideways smile and tossed me a new wood staff.

I took hold of it and closed my eyes, trying to concentrate. I wondered what I was supposed to do to make my emotions flow. It should be second nature. But not when you're thinking about it so intensely. I felt like I was trying to conjure spells or charm snakes — like I had ever done anything like that. I felt like a fraud.

Love. Right. I loved my mom and dad. I loved Kim, and oh,

how I missed her. She was such a ham, and I sure could use a good laugh right about now. Michael then flooded my mind, and I could see his eyes. So very blue and welcoming.

I could feel him looking at me, and remembered the way he brushed against my arm whenever he was near; it was always so incidental and natural; whenever he helped me out of the car or walked with me, or gestured while he talked about something.

It was the way he was. All the physical considerations aside, he was an amazing person. I loved his heart, his kindness, and the way he loved so honestly. I wanted to be with him for the rest of my life and I wasn't ashamed to admit it, even to myself. He would be my one and only; ever.

Okay, this might actually work. I thought back to our date. I remembered how he had looked over at me and smiled as we drove off to the restaurant. He had just stunned me with that line about Audrey Hepburn... my heart melted and I pushed off the wall that marked the safe zone of my thoughts, drifting out into the pool of all things Michael.

Kale's voice was soft and low. "What are you thinking?" I stood, eyes still closed, hands on the weapon. When I comprehended his question, I blushed. He prodded gently still. "Tell me."

"I'm thinking of love." Warmth washed over me, but this time it was different. I could feel Michael's arms around me. I began to overflow with joy. It just kept coming and coming. After a while, I couldn't stand it anymore. I opened my eyes and saw everything around me awash in a warm foggy light.

I watched as my hands effortlessly shattered the staff like clay on my uplifted left knee. I was shocked. I thought we were done, but before the intensity of the emotion passed away, I heard Kale from what seemed like a great distance: "Now the metal one, Airel; hold the power at your center and do not let it go! Concentrate!"

The silver metal staff appeared in my hands, blinding and almost transparent with light. I spun it over my head expertly before bending it into a horseshoe over my knee. I was smiling when I turned to see Kale standing in front of me. Something about him was impossible to take in — like looking at something in the dark. I could not see him if I looked directly at him. He held out a solid square chunk of steel — at least that's what it looked like. It was probably half an inch thick.

"Punch through it, Airel. Direct and focus the strength you feel and punch a hole right through it." I could hear his excitement, and I didn't want this feeling to fade, so I held it close. I drew back my right hand, made a fist, and punched from the tips of my toes to the back side of the steel plate. My fist hit the plate and I cringed as hot pain reverberated through my shoulder. "Owww!" I screamed.

The beautiful light slipped away from me, and I fell to the floor, exhausted. I sucked in the sweet, cool air and lay on my back, looking up at the wood rafters of the training room. Kale leaned over me with his sideways smile again.

"Don't worry, it's your first time. You show more control than I had expected." He turned away. "There is hope for you after all."

I was still out of breath. "Thanks. It was so wonderful! Nothing like anger."

He nodded and furrowed his brow. "Anger is a dangerous emotion; the hardest to control. You must learn to use the pure emotions first. Limit your use of the unclean emotions unless absolutely necessary. They are powerful, indeed… but raw power can destroy its user."

I sat up, glad to discover that I was catching my breath. "Can I die?"

"Yes, you can die, but it is difficult. You will heal from almost any wound. Your heart cannot survive if it is pierced. And again, how can the body survive if the head is severed from it?" He smirked at me. "So don't go losing your head. If you stay out of trouble, you will age at a very slow pace and live for a very long time."

I felt like he wasn't telling me the full story. "What do you mean a very long time? Like forever?" I didn't know what to think of this. I'd never even considered the question of living forever.

"Yes and no. You may live for eight thousand years and die of old age. Then again, you may only make it to eighteen, dying in a bombing, or drown… no one knows." His statement was loaded, but I had learned enough at this point to keep my tongue in check. If he didn't say something, he meant not to say it.

"You do age, but very slowly. When you're two hundred years old, you will look much the same as you do now." He began cleaning up the dojo, putting the equipment away.

I didn't know what to think. This changed everything. My friends, my family would all die, and many times over. I would be alone for so very long. Just when I thought I was going to like the idea of — well, immortality — the catch landed on top of me.

CHAPTER VI

1250 B.C. Arabia

THE HORDE CAMP WAS quiet. A few guards patrolled the perimeter carrying torches. It was easy for Kreios and Yamanu to creep past them into the main part of the camp, the fog moving in subtly with them. Kreios was waiting to feel the pull and drain of his power, but because of the Sword, he did not. He hoped Yamanu was doing fine as well.

His hope was not returned to him void; as Yamanu shaded them from enemy detection, he also read Kreios' worry and reassured him. *"I think El is for us this night, my friend."*

"I count over one thousand; does that sound right?" Yamanu agreed, and they moved on to the edge of the camp. *"We will sweep from one end to the other, killing as many as we can without drawing attention to ourselves. When we are discovered, we fly."* Kreios wanted to break the will of the horde and see if he could turn fear upon them for a change.

There was only one variable outside the scope of their control. If the demons that owned the men remained unmanifest — that is to say, lying dormant within the men's flesh — then all Kreios and Yamanu would need to do would be to kill the men; the demons would follow them to Hell. But if the demonic pairings of the Brotherhood *were* physically manifest, and resting alongside the men — or elsewhere — their task would become complicated.

Kreios tossed his invisible dagger from one hand to the other and stepped silently inside the nearest tent. It was large, composed of rotting hides tied to long wooden poles. Flies buzzed about, even though it was cold.

A cluster of men, six of them, slept snoring like wild beasts. This was the smallest component of the enemy army; a group of six that ate, slept and fought, side-by-side. Stench filled Kreios' nostrils, reeking of sweat, filth and the sweet tang of urine. The men were not clustered in pairs, which meant that the demonic controllers of the enemy men remained inside them, dormant.

Silently communicating with his partner, Kreios took the left side, and Yamanu took the right. They moved quickly, cutting throats like butchers. The men flopped and kicked, gasping as blood poured into their throats, simultaneously bled dry and drowning. The demons within made them convulse, making one last vain effort to break free and escape as they were dragged off to Hell, kicking and clawing.

The angels had their way in the camp for a good portion of the night, despoiling and irradiating the pestilence of death and judgment. With each kill, Kreios grew more and more hopeful. Yamanu did not make a sound through it all.

Kreios turned from slicing the neck of a short man, the last in a group of four in a smaller tent, when an enormous man entered, clad only in a loincloth. A tangled, matted mass of thick brown hair clung to him like a shrub to the face of a cliff. His enormous belly overhung his loincloth, the picture of sloth.

The two angels were invisible to him, but his eyes grew wide as he realized that his comrades lay dead at his feet, their blood soaking into the ground. One, the last one to die, twitched, his left hand jumping. The giant man screamed like a wild cat, sounding the alarm.

Kreios was quick, stabbing his dagger into his throat, cutting the cry short — but it was too late. The sound of voices and angry grunts rippled through the camp. Yamanu knocked the man aside, who was dead where he had stood, and sprang from the tent. *"Time to fly!"* Kreios followed him out. Into the middle of the row of tents flowed hundreds of half-naked men, swords raised.

Torches blazed, captains issued orders in gruff shouts, and the guards on the perimeter began running toward the noise. It was like being trapped inside an hourglass. Kreios bent his legs to take to the air, but something held him back. Yamanu looked to Kreios and he nodded: he, too, was unable to fly.

Within the gathering mass of enemy combatants, there came a thick, dirty sound — flesh tearing from flesh. The men twitched and jerked as if being rent in two. Black hooded demons with glowing eyes wrenched and twisted from the mouths of the men, as if their tongues were tombstones that guarded the wretched, stinking, open sepulchre in each one.

The dark forces came free. They drew black swords that dripped, wet. The earth beneath turned to boiling tar. Kreios felt distress in Yamanu. It had become too late now for them to flee. One course of action remained. Kreios erupted with a shout: "For the Sons of God and for Ke'elei!" He unsheathed the Sword of Light, blasting a shattering hole into the very heart of the night.

Kreios charged through the horde as an enraged bull. Men and demons flew in all directions, felled beneath the crush of his mighty arm. The fog vanished in an instant as Yamanu withdrew his shadow, drew his sword, and fought bravely in the light of the Sword.

As Kreios maneuvered his way through the onslaught, he kept a steady eye on the tent of the Seer. A cry came from his left side, and Kreios could feel the pain in Yamanu's thoughts. He turned to see a large demon standing over his friend, a curving black sword held high overhead, ready to deliver the final blow.

Instinctually, Kreios threw his Sword, cleaving the demon into a disemboweled wreck. The Sword of Light passed through its target as if it had been nothing, lodging firmly into the trunk of a tree on the edge of the enemy encampment. Yamanu stood; the horde army closed in. Kreios sprinted for it, alarmed at his rashness. Perhaps now that Yamanu was freed, they could work together to regain possession of the Sword.

He heard a distant but immediate voice. *"Take them alive. And you, Kreios: stand still where you are, or I shall remove this one's head from his body."* Kreios whirled and beheld the Seer in all his evil glory, standing with a small jagged sword to Yamanu's throat.

He froze.

Kreios thought about so many things in that instant that only one mattered, for all its importance: he knew that he might never see his little girl again.

The Seer burned a hole in him with malicious eyes. Was this Lucifer? — Kreios wondered — or just another piece on the game board? He locked his gaze onto the Seer's eyes once more, determined to see if he could recognize anything at all. He held there... until the creepings of fear consumed him. He was not going to escape this time.

Kreios turned toward the Sword that stuck out of the distant tree and noted that its light had been snuffed along with his last hope of deliverance.

Two enemy warriors grabbed his arms in the darkness and held fast with inhuman strength, their demonic counterparts nearby, faces hooded and black. It was like firelight flickering where their eyes might have been.

He was dragged toward the Seer's tents at the center of the camp, quite a distance away. He struggled, but it was no use. They took Yamanu somewhere else, which completed the crushing of Kreios' spirit. Each moment was more and more draining; Kreios could feel it. His breathing became ragged and harsh. He slumped to the ground, spent, and the two enemy warrior-slaves who had been carrying him, tossed him like a rag doll into the Seer's tent.

Kreios landed on his face, his body a crumpled rag. Bright white stars flashed before his eyes, and for an instant, he thought he was going to fall out of time. The Seer materialized in front of him, hiding under a hideous, dripping hood. The stench that followed him was almost unbearable; it smelled like a pile of corpses in the dark. *"I would like to thank you for bringing back my Sword. I have missed it so..."* He laughed, high and wheezing; a whine. Kreios shivered and closed his eyes.

Kreios felt Yamanu, wherever he was, would die soon if something didn't happen. He felt him fading from his grasp. He decided to address the evil presence in front of him. He raised his face from the dirt and said, "Why me?"

The Seer laughed once more, wheezing and rattling. *"You think I want you? I thought you a worthy foe... but you are a dumb sheep playing with wolves."* The laughter continued, more intense and disturbing. At last, the Seer regained a trifle of self-control. *"Are you growing weak, slave? Yes... yes, you are. Perhaps amendments can be made to prolong your stay with the sentient — though you're quite pitiful, aren't you? Yes, you are."*

Kreios was sucking air and filthy dirt into his lungs when a thought came to him, light and terrible. He tried to put it from his mind. *It has to be a lie!* This was a sick game the beast wanted to play; and if Kreios was to survive, he knew that he had to begin playing it.

The Seer began speaking unclean incantations in one of the lost tongues, binding and loosing. The end result, though his ears burned for hearing such unspeakable atrocities, was that the drain on the strength of Kreios was stopped. The Seer knelt to the ground and brought his face near. Kreios nearly vomited from the stench of it, thinking perhaps the Seer would try to speak a curse over him. Instead, he spit on him as he stood and took his leave, hissing, disappearing through the folds of the tent. Kreios sighed with relief and began to pray.

CHAPTER VII

Boise, Idaho. Present day.

STAN THE MAN GIGGLED like a little girl, cleared his throat, and adjusted his sunglasses. "I am a fan of your little plan, Stan the Man," he said cheerily. He repeated it again and again. It was a stupid little rhyme, but he needed it. He wanted it. He was the *man,* especially with his latest prize knocking around in the trunk. He had the world by the tail.

It had been enjoyable, his time with Lopez. The detective had been so very trusting, after all; it made the irony so very delicious. *He had actually thought that I would let him go after he told me what I wanted to know.* That boggled what was left of his mind.

"Let me out, you pervert!" The voice in the trunk was angry, sure. But there was fear there… and innocence, too. Stan loved innocence, loved to misuse it, turn it back on itself.

The detective had been last — the super-enjoyment of that moment would live on in infamy with Stan. He had become engorged, not just from bloodlust, but from his poetic desire to manipulate and target the innocent. He preferred to kill first those who did not deserve to die, preferably with someone watching — someone whose pain would drive them mad before he finally showed them to the edge of the grave and turned them loose within it.

Stan giggled again. *That's just what happened to Lopez!* He had been so *very* helpful. And Stan the Man was sated now. His mind was at peace, and all was right with the world. And all was *going* right as well. The address that he had taken from the detective, the Mexican *bandito,* was just as good as gold. He had made his score, all right.

The voice came from the trunk again. "You know what I am going to do when I get out of here…!" It thrashed in the trunk like a drowning kitten; all screeches and howls, nothing more. The louder she screamed, the better he felt. "I'll tell everyone; the police, my school, the news, my parents — they'll be very interested in a middle-aged pervert that kidnapped a high school student!"

Silence. She was thinking it over. Stan drove on.

"You think you're going to get away with this?! You're a fool!"

Stan was smug, and he smirked. He spoke calmly, soothingly. "Yell all you want, Kim. Where you're going, no one will ever hear you." He spoke in a sing-song voice. "Screaming will only get you a slower and much more painful death!" That shut her up. *Stupid kid.*

CHAPTER VIII

1250 B.C. Arabia

KREIOS WAS LAID OUT where he had landed, eyes closed. He entered deep into the part of his mind where he knew it lay in wait. It might help him — or it could take his soul — leaving him to wander, forever lost. He could still hear the Seer, the guards, other sounds from the outside world. But they were far away, as if they were in another time and place.

Heavy darkness filled his vision. He felt his life wavering. Kreios knew that if he did not do something decisive soon, he would die along with Yamanu. At the far end of the maddening blackness that reached for him, Kreios saw a glimmer flickering in his mind. He moved toward it. As he moved closer to the light, he knew what he would find there, before he actually saw it: the frameless door.

Kreios, like anyone, had seen many doors, had walked through them. He had been faced with them both at journey's end and at inception. He had been invited through them into warmth and fellowship, had banged on them in the cold of winter, and bellowed to be let in. Doors had stood in his path as open gateways to his furtherings, but doors had also stood in opposition to him on his pathway, as well. Some, he had never passed through.

What was beyond it? Was it good or evil, and why did he feel that whatever lurked behind it might kill him? He didn't know, and as he circled around it, he noticed that only one side of the door was pierced with a hand hold — the other side was smooth, unblemished.

Kreios could feel Yamanu feebly projecting his thoughts toward him. The time was short. He would have to risk his own life in order to save that of his friend — he would pass through the door. All of his options had been reduced to this choice.

The door changed color, as well as shape, from the corner of his mind's eye. Reaching out with a strong hand, Kreios grasped the handle and turned it. It yielded smoothly to his touch, swinging open of its own accord, as if there was a pressure difference, and he could feel the gentle rushing of wind passing by him from behind.

The slight breeze that pulled at his robes made him think of the long autumn weather he loved. Memories of his courtship with his beloved wife flowed over him in cool, refreshing rivulets. The smell of orange-red leaves, of pines dropping needles, filled the air. Kreios stood before the open door, breathing in deeply. A small smile took the right corner of his mouth.

Beyond, the sun was shining. The beauty of the place called aloud to him. Kreios peered in without stepping over the threshold. There, lying on the grass only a few steps beyond the open door, was a sword. He glanced back and took a tentative breath. He looked in again, knowing already: the sword lying naked on the grass was the Sword of Light. It reflected liquid sunlight off its blade.

There was no more time for wonder. He leapt forward, dove to the earth, and rolled to his feet with the Sword once again in his hand. His back to the door, he was becoming overwhelmed. His will to return diminished with each breath of pure, sweet, perfect atmosphere. The memory of his sweet Eriel called him back.

He turned, and in three powerful strides, made it to the threshold. He could hear voices calling to him, begging him to stay with promises of undying happiness, and it caused him to stumble. Kreios knew one of the voices in the sea of calling. It was his departed love. Tears streamed down his face as he felt her tugging on his heart, pleading for him to stay.

"NO!" Gripping the door edge, he pulled himself through and almost dropped the Sword. As soon as he crossed over, the door slammed shut powerfully, with finality.

He became aware of his limbs again, his heart beating, and he felt the soreness of his face. The sounds of his attackers came from afar, in the distance. He lay motionless, taking care not to betray the change within. He projected to Yamanu his plan, and could feel the life and power from the Sword fill his body once again.

He did not understand how he could go into his own mind, to a place he had seemed to have imagined, and retrieve the Sword of Light. Nevertheless, he was sure that when he opened his eyes, he would be holding it in his hands. He was ready to risk his life, the life of his friend, ultimately the life of his daughter, on that.

The smell of dirt and sweat filled his nostrils. He kept his eyes closed tightly, waiting for the right moment. He soaked it in, felt peace fill him with power. The strange thing to his mind was how he could feel the Sword at hand — and yet, as he flexed his fingers, it was not there. He wondered how long it could balance in between realities before it was lost completely.

Yamanu must not have been far, because as the Power filled Kreios, he could sense his friend and warrior brother rising up. The Shadower's gift was augmenting and he was storing it, damming up the potential, making ready for a massive flood. He and Kreios were walking a narrow edge as they coordinated the timing of their one and only opportunity to break with the doom that the Seer desired to visit upon them.

Kreios opened his eyes and jumped to his feet. He was the embodiment of the Angel of the LORD, that enigmatic identity, before whom, prophets would fall down and kings would tremble. His body was awash; waves of spiritual power rippled throughout. He did not look to see if the Sword of Light was, indeed, physically at hand, but he clenched his fist, and he could feel its grips, more real than ever. His only hope was that his faith was strong enough to *make it real.* He swung it high and held it there.

The tent exploded, ripped asunder and dissolved in light as demons and their pet slaves were thrown like toys. Simultaneously, Yamanu arose, swift and terrible, and though Kreios could feel him near enough, he could not locate him precisely. No matter: crippling cold and inky darkness descended upon the enemy camp with such ferocity that even the demons trembled.

Contrary to conflicting with the gifts of the Shadower, the Sword complemented and increased them, and heavy black fog exploded over and through the enemy camp, throwing the Seer's horde into wincing grief. Some of the men became mute with it and could not remember why they were there or what they were doing, wandering helplessly.

Kreios stood at the epicenter of what was left of the travelling residence of the one he hated. He looked for the Seer, vengeance ripping through his veins. The demonic horde army was scurrying every which way. There were screams of incomprehension, vague orders and countermands, as the enemy attempted to gather itself together out of confusion. He searched, urgently, kicking bodies out of his way, hacking through obstacles, stirring the wreckage, but the Seer was not there. Kreios filled his lungs and reared back, raising his voice to the heavens with a roaring battle cry, calling out the Agent of Darkness.

"Come out and fight me, Seer!" The cry did not produce the intended result. Kreios and Yamanu, now standing side-by-side in the wreckage of the Seer's tents, were faced not with a sporting contest with the disobedient deserter, but with a wave of filthy demonic infantry bearing down upon them.

Yamanu recovered his stolen sword from the ruined body of one of the guards, and with weapons raised at the ready, their eyes blazed with holy fire.

They became encircled by enemy forces, rallying against the battle cry that Kreios had delivered. The enemy could not perceive beyond the vagueness of the upside-down hope they had, where they were going — where they were being driven.

Kreios and Yamanu waited to spring the trap. The enemy drew nearer still, their pikes deployed horizontally, pointing inwardly at the angels. When they had drawn within a stride or two, Kreios launched himself from his defensive position, smacking aside enemy combatants' weapons with the flat of the Sword, which flowed fluidly back around to the attack, slicing with ease through muscle, bone and marrow.

Whirling angrily through their midst, Kreios downed enemy

after enemy with his Sword, arcing high, then low. He swung upward, slicing a demon from groin to chin, producing a horrible truncated shriek.

Yamanu moved independently but kept close by, hacking and slicing at demons and evil men. He waded through them, swinging his weapon like a harvester, growling and screaming maniacally only once — at the onset of battle. From then on, he was silent, concentrating, and all the more deadly.

The angels worked steadily through the advancing enemy army, simply cleaving its members in two, drenching themselves in acrid blood that stank and burned. Sparks of black and red flew from demon mouths.

Soon, the angels had run through the initial wave of attackers. They stood, panting gloriously, drenched in their own sweat comingled with the rank blood of the vanquished. They awaited the second onslaught, and as they did, Kreios closed his eyes and probed the invisible realms for his opponent.

As he searched, he beheld the tree into which the Sword had been lodged. The Sword was not there, which was absolutely perfect. Kreios held his hand high, and there, manifest before him, was his weapon: the Sword of Light. He clenched his hand around it, felt its heft, spun it deftly, and the blade hummed and buzzed through the air. Now victory was assured to him.

But it did not take long to assess the outcome of battle: the Seer had fled, had sensed the coming battle when Kreios had been filled with the holy fury that fueled him. The skirmish the angels had just endured was sacrificial; a diversion away from true intent — that the Seer, coward and dog, was rallying elsewhere, gathering more and more thousands to his side.

Yamanu sensed all of this as well, yet they hedged on the side of caution, standing at the ready in the midst of Yamanu's icy, pure black fog for quite some time, awaiting some new treachery. But it did not come.

At last, on toward the dawn, the angels relaxed their vigilance. Setting fire to the remains of the enemy camp, which burned vigorously, they advanced to the lake to bathe and to clean their

AIREL

weapons and clothing. The Sword of Light was clean already. The acid blood had dripped from it as it was being used — it was like mixing water and oil. Nothing could cling to it.

When they were clean, they came ashore and sat under a tree in the broadening sunshine of midmorning. Yamanu lit his pipe luxuriously and puffed at it, sending strongly-scented smoke curling into wreaths in his lap and spilling onto the ground, dissipating. "So," he concluded, "that went well…" His words fell off, and Kreios could see a grin on his face.

Kreios never did have much of a sense of humor. All he had on his mind was the mission, and how they would complete it. "We must kill the Seer or all is lost." He did not give much time to vain things, including the typical victory strut — no matter how small.

Discomfort moved in on the pair. At length, after Yamanu was finished with his pipe, Kreios gave a sigh. The enemy horde would be on guard from now on. Surprise attacks would require more… creativity. Kreios took to the air, hovering at treetop height, waiting for Yamanu to follow him.

"What now, Chief?" Yamanu asked as he joined him.

Kreios was stone-faced again. "We make camp. Then we find a way to persuade our brothers in Ke'elei to help us. I believe I know how to convince them."

CHAPTER IX

Eagle, Idaho. Present day.

GIDDY, UNNATURAL, OVERPOWERING, WONDERFUL joy! Only the act of watching someone squirm in their bonds with a look of raw hatred on their face could bring these lovely emotions to bear.

Stan glowered back at her. He grandly produced an enormous Cuban torpedo from his coat pocket, felt its moist firmness in his fingers and sniffed it. Snipping the end, he lit it with a match. Smoke billowed up in his face. Stan looked like a ghost in the pale light of the single bulb.

Stan stood in his own garage this time. It struck him that he didn't know how long it had been since he had been home. *Home?* His suit was tattered, his fingernails dirty. He couldn't remember his last shower. He didn't care. He had walked out of his old life — and his new one, far more exciting, meant he had to give up certain things to get what he wanted. He licked his lips.

Kim was bound to a wooden chair with duct tape. She had a strip plastered over her mouth, as well. Stan looked at her with mild interest. She didn't know where her best friend was, he knew that. But he had other plans for her. Bait. White female bait.

The peace that killing brought him could only last so long. He needed more; the bloodstone demanded more.

Kim was looking at him with big round eyes. No tears. No downcast obedience. Just hatred.

"We're friends, aren't we, Kim?" He stared at her with wild, bloodshot eyes. "Yes… yes, I can see that you agree. Good, good… I knew you, of all people, would understand." Stan let his words reverberate in the silence. Then, as if remembering something, he ran from the dimly lit garage into the house.

He returned with a video camera in his shaking hands. "You wanna be in a movie? I know you do. Every girl your age wants to be a movie star." His voice pitched higher in excitement as he set up a tripod. After a few tries, he successfully mounted the camera and turned it on.

"Say 'hi,' Kimmy."

Kim sat, frozen.

"Good… very good. Kim, you get to be… *helpful*. You get to help me find your little friend. Won't that be nice!"

Mental gears were grinding in his head, and he slipped into a stupor momentarily while everything got sorted. When he came out of it, he was addressing the audience in the camera. "My old friend!" Stan exclaimed in a joyful voice. "It *has* been too long. I've got a prize for you here, a token of my love, if you will." He descended into crazy laughter. "I'm —" he hacked out a further giggle, "I'm not asking for a lot. All I want is a little fair trade." He sang out his next words from behind the camera: "I — just want — to trade! This for that." He took another long draw on the torpedo as Kim squirmed in the chair.

"Or I could just kill her." He laughed again, but then he got serious and began to gesticulate. "If you decide not to give me the girl, I will kill this one and ship her piece-by-piece to her mother." He was twitching. "But no more secrets about the plan!" He lowered his voice to a whisper and came close to the camera, still behind it. *"You know where to find us, slave. You have twenty-four hours."*

Stan turned off the camera, picked it up, and walked out of the garage, turning off the single light as he went. Kim was alone in the dark. For the first time since she had been kidnapped, she let her guard down and allowed herself to cry. Tears dripped down over the duct tape gag and collected at the tip of her chin.

Stan listened, just on the other side of the door. He suppressed a giggle. He could skip down the sidewalk chasing after the ice cream man, he was so ridiculously happy.

He went to his study and began to scratch out a wretched note:

Dear fools,

Play this tape on the news tonight. If you do not, I will kill this poor helpless girl — and you will all be responsible. If you refuse to OBEY, *everyone will know you are the ones who killed her.*

Stan's the Man

CHAPTER X

Somewhere in the mountains of Idaho. Present day.

I WAS SITTING READING when an overpowering fear stole into me. Something was seriously wrong, but I couldn't put my finger on *what*. I closed my eyes and tried to think of what to do. Far in the back of my mind, I could hear *She* whispering, but I couldn't make out the words.

"Come on, what is it?" I was shaking now, cold and scared. But what was I scared of? Then it all hit me. The feeling, the smells and the sounds.

"KALE!" I screamed. A minute later Kale burst through the door.

"What? Are you okay?"

"Kim! She's in trouble. He has her." I could not place a name, but his face loomed in my mind. "We have to hurry; he's going to kill her."

The shadow of pain crossed his features. "I believe I know who has her. How do you know she is in danger — can you feel it?"

"Yeah! It's as if I'm right there with her. Please, we have to do something." I tried not to panic, but the feelings of fear and worry were powerful.

I gathered myself together a little and asked, "Who is he?"

"His name is Stanley Alexander. He is the reason I took you; or as I like to see it, rescued you. He was watching your house, stalking your family. If I had not stepped in to save you, you would be dead now."

My heart crashed. An icy wave washed over me and I gulped, trying to keep things in check. I wanted my voice to be small as I said, "Is he Michael's father?" I knew the answer.

"Yes. Stanley is in the Brotherhood."

I recalled what I read about them and shuddered.

"Okay, you have *got* to tell me what's going on! No more secrets, no more mysterious 'you shall know in time' crap. I need to know who you killed in that theater and what I am, *really*. Am I one of the Sons of God? Am I related to this Kreios? And why is all this happening to me?"

"I know you're confused, Airel."

"Please, we need to go save Kim, can't we leave now?"

"Airel, you have to know what you're getting into, there is more you must understand. May I start from the beginning?" Kale inhaled deeply as if to prepare, and I sat back down — I had stood up during my tirade and didn't remember having done so.

Kale began. "You are a descendant of Kreios. He is your grandfather. Great to the tenth, at least. You, as well as all of your ancestors on your father's side, all the way back to Kreios, have within your genetic code the gift of the abilities you're just beginning to see. These gifts lay dormant, however, until triggered directly — spiritually — by contact with one of the Brotherhood."

He stopped. I nodded for him to continue. "It's like a switch. It's off until you happen to meet the wrong person in the supermarket. Then you begin to manifest supernatural abilities. That's why you don't have any relatives with these abilities. They're only awakened in adolescence. Once you pass into adulthood, the chance is gone forever."

I thought back to my dad and everyone on his side of the family. I couldn't remember any weirdness happening with them.

"You are a Daughter of God. The last one was Eriel, in the line of Kreios. I know this is quite a lot to take in, but you need to understand: our time is running short." He paced the room.

"Tell me about that night in the theater." I wasn't completely sure I wanted to know, but my mind was driving me forward, hungry for resolution. I had to know or I would go crazy.

"The man I killed was one of the Brotherhood. He was latched onto you strongly. I had to kill him before he killed you. You see… they know when someone is turning. They can feel it; sense it. Once you started to get sick, it was like blood in the water." He paused and reflected. "There are laws of the land for a reason, Airel — but the letter of the law is dead. It's not always an act of evil to take a life. Especially in cases like this. These do not understand reason. They do not understand our ethics. They only understand violence. Death. Destruction."

I nodded again, knowing there was more; almost ready to beg for it.

He looked deeply into my eyes. "The Brotherhood is not just some criminal underground. *They* are the real half-breed. Part human and part demon. Every man has a demonic counterpart, a Brother. That is what makes them so very strong. Being in proximity to any member of the Brotherhood will drain you — they feed on your power; and if you engage them in a long battle, you will be defeated. You see why, now, as soon as I discovered he was one of the Brotherhood, I had to kill him quickly. No time to wait. Not even if the movie was interesting." He smiled, and the smile was true, honest.

"I understand. So you're like my advisor, my guardian?" I asked.

"Yes. I am a servant of El — God. We have been fighting the Brotherhood for thousands of years. I am here to train you, to help you. I would have liked it to have happened under better circumstances. But this was the best I could do. I have tried to give you every good gift since you fell into my hands."

"Now it seems that Mr. Alexander has found a way to draw you out, and I must leave the decision in your hands. If you want my counsel, it might be better to allow her to die than to give yourself up — you're more extraordinary than you realize. We cannot lose you, Airel."

I flushed with anger at the thought of ever abandoning my best friend in her hour of greatest need to the whim of some lunatic. After all, to what purpose had God gifted me so radically? So that I could lay it down when it was most needed? I didn't yell at Kale, though. I held my anger in check for once. "I don't care if you can't lose me. I can't lose Kim! I understand what you're saying, but I can't just stand aside and let Kim die because I'm 'so important.'" I took a few deep breaths.

Then a thought occurred to me that should have been obvious. "Will you help me?" For a moment, as silence filled the gap between us, I wondered if he would.

Then something else crossed my mind. "Kale, what's Michael's role in all of this?"

Kale stood like a statue, looking at me with clear hazel eyes. He did have beautiful eyes — sometimes. "Do you really want to know?"

He didn't need to say it. I knew what he was going to say, and yet I couldn't believe it. Michael loved me; he couldn't be in league with his father. "I don't believe it. He... he..."

"Loves you? No. He doesn't. He used you and now he's gone. He left last night. And I let him. If we do not confront Stan, he will come to us. Do you not see, Airel? Michael is part of the Brotherhood. He was sent to your school to get close to you, to find out if you were really what they thought you were. He is the reason why you were awakened — the day he came into your life was the day your old life ended."

CHAPTER XI

I COULD NOT FEEL my legs as they ran. My arms flailed at empty air. I was swimming in grief, running blindly, my vision blurred and became kaleidoscopic with my tears. This just couldn't be. I found myself in Michael's room and I landed on his bed, which was unmade and still carried his lovely scent. But he was gone.

I saw a note on his pillow and reached for it, stretching and swimming through the comforter. I couldn't even ask why. I looked at his handwriting and started to cry again. The words, the feelings. I had fallen for all of it. The love of my life crumbled to pieces, into meaninglessness. He had been planning on leading his demon father right to me — or maybe he had even planned on killing me himself. I wiped my tears away with the back of my hand and looked at the note, the only piece left to me; the only evidence of the love that never was.

Dearest Airel,
I am so sorry if I ever hurt you. I have to go, and by now you know why. If I could change who I am I would; but I'm in too deep. Run, Airel. Run! Please!
Michael

I burst into deep heavy sobs and fell back on his bed. My hands shook in anguish as I crumpled into a ball. How could he do this to me? Didn't he know how much I loved him? Didn't he know that I would die for him? But he had told me to run. Was I supposed to run from him? Like this was some sick game?

I couldn't think; it was all so wrong. I shivered in remembrance of his gunslinger eyes, those painfully blue eyes. The whole time I was falling in love with him, and he was encouraging me in it, he was thinking of how best to kill me. This was a game I had never played before, one I never wanted to learn, and one I was determined never to play again.

A hand touched my shoulder. Kale sat next to me. He pulled me into his arms. And in his arms, I found my solace, my thoughts appropriately turning to destruction and fury. But that fuel was quickly spent, burnt, and I fell into despair. All of it was accompanied by a maelstrom of tears. The man I had loved to hate was now my only friend. The man I once loved was now my worst enemy. My body shook, wracked in spasms of pure white grief. I sunk low. I reached out looking for *She*. *She* could have told me; *She* could have warned me, and none of this would have happened.

I screamed to her in Kale's arms, "Where are you?! Talk to me! Why?! Why didn't you tell me?!" I screamed until my voice gave out. *She* was there, and just as Kale had taken me in his arms, *She* did as well. Her warm wings covered me, and I let everything go. All my emotions, hurts and fears fell from my heart and soul, and I cried like I'd never cried before.

I was rebirthed in that moment. That's the only way to describe it. I had to be cut so deeply that I felt my own death was imminent.

I saw clearly that everything from my birth to the day I had been kidnapped had been planned — foreseen — and provided for. There were no accidents, no coincidences; right down to whomever I met and what school I went to. And then, from the expansive view of my lowest moment, I could rest in the fact that there was a purpose for everything.

I had never asked for it. But there I was. I didn't know what the end would hold for me, but I had to try. The pain of losing Michael threatened to crush me, but I understood now that I had never lost him. I had only lost who I thought he was. Simply knowing that I *could* love so deeply helped me begin to work past the pain, in a way. It would be a long, long journey, and I knew that my confrontation with Michael would be telling.

I didn't want to think about what could have been. It wasn't *Why*, but *What*. What was I supposed to learn, and would I become a better person for it or let the pain and loss consume me?

CHAPTER XII

1250 B.C. Arabia

THE SEER PEERED INTO the red light pulsing from the bloodstone, as if in the midst of it was the answer for which he was searching. He was filled to brimming with black rage. Within his tortured mind, the staccato ringing of his Brother, his master, resounded: *"Slave, fool! The Sword was within our power — and you failed to keep it!"*

The face of the Seer became old and withered again: "I have not failed us. It is you who failed to foresee what Kreios would do —" He doubled over in mid-sentence as scalding pain ripped through his body. He coughed and spat, and thick blood boiled on the ground. *"Where are our nine spies? Have they returned?"* He was writhing in agony until this new thought opened his eyes.

He did not know where they were. They should have been back with prisoners by now. The Seer struggled to his feet, the pain ceasing. He pulled his hood up, so as to hide the face of the almighty Seer from those who might want to see what he actually looked like. He walked out from his tent into the night air. It was disgustingly fresh, even in the midst of their encampment.

On a distant hilltop, a small fire was dancing, sending its light up through the night sky. He could hear singing — the two escaped prisoners mocked him. No fool would sit and sing around a fire in plain view so soon after escaping from the most powerful horde army in the world. *"And where are my nine?!"*

Yet there it was. No shouts. No sounds of battle. Only singing, and the flicker of a campfire, star-like from this distance. The Seer growled, turned, and grabbed his newest replacement captain of the guard. "Send twenty more Brothers with their hosts and bring me back the Sword — kill anyone in the enemy camp and bring me their heads. Tell them not to return empty-handed unless they wish to die." He spit out the words with so much hatred that some blood sprayed against the guard's face.

"Yes, master." He scurried off and spread the word. In the next moment, twenty of the Brotherhood stood before the Seer, ready for battle. He waved his hand toward the firelight. The group moved out and disappeared into the forest.

୧৭

Kreios and Yamanu had made camp for the night on the rise of a small open hillock, in perfect view of the enemy, and had lit a fire, not worrying if horde scouts saw them or not. The idea was to attract some attention and leave a trail. Besides, they were hungry. Yamanu stirred a stew made from fresh herbs, select roots, and a grouse he had killed. They talked and sang in thanks to El with loud voices as the stew simmered.

Kreios, a resounding baritone, and Yamanu, a tenor, sang songs they had used to sing as children before they had left paradise. Their voices rang out clear, strong, over the ravine, and reached all the way to the horde camp — making the patrols uneasy. Kreios knew there was power in the songs of angels.

Yamanu dipped his finger in the warm stew and a look of pure delight crossed his face as he touched it to his lips. "Wonderful, my friend. A few more moments, and we may even draw out the Seer with this fine stew." Yamanu breathed in the aroma and closed his eyes, savoring the smell. They began to sing again.

୧৭

The Brotherhood twenty made a clicking sound as their wings twitched. They found the nine that had been dispatched prior and joined them. The intelligence the nine had gathered confirmed that, indeed, there were only two angels. The horde contingent agreed to a multi-pronged attack on the escaped prisoners: they would surround them and destroy them.

Before long, the Seer could observe their black forms ascending the hillock against the far-off camp, and he rubbed his hands together in anticipation.

As he expected, the singing stopped. A flash of white light lit up the night sky. After a mere instant, all was silent once again. The sound that reached the Seer's ears made him tremble deeply: again, it was the sound of singing, only this time more intense.

He cursed and coughed, and in a fit of rage, began to attack the four guards that had been assigned to keep watch over his tent. All four were soon dead. Blood ran down the Seer's robe. He breathed raggedly and allowed black saliva to drop freely from his mouth. Kreios was mocking him — and for that, he would pay — dearly.

§

As Yamanu and Kreios sat cooking their quaint dinner over a warm fire, singing childhood songs with happy hearts, the twenty and the nine drew near, encircling them. Kreios and Yamanu could smell them over the stew, and the mingling of stench with savory scent turned their stomachs.

Kreios had only to draw the Sword. Nearby, hiding in the forest, were the one hundred Shadowers Yamanu had promised; the best and most gifted. With them stood another seventy angelic warriors who did not agree with the council's decision, and insisted on following Kreios and Yamanu into battle. As he drew the Sword and held it high, the skirmish began.

There were not enough members of the horde to go around, and the angels made quick work of them. It was over in an instant. The one hundred Shadowers and the seventy warriors then ascended to the campfire, and offered their allegiance to Kreios and Yamanu.

"Kreios, friend of El and brother to the host of heaven. We heard your beautiful singing. May we join you?"

§

The Seer flew into a rage and screamed for the entire army to assemble, to make ready for war. Fear and anger had a common friend: blindness. One can make grave mistakes under their influence. The Seer was now doing precisely that. The tools that he knew how to use so effectively against his enemies now turned against him, naturally.

❧

Kreios reached out in his thoughts to the gathered angelic army. He would exercise command in this way. He first searched them to determine if they were valorous warriors, intrepid and thirsty for victory. He found, to his delight, that all of them were indeed of solid stock, some even angry at the council's decision. All of them wanted to destroy the horde almost as much as he did.

The risk of opening up his own mind could not be helped, but he closed off as many irrelevant passageways as he could, in order to make his commands clear and concise. He did not want to clutter the field of battle with thoughts of Eriel, with his fear of losing the Sword.

He looked down into the ravine from the hill. It was writhing with the creeping light of enemy torches. The sound of tearing and ripping flesh broke the stillness: the horde had just doubled its size. The demons now stood apart from their hosts. They would act as lightning rods, filtering superhuman power to the men under their control. It was a wet and sickening noise, the reek of the stinking demons wafted up the hill. Kreios complained lightly that he would not get to enjoy Yamanu's fine grouse stew.

"Some other time, friend and Captain. Save your hunger for the roasting of demon flesh in the fires of Hell. Besides, I already ate most of it." Kreios nearly laughed at his comic friend. He only shook his head.

Then, in a loud, resonant, commanding voice that shook the very rock of the hills, he said, "Stand ready the Trumpeter! Prepare the attack!" The angelic host drew sword, bow, spear and axe, and the hills of the theatre of combat rang out with the sound of it. "Angels! Hear the sound of the voice of the Father, and do not fear the cleaving of flesh from bone! Fear not the dark enemy that hides in shadow and deception! Fear only the shame of ignominious and unworthy death!" Shouts and warrior grunts and growls showered down upon the enemy horde.

Then Kreios issued his first order: *"Demons first. The strength of the men will then fail and their desire to fight will crumble."*

300

The thought rang out in the minds of the angelic army, and the earth beneath them began to shake as the Sons of God assembled themselves in battle formation. *"You will join the battle in waves so that we can minimize the drain of the horde. Half of you will take to the air with your Shadowers, while the other half engages the enemy in combat with theirs. Keep your distance until my signal. I will lead the attack. Yamanu, you will lead the angelic host in the air. When the time is right — we merge and destroy the horde."*

"What about the Sword?" Yamanu queried Kreios privately. Everyone within a small radius of the Sword would not lose strength. *"Thirteen of the best fighters will stay with me throughout the battle. That many will stay strong if they stay close to the Sword."* The thirteen angels, singled out and now assembled, agreed to fight at Kreios' side, to the death. He was deeply touched by their willingness to sacrifice themselves. He knew that this was about more than Eriel, or even him and the Sword. These few men knew that. He wished he could grasp the hands of the angels in his little army to show his gratitude — but he could not.

Yamanu turned to Kreios, and they embraced like warriors. A billowing mass of fog appeared, obscuring the angelic army. Kreios unsheathed the mighty Sword.

CHAPTER XIII

Somewhere in the mountains of Idaho. Present day.

I OPENED MY EYES, though I didn't want to. Nothing this day could hold appealed to me. Kale and I left at four in the morning, and I passed out in the front seat. Crying was hard work, and my eyes felt crusty and swollen.

My head hurt so badly it felt like someone had used it as a drum, pounding on it all night. Rubbing the sleep from my eyes, I looked over at Kale. He turned and gave me a sort of half smile.

"You were talking in your sleep."

I groaned and pulled the visor down, and gasped at my reflection. In most cases, after a night of crying and sleeping in a car, I would be a hot mess. I was not, in fact. I looked fine — good, even. I ran my hands through my hair and sighed. "Sorry. I hope I didn't say anything embarrassing."

"No."

I tried to block the memory of Michael standing in the kitchen. He had turned toward me, looked me in the eyes, and lied, straight-faced. To think that I almost kissed him. I had wanted to kiss him. Even now, I still wanted simply to be with him — that was the worst part — I still loved him. How could he have done this to me? And how could I still love him?

"You okay?" Kale asked. He was looking at me with a concerned expression on his face.

"Yeah. Just having flashbacks." I wiped a tear that had slipped past my defenses and smiled as best I could. I wasn't okay; not even close. I wanted to run and curl up to die alone. *But I might not die. I might have to live for thousands of years.* It felt like I stood before the yawning chasm of eternity, and it was fast filling up with misery. A change of subject: "How long was I out?"

"About an hour. We're still two hours out. I did some digging and found out that Stanley Alexander is a defense attorney. He's widowed; his wife died of cancer, according to her medical records."

"How did you get all this information?"

"I have a source." He let a smirk cross half his face.

"A source?" It was clear that he was not going to let me in on this secret.

"I think I know where he will be. He has two homes. One of them, he rents out, but it's been vacant for the last six months." Kale took a sip of his coffee. "No one knows what he's done yet, but that won't last long. People he works with, friends, neighbors, will have seen that video on the news and recognized his voice, put two and two together and called it in. He hasn't been seen at work in quite a while."

"What video?"

"He sent a video to the newspapers and TV stations. It was aired last night."

I had a sick feeling in the pit of my stomach. "Kim?"

"Yes, she was on it. Which proves that she's alive. But we need to find her before anyone else. If the police show up, she's as good as dead."

"It's like he wants to be caught." I wondered if the video was an attempt to flush us out.

"Maybe he does. If he's as far along as I think he is, God help the police if they try to arrest him."

I wondered what he was talking about. "What do you mean? How are we going to get Kim back?"

"I think he's the Seer. You would have read about him in the book I gave you." I nodded. But I wondered how someone who had lived thousands of years ago could still be alive.

"The Seer is a spirit. He can be killed, but only by one of the Sons of God. We must be careful how we go about our business,

Airel. If we kill Stan and leave the Seer without a host, he will be driven into the bloodstone." Kale looked at me with a raised eyebrow. "Do you know what that is?"

I shook my head. It was too much to take in. If I had read something about it, I couldn't remember it now.

"The stone was stolen from Paradise when the Sons of God fell. It is a pure union of diamond and onyx that glows red in the presence of the spirit of the Seer on earth. It does not belong here in the earthly realm. It is a talisman that allows him unnatural power, power that he continually consumes via the bridge enabled by the bloodstone, between the spirit realm and this one. He uses this power to try to subjugate any created thing he desires to control. He is a demon prince from the substructures of Hell; some believe he may even be Lucifer himself — it is difficult to discern these things. The spirit of the Seer is confined to the immediate vicinity of the red bloodstone. If his host is killed, the Seer will be recaptured by the bloodstone until he finds someone else to enter."

"So Stan invited this Seer to possess him?" I couldn't believe someone would be willing to do that.

"He can be very convincing. He will say anything, as I said: you name it, he will promise it. A person who's drunk or high will let him in without even realizing it. All the defenses of the mind, the gateway to the spirit, are nullified and the doors stand open wide."

I shuddered. *She* fluttered in my mind, as if asking for my attention. "What about me? I'm not possessed, am I? I hear this voice in my head — like my conscience, but almost audible to me. I call her *She*."

Kale's eyes narrowed. "I have one, too. *She,* as you call her, is your inner man. Or woman. I keep forgetting that these days, man means *a* man, not *the race of men.*" He gave me another smile, and I was struck by it — there was something in it that I couldn't quite figure out. It felt warm.

"When you were awakened, your inner *woman,* your angelic spirit, was awakened in you at the same time. It's like a sixth sense, only separately cognitive. *She* is there to help you and protect you. In battle, for example, *She* will warn you in advance of any threat to your life."

"So, it's a good thing." I could feel her sitting back down and fluttering her wings, folding them under her. They sounded like the pages of a book sometimes, like the fluttering of a bird at other times. It was so bizarre how I could visualize what she looked like, and simultaneously be unable to see her.

"Yes. It's a very good thing, if you listen to her. In time, she will blend with and complement all of your other senses. It will be simple instinct to trust her and respond to her leading. She also heightens your other natural senses. You may have noticed this already."

Those were the times when I lost my breakfast. I figured that I started to get sick the day Michael came to school. As I thought back, I recalled that every time I got sick, Michael was close by. Then the last time, at Kale's house, when I passed out for eight days, must have been an overload. Maybe one of the reasons I had always gotten sick around Michael was because *She* was amplifying my sense of smell, and the scent of the Brotherhood, Stanley, was probably all over Michael. "So why did I get so sick?"

"When you began to change, your body was rejecting your angelic side; it makes you sick. Being close to someone in the Brotherhood will start the process — Michael's job is to find our kind — he can feel when someone is turning and feeds off the power. You, however, somehow resist him, and his drain on you is not as strong as it should be."

"Sometimes I would get sick, and a second later, he would be there, but other times I was fine."

"I think when you were out for eight days, that was your system adjusting, allowing your angelic side to take over. I'm not sure if this will make it better or worse for you around one of the Brotherhood."

"So, what do we do now?"

"Airel, if I had my way, you would not be here and I would go get Kim by myself. However, I don't think you will listen or obey me on that particular point, so we'll go in as a team. I will provide the diversion, and you will keep yourself alive. Your job is simple:

get Kim out. I will deal with Stan."

"But you could be killed! He has super-human abilities; you said so yourself."

"I know. This is not about me, though. All you need to know today is what I have already told you." His eyes softened to a washed out blue-hazel, and his voice flowed freely with compassion. "Obey me." I flushed at being talked at like a child, and shook my head. I didn't want Kale to put himself in harm's way, but I couldn't stand by and let that monster kill Kim either.

"No, I'll listen. Just tell me what to do."

Kale nodded, obviously pleased.

I looked over my shoulder to the two seats and the straps and tie-downs. My stomach turned.

Kale noticed and gave me a smile in excuse. "I had no choice, Airel. You understand I was never going to hurt you."

I nodded. "I know; it's just that it seems like *forever* ago. My family must be beside themselves. What am I gonna do about them?"

"We can talk about that later."

Great. More mysteries.

I sighed and thought about what my parents must be going through. I bet the police were involved by now. I could see my mom sitting on my bed looking at a picture of me and crying. God only knew what Dad was doing. I needed Mom, especially now.

My whole world was being torn apart, but I didn't have the luxury to dwell on the past. *"Past is perfect; what's done is done. You must leave it where it is and move on today. Only learn."* I wanted nothing more than to go home and cry on Mom's shoulder, lie in bed for the next month, and bathe in my sorrows.

I started to recognize landmarks and saw a sign: *Now Leaving the Sawtooth Wilderness Area.* My stomach was tight, balled up, and butterflies flipped and flopped inside it.

I had wanted to bring some sort of weapon: a gun or a sword, but Kale refused. "You will be going after Kim, not Stan. Remember that. You should have no use for a gun or any other weapon." I protested, but it fell on deaf ears. I thought *I* was stubborn, but compared to Kale, I didn't stand a chance.

He armed himself with a small black dagger that ended with a wicked curve at its tip. He put in its sheath on his belt. He was still wearing his white robes, and he looked positively out of place behind the wheel. "This is comfortable," he said, catching my disapproving glance. I guessed men were all the same; it didn't matter how they looked as long as they were comfortable. *Fashion? What's that?*

I was nervous. I didn't know what to expect. I checked in with my little winged friend and she sent me a wave of comfort, for which I was grateful, and I tried to remember to breathe. I focused on Kim, thought of her face in my mind, and recounted all the fun we had together. She was like a sister to me, my best friend.

"Some things to remember," Kale interrupted my reverie. "If you fight Stan, you will lose. Most likely he will kill you. If I fail, you must get Kim out of there and hope that Michael did not tell his father where my home is. Do not try to fight. You have not been trained, and you will lose. Do you understand?" Kale's face was somber and I could tell that he was not joking. *Not that he ever would.*

"Yeah, but…"

"Promise me. Run. Do not fight." I thought in my heart that I could beat him, but Kale was not backing down. I promised.

Kale looked at me.

Again, there was that old feeling, the same one I felt when I first saw Michael in the coffee shop: Destiny.

PART FOUR

REVELATION

CHAPTER I

Eagle, Idaho. Present day.

I SIGHED LOUDLY AND looked out the window. We had pulled in four houses down from where Stanley Alexander lived. Maple trees looked like they were on fire in a spray of yellow, orange and red — with only a memory of green from the summer. Pines stood dark green against gray skies, and it felt as if I was on the edge of something.

I climbed down out of the Yukon and shut the door as quietly as possible. The neighborhood seemed empty. Fittingly, there were no signs of the police — they were busy cruising the blue collar areas. There wasn't even an Eagle soccer mom running behind a stroller. It was lifeless and foreboding. Kale pointed with a subtle jerk of his head up the road. I followed him along the little bike path.

The Alexander residence was all stucco and wrought iron. Fake Italian, like those wretched casinos in Vegas — my least favorite town in the whole wide world, because literally *everything* is fake. This house seemed to have a similar scent. I wasn't sure if *She* was helping me or not, but I smelled stench. Cigarettes — no, stale cigar smoke. I searched for Michael's scent.

We approached the house. A three car garage was attached to the right side, and a black BMW sat in the driveway, looking like it hadn't been washed in quite a while. It was just like a horror movie, when the camera shows something completely normal and innocent, but the mind processes all of it in a different context. It chilled me; the wind gusted through a drift of leaves, and *She* stood up, taking it all in just as I was.

What do you see? I asked.

"Be careful; he's sleeping, but not like you think."

I could feel a warm augmentation filling my veins with power. My vision became much clearer, richer. Colors seemed bolder, sounds louder, and I could even hear Kale's heart beat through his silly white Moses robes. *I guess it works… Halloween is right around the corner.* I reached out with my mind to try to read his thoughts. I didn't know if it would work, but I had to try. All I got was static; nothing worth anything, so I gave up.

I followed Kale to the back of the house. Everything was wide open in this ritzy neighborhood. No fences or anything between houses. The grass was deep green, having come back from the oppressive heat of summer, and smelled like it had just been cut. I filled my lungs with it. Kale elbowed me to pay attention to what I was doing. I apologized with my eyes.

Before I knew it, Kale had drawn his sword-dagger thing. We entered through a sliding door into the kitchen of Stan's house. No one sat eating lunch; no one had washed any dishes in quite a long time. Something was rotting in the sink. Probably in the trash can, too. Kale motioned for me to go to the garage while he stood guard. I knew, even without the benefit of reading his mind, that he preferred to avoid a confrontation with the Seer if we could.

I crept silently toward the white door that I assumed led to the garage. It was unlocked. When I opened it, I saw Kim's back, her head slumped over on her chest, her body still taped to the chair. My heart failed me. *Too late!* She was limp. *Dead.*

◈

Upstairs, Stanley Alexander was sleeping. As he lay there, the creature within poked, prodded, and slid free of his body like excrement. It was not the biggest demon by any means, but covetous ruthlessness and the will to act where others would not dare, gave him rank and title. None knew his true identity.

He was called by many names, 'the Seer' one of them, and that because of the bloodstone. His wings were long, black and ragged, and hung around his twisted body like tattered sails on a forgotten ship. He pulled the left one free of the host and noticed for the ten thousandth time that it had been clipped. The memory of how he had lost part of it made him seethe with anger.

He stood over eight feet tall when hunched over. His eyes were dark red and glowing. A black fume fell constantly from his mouth. Two horns curved downward from the top of his skull and protected his face from the edge of the sword. The thin tail twitched and bobbed like that of an excited dog. The tip was barbed with a mace-like hook. Thorny scales ran up the length of his back, ending at his short neck.

The Seer took the red stone from the sleeping, weak husk of a man and held it. He looked into it and frowned with thin black lips. He sneered, and yellow and brown rotten teeth exposed themselves in a menacing grin.

"You have come at last, my daughter. Now I claim and take what is rightfully mine." The voice was guttural. The stone throbbed, humming, and he watched through it as Airel opened the door to the garage, finding her best friend. The gasp that escaped her mouth made him smile, revealing crooked and gnarled teeth as he crossed his arms and embraced himself, shivering with excitement.

Then the stone showed him something else in the house — Airel's guardian companion. The Seer howled in a shriek of delight and fury. Thick smoke vomited out from his mouth as he crouched, then he threw back his massive head and roared, *"You return to me! My old friend — Kreios! KREIOS!"*

The cry of the beast woke Stanley from the sleep of the dead. The house shook from footing to rafter. Dust rained down on the Seer, and Stan sat up in utter horror — he had never quite gotten used to it — as he saw what was standing next to his bed. Before he could gather the breath to scream, the Seer dove at him, grabbed his frightened face, and looked into his bloodshot eyes.

"Look at me, you sniveling slob. Look into my eyes. You will bring Airel to me; do not kill her, do you understand?"

"Do not kill her; yes master, I understand." Stan's voice was low and droned on. He was a man who had lost his soul and replaced it with nothing but darkness. He stood up and clawed at the open sores that refused to heal, covering his body from head to foot.

He was already dead; his body was trying to tell him so, but he would not believe it. As his body decayed and rotted, he still moved, he continued among the sentient, he was autonomous — this was evidence enough of his power, at least to him — which made him useful enough for the demon who pulled his strings. The Seer unfurled his ragged wings, enclosing his slave within them. A boiling pool of blackness collected at his clawed feet.

Stan smiled as he felt his strength returning. He felt unstoppable once more. *Stan is the man* — true master of the Brotherhood. It was his destiny to destroy Airel before she could discover anything more of her true identity. Michael had done a *wonderful* job. Stan swelled with fatherly pride at the thought of his only son. He would move quickly through the ranks, indeed.

The Seer placed the bloodstone into Stan's hand. Stan replaced it around his neck. He felt like he was naked without it. Of course, he had plans of his own that did not involve the Seer. He would keep it. With it, he could do anything, go anywhere, and rise to be the most powerful being in the world.

Slave would be master.

The demon withdrew the shroud of his iniquitous wings, discharging Stan to his work, newly empowered by the unnatural. Stan fished out an ancient dagger from under the bed. He had stolen it; from where, he could no longer remember. These days, he could not remember much — his memories had been mixed and adulterated with those of a thousand hosts before him. In the final analysis, he had no idea who he was anymore. But it didn't matter. Stan was the *new* Seer, *de facto,* and soon he wouldn't need the wretched lizard to call the plays, to direct and control the power. *Soon…*

‑‑‑

I stood in the doorway to the garage frozen in horror — my best friend, dead. I felt like throwing up but held it down. *How could…?* This was all wrong; this kind of thing was not supposed to happen. Reverberating through my bones, calling me back from the nightmare, I heard an unearthly scream that chilled me absolutely — and more than the sight of Kim's lifeless body.

"Kreios? KREIOS!"

Images superimposed themselves on top of each other, of the man I was growing to love in the Book, and of the man named Kale who had abducted me and kept me prisoner. His marble skin, blond-almost-white hair, and his odd ways — he seemed so old, but at the same time looked so young. It all crashed into me with violence, stopping me.

I looked at my hand on the door jamb, but my mind saw beyond the physical. What I saw... angels, half-breed offspring, demons, Ke'elei, an immortal race, Kreios, Kale, Airel. *Could it be? Could he still be alive?* Why had the Book withheld that part of its story from me? Kreios was not merely one of the Sons of God; he was an Angel, descended from heaven itself. He would live forever, unless a demon like the Seer killed him, which even then was not an easy task. Kreios was a fearless warrior, with more skill in battle than I could dream of.

"KREIOS!" The roar grew louder, and I would have stood there dumbly, frozen, if Kreios himself hadn't yelled at me.

"Airel! Move! Get Kim out the back!" His voice had changed, ripping through me with the essence of deadly command. It had real physical weight to it.

My head cleared instantly, and I bolted into the darkness of the garage. To my utter disbelief, Kim was moving. Her head came up slowly, and she opened her eyes as I fell on my knees at her feet. Blue and purple bruises covered her face, masked partially by the gag of duct tape. Her left eye was swollen shut, yet she managed a smile.

"Oh, Kim! I'm so sorry. Oh baby, hang on!" I tore the tape from her mouth, and before I knew what I was thinking, I had torn through all that bound her to the chair, including part of the chair itself. I let my instincts take over, and shreds of tape littered the garage floor, along with whole chunks of chair.

Kim's head lolled and she opened her eyes in a groggy slow fluttering. I felt sick to my stomach.

"Oh how I missed you, Kim." She stood on very shaky legs, and I could tell she was not strong enough to run with me back to the SUV. The sound of a fight erupted from upstairs in the house, and I heard a scream of pain. The sound was like fingernails on a chalkboard. I cringed and took my bearings, looking around for a way out.

"Look," I said in a whisper. "We've got to get out of here! I'll explain later; so just go with it, okay?" Kim looked at me with raised eyebrows; she had no idea what I was talking about.

I grabbed her and threw her over my right shoulder, like firemen carry fire victims. Leading with my left side, I lowered my shoulder, and like the would-be hero, lunged at the garage door, punching through it like paper. Unlike the would-be hero, I tripped on one of the steel spars that reinforced the door and lost everything. Kim and I tumbled out like rag dolls. *Oops.* I scrambled to my feet and moved toward Kim — we had to get out of there before we were discovered.

Standing in the driveway like a bent-over zombie was what I could only imagine was Michael's father, Stan. He was grasping a large curved black knife and had a wicked smile on his face.

"Going somewhere, Airel?" Black goo dripped from his mouth. "I've been looking forward to meeting you. I must admit… I thought you would be taller." He laughed and began choking and coughing. I knew I was out of time. I had to do something, so I rushed him, again lowering my shoulder like a battering ram.

Stan was doubled over with both hands on his knees, spitting out blood or something worse as I made contact. The blow landed between his neck and collarbone. I felt a *crack* sound as something inside him broke, dully. That sound filled me with something that had to have come from all the warriors in the line of my family — satisfaction.

The next thing I saw was his body wildly flying, landing on and skidding across the lawn across the street. He was up and on his feet so fast that I wondered if he was as old and broken as he appeared.

I didn't have any time to waste. I turned, scooped Kim up

again, and ran to the SUV. Everything was just a blur of colors, but I could still see everything in crisp detail. Kim was screaming, but I tuned her out. I had dumped her onto the passenger seat and slid myself behind the wheel before Stan knew what was happening.

Like the voice of *She*, I heard the command ringing in my mind — but it was decidedly not *She*. *"Go, Airel; take Kim and go! I'll meet you at the house — can you find your way back?"*

I think so.

"Be careful."

I turned the keys in the ignition and the engine roared to life. Kim had buckled up and was looking at me with mouth wide open. I just looked at her, dropped the shifter into drive, and floored it. The rear tires lit up. I aggressively yanked the wheel left, and executed a totally pro-style burnout u-turn. We were *outta* there.

I scanned the rearview mirror to see Stan standing like a drunk and screaming curses. I smiled, and somehow his outrage made me happy. *Next time, Stan... Next time.*

CHAPTER II

WE GOT ON THE freeway. I didn't begin to relax until after we were headed out of town and on our way to Sun Valley. I didn't hear a single thing more from Kreios. I was still in awe and speechless about that whole thing.

The road was long and wide open out there, just desert. We flew on at a comfortable 85, ten over the limit, which was as far as I wanted to push it. I was in my own world. I didn't look at Kim the whole time, and it wasn't until we had stopped for gas outside of Mountain Home, an Air Force base town, that an opportunity presented itself.

She had just come back from a much-deserved break in the powder room while I searched the Yukon for a way to buy gas. Her voice was slow and shaky — not at all like her. "Are you going to talk to me?" She let the question fall to the ground, flat.

"Are you okay?"

"Fine, nothing's broken. Now talk to me."

I paused. "Kim... I can tell you some, but not all. It's just too much to take in all at once." I heard in my voice the *exact* same tone and attitude that Kale — Kreios — had used on me, and it burned my pride fiercely. I tried for the save: "Anyway, some things I just have to show you."

She didn't look like she was buying it.

I wondered how much I could tell her — would she reject me as a friend now that I was a proven freak? Not all human? I considered it. I didn't think she would, but the thought of how important it was to keep this a secret; and with Kim's big mouth,

319

everything was in play. Never mind my feelings. Could I trust her to keep this under wraps?

"Airel, I won't tell anyone. I swear on my life!"

What?! You're reading minds, too, now? I sighed, swiped a card in the reader that I had found in the console, and started the pump. "The only way to tell you is to start from the beginning. Do you remember when I started getting sick?"

"Yeah, I asked if you were preggers." She laughed.

This girl is resilient. "Classic…"

The rest poured out over the next few hours as we drove on. I told her everything — everything I knew up to that point.

I told her about the Book and the way it kept changing, like how I could read a story one day, and the next, a new one would be in its place. I wanted to write in it so badly that a few times I almost had. I didn't know what that might do, however, and I wasn't sure if the book would work that way.

Kim had put her hand to her mouth, shaking her head in protest. The way she received it was all amazement and joy, just like a child. She was more excited than I was, and wanted to see for herself how I could heal.

The cigarette lighter and my sizzling hand cured her of that particular curiosity, and she clapped in glee when my hand returned to its fair, milky color. She had already noticed my clear complexion, as well as the life in my hair. I wondered if my metamorphosis from what I *was* to what I was *becoming* would end soon, or if it would be ongoing. *For how long?*

It was difficult when I got to the point in the story where Michael's total betrayal was realized. She had trouble believing that part. "Airel, for what it's worth, I think he really did have feelings for you. Otherwise, why would he leave you that note? If you were just a job, a mission… then he would have just gone, without a second look."

"Yeah, well… I don't know how to trust anymore." The truth was that I was vulnerable, and it wouldn't take much either way.

"I just want to hate him, to forget I ever met him. Is this pain worth the love I have for him, to know it was all a lie?" My heart was so broken, and with each memory, I felt like it was just breaking all over again.

Why couldn't I get past this? All I wanted was to move on and be done — it hurt far too much, and I couldn't make sense of it. I wanted him to disappear completely, as completely as he had betrayed me.

"I don't know Airel, it just doesn't make sense."

"Why did he do it, Kim?" I was having trouble seeing the road. "Why did he try so hard? Why did he let me fall in love with him, knowing the whole time that he was baiting me into a trap? Why not at least just be a friend, and get close that way; why lead me on like this? Does he hate me that much?"

Kim didn't have any answers, and neither did I.

CHAPTER III

1250 B.C. Arabia

"HOLD UNTIL I MAKE contact." Kreios stood alone, the Shadowers' gift cutting a divot around his position, leaving him exposed and fully visible to the enemy on the moonlit little hill. *"I want them to believe they are fighting only one."*

The clanking, ripping sounds of the demonic army came through the night to the angels, much clearer now as the horde began to emerge from the forest in a swarm, torches held high.

This was the kind of day for which he had been made. Kreios felt the leeching pull of the horde begin to try to attack him, but the Sword deflected it, even adding to his reserve. *"Stand ready the trumpet..."*

The army ascended the hill, weapons and teeth bared.

Kreios stood still, resolute.

Like the point of a spear, the first wave of the horde attack converged on Kreios, assuming he was ready to martyr himself, and that the fight would be over before it had started. Wicked men and demons ran on top of each other and killed one another in order to be the first to reach Kreios and snuff his life.

"Trumpeter, sound the attack." Kreios held up the Sword, and Glory sprang forth from it in long spiraling webs of light. The enemy army threw up their hands to cover their eyes, but it was too late. Blindness overcame them and they fell, crying out in agony, crashing to the earth, clawing at their eyes. Their coming damnation was revealed to them by the light of the Sword; the

trumpet resounded, and the Shadowers covered Kreios. The first angelic wave charged immediately, killing two or three of the cowering horde with each strike of the blade, axe and mace.

Kreios moved lightly, wading through the horde, parrying, stabbing, cutting. The thirteen at Kreios' side were unmatched. One of them, Veridon, at least a head above the rest, wielded the mace and took three or four of the enemy with each swing. The demons attacked each other in panic as they tried to meet with their invisible enemy.

A monstrous man worked his way toward Kreios, keying on the body parts that were being thrown outward from where he stood. A massive club was in his hands, dripping with blood. Spikes protruded from its working surface. Kreios leaped into the air, Sword held high, and brought it down squarely on the man's crown, splitting his massive head in two. A fountain of black blood rushed forth from the man's wound as he fell to the earth, flopping like a headless fish. Kreios saw that this hordes man was still unmanifest, his Brother still hiding within him. *"Some have not yet divided their forms!"* The message was received, and the angelic army engaged the deception.

The Seer hovered above the trees, robes billowing wickedly, chanting in ancient tongue a powerful spell. With upraised hands, he finished the incantation and red flame sprung up from his feet, licking at his body to a point well above his head, removing his human form from view, and casting an eerie light on the battlefield. The incantation created a massive shroud over the field of battle.

Slowly, the gift of the Shadowers began to recede. The angelic army on the ground was no longer hidden, the protective shadow pierced by the power of the Seer's diabolical shroud. The angelic army at Kreios' side came into full view of the enemy. The tide on the battlefield turned, and Kreios saw his warriors begin to fall quickly before the demonic horde.

Kreios could feel his anger rise; he could sense each one of his men as they died, could hear them cry out in his mind. *How could the Seer have known of our Shadowers?* He did not allow himself to think about the treachery of the council now.

He searched through the ether for the mind of Yamanu. *"You must engage your troops now, Yamanu. We fight to the death from here on."* The angelic second wave moved in thunderously, and there was the sound in the treetops of a great army. Kreios breathed more freely as fresh troops landed at his side, and the spent troops retreated to the safety of Yamanu's shadow in the air. The angels were much stronger than the Brotherhood, but the advantage was short-lived. If not for the Sword, all would be lost.

Kreios took stock again. The thirteen at his side were still strong. They did not feel the drain. Veridon, to his right, stood face-to-face with four hordes men, bleeding them in a single stroke, hewing them where they stood. Kreios dodged an enemy stab from his left, spun fluidly, brought the Sword back around, and took the fool's head off.

The angels on the ground, refreshed, roared lustily and charged into battle.

The troops now moved like lightning, but Kreios could feel the death of yet another number of angels from behind him.

His hand was forced. *"Assemble, Army of El! Rally to my position!* — TO ME!"* His voice rang out into the red night. An answering roar came from the horde and they charged forward.

Down from the heavens came Yamanu's contingent, barely refreshed. Gladly, they came back to the restoring source of the Sword; a veritable link to heaven itself. Kreios quickly counted heads and estimated that their numbers had been cut down by nearly one hundred.

Together, the angelic army made progress. Though they made an easy target being grouped in a single unit, the problem for the horde was being able to get at them — the angels were very strong in the vicinity of the Sword.

Attacks were repelled with ferocity, and the horde army lost hundreds as they threw themselves against the bulwarks of the angelic formation. It threw them into confusion for some time. Kreios exploited the situation by retreating to the high ground, forcing the horde to come and get them by climbing up the little open hill after them. It seemed the advantage in battle was swinging back to him, and he considered his options as he lopped off yet another enemy head.

The horde flowed up the side of the small hill like water, and the Seer hovered over the mass of men and demons like a protective father. They kept coming and coming; as if in the forest they were breeding and multiplying. Kreios was amazed by their numbers. He only wanted to get to the Seer and finish him, but that was not yet an option.

Blood and gore covered the glowing angels as they fought in the open, exposed, the Shadowers unable to overcome the Seer's powerful incantation of black magic. The horde then regrouped at the rear of their formation, their strategy changing.

The demons reentered their hosts, the possessed men grew wild, and their eyes blazed: together they were stronger. This new concentration of force was then sent against the angelic army and smashed against it with great force. Kreios felt the pain of many more of his army fall in that moment. They tried to hold the horde at bay, but their defenses were failing and they were weakening. He counted again. He was down to only around twenty. Of the thirteen that had fought by his side, only three remained, including Veridon. To his great joy, Yamanu was still among the living.

Kreios' mind was invaded with the thought of death and walking through the door. Even now it called to him.

He paused for an instant as the battle continued to rage around him. Weapons clashed; oaths and curses were flying.

He inverted his Sword and rested the tip of the blade on the ground, kneeling, bowing his head, resting it on the pommel at the opposite end in prayer. He closed his eyes as warmth and power from the Sword radiated throughout his body. He ran down the corridors of his mind to the Door.

He could see it with his eyes closed. It was standing there, solitary, precisely how he felt: alone, exposed. Time was relentlessly flowing past him as he paused between realities, and he knew that the longer he tarried, the more dangerous the situation in battle became for all of them. He ran to the door and opened it. Beyond, was a dark hole, nothing visible on the other side.

He stepped through, knowing that he had been driven to the ends of his choices, that this was the last one remaining to him. It felt like he was falling, but the darkness was so thick it was impossible to tell. He reached out into the dark void in his mind. Suddenly, it was there, not in fields of grass, but in the dark this time, and invisible: The Sword of Light. His eyes flew open, and he snapped back to his body, knowing what must be done.

Standing, he took the Sword in his hands. With a great battle cry, he launched himself upward, the Sword held above him, pointing menacingly at the shroud concocted by the Seer. He rocketed straight up into the heavens on a trail of pure white fire, and lodged the Sword deeply into the shroud itself, sinking it all the way to the hilt. It had pierced the Seer's wicked spell.

Cracks appeared in the firmament, and light was breaking through, ripping the shroud of the Seer's black magic asunder. Great chunks of it broke free and began to fall on the horde, dousing the red fire in pure heavenly light. The horde army stood in stark terror as the light began to filter through, revealing all; and even the Seer cowered, raising the sleeve of his garment to cover his face. He fell to the earth awkwardly, landing in a heap.

White light flooded down from the Sword as the night began to crumble away like rubble. Kreios was lifted up, the grips of the Sword in his hand, and as he wielded it, awaiting the coming rout of the enemy mob, power and light like the sun poured from the blade over the remnant of the angelic army, enfolding them in its invincible protection. This, then, was the Presence of God — despite their decision to leave Paradise for their other love — El never abandoned His children, especially in their darkest hour.

The Sword began to hum a high-pitched song, and as it did, even the rocks of the dark dome of night cried out, broke apart, and fell to the ground. Shining brightly, Kreios descended now, and landed with a stone face set toward the battle.

The horde army was stunned. They stared at it like children, and a new feeling washed over them: deep and abiding fear.

All was deathly quiet and still for an instant. The battlefield stood frozen. The angels on the high ground, about twenty in number, and the horde masses on the plain and in the forest, were all still. The Seer regained his feet, limping, trying to heal, seeking the power of the bloodstone. The Sword was raised in Kreios' hand, and he spoke simply, quietly, eyes blazing. "Trumpeter, sound the charge."

The Trumpet sounded forth with a mighty blast, and it shook the hill. At its sounding, the angelic remnant took to the air in an instant, hovering at the ready, motionless again in brief pause, bristling with weapons. The horde army stood in shock, for all their numbers, and defeat called soothingly to them, begged them bow down with her and die.

The angels blasted out into the horde with the force of a powder keg, wilting the enemy infantry, breaking their line, decisively smashing and crushing them into oblivion as they went.

Kreios noticed Yamanu; his weapon shone like the Sword of Light — in fact, as he looked around him, he saw that all the angelic weapons had the same halo around them. Angels were arcing on shallow trajectories into the air in short bursts, careening back to earth, and enemy body parts and blood flew outward from their impacts. They would loop up into the air again, readying to deliver their next blow. The angels were killing over a hundred of the Brotherhood at a stroke, and soon, inevitably, the will of the evil army was broken. Command and control of the Seer hung by a thread.

Atop a heap of the bodies of his own men, the Seer stood with black robes billowing in the light of a supernatural midday. For the first time that many of the angels had seen, he had a weapon in his hand: a staff of obsidian, which emanated darkness.

Kreios said to the remnant in a small but commanding voice, "Go and find any who have escaped. Kill them; there shall be no mercy for these." Yamanu took them and flew to reconnoiter the remains.

Kreios removed his blood-soaked and stinking cloak, letting it fall to the ground at his feet, revealing his gleaming burnished breastplate. He pointed the tip of his Blade directly at the Seer, and from the distance between them, called him by name. "Tengu!

You *shall* bend the knee!" A howling screech of agony greeted him in response. Kreios' body rippled with white light, making his birthmarks gleam in silver and gold. The Sword was perfection, glowing as if it had just been drawn from the forge.

"No, Kreios!" He spoke in spitting disgust, firing out barbs of speech like wet wood on hot coals. *"I shall not bend the knee!"*

"You are wrong; you have been marked, and you have been overmatched. Bend the knee you shall; if I must kill you to bring it about more quickly — I am ready." Kreios took to the air very slowly, sizing up his prey, waiting for him to show a chink in his armor.

The Seer laughed raucously. *"You cannot kill me, Kreios!"* There was a long pause as they sized one another up; the Seer on his mound of flesh, Kreios riding the air. *"You would not kill your own brother... would you?"* He held his staff aloft, brushing his dripping hood back, letting it fall around his shoulders. He moved the head of the staff in a hypnotic series of circular motions, bathing himself in the light that now streamed down on them from heaven above, raising his face to it, feeling the unfamiliar warmth. The act was sacrilegious. It was clear in that light that he bore a likeness to the angel Kreios.

The Seer called his name, singing it like a child's lullaby. *"Kreios,"* He laughed hideously, his face marred by beauty; its features uncomfortably hung and draped over emptiness. He was a picture of what once might have been lovely, but the thought of such things was fleeting and repulsive, out of place.

Without any warning, the Seer's host changed in appearance, becoming a withered old man, and he cried out in agony. Kreios lunged forward. The Seer was manifesting into two forms, and he needed to kill the host before the demon Brother could emerge. If he successfully split, the kill would be much more complicated.

A black bat-like wing protruded. Kreios was closing fast; he raised the Sword and hacked it off as he landed on the heap of bodies, the end of the wing skittering off, curling inward upon itself, rolling into a ball and finally exploding in a pungent whiff of sulfur. The Seer's scream was surreal, being a mix of host and demonic parasite.

He wheeled around to face the angel, furious. As Kreios recovered into his ready position, bringing the Sword up to guard, the demoniac completed its manifestation. Kreios' heart fell in that moment, knowing that he might have missed his opportunity to put an end to all of this madness, and only by a hair's breadth.

The old man, a shell, screamed wildly at Kreios, wielding a short black dagger. He lunged very quickly, driving it into the angel's side. Kreios smacked him, sending him flying into the forest of corpses that lay scattered round about them. He bounced up, a good distance away, and started rushing back to the fight. Kreios turned back to the demon, moving quickly.

The Seer was now holding the long obsidian staff in his hands, and he made it weave a pattern in the air. Kreios guessed that he was conjuring some hellish shield and decided to put a stop to it. "Where are your masses of troops, boy? They no longer stand between us; you cannot hide behind them now. You should surrender, and be sensible."

The old man behind Kreios was tripping over bodies, but approaching quickly.

The demon hissed defensively at Kreios. The angel closed his eyes and concentrated on his target, focused on the Sword, light in his hand. Without drawing it back before the strike, he lunged, eyes closed, willing the tip of the blade through the belly of the beast and out his back.

The demon groaned loudly but shoved him away, and the Sword pulled free. *"I told you, big brother, you cannot kill me — certainly not with my own Sword!"*

Kreios heard the old man, the host, coming for him from behind, panting sub-humanly. He did not turn to face him; he merely backhanded him and sent him flying again. He knew if he killed the host, the demon would shelter in the bloodstone, beyond his reach.

He turned back to the demon, his nemesis — and spoke. "Engage me. Show me what I taught you when we were young together — before the precipitation. Bring to me the hollows of your putrid and spurious heart, so that I may fill them up with the dregs of the cup that has been prepared for the traitorous!"

The demon simply laughed. "*Talk of traitors! Hail — the king of fools: Kreios. How dare you speak to me of traitorousness, you adulterous Cain! At least a third of us had enough honor to declare war outright. You shall not speak at me of betrayal — ΥΠΟΚΡΙΤΗΣ!*" He swung the black staff maniacally.

Kreios dodged the blow, reaching in with the sword and slicing at the neck of the beast, but not deep enough. He spun and parried a second, a third, then took to the air again. He looped around quickly, Sword overhead, and barreled into the demon headlong. As he did, he brought the edge of the Sword down upon the staff with a thunderous *crack*, shattering it powerfully and knocking the demon senseless, onto its back.

Kreios again took to the air, this time with a vengeance. Like a comet, blazing with speed, he shot up in an arc, peaking high up, directly above the immobilized body of the demon, the Seer, his brother Tengu.

Sword drawn and at the ready, hands grasping the grips like a dagger, the point of its blade aimed squarely ahead, Kreios saw the target blur as he broke the sound barrier — yet his aim was true, and the target was not moving. He would bury the blade of the Sword into mountains of rock if it meant that, in doing so, he would sever the head from the body of his nemesis. He was seeking the end relentlessly; he could taste it.

The Seer, recovering, bared jagged and rotten teeth at him from below, and opened his arms as if issuing an invitation to Kreios to give him the worst he could imagine.

Kreios suffered himself to smile. This was, in fact, the end of the Seer, an end to the dogged pursuit of his people by the horde army, a chance for peace at last.

The Seer below was visibly delighted as Kreios streaked toward him, lifting his chin slightly as if begging for the inevitable, daring to lift his horns and bare his neck to the Sword.

The moment stretched out.

Kreios was within striking distance; the collision stood on the cusp of itself, and he moved closer still. The tip of the Sword touched the folds of skin on the Seer's foul throat. Then, he vanished. Smoke exploded in great billows, and in the same instant, Kreios smashed into the earth, scattering dead bodies, limbs, congealed blood, earth, rock, and smoke everywhere.

Scrambling to his feet, Kreios searched for his enemy, glancing everywhere, finally seeing the old man, the host of the Seer. He thrust the dagger that he held at his own neck deeper, gurgled, and fell to his knees.

Red with rage, Kreios bellowed, "No!"

Blood ran down the old man's hand and dripped to the earth, mocking Kreios as the last few bits of smoke that once were the embodiment of the Seer disappeared. Kreios screamed and charged the old man, Sword drawn. He hacked off his head, arched his back and screamed into the sky. The Seer had escaped into the bloodstone.

Kreios searched the body of the old host for it; it was not to be found.

The angels returned to Kreios; Yamanu reported: victory. *Though with heavy cost.* They set fire to the fields and watched as the flames crept in upon the dead, consuming them. The smoke of it would rise and darken the sun for some distance around for many days.

There were thousands upon thousands, and the bodies of his comrades were hopelessly entangled with them. It was a shame to burn all of it together. But these would return to peace, even if they must sleep until the end before they arose.

Kreios lamented his failure. And though the small company of angels regarded the battle as a victory, he could not abandon the memory of so many brave angel warriors. They had stood by him to the death, and had tasted consequence... in a great many ways. He stiffened his resolve, that by refusing to dwell upon himself too heavily, he would honor the memory of those now lost.

He knew that this was not an end, but a beginning. They flew to Ke'elei. To home. To the beloved who remained. To bitter sweet days.

CHAPTER IV

Eagle, Idaho. Present day.

WHEN STAN HAD HEARD the name of Kreios uttered, it shook him to the core. *Kreios? Here?* The memories of Kreios were his inheritance as host of the Seer. He had cursed and gritted his teeth. He was both angered insensibly and pierced with fear. Kreios was supposed to have been killed millennia ago — or slinking in the shadows, hiding. Stan had assumed, as had the Seer, that he had succumbed to death somehow.

He growled in pain. His shoulder sagged and his collarbone stuck out, making a little tent under his shirt.

Airel was gone. No matter what he thought or how strong he believed he was, she was faster and much more powerful than he had ever imagined. She didn't look strong or fast.

He could hear the Seer cursing. Stan forgot about his broken collarbone and ran toward the house — he had no choice but to obey — *for now.*

The front door hung open and he caught a glimpse of his winged beast master flashing across the living room in a tangle of light and smoke. Gripping his dark dagger, he peered around the corner and saw Kreios. His body was glowing with a brilliant white light, and Stan had to cover his eyes to keep from being blinded.

The angel was armed with a long hooked dagger, and as he stabbed it into the demon's gut, Stan felt the pain rip through his own midsection. He looked down to see that his shirt was soaked in blood. Could he die if the demon died? He didn't think so, but he wasn't taking any chances. He leaped into the fray and slashed with his dagger downward across the angel's back.

Kreios turned, almost casually. The look of calm on his face stopped Stan in his tracks. He beheld the brightest eyes he had ever seen; they were steeped in more history and wisdom than he could possibly imagine.

The moment Kreios turned his back to the Seer, it seized its opportunity and lunged. Long rotten teeth sank deeply into his neck. The angel closed his eyes and bent at the knees, and for a second, Stan thought he was going down.

"Kill him, you blubbering pig!" The voice stung his mind and sent sharp needles into his skin. In the time it took Stan to grip and draw the dagger back to put some force behind the final blow, Kreios launched.

The angel shot straight up through the second story and out the roof like a rocket. Plaster, wood, fiberglass insulation and dust ejected out and rained down through the gaping hole, and the whole house skewed off center.

Stan was left earthbound, peering up at them as they twisted left, then right, trailing black smoke. He could not make out much detail, but he sensed through the demon the panic that flooded over its mind.

In the launch, the demon's jaws loosened their grip, and Kreios used inertia and the resistance of the wind to keep the beast at bay. He tore loose from the demon's arms, spinning him around so that he could grasp him from behind. "I've been waiting a very long time to clip your other wing, brother," he said as they flew higher.

Kreios grasped the Seer's lone intact wing and wrenched it out entirely by the root. Stan fell to the floor, arching his back in unbearable pain, howling madly. The Seer was wild with unspeakable rage, spitting and howling furiously.

Kreios punched the top of his head, released him from his grip, and let the struggling demon fall, flapping impotently.

Stan could hear the wind rushing by, the flapping. As the body of the Seer impacted the earth, Stanley Alexander passed out, his body convulsing, then rigid. He could feel his mind straining to make sense of it all, but came up empty.

Is this the end? There was no answer.

CHAPTER V

Sawtooth Mountains of Idaho. Present day.

KIM HAD FOLLOWED ME through the dark tunnel in silence. It seemed we were both a little off; she was speechless for once. As for me, I had just fought a man who was not quite human and held my own. The huge house was utterly empty without anyone there. Kim gasped in surprise and wonder as I gave her the tour: the great ballroom, the massive library, and my room. We didn't even consider entering Michael's room. It was too close to the wound, and the pain was still fresh.

Kim spent some time in my bathroom so that she could at least clean up and feel human again. It's good that we were, along with all the other things we shared, really close to the same size. She looked much better in one of my favorite outfits, and aside from the bruises and her stiffness, she was herself again. Nothing a little Advil and time couldn't cure.

One of the first things we discussed, once we had caught up, was when she could go home.

"Same as me," I said, "whenever it's safe."

"What's *that* supposed to mean?"

I was amazed at how much like Kreios I now sounded, and how much like me she sounded. Things were starting to make sense for me now that I understood some of the reasons why — but not for her so much. "We'll talk with my... with Kreios, when he gets... home." Old words were hard to fit into new definitions. I was trying to roll with it, Kim style.

She changed the subject rather effortlessly. It's one of the reasons she was my best friend. "You know, since you and Michael went missing, I've been looking for you like a mad woman. Your parents called the police, but that seemed to make things worse — the detective that was in charge of your case was murdered! Everything changed after that. They've got everyone looking for you now. I was expecting to see your face on the milk carton soon." We didn't laugh very hard at the joke; it only made me think of how we would have to launch a massive cover-up if we were to survive for long.

Since Kreios wasn't back yet and we were getting pretty hungry, I put together some dinner out of whatever was around. If there was ever a time when I wished for the modern conveniences (such as frozen pizza), it was then.

The sun was sliding behind the mountains when I heard something far off. Kim obviously didn't hear it, and I wondered if I should be alarmed or get ready to defend the castle or something. I wished Kreios had showed me more. It was the sound of rushing wind, but faster, quieter. Kreios appeared seconds later, landing on the back porch, graceful and feather-soft. Kim and I stared through the big windows, awestruck. We were in the company of an angel.

"Whoa," Kim muttered.

"I know — too bad I can't do that." Kim looked at me, her face scrunched.

Kreios opened the glass door and walked into the room. I ran to him, barely aware of what I was doing, and threw myself into his arms, asking if he was okay, if everything was alright. It sure seemed like there was nothing to worry about, the way he shone — but I couldn't help being concerned. This angel in the room was my grandfather.

As I drew away and looked at him, I could hear his voice in my mind. *"Airel. Do you understand now?"*

I nodded, slightly, not wanting Kim to feel like a third wheel attached to a private conversation. For the first time, I saw my grandfather — Kreios — and I heard him in my mind once more. *"This is just the beginning."*

CHAPTER VI

THE NEXT MORNING, WE were up early, except for Kim, who was sleeping off the bruises and soreness. I sat with Kreios before sunrise in the library, by the fireplace.

He wasn't one for small talk, and that seemed especially appropriate now, given that we were up against so many negative possibilities, including the Brotherhood.

"I want to make sure you're okay. I know all of this is a lot to take in." Kreios looked over at me, and I felt for the first time, he was a real friend. Not just that; everything he did was for me, to help me. Knowing that he was also my grandfather made it that much more real.

"Yeah, I'm good. Just trying to work it all out in my mind. I feel like I know you; as if a part of you has been inside me my entire life." I could feel my heart tighten as I tried not to think about Michael. It was hard not to think about the man I was in love with.

"Airel, I know that all of this is difficult for you. You have enough to deal with on top of your realization that you have supernatural abilities. You were kidnapped and taken from everything you know. Your friend was abducted and nearly killed, your life has been upended, and…" I was glad he didn't mention the primary crisis in my heart. He continued, "Well, any one of those things would be hard for an adult, much more so a young lady like you." He folded his hands around a hot cup of tea and sighed.

My eyes burned. I tried to hold back the dam that was ready to break. I missed my parents, my school, and my life. I never asked for any of this. The one person I needed most, after all of this, was my mom. I needed to cry in her arms and to feel her love, to tell her how broken I was. And what sucked about it was that, no matter how bad I wanted to feel her near, I couldn't. "I'm so scared! I feel so alone right now."

Kreios touched my hand with gentle fingers. "Love is a different kind of thing, Airel. We can give our hearts away and lose ourselves in someone we love. I know what it's like to love and to lose that person."

"Yeah, but she died; she didn't betray you. She didn't lie to you, or lead you on about caring for you and then leave you!" Tears were now streaming down my cheeks. I wiped at them with the back of my hand.

"Yes, that's true. I did love and still love my wife. I left everything I knew for her. I left the God who made me; I was the one who betrayed his love for me. For love, we do things we would not otherwise do. But one thing we have to understand is that true love is freedom."

I looked at him and sucked in a deep breath. "What does that mean?"

"It means that you have to find out who you are. Who are *you*, Airel? Do not be defined by the man you love; do not lose who *you* are in the love of another. We can only love the way we were created to if we are first whole in ourselves. If you drown in your feelings for someone, it will turn to obsession and it will cloud your mind to reality." He took a slow sip of his tea.

"I don't know who I am. I'm confused, alone, hurt… and I feel like the one person I trusted most just cut out my heart. I know deep down that Michael loved me. I saw it in him. But he threw it all away, and for what? How can he just toss me aside like that?" My heart hurt so much I felt like it would burst. Hot tears flowed and I let them fall. I had to deal with my pain; I couldn't hide it inside anymore.

"I don't know why he did what he did. Maybe he did love you. Maybe there is more to the story than we will ever know. But even if he did love you and you were going to be together, you have to step back and look at how you loved him. Do you see that it was unhealthy? Do you see how he was overtaking who you are as a person? You are bound for failure if you allow yourself to drown in each other."

His eyes were very soft. "I love you, Airel. I have been looking after you ever since you were born. I want what is best for you and this pain — this need you have for him — is not love."

I became angry with how he was turning my pure love into something it could never be. "I love him! Don't you get it? It was him, not how he looked or what he said, but *him*. He is an amazing person! And it's my choice to love him. Don't you think I want to forget, to hate him for what he did to me? I want more than anything to erase him from my memories." I was sobbing now, and I buried my head in my hands and wept.

I looked back on every conversation, every look, every word spoken. The truth of what Kreios was saying came shining through, inevitably. I decided to love him, yes — but then I had begun to lose myself. I didn't want to see it, didn't want to admit he was right. How could this happen? I wanted to drown, to drink in Michael and die, consumed by him. But was that real? Was it something I could count on?

Kreios let me cry. He didn't reach out to comfort me, but sat back with accepting eyes and let me get it all out. It flowed like water through the imagined man I had created, dissolving him into nothing.

"Tears never lie, Airel. What you're feeling is part of who you are. You are a strong, beautiful, intelligent, loving woman. In you, there is more than you can imagine. You don't need a man to love you to make you special. You are special because you are *you*. Don't you see? See and believe you are one of God's children; that is what makes you special."

My shoulders shook as I poured out all my hurt, all my love and all my hidden hate for Michael, for myself. A part of me didn't want to feel; I wanted to shut it off, to run and hide from this overpowering pain. But what would that do? Would it stay buried? Like oil, it would always come to the surface.

"I just want it to go away. I can't live feeling like this." My voice cracked, and I let the wave of thoughts and memories cover me. "Kreios, I need him… I want him… but…"

"You have to let him go, Airel. You have to feel the pain, the hurt, and let him go." Taking me in his arms, Kreios held me and I cried out of my soul. Never before had I opened up my heart to my own fears and feelings. It was the worst and best experience of my life.

I'm not sure how much time went by, but after it was all over, I fell into a deep sleep as Kreios ran his hand through my hair. He was my connection, the one person who understood what it was like and what I was feeling. *I don't know if this will change my life, if I can move on and be strong, but I know that I will be fine. I will be okay in the end.*

Because I am enough.

CHAPTER VII

WE HAD A LONG breakfast. I talked with Kreios about when we could go back home. I blamed it on Kim and how her parents, too, missed her terribly by now. I felt caught between two totally unknowable things: my desire for everything to get back to normal as quickly as possible, and my need to reset and find out how to be who I needed to be from now on.

I asked Kreios about the Seer, and he didn't really say much. Stan had escaped, and Kreios had been worried about me — so he flew straight home to check up on me instead of hunting down the monster. He told me that he would be leaving soon in order to be sure of a few things, to wrap up the loose ends. I guessed that meant that we still had to be careful and stay hidden until Kreios could force an end to all of it. I didn't try to push my luck with him. I knew he would just tell me that I needed more training.

Kim walked into the kitchen around 10:30, changing our conversation and giving Kreios the cue he was looking for to leave. He said he wouldn't be long, and to stay on the property.

Kim and I had a decently normal conversation, considering everything that had happened. Kim was somebody who could do small talk, and with a vengeance. Once she had got her fill of the usual breakfast fare — except that this food tasted so much better — we decided to take a walk.

We ended up following a trail I hadn't explored yet, which was nice, because the other ones were haunted for me by Michael's ghost.

The trail led up into a thick forest of quaking aspens that were holding onto the last of their bright orange leaves. Their chalky white trunks and branches were a feast for the eyes. It was an Indian summer kind of day; autumn, but warm. The trail took us through the trees and ended abruptly at the top of a cliff, probably forty feet tall, that overlooked a little mountain lake. We could see fish jumping occasionally, making silvery splashes and ripples in the placid surface.

We decided to sit down, each of us 'pulling up a rock,' to soak up the rays. The sun was high in the sky, deep azure blue contrasted sharply against billowing white clouds. I thought about my mom and dad again. It was ripping me apart that they were worried sick about me, and I felt like it was within my power to go to them — it filled me with guilt. I wasn't a prisoner, not anymore. I could just grab the keys to the Yukon and be done with it.

The only thing that kept me from going was that nagging feeling that I would do to my family what I already had done to Kim. Indirectly, sure, but still. If it wasn't for me, Kim would never have been taken hostage and used as bait.

Then again, if it wasn't for Michael...

"What is the great angel thinking about now?" Kim asked as she lay on her back on a huge granite boulder, sunning herself like a lizard.

"Oh, Mom and Dad," I lied halfway. "I miss them." Echoes of the hurt Michael had caused, along with my ebbing feelings for him, faded into the background as I forced myself to talk about something else. "And I miss my own bed and my own room. I think I won't be graduating this year; missed too many classes."

Kim shrugged. "No worries. You're smart enough." I wasn't sure I agreed with Kim's attitude. "Besides, Kreios can teach you anything you ever wanted to know. He's like what, four thousand years old?"

"Something like that. I hope this'll all be over soon. I don't know how much more I can take. We've gotta get you back, too —"

"No way. This is the best vacation I've ever had."

I knew she was lying for me, trying to ease the pressure.

"Besides," she continued, "until Stan is caught, we're safest here. Kreios has something cooking, I can tell." Her hands brushed away a bug that had found its way up to her cheek. I closed my eyes and tried not to think, tried not to worry. It was nice, anyway, to just lie still in the sun on a big rock. I decided to enjoy the moment.

"So what ever happened with James after we went missing?" I was curious. I hadn't thought of him at all, but I remembered that Kim had a huge crush on him.

"Oh, James," she sighed. "He took me out one time after, but something was not the same. He was like a shell of what he used to be. He missed Michael, and I think he took it very badly. He never talked much to begin with, but this was different. It was kinda pathetic, really. I felt like all he could think about was Michael. I just let it go; I didn't want to be around someone who was so down all the time."

"Well, they *were* best friends." I wondered if James knew who Michael really was. I doubted it; he didn't seem to let anyone in, even me.

"Whatever, though," I said, trying hard again to relax and just enjoy the moment. I closed my eyes and lay my head back. It was a lazy day, and nothing to do but watch it amble on past, like an old man with a cane. It was weird, like I could hear the footsteps of the old man in my head, shuffling past in the dirt. When I realized what the sound really was, it was far too late to do anything about it.

"Hello, Airel. Did you miss me?"

CHAPTER VIII

STAN STOOD HUNCHED OVER, his lips wet with blackness, a smirk on his bruised face. I could see the glowing red stone dangling around his neck. "You are an abomination, a curse, and I am here to carry out my orders." His bloodshot eyes twitched back and forth like a whipped dog.

Kreios! I searched for him frantically.

Kim struggled to her feet and scrambled to my side. "You must have a death wish, you creepy little man!" She was trying to look tough. "Airel will tear you apart!" I elbowed her in the ribs and muttered under my breath.

I swept her behind me with my arm and instinctively crouched in my fighting stance. *She doesn't know what she's saying and I don't know what I'm supposed to do.* Kreios had told me to run if I ever met Stan alone. He was speaking in two voices, so obviously the Seer was with him. My spine tingled as my body poured adrenaline into my fear.

"Come here, girl," Stan's eyes glowed red even in broad daylight; his pupils cat-like and piercing. He held a length of heavy chain in his hand.

"You really think I'm just going to go with you?" I could hear Kreios coming. I stepped forward slightly, to try to fend the villain off, but he didn't budge an inch.

"You're crazy," I said through clenched teeth, trying to signify my courage. I could feel everything; every beat of my heart, every fiber of nerve and muscle in my body. I was a coiled panther ready to unleash raw fury — and deep within me, I could feel

She gathering up all the frustration, anxiety, disappointment, and crushing powerlessness I had felt ever since I had begun my change, and distilling it into hate for the evil one that dared to stand before me. I wanted to kill, for the first time in my life, and what's more, I was ready to do it, couldn't wait to begin.

When Kreios landed, it was a seismic event. There was maybe twenty feet of open space between me and my attacker, and Kreios landed right in the middle of it, cracking the earth deeply, making the boulders shudder. The swirl of light that danced around him almost looked like wings, but it moved around his body as if the light itself was protecting him. His jaw clenched.

He held no weapon in his hand, and he was clothed in the same simple robe that he had worn for my training. "This time, brother, you *will* bow to your Maker or I will take more than your wing."

The Seer laughed maniacally, extricating himself out of Stan as if his body was a used container, kicking him aside when he was through, sending the heavy chain he had been brandishing into the grass. Kreios lunged in attack, and the thing backhanded him with one massive movement. Kreios flipped over, righted himself, and hovered in the air.

"Airel! You must take Stan; it is the only way." He looked at me, and in his eyes was strength and trust. *"You must walk through the door, child. Walk through it and take that which awaits you there. It is your destiny."*

This is getting real. And it was getting hard to believe.

Time stood still in that moment of my existence. My eyes wide open, there appeared before me, somewhere or somehow between the real and the supernatural, a door. It was made of a single piece of wood and stood apart from everything. There were no handle or hinges, as far as I could tell. I looked at Kim; she was frozen and didn't seem to be able to see me. The trees were stuck, motionless. I reached my hand out to the door, and as I did, it opened to me.

I could only believe one thing as it swung open and revealed what was on the other side: this was the Sword of Light; the Sword of my grandfather, an angel of God, who had once lived in Paradise, heaven, in the company of God Himself.

The Sword was brilliant; it illuminated me, my spirit, my mind, and called to me. I strode through the door, a petite girl of seventeen, and wrapped my hand around the grip. As I passed through the door, it evaporated, leaving me once again at the top of the cliff, Kreios, the Seer, and Stan before me, Kim behind me, all frozen as if I had been taken out of time. And the Sword was immense, but seemed to shrink and grow light in my hands. I sensed that it would do the work; all I had to do was hang on.

I moved the blade in a wide arc over my head, feeling far more wise and graceful than I ever had; I felt like a warrior. And I *knew* that I was. I took to my fighting stance, this time with the Sword in my hands, and closed my eyes.

When I opened my eyes again, I was still holding the Sword. Everything was slowly starting to regain its momentum around me. I saw a branch move in the breeze. I looked at Kim, who was looking at me as if she had seen a ghost, her finger trying to point at the Sword, but failing, shaking and falling back to her side. "Kim. Stay out of the way, okay? Go hide!" She ran to a nearby stone outcropping and disappeared.

The Sword was feather light in my hand. I felt warmth and power filling me. It was not red like anger, or white and wonderful like love — but something else entirely. It didn't even have a color — not one I could put into words.

Stan sneered, unsheathing the same black dagger he had had at his house, stepping toward me in a sideways crouch, dagger in his leading hand. "The Brotherhood wants you alive. They will have to understand if I bring you back dead — I had no choice, you see — you attacked me!" He snarled, snorted and spit.

Kreios barreled right at the Seer, taking him on without delay. The two tumbling bodies fell out of sight in the forest, behind a small rise. I could hear branches breaking; maybe whole trees from the sound of it.

I studied my enemy. Stan was not just any man. Not only was he being propped up by supernatural — unnatural — power that found a home in the Seer, but he was also the father of the love who had left my heart in a heap of ashes.

My enraged heart was now looking at the target for the blame — Stan. And not only Stan, but the *being* known as the Seer. I focused my pain on him as the cause of it and charged forward with a shout that surprised me.

Stan's guard was inadequate at best, and as *She* guided me through my body's motions, I stabbed with a thrusting motion and felt the Sword take over, driving the point of the blade in. I could feel ribs break under the force of the blow.

Stan howled in pain, dropping his hands. I moved fluidly to the side, forcing the point of the blade to pivot on the rib, ripping him apart inside and opening him up. Stan fell to one knee and gasped, eyes bulging. The Sword was withdrawn from his wound. I felt almost like a spectator as I watched myself move like someone who knew what she was doing; who could handle herself with a weapon like this. I swept the Sword out and around to the side, spinning back to my opponent, keeping the Weapon between us. It was amazing how easy it all was.

"You think you can kill me that easily," he croaked. The wound began to heal right before my eyes, though a deep crimson scar remained. "As long as I have this —" His voice cut off as he fondled the red bloodstone that hung around his neck. Then a new cut emerged on his neck: long, with five points at its end. It began to bleed. It looked like claw marks, or maybe invisible strong hands.

Kreios.

If I killed Stan, the Seer would die as well... *or will he just retreat into the red stone?* I couldn't remember. Stan got to his feet and smacked me with more force than I would have thought he was able to muster. I thought I would fall, but my body moved into the motion his strike had created, moving with it, spinning back around, using it to reset my fighting stance.

"We must coordinate our kills, Airel! The Seer must perish first; otherwise he will escape into the stone."

In our macabre dance, we had exchanged positions; the rocky cliff now stood behind the wild-eyed man. *Maybe I can back him up and push him over. Will a fall of that height kill him? It might knock him out and drown him...*

I swung the Sword powerfully, meeting the edge of his jagged dagger in a spray of sparks. The tip of his weapon was cut; it sailed off into the lake below. He tried to counterattack with a quick jab, but missed. I swung again, bringing the tip of the blade in an arc up from the ground to the sky, pushing him back.

Stan twitched and cried out, slapping at new wounds on his body. He was limping and favoring the side where I had hit him and smashed his ribs. Evidently the healing power of the bloodstone was not working fast enough. *His ribs are still broken.*

I pulled up and kicked him in the gut, knocking the wind out of him. He doubled over; I raised the Sword high overhead, and clubbed him on the back of his skull with the end of the handle. He slumped to the dirt in a wrecked pile. Unconscious.

I wasn't even breathing heavily.

And then the Sword of Light vanished right out of my hands. It was gone. *Was it ever there?*

☙

The angel and the demon tumbled into the undergrowth, away from Airel. Kreios knew that he must be quick if he was to be victorious. A massive aspen broke their progress, snapping off three or four feet above the ground, the tree top falling with a shiver.

Kreios grunted, grabbing the Seer by the neck, ripping at it, feeling the black blood trickle and spray, and the smell that rode along with it.

Clods of dirt flew through the air. They struggled, Kreios climbing onto the demon's back, but Tengu flung him off. Kreios rushed him, then faked left and lunged right, striking again at his neck with his left hand, using the hold to swing himself around onto the demon's back. Kreios could feel his strength begin to fail; the demon soaking it out of him quickly now.

Kreios got a foot planted in front of him, shifted his weight, then forced Tengu forward mightily, sending him headlong into the dirt; the angel riding the back of the demon. The Seer choked and gagged, holding his ribcage. A gash appeared there, and Kreios could see the broken ribs jutting out. Airel was doing better than he had hoped.

Tengu tried to flop over onto his back, arching himself desperately, trying to extend the seconds, to weaken the angel. Kreios simply enlarged his grip on the neck of the demon, holding his head now in the crook of his elbow. He reached and dug thumb and forefinger into both of Tengu's eye sockets, digging them in as deeply as he could reach.

The Seer screamed in total agony, blinded and bleeding from the damage, his eyeballs ruptured and leaking.

Now that the demon had been immobilized, Kreios changed positions. He wearily placed a knee on each shoulder blade, pinning him to the forest floor. Kreios then grasped with iron grip the horns of the Seer's head that sprouted from the top of his skull and wrapped around in front of his face.

"You ceased long ago to be my brother," he said. "The war of endurance is over. And I put an end to you at last." With one powerful motion, Kreios wrenched Tengu's head to one side, pulling upward, snapping the neck of the demon, killing him, and ripping his head off.

Now, like a scrap of discarded snake skin, the body of the demon withered, shriveled, and became dust, blowing away in a sudden strong gust. Kreios discarded the large head, letting it roll down the gentle slope a little ways. It came to a stop, then exploded in a whiff of inky darkness, pitifully vanishing as vapors into the wind.

CHAPTER IX

I WAS STANDING OVER the crumpled body of Stanley Alexander when I heard the most awful wrenching sound; a scream that ripped at the heavens and was cut short, as if the soul of it had been torn right out midstream. I was still trying to figure out what was real and what was not — vanishing doors, then disappearing Swords — *seriously, what's next?*

As soon as that unholy scream had rent the air, Stan jolted wide awake in a spasm, lurching up from the ground. I jumped back defensively. I reached out in my mind to Kreios and got nothing. *Is he dead?* I didn't know.

When Stanley Alexander opened his eyes, something was different. It was very bad and it was very new. *She* was sending me warning signals without words, and I understood that what I was looking at in Stan was unprecedented. What he had become then had never been seen under the sun before.

He got to his feet wearing a wicked smile and said, *"'We' is now me."* He moved so quickly that I couldn't do anything. Before I knew it, he had stabbed me. I felt overwhelming pain dashing against my chest. He stepped forward, pushing with the blade. I heard Kim scream from a long way off.

He pushed harder, the black blade digging in further, and I fell to my knees. I gagged, wrapped my hand around the blade to try to stop it from going farther. I felt a pumping, gushing, leaking sensation in my chest that was all at once hot and cool, and my strength faded rapidly.

Stan pulled the dagger free and walked slowly around me as

351

my wound gushed, blood running down my skin and soaking my clothes. He stood behind me then, with his dagger raised. I sensed what he was going to do, heard the voice of *She* screaming out in agony and grief, and searched with all my heart for the mind of Kreios, but I couldn't move. My heart had been pierced. I was mortally wounded.

In the background, I heard Kim screaming, footsteps running toward me, but her voice sounded distant and vague. Somewhere deep within, I knew she would be killed — it was inevitable — but I was now bound to my fate, and a prisoner of the events of my life. *So short!* I turned to face the unspeakably evil thing that had stabbed me, that would finish my life and end it. His eyes had become livid, death had skinned them over. I fell to the earth on my side and rolled to my back, my legs askew. He was crazed and twitching, his muscles stuttering as if fighting rigor mortis. He raised the dagger for the final blow, the severing of my head from my body, and all I could do was wait for it.

The sound of tearing flesh, a sloshing wet sound, filled my ears. I couldn't tell what was happening, if the sound had come from inside my body as my heart tore itself apart on the line that had been cut into it, or if the sound had come from somewhere else. I wondered abstractly how long a person stays conscious after they're beheaded.

I now began to long for the end. My life had been so very confusing. And filled up with pain. And short. It made, all of it, no sense to me. The most random bits of memory flashed into my mind and skipped right out again. Things I would have sworn I had forgotten, things that did not exist to me anymore. Memories of old classmates from kindergarten, a lonesome bike ride when I was seven, an old book I had held, a doll I used to love. Everything around me was becoming faintly hazy.

A garbled exclamation broke the silence. My eyes flew open. From the open mouth of Stanley Alexander, protruding like an obscene black tongue, was the tip of a sword. His eyes rolled back in their sockets and blood dripped from the tip of the blade.

The immense and crushing drain on my strength stopped —

but I was left with a shattered heart, the violence done against it now complete and total. I both felt and believed that my life had now run its course; the time left to me now a handful of moments.

But Stan had already found his own end. The line he had drawn finally ran out. He fell to the earth and shattered like crystal on impact, the shards metamorphosing into vermin and creeping things that fled to the undersides of rocks, there to hide from the light and warmth of the sun. The bloodstone, in the dirt, rested alone and unposessed, glimmering a deep and blinding red.

I tried to find my bearings, fluttering my eyelids and struggling to sit up. *Was it Kreios?* Who had killed Stan?

"Airel! You're hurt!"

It was the voice of the one who had struck down and defeated my treacherous foe.

Michael.

The black sword that he held dropped with a dull clang to the ground, and he rushed to my side, and fell to his knees. "Airel." The sound of my name on his lips warmed me completely.

He had come back! He had struck down his own father to… emotion flooded me, drowning my senses utterly.

"Airel, I'm so sorry…"

I looked into those eyes once again, and instantly I knew the truth. Michael Alexander *did* love me. He had never wanted to hurt me. He had been forced to betray me, and was probably as confused about all of it as I was.

Michael's face seemed weathered, however. There was a muted look of horror there underneath it all, and as I searched him with my eyes, I noticed James was with him, looking like he had just arrived, standing just behind Michael in his varsity jacket. He had a strange look on his face.

Kim was at his side, saying, "James, what's going on here?" I turned back to Michael, a million questions popping up, and saw something else: fear.

Michael struggled, looking tortured. I looked to James.

Michael reached quickly on the ground for the piercing bright bloodstone, and brought it closer, holding its dangerous and intense light between us, not far from my chest wound.

I was seized with the most unimaginable horrors. My heart felt like it was being welded back together, patched and bolted, and I died a little more, seeing impossible things. I cried out in my distress.

James leaned forward quickly, with glowing eyes, and knocked the bloodstone from Michael's hand, sending it skittering across the dirt, giving me a reprieve. I gasped and tried to gather myself together so that I could thank him, but he looked at me with extreme hostility. "Kill her, Michael! Redeem your mistake."

Mistake?

Michael pulled back from me, intense sadness filling his empty eyes. He looked soulless, an automaton on a short leash.

"Take up your sword and strike her down!"

I still didn't quite grasp the situation. I felt as if I had been blindfolded and handcuffed to a carnival ride. James's harsh words were still not making sense to me.

Michael appeared to be severely distracted as he looked askance toward the weapon; he seemed to be suffering an internal civil war. With sagging shoulders set in the frame of purposeless behavior, Michael bent down for the sword, but stopped short of taking it up.

James growled like a dog. He was enraged; his skin fell away in shreds that looked like old newspapers and torn photographs. Smooth black wings unfurled from his back and enfolded us in a threatening semi-circle. He shook, his arms growing long; huge round paws with long curling claws emerged from his fingertips. The boy I had known as James burst apart from the inside.

"Love-infested innocent! If you lack the strength, allow me." He snatched the sword from Michael's limp hand as dark steam fell from his mouth. Michael stood there, completely whipped, and looked at me with sad eyes.

A single tear fell to my cheek as I realized the ultimate loss in the situation. I pleaded with him, screaming at him in my thoughts, *Michael, don't stand aside and allow this!* "Michael," I spoke, my voice choking me, "have you already left me?" *Again?*

My eyes burned with tears. I didn't see the demon. I didn't see Kim. All I could see was him, my soul, my life — Michael. I *would not* believe that he didn't feel love for me. He had killed his own father to defend me; there had to be something else that held him bound beside his own broken will.

The demon struck Michael in the face with contempt, sending him sprawling, then turned back to me. "Enough talk! You have been alive for far too long. Today you, Airel, daughter of El, shall die!" I was reaching up to Michael, trying in vain to sit up. The hideous demon leapt straight at me, colliding with such great force that I could feel my almost-immortal body begin to give in to what was becoming inevitable. We skidded off the top of the cliff in a plume of dirt and dust and stones, falling. The water, far below, was going to hurt.

I couldn't fight, couldn't breathe. All of the strength I once had deserted me. I saw Michael rush to the cliff's edge, reaching out to me as I fell, his eyes shouting a love and sadness so deep, so stricken, that I thought for an instant that he was in more pain now than I ever was. Hate was life to him; he was bred, raised, trained to hunt us down, to kill us. Even as I fell to my death, I decided none of my injuries, be they physical or emotional, mattered. *Michael...*

The force of the water on impact further sapped my strength. My eyes instinctively closed as I went hurtling into the surface of the abyss, the demon astride my dying body, the water bubbling around us as we sank. The depths reached for me, to take me down, and down.

I opened my eyes for the briefest of an instant, searching the cliff top for a final glimpse of my love, his love unrealized. *We never really had a chance, did we?* I realized how thickly bitter rust had covered us, locking away lovely possibility beneath a hideous mask.

There was only one thing left to me that was in my power: *Michael, I forgive you.*

I saw him standing rigid at the edge of the cliff, grasping the black sword in his hands. The blade was inverted back upon his abdomen, and just as I began to sink beneath the spray of the water of the lake, he drove the point of it home, crying out in pain, doubling over. The demon jerked suddenly, releasing me, roaring in fury and pain.

I could feel the water pour into my lungs, relentless.

MICHAEL! NO, MICHAEL!

My heart and mind screamed out at the one I loved, ripping against the grain. The waves crashed in upon me, and as they did, my eyes met with unspeakable horror: Michael drew the blade out and then plunged it back in, again, again, again. My heart burst inside my chest as I watched.

The demon James writhed and flopped on the surface of the water as I sank below. I could hear its ungodly shrieking through the boiling and squalling waters as I sank. Still, I looked to the cliff's edge, holding out hope as a candle to the hurricane, begging God for mercy — and I saw Michael deliver the final blow, becoming limp, falling from the cliff, tumbling end over end, the sword pulled out and away, tumbling wildly, and Michael hit the water with a sickening smack as I sank.

Blood and water mixed in a drink of death.

CHAPTER X

THE SUN BLAZED OVERHEAD, warming the forest glade unseasonably. Kreios could feel his strength returning slowly. His heart stutter-stepped in his chest and he cocked an ear to the disturbance: A scream. His body stiff and wooden, stubborn, he nevertheless jumped to his feet and began to run toward the cliffs.

He reached out but could not find Airel. He sprinted, forcing his body to wake up, straining it.

He arrived at the top of the cliff in time to see Michael toppling over its edge. Kim was there, standing still, dazed and in shock. Kreios was at her side quickly. He laid her down on the earth before she could hurt herself.

He then noticed the bloodstone beside her. It was shining in a constant, piercing crimson light that called to him like the fondest memories of his childhood. He did not dare to touch it. There were more important things — he would not lose another fair, young princess in his family line.

He rushed to the precipice, looking down. Beneath him were Michael and James. The demon was struggling as if injured, and Michael was sinking quickly. He was injured as well. *No sign of Airel.*

Water was a difficult element. It posed a singular set of challenges for one like Kreios. Flight through the air was effortless, second nature. Moving in water slowed everything, made difficult what would be easy in the air; it was like thousands of grasping hands pulled against whatever course of action was decided upon. And drowning was a mortal risk, even for an angel.

He searched again in his mind for Airel, and could not find her. He cursed what his eyes beheld: two of the Brotherhood. And though they were far below, struggling and thrashing in the water, quite possibly even at that moment moving toward their eternal damnation as the jaws of Hell opened wide to receive them, Kreios could not justify simply watching the boy die. He could not separate himself from this chain of events.

Michael was beginning to sink beneath the surface. *He doesn't have much longer.* Kreios leapt into the air, and far from giving himself over to mere gravity, shot on a bullet's trajectory into the water; his body stretched out, punching a hole in the surface at impact that yielded the smallest splash.

He was deep before his momentum was checked. There was blood; and the fume of cursed demonic detritus filled his nostrils even here. He looked; and in the distant darkness, a chance ray of sunlight played off the dark brown hair of his Airel, the last in the line of his heirs. *No!* He moved quickly to her side and looked into her face; he feared it was too late. He took her anyway, pushing off the muddy bottom, gaining speed and momentum in the molasses, aiming directly for Michael, who was now sinking toward them. *Too late for both of them.*

Kreios did not slow as he intercepted the boy. He simply ran into him, gaining speed, a limp body hanging over each shoulder, and when he broke the surface of the water, it erupted upward, outward, droplets and mist, and Kreios flew right out of the center of it.

When he had reached the edge of the cliff, he dropped the body of the boy with contempt, allowing him to land clumsily in the dirt. To Kreios' shock, Michael rolled and coughed, sputtering, gasping. He landed gently at the lookout point where the whole drama had unfolded, and laid Airel on the ground alongside Kim, whose eyes were closed. He looked from one to the other. Michael was nearby, coughing up blood and water.

Airel was limp, her mangled heart not beating. Kreios began CPR. Michael dragged himself over to her side and left a blood trail behind him in the dirt. "Airel! Is she dead? Will she be okay?"

His voice cracked, and Kreios filled her lungs with air, not looking at Michael.

The boy was beside himself and started crying with big long sobs that wracked his pitiful body. "This is all my fault. I killed her; I betrayed her! Oh God, please help her, I can't live without her; please, *please!*" He groaned, finally, and fell next to her, his wet arm draping over her lifeless body. He did not move, and his breathing was shallow.

Kreios stopped his CPR, knowing that it was no use, and looked at the boy, Michael. He pushed him over onto his back. "Let me help you, Michael... hold still." Kreios wanted nothing to do with the boy. But he knew that what he was about to do was what Airel would have wanted.

Michael was almost gone.

Kreios retrieved the blazing red stone from where he had left it, and against a great pulling and tearing at his will, brought it to the boy, resisting the caressing whisperings of blasphemy that were flowing from its core. "Receive your accursed burden," he said, softly, sadly, as he touched it to the boy's skin, then tossed it away. The wounds closed up, leaving many red scars — not healed, but repaired. Michael's eyes snapped open; he gasped and screamed and pushed away from Kreios.

He looked down at the marks of his wounds in horror as he realized what the angel had done — had damned him to a life of bitter emptiness, shame and regret. "I don't want to live! Why did you help me? Why did you do that?" He broke into long, fitful sobs. He collapsed onto Airel's body, sobbing, saying again and again, "I'm sorry," in her ear.

Kreios stood and turned from him. The burden of pain that had been laid upon his back over many thousands of years was indeed heavy. Tears filled the blackness of his vision as he walked away into the forest. He sat alone, and the tears came once again.

Airel was his blood. His daughter. Kreios roared softly as the worst of his fears became realized. Now he had lost her, too. It was a fitting gall that they had been driven, all of them, inexorably to this sad and shattering end. He could not see her anymore; he did not remember her face; he was unable to recall anything of joy. Kreios buried his head in his hands and wept: for Airel, for Eriel and for his wife. All he could see was the grave, yawning wide and consuming all his loves.

౭౧

Michael stood, finally. Far too late. Eyes marred by grief, he gathered to him the body of his only love and carried her in his arms. He looked to Kreios, who did not acknowledge him. Wordlessly, he passed him by and started on the path back to the house, holding Airel in his arms. Life and purpose dropped away from his soul, leaving him naked, in exposure to the wicked ravages of the world. He welcomed them. He looked on what he had done with emptiness.

౭౧

Kreios was alone. Again.

He stood and walked to the edge of the cliff, looking out over calm water that erased everything, and his whole life was not real. What had he done? He felt bound to loss. Every choice that was made under the sun, no matter how perfect and good when birthed in the confines of the heart, was destined only for an inevitable end and death. Joy was fleeting, and after thousands of years, time sped by far too quickly. The years had become seconds, and the hands of the clock, that malicious machine, were relentless and devoid of any mercy. The water was glass once again. It had no memory, and showed nothing.

And yet, he would refuse to ask why. He knew such a question had no answer. The deeper one penetrated into the deep and the void, the more obvious it became that every question found its beginning and end in El. Now, yet again, Kreios had been brought back to the bedrock. The foundation of All. It was unglamorous and it was unlovely; and yet — for some reason that he did not yet understand — that did not matter.

He thought of Airel. In a very short time, she could have been, could have done, so much. The waste was vile and unspeakably bitter. He had been so foolish to hope that hope would bud and bloom into peace, once he had put an end to the Seer.

His poor, wretched, wicked brother had chosen a far different path, one that had burned with fire and fury and the self. Kreios had dared to believe that he would be filled with relief. But the cup he now drank was not what he had expected.

Light flowed outward from his body on feathery strands, waving in the breeze. He slowly became lighter, the earth releasing him from its hold, and he took to the air, gentle as the breath of his newborn baby girl so very many years ago.

He spread his arms and raised his head, rising up above the trees. He gathered his resolve as he gathered speed, launching himself into the sky, flying straight up, leaving thunderclap behind.

The sound scattered a few birds. Michael stopped along the path through the woods. Kreios headed north.

There were still enemies to vanquish. The Brotherhood was leaderless. There were many yet to kill. And Michael would be the last.

ભ

Kim's body lay silent, her breathing rapid, the shock claiming ownership over her. Beside her, by a tuft of grass, the bloodstone lay blazing red, whispering. Alone, abandoned, and left. In an instant, she awoke, startled, and looked: red.

EPILOGUE

AIREL'S BODY WAS COLD and wet in his arms. The shiver that he waited for, that should have come from her chilled body, never came. She was completely still, eyes closed. She *looked* like an angel. Her skin pale, smooth, fair; her lips full, the faintest red flushed within. *What have I done?* Why was he so confused and mixed up over this girl? It was just another job. He couldn't count how many times he had had to do something just like it in the past. He was even good at it; had been doing the same things for far longer than he could remember. He could make instant friends, could find out if the target was one of the Sons of God in a week or less.

But Airel had been different. He had wanted that, though. He had wanted her to be different. He had hoped it was just a mistake, a wrongful mark. They had to have botched things somehow; it had to have been a case of mistaken identity. But then he had fallen for her. *Stupid, stupid, stupid!*

If you love her so much, why did you betray her? His mind flickered backward to his mother — how his father had murdered her in cold blood while cursing her to a slow and painful eternity in Hell. The next thought was inevitable, and it hurt more than he could express: *like father, like son...*

He had known that trying to negotiate with his father was pointless, but he tried anyway. After a horribly long night, he had barely escaped with his life, leaving his mother to die. James had sealed it up, had demanded and extracted his complete and utter obedience.

Michael walked into the open meadow and began to climb the long, winding stone stairway that led up to the back of the house. He didn't know he was sobbing, that his tears were falling onto Airel's face, until he walked up to the big windows and saw his reflection in the glass.

He abhorred his reflection, felt guilty that he didn't hate it enough. He pushed the door open and walked into the large ballroom. He then carried his one and only up to her room and laid her gently on the bed.

Michael was not expecting the fury of the storm of his own grief as it overtook him. He collapsed over the body of his beloved, whom he had murdered, and he buried his head in her wet hair, sobbing, "I'm so sorry! My love, I'm so sorry!"

He tried to breathe in the sweet smell of her hair and skin, but only caught the scent of death. All he desired was to join her, and he cursed Kreios for bringing him back to a life he no longer wanted to live.

Some things cannot be undone. Some words cannot be rewritten, and some wounds cannot be mended.

Michael raised his head, blinking. He looked at her face, still beautiful in death. A thought, both rash and bold, was blooming upon the face of his consciousness. *Would it be possible?* He rose to his feet, half-turned from her, as if pulled in some new direction, yet not willing to depart. *No.* He reached down to her figure, lying motionless before him on the bed. "No!"

He moved toward the door, slowly at first, walking backward, then turning, increasing his pace, and reaching the door. When he passed through it, he turned and ran down the hallway to the stairs, racing down them, half falling with the speed he carried.

When he reached the bottom, he turned toward the library. "No!" He was racing. He crash-landed in the room before the great fire, which was always lit. Frantically, he searched. "No, No!"

Running wildly throughout the room, dodging from shelf to shelf, he looked. He searched high and low. *It is here somewhere; it must be; I feel it to be true!* And yet the lines from Shakespeare echoed back to him:

Truth may seem, but cannot be;
Beauty brag, but 'tis not she;
Truth and beauty buried be.

"I *do not* believe it!" he hurled the words against the real, dashing them against the rotten powers of his mind. He searched frantically on for a moment, then stopped — still.

Slowly turning, he fixed his gaze on the great roaring fire. Above its licking flame, there stood a mantelpiece. On its ledge were a few books, an old-fashioned inkwell and quill pen. He walked toward them.

Each step produced in the air a shockwave of foreboding, each step radiating outward momentous importance. His hand reached up and out; he closed his eyes, sensing. Farther and farther it reached, fingertips extended. Closer it came, the reach of his hand cutting against time and possibility. At last, the tip of his forefinger brushed the surface of a book, and he heard, ringing out into the wilds of his mind a single word: AIREL.

Michael understood in an instant what was to be done. Taking the book down, he opened it. Taking the quill pen from the inkwell, he wrote three simple words:

"But she lived."

COMING SOON
BOOK TWO IN THE AIREL SAGA

MICHAEL

There is never an end,
Life breaks in with gentle force and the old is made new.
Death is the beginning of life,
Before we can truly live, we must all die.

CHAPTER I

MICHAEL COULD PHYSICALLY FEEL his heart rip inside his chest as he was crushed under the weight of his decisions. But what choice did he have? Writing in the book had to be wrong, but he could not lose Airel this way. Not like this; not after he betrayed her to his demonic father, not after all that had passed between them. He had trampled his love for her, had trampled *her* — and for what?

His pen scrawled the words:

"But she lived."

Michael watched the page crinkle under his tears as they dropped to the parchment, smudging the ink. This was not what he had wanted, not what he would have ever believed could happen.

Airel was just another mission, just another cursed threat that needed to be cleansed from the dominion. She was a job, like so many others. But Airel somehow got in, broke past all his defenses and took hold of his heart.

He had never known love, never really cared about it — not with his demon partner. Airel broke the rules like they'd never even existed. He now was certain: he would kill and die for her.

He turned and set the book down, closing it. The name on the cover glistened like stars in the coldest sky:

AIREL.

It was her book, The Book of her life. Every thought, dream and nightmare.

He left it there in the library and walked the lonely trek down massive halls of splendor toward her room. It was the most tortured he had ever felt in his life, and he felt the heat of self-hatred grow with each step.

Michael did not know if what he had done would work. He walked reverently into her room and stared at her as she lay cold and wet on the bed. He was so numb that he didn't know what he had expected: did he really think she would just wake up and live out a happy, normal life?

Airel's corpse was pallid, blue and cold. Michael could feel his gut tighten into a hard ball; he could feel fresh tears well up and sting his eyes. He muttered a curse and ran a hand through his hair. His legs shook and he collapsed and fell to the floor under his overpowering grief.

"No... please, God," he prayed sacrilegiously, but honestly — and though it was the first time he had ever called out to El in submission, he held tightly to vague hope. "I can't go on without her; she's innocent. This is all *my* fault!" His voice shook, but through the distortion of tears, he looked and caught his breath.

Airel bolted upright, hacking and spitting water, arms clawing, lungs sucking air. Wet and tangled hair flew with the force of her gasping.

Michael froze, stunned, not believing what he saw. He tried to get up off the floor but could not.

Airel looked around, crazed, as if she had just awakened from a horrific nightmare. "Airel!" It was a whisper that he managed to force past his lips; the only word that said it all. It said, "I'm sorry;" it said, "Please forgive me;" and most of all, it said, "I love you!"

ABOUT THE AUTHORS

Aaron Patterson is the author of the best-selling WJA series, as well as two Digital Shorts: 19 and The Craigslist Killer. He was home-schooled and grew up in the west. Aaron loved to read as a small child and would often be found behind a book, reading one to three a day on average. This love drove him to want to write, but he never thought he had the talent. His wife Karissa prodded him to try it, and with this encouragement, he wrote Sweet Dreams, the first book in the WJA series, in 2008. Airel is his first teen series, and plans for more to come are already in the works. He lives in Boise, Idaho with his family, Soleil, Kale and Klayton. His daughter had an imaginary friend named *She*.

Chris White has an award for reading 750 books in one school year — from the 3rd grade. So yes, he's more of a nerd than Aaron. Chris loves history, Sherlock Holmes, and anything that's not virtual, like old motorcycles and mechanical typewriters. He also doesn't get why we have these things called "smart phones" when all they do is make people dumber. Chris recently celebrated 10 years of marriage with his wife, April, and has two boys: Noah, age 8, and Jaden, age 3, who inspired the Great Jammy Adventure series; the OK-to-color-in picture books. Chris is working on a short story called The Marsburg Diary that will further explore the prologue to Airel, and he is finishing up his first novel, entitled K: phantasmagoria, due out in 2011. Chris has a major crush on Audrey Hepburn, who is now dead. His wife is okay with all of this.

EXTENDED CUT BACK STORY:

Stuttgart, Germany: 1897

William Marsburg had risked everything for this. He had journeyed over the frigid sea from his home in London, endured horrible weather, wretched roads, and terrifying unexplainable occurrences. But the purpose of all the misery that had come before, that he had endured with his reward in mind, slipped into the void and faded away. He wrung his hands — the book was lost.

He had been in correspondence with Herr Wagner, who lived in a large house in the country near Stuttgart, for well over a year. Marsburg had been following a lead on a rare book that was in Wagner's care. They had written back and forth in detail on the subject. William Marsburg had come through the fires of Hell to get here, and probably still smelled of brimstone as he stood talking to the German in utter disbelief. His blood was boiling.

"I can apologize to you again, sir, if you require it," Wagner remonstrated in heavily accented English. "But the book is not here."

"The book is not here," Marsburg said.

"I can state with certainty that you were not the only party of interest…" Wagner looked past him through the window to the rapidly darkening landscape, eyeing the already black forest. He took a large drink of brandy.

William Marsburg had not yet touched his own brandy, though he could have used it — he was chilled to the bone. "No matter," Marsburg blurted. "I can only thank you, sir, for being kind enough "to allow me to prevail upon your hospitality as my host."

"Certainly." Herr Wagner was still marveling at the fact that Marsburg had evidently arrived at his isolated doorstep on foot.

"I shall leave early tomorrow. I do not wish to put you out in the least." Marsburg *wanted* to say far more than propriety would permit — he wanted to interrogate the man, make him pay, cause him pain, beat him, bind him and extract the answers he sought; that he valued more than his own life. And though Herr Wagner made a show of protest and offered him his house for as long as he required it, Marsburg knew he was being insincere. The German had wanted him gone as soon as his identity had become known to him.

A servant showed him to his room. He turned into bed and slept fitfully.

He awoke in the morning to find his host missing, as was the book for which he had come. The valet, however, soon came howling into the drawing room in hysterics, screaming sacrilegious oaths in frightened German. Wagner was in his room, murdered; flayed like a beast and strung up by his limbs above the bed, dripping. William Marsburg could not stifle a shudder, knowing more than he would readily admit.

Police came to investigate and found nothing but the unspeakable realities. They instructed Marsburg to remain in Stuttgart until further notice. That night, if he had been unable to sleep well the night before, he slept not at all.

In the morning, feeling on the edge of illness, he arose for breakfast, courtesy of the late Wagner's servants. It tasted horrible. He knew, of course, exactly what he intended to do.

As soon as there was reasonable opportunity to take his leave, he dismissed the servants to quarters and began searching the house. He was not a man to be kept from what he wanted, especially after having traveled through so much adversity. And he could not allow himself to flee, though he could taste his desire for it, until he had, at the very least, satisfied a lust far darker and more compelling: his lust for the book.

It was a dark day; the heavens seemed to mourn both the loss of the master of the house and the manner of his passing.

Down long corridors, past hideous wooden gargoyles and demonic statuary, over creaking floor boards, he crept. He searched using only what daylight made its way past the shutters into the house. After hours of searching, only one possibility remained: the cellar.

His breaths came in short intervals as he realized what he must do. He risked discovery by the servants as he exited the back of the house and stepped into the snow. Though only fine rays of sun filtered through the thick clouds, the light was focused on him, as if announcing his plan to the world.

He stepped lightly toward the side of the house, where a single heavy door was situated over the steps that led to the dankness of the cellar. Brushing off a crust of snow from the frozen iron ring on the door, he heaved upward, snow sliding off noisily into a pile beside it. He glanced roundabout him, and seeing no one but the dog, descended quickly down the stone steps, allowing the door to close softly over him. It was like, he supposed nervously, being buried alive. He wondered off-hand if that was what his own funeral would be like — with none in attendance, none to mourn his passing but the dog.

In the stifling darkness, he reached his trembling fingers into the pocket of his greatcoat and found his sterling matchbox. He struck a match and it flared up, revealing the icy puffs of his breath, then a taper candle set on a ledge. He could not see much in the darkness beyond. He took a deep breath and tried to reject the overpowering idea that he would share Wagner's fate, only in slightly different gruesome detail, down among the roots, stones and mud.

He lit the taper and stepped forward cautiously into the icy darkness. It did not take long to look past barrels of flour and barley, jars of pickled beets, bottles of wine, toward a single wall with bits of plaster peeling from it.

He moved toward the wall, examining things closely on the way, as he looked for clues. Behind a large barrel, he saw what he was looking for. There were cracks in the plaster in the shape of a square, where it was darker, fresher. He rolled the barrel aside with his free hand and set the candle on top.

He ran his fingers along the edges of the cracks. The plaster was moist, crumbling off and smearing on his fingertips. He cursed the old German, so freshly dead. "He hid the book here for some selfish reason, no doubt," he whispered his abuses into nothingness. He wiped his grimy, sweaty hands against his clothes.

He searched for something to scrape the wet plaster from the wall, finding a stave from a whisky barrel. He looked around for enemies, deciding in the end that surely he had not been fated to get this close only to be struck down. He turned to his work and began to scrape the plaster away, revealing the lath boards beneath. As he stabbed at the crumbling wall, one of the boards broke, revealing a hollow behind.

He broke more boards away and gasped. There, revealed by the light of his candle, was a dark chest. It was small, about the size of a book. "At last!" he hissed, then cursed himself for making so much noise.

He pulled the box from its stealthy hole with a little effort and laughed in spite of himself. "This is it!"— he knew it. The bronze clasp gave way easily as he opened the lid. Inside was an antique book, hide-bound. It was glorious, and he gasped again in worshipful awe. Once more, he looked around into the edges of the darkness for sinister signs that the enemies he had made over the course of the last year of his life were awaiting him. His hands were dirty and sweaty, and he knew that he should not touch such a treasure with such hands... nevertheless, he proceeded. His whole body shook as he reached slowly into the chest.

His finger grazed the cover, and he shouted in shock, recoiling in horror. Eyes wide, he froze and cowered, shame-faced that the game was now over. Or was it? He looked to the door, then back to the book in awe. "What is this?" His whispers licked the gilded edge of the book.

Had anyone else heard it? He waited — for what felt like eternity — for the servants to come running to investigate. He shivered, feeling suddenly colder. He looked down at the chest that held the object of his desire and considered. This had been such a simple little quest. So innocent. He could never have guessed at any of this. In fact, he felt small… and did not like it. Resolved, at last, he reached down and closed the chest with malice.

He stood and regarded his situation for some time, running over his "choices" in his mind. What happened, however, was inevitable. He reached down, grabbed the little chest, and placed it inside his greatcoat.

He burst from the cellar, leaving the door to crash down on its hinges, muttering profanities in his haste. The candle's flame was now the only life in the cellar.

He walked straight into the house and very hastily packed his only bag, burying the chest deep inside. He grabbed his satchel, with its own newfound valuable contents, and rang for the valet. When he came, Marsburg informed him that he would depart "at once." Servants and footmen were soon scurrying every which way in the now heavily falling snow in front of the house. Marsburg looked on with impatience as the coach and horses were made ready.

He raced to the Stuttgart station and the soonest departing train to anywhere. He had taken that for which he had come.

The candle had been knocked askance by his frantic exit, finding a bit of cheesecloth, broken lath boards, dry timbers; and flames were spreading in the cellar. Soon, it would consume the entire house, leaving nothing but a smoking black crater.

But as William Marsburg took to the rails to fly away, his mind was ringing with a single deafening word; the word he had heard when his finger grazed the cover of the book:

KREIOS.

London, England: 1977

William Marsburg coughed so hard that his lungs felt lit by Hellfire in his chest. He was hunched in a large four-poster bed in a room not quite dark, but full of the gloom of death.

He fell back in an exhausted heap, and the pillow accepted him with the warm softness of goose down. Marsburg had a full head of white hair, and even on his deathbed, he looked far stronger than he should have — not a day over fifty. Time, it seemed, had been good to him, but now his life was precipitating away at an alarming rate. It would not be cheated, he surmised; or was it death that was the jealous lover?

A slender nurse came into the low-lit room silently. She had heard the coughing and placed a cool cloth on his damp forehead. His fever broke the night before, but he knew he would not make it to the weekend.

Marsburg gripped her small wrist, croaking out two words, then fell into another fit of hard hacking. "My... son!"

Ms. Naples shushed him and cooed in a soothing voice. He relaxed and laid his head back down, gasping at the air, seeming not to be able to get enough.

Ms. Naples turned and left the room to fetch his son.

Marsburg closed his eyes; the cool lids quenched his hot eyes. Had he been consigned to Hell? Was this the precipice of his eternity? He hoped not, but deep inside the psyche where most feared to tread, he knew that he might very well deserve the lake of fire.

England was in the throes of a harsh and long winter, and William Marsburg felt its desolation deeply. He remembered the time he first laid eyes on the Book. He could still feel its presence! The voice was ever-present in the back of his mind, even now — it was a disease of thought he had never been able to shake. Nay, indeed: he hadn't wanted that. And now that the finish actively stared him down... "Ah..." he sighed, and he could not shake the heaviness that haunted him. Perhaps he had been mistaken all those years ago. He still heard it as if for the first time:

KREIOS.

He shivered and pulled the covers up around his neck, praying for death to come, for freedom from this burden.

The Book was in a safe place, but he had to make sure it stayed that way. No matter the cost, the Book was worth more than one man's life. He let a tear escape at the thought of his son and the long life he had yet to begin to bear. Now, at the threshold himself, he began to understand Wagner's reluctance. "Oh God!" His plea was but a breath.

He turned as his son entered the large and well-furnished room. Marsburg had done well for himself. He was, after all, the master of rare antiquities. The people of England, the royals too, had enjoyed them. They could see it all, his entire collection. But not the Book.

"Father." A tall well-built man stood over him with pure black hair and a jaw thick and heavy. Many women had fallen for his eyes, the flame that resided there inside them.

"My son." It was a simple greeting, but it brought more tears to his eyes. As he gazed upon his only son and saw what lie in wait for him, it pained him. "I have to tell you a story."

His son shook his head in protest. "Father, you need your rest, please..." His voice dropped off, and Marsburg knew in an instant that this would be the last conversation he would have with his son.

"No, my son... I must tell you this story before I go. It is more important than anything you could imagine. You must listen and heed what I tell you." He struggled to a sitting position and his son pushed a few pillows behind his back. The move was exhausting. His back ached and his mouth was dry. He gestured for the tall glass of water on the nightstand. His son handed it to him.

After a few sips, he began. His boy took a seat on the edge of the bed and looked sadly at him, feeling, too, that this would be their final moment together.

"I am an old man; much older than you think. I was born in July of 1856. It snowed in July that year... who would have thought it could snow in July?! But it did. That was the day I was born."

William Marsburg began to weave his tale. The Book was secreted close by, perhaps five miles distant, in a chamber known only to him. It pulsed, supernatural protection and long life emanating to its guardian in symbiosis. Soon, the guardianship would pass to Marsburg's son — he would have to decide if he would take up his father's mantle.

Even in that moment, as William began to fade, the Book began to call to Jack Marsburg, lowly, insistently:

KREIOS.

AIREL

Aaron Patterson
&
Chris White

CPSIA information can be obtained at www.ICGtesting.com
Printed in the USA
LVOW121453210312

274154LV00002B/73/P